**"Nothing you change on the outside can change
the way I feel about you in here."**

Jason tapped his chest. "Darcy, you could be eighty, and you'd still be beautiful to me." Jason's voice was deep and low, his tone heartfelt. "If you need anything, call me."

"I can't." Steeling herself against their attraction, Darcy lifted her gaze to Jason's. "Things have changed. I can't go back to who I was." The woman who loved Jason Petrie unconditionally and put herself second to his career.

"Things *changed*. Past tense." Jason gave her a small, hopeful smile. "We can meet later and talk."

"Talk." She rolled her eyes. They both knew, when they were together, they never just talked.

"Just talk, I swear." Perhaps to prove it, he put his hands in his back pockets.

"I…" It was tempting. "Jason, I…I can't."

Jason inched closer until she could practically feel his warmth. "But—"

"No." She pushed past him and on to her new life.

Dream a Little Dream

MELINDA CURTIS

FOREVER
New York Boston

Forever
Hachette Book Group
1290 Avenue of the Americas, New York, NY 10104
read-forever.com
twitter.com/readforeverpub

First Edition: February 2021

Forever is an imprint of Grand Central Publishing. The Forever name and logo are trademarks of Hachette Book Group, Inc.

The publisher is not responsible for websites (or their content) that are not owned by the publisher.

The Hachette Speakers Bureau provides a wide range of authors for speaking events. To find out more, go to www.hachettespeakersbureau.com or call (866) 376-6591.

ISBN: 978-1-5387-3348-6 (mass market), 978-1-5387-3349-3 (ebook)

Printed in the United States of America

CW

10 9 8 7 6 5 4 3 2 1

This book is for Alex, my editor. Thank you for everything.

Acknowledgments

Writing a book is a journey that begins with the seed of an idea. A writer's goal is to have that idea grow and unfurl along different steps of a trellis with interesting twists and charming flowers. Yes, I'm a gardener. But recently, I moved to a different climate where much of my go-to gardening knowledge has been put to the test. Like my plants this season, this book began with a new-to-me seed. And let me tell you, I was dreaming a little dream, hoping my trellis was strong, my twists were interesting, and my humor would flower in charming, unexpected ways.

Several folks were instrumental in cultivating this story into what it is today. Thanks to my family for patiently listening when I needed a sounding board. I can't count how many times Mr. Curtis muted the television so I could talk through a plot point. Hugs! Thanks to Cari Lynn Webb for reading those holey first drafts and helping to shape the bones of the story. Hugs! Humongous thanks to Alex Logan for helping to give Pearl hope, Darcy heart, and Jason heat. I'm not sure either one of us ever pruned and nurtured a story so much. Hugs!

Thanks to the team at Forever Romance for all their rays of

sunshine and excellence, from cover concepts to copyediting to ideas for getting the word out. You make everything look so easy when I know it's not. Thanks to my team members— Pam, Sheri, Nancy, Diane—for providing me with a safe space for gardening...er, writing. When I don't know how to do something, it's awesome that you guys do.

And finally, thanks to my readers—both those who've loyally picked up my different series and those who've just found me because of an awesome cover or intriguing review. I take my promise of providing a little laugh, a little cry, and a little sigh very seriously. Enjoy a walk through my writing garden!

Prologue

♥

I hate poker."

"Edith." Bitsy Whitlock ground her teeth. She loved poker, and she'd come to Mims Turner's house for precisely that purpose—to play poker with the Sunshine Valley Widows Club board and take her mind off the two-year twitch.

Not the married seven-year itch. This wasn't about straying. This was the two-year marker of widowhood when grief was mostly conquered and the heart came alive again. Bitsy was considering trademarking the term, because the two-year twitch was a thing. A real, distracting, body-temperature-raising phenomenon. She should know. She'd been widowed three times. She could feel the impulse to love coming on like her joints heralding the changing seasons.

But right now, Bitsy felt a cuss word coming on. Not from her exasperation over the twitch but from her annoyance with Edith. "Shiitake mushrooms."

In the chair next to Bitsy's, Edith Archer jerked in her seat as if she'd been administered the paddles of life. "Bitsy, I hate poker," she said again. "Why can't we play Yahtzee? Or rock, paper, scissors?" She pounded her fist into her palm three times. "I'm good at those games."

It was difficult to smile while grinding her back molars, but Bitsy tried because smiling and being pleasant was what she was known for. And in the small town of Sunshine, people expected you to live up to your label.

"We're adults, Edith. We play poker." Clarice sounded just as put out by Edith as Bitsy was, only louder because she'd forgotten her hearing aids again. "We've always played poker. And our winner always decides who in town needs Cupid."

Cupid. Standing in for the cherub was the favorite pastime of the four elderly women making up the Widows Club board. But before Cupid's arrow struck home, someone had to win a pot of pennies to decide who would pick the lucky couple.

"Has anyone else noticed that Jason Petrie hasn't left for the rodeo?" Mims hadn't been dealt a card yet, but she was tipping her hand as to whom she was playing for.

Bitsy ground her molars some more. Jason Petrie? He wasn't even a widower. Although...perhaps Mims was playing for someone she thought Jason should be with...

Jason's longtime girlfriend Darcy had dumped him last spring. Adding to his heartbreak, she'd rebounded into the arms of a much older man, her mentor Judge George Harper, who had also been on the rebound from a relationship with Bitsy's mama. Now George was dead and buried, Darcy was a widow and the town pariah, and Mama was in mourning. Mims wanted to match Darcy to Jason? She'd have to unravel last year's love quadrangle.

Good luck.

"Hold off on your matchmaking suggestions." Clarice's voice grew louder as she shuffled the cards. "Club rules. You can't talk about your matchmaking choices before you win."

"Just because you've always done something doesn't mean

you always have to." Edith's fingers drummed on the table. "What are we? A bunch of stuck-in-a-rut old widows?"

"Yes!" Clarice dropped the cards. "Who wants to change their ways at our age?"

"Me." Edith jerked her shoulders back.

Me. Bitsy was surprised she agreed with Edith about anything. But there it was. Bitsy was restless in her widowhood, which was saying something since she was pushing sixty-five. She glanced around the table at the others, who were older and seemed content with their widow status, with hobbies and good works. At Mims, who no longer dyed her hair. At Edith, who'd embraced eye-popping hair colors, currently dark red. At Clarice, who'd let her gray hair grow, braids reaching all the way down to her waist.

Bitsy touched her bobbed blond hair, suddenly painfully aware that she was the only person in the room wearing makeup and heels. Did taking pride in her appearance fuel the twitch? Bitsy rubbed her temples. She should be happy. She was recently retired and had a cozy home. Her mother lived in the separate unit in back. The thermostat was always set on seventy. The television was always tuned to the Food Network. She'd redecorated when she'd given away Wendell's outdated recliner. And yet she'd lain in bed last night unable to sleep, one arm outstretched into the empty expanse of bed. She should be worrying about her mother and instead...

I haven't given up on love.

"I may be a widow, but I'm not dead." Edith was still on her roll, her intense auburn hair as brash as her personality. "Come on, Mims. Support me on this."

Mims, their fearless leader, hesitated.

And in that hesitation, Bitsy knew what she had to do. She

adjusted her bright-pink sweater set on her shoulders with fumbling fingers. "You should match me."

The three other widows gaped at her. And then everyone spoke at once.

"You have to win the poker pot to choose who we match," said Clarice, the club secretary and keeper of the rules. She pounded the deck of cards on the table.

"We can't match a board member," said Mims in a tone that brooked no argument. She crossed her arms, signaling an end to the discussion.

"Holy fudge nuggets." As usual, Edith had other ideas. She leaped out of her chair and hugged Bitsy. "Bravo, my friend. Bravo."

And then the room settled into silence.

Bitsy's cheeks felt warm. "I...uh...I should resign as treasurer. And...uh...leave. So you can match me with someone." Despite her halting words, she rose smoothly from her chair and headed for the door with steady steps.

"Are we really going to match her?" Edith whispered, although loud enough for Bitsy to hear in the foyer.

"No," Mims said firmly. "Bitsy is just in a funk. Besides, we always choose young widows. We're going to match Darcy Harper."

This was apparently too much for Clarice, who cried, "But we haven't played one hand of poker!"

Chapter One

♥

All her life, Darcy Jones Harper had had a love-hate relationship with Sunshine's courthouse.

A year ago, she'd been in love with it while she worked inside as a law clerk. But that was before she quit to study for the bar exam. Before she married Judge George Harper. Before he died.

If she'd had her druthers, she'd have preferred never to set foot inside Sunshine's courthouse again. But she'd been invited to attend a meeting to appoint a judge to replace George, and she felt as if she had to show up to honor him and their unorthodox relationship.

"If you marry me, I'll die a happy man," George had told her while seriously ill last spring.

It would have been hard to say no to anyone's last wish, especially someone who had been as kind and generous with his time and influence as George had been to Darcy.

Ronald Galen, the burly court bailiff, bumped Darcy's shoulder as he passed her in the hallway and didn't apologize.

Her father would have used the collision to lift Ronald's wallet, the one peeking from his back pocket. Darcy wasn't that strategic. She tugged the lapels of her suit jacket and imagined the satisfaction she'd get from taking a swing at Ronald with her hobo bag. Not that Judge Harper's widow would ever do such a thing.

Darcy hesitated outside the door to the judge's chambers. Sunshine was a one-judge town. For the past two months, a justice from Denver had filled in once a week—first because George was dying and then four weeks ago because he'd died.

But the placard next to the door hadn't changed. JUDGE HARPER.

"She's got some nerve."

Town opinion hadn't changed either. A group of clerks walked past. It was impossible to tell who'd spoken.

It didn't matter. All Darcy had to do was attend this last official meeting as George's widow. Then she could leave Sunshine, find a place where she could live without being ostracized, and use her law degree for the good of a more accepting community.

Darcy held her head high as she entered the reception room for the judge's chambers.

Tina Marie gave her a cool perusal from behind her large oak desk. She was a lifelong public servant. She proudly wore an American flag on the neckline of her beige sweater, and her disdain for Darcy on her penciled-in, lowered brows. Next to her, the desk Darcy used to occupy when she'd clerked for George, and been higher in Tina Marie's opinion, sat empty.

Tina Marie leaned over the ancient green intercom, pressed a button, and said, "*She's* here."

Shoulders back, *she* marched into George's office.

Darcy's reception from the three men inside was mixed. Her two stepsons, Rupert and Oliver, were in their late fifties.

They spared her brief, dismissive looks. A gray-haired gentleman sat behind George's massive walnut desk. He gave her a once-over and what seemed like an approving nod.

"Mrs. Harper, I'm Henrik Hamza from the Judicial Performance Commission here in Colorado." The gray-haired gentleman indicated she should take a seat and waited for her to be settled. "I'm here today to announce who will temporarily replace Judge George Harper."

Darcy silently rehearsed her brief words of congratulations for whichever of George's sons received the appointment.

"You're here because you're the only private-practice attorneys in Sunshine. Obviously, there's a desperate need to temporarily fill the position left vacant by George's passing." Henrik paused and gave them a compassionate glance. "In a situation like this, our commission is tasked with appointing an interim judge until the next election, which is in November. We took George's recommendation into account when we made this weighty decision."

Darcy held her breath. In a moment, one of George's sons would ascend to the judicial throne while the other would know exactly what his father had thought of him. Rupert and Oliver preened, each trying to outrival the other. Both wore expensive wool suits, designer ties, and pointed Italian loafers. Oliver wasn't as polished or as handsome as Rupert, but each sported the slick smile of a confident con artist, as if they came from a branch of the Jones family tree.

"I may as well cut to the chase." Henrik smiled at Darcy. "George recommended that his successor be his wife, Darcy Harper."

Darcy was knocked back in her seat, shocked. *George, what have you done?*

"No!" Oliver shouted, red-faced. He gripped his silk tie as

if he were holding himself back. "It was bad enough that Dad couldn't distinguish between the book and his imagination when it came to sentencing but this..."

"You've got to be kidding me." Rupert was more refined in his reaction, staring down his regal nose at Darcy. "*Her?* On what grounds?"

Henrik came around the desk and shook Darcy's cold hand. "On the grounds that his sons were more interested in profit than the good of the community."

Darcy almost nodded. George had frequently said, "My boys only practice law because the hourly rate is better than hooking. And I don't mean fish."

"But...but...Darcy's a gold digger!" Oliver yanked his tie like it was a bellpull. "She married our father for his money."

Not true, although George had left everything to Darcy. A fact that still made her uncomfortable.

Oliver wasn't done protesting or tugging that tie. "Dad would still be here if she'd agreed to put him in a home."

Really not true. George hadn't wanted to decline in a hospital when it wouldn't change the final outcome. A fact that had made Rupert and Oliver uncomfortable.

Rupert sneered at her. "She had Dad under her control."

Completely untrue. But no one would believe that if she accepted the appointment. A fact that was going to make the entire town uncomfortable.

"I'm not just going to stand idly by and let her take my seat," Rupert continued to vent.

"I'm sure she won't pass the background check." Oliver eased the grip on his tie.

"She won't." Rupert leaned closer to Darcy, speaking half under his breath. "She's a Jones."

Darcy stiffened, suddenly grateful her juvenile record was sealed.

"I can assure you that Darcy passed her background check with flying colors." Henrik opened the door. "Gentlemen, if you're interested in the position, you may run for the office next fall. Thank you for your time. You're dismissed."

The two Harper men glared at Darcy as they got to their feet.

"This isn't over," Oliver promised.

"Not by a long shot," Rupert agreed just as darkly.

Henrik closed the heavy door after them.

Darcy wanted to follow them out and never look back.

Instead, she leaned forward and told Henrik, "There's been a mistake."

* * *

Spring, the herald of the rodeo season. The official beginning of sweat and blood and broken bones.

Former three-time world champion bull rider Jason Petrie had yet to leave Sunshine to join up with the tour. He was spending his first May in his hometown after fourteen years on the rodeo circuit.

"What are you doing here, Jason?" Noah Shaw, owner of Shaw's Bar & Grill, frowned at one of his best customers lately. "It isn't even happy hour."

"Close enough." Instead of sitting at the near-empty bar, Jason slid into a booth with a good view of both the door and the rear section near the pool table. He tipped his straw cowboy hat back. "Good things come to those who wait."

Word around town was that Darcy Jones Harper had a big meeting at the courthouse today. He and Darcy went way back, to middle school. Up until last year, she'd been his. If she was coming out of hibernation from that gated fortress just outside of town, she and her friends would most likely meet up at Shaw's for happy hour.

Jason's cell phone rang just as Noah set a beer in front of him. It was Ken Tadashi, his sports agent. Jason let it roll to voice mail. Almost immediately, a text from Ken arrived. YOU NEED BUZZ OR A BUCKLE. CALL ME. Jason turned his phone over, flexing his scarred leg to rid himself of a sudden, deep ache.

He'd missed most of last year's rodeo season because of a compound fracture in his right leg. He was missing the start of this year's rodeo season partly because of that leg pain but mostly because of Darcy. Things had gotten out of hand between them last spring before a bull busted his femur. She'd seen a corporate buckle bunny kiss him on television after a fantastic bull ride—a smooch he'd been paid for—and instead of waiting to hear his explanation, she'd married old Judge Harper. Jason had been gutted.

He still was. He wasn't returning to the circuit until he won Darcy back, which was hard to do when she'd been hunkering down behind locked gates for the past few weeks.

Three members of the Widows Club board entered Shaw's. The elderly women paused in the entry to take stock.

Uh-oh. Jason recognized the ambitious look in their eyes. The Widows Club ran numerous events throughout the year to benefit good works and charities. In spring, they went on the hunt for volunteers. Jason slouched in his seat and tugged the brim of his cowboy hat lower, not that he expected to escape their notice. There was hardly anyone else in the bar. But he tried to look like he wanted to be alone.

Didn't work.

Mims spotted him and headed over. The club president defied the label of grandma in all but appearance. She had white curls like Mrs. Claus but was an avid hunter and fisherwoman. Rumor had it she packed heat in that pink purse of hers. Edith motored behind Mims, short legs working as quickly as her mouth sometimes did. Clarice brought up the rear, slowed by her walking stick. Bitsy, the fourth woman on the board, was nowhere to be seen.

Mims slid into the booth across from Jason, followed by Edith. Clarice hip-checked Jason toward the wall, simultaneously adjusting her embroidered overall straps.

"So, Jason," Mims said solemnly, "we've read your column."

"Column?" For a moment, Jason was at a loss.

"Your advice to Lovesick Lily in the *Cowboy Quarterly*," Edith clarified briskly. "You told me about it last December."

"Right. Yes." Jason's agent had arranged a few public relations gigs while he was injured, one of which was writing a love advice column. "Hope you liked it."

"It sucked," Clarice said in her outdoor voice. Her ears were unadorned by earrings or hearing aids.

"Truly dreadful," Edith echoed in a much quieter, but still disparaging, tone. "You have no idea what women want."

Jason set his jaw.

"I believe a kinder way to deliver our critique is to say it left much to be desired in terms of valid relationship perspective." Mims produced a copy of the thin magazine from one of her fishing vest's utility pockets. She unfolded it and opened it to the page with his column.

"Thanks?" Jason sucked down some beer and looked toward Noah for a save.

The wily bar owner was making his escape, carrying a tray of glasses toward the kitchen.

Chicken.

"If you take our advice," Edith said, as if Jason should do so without question, "you'll be thanking us before your next column."

"There will be no next column," he said succinctly.

"Jason." Mims stared down at the magazine and tsk-tsked, much as Mrs. Claus might upon reviewing Santa's naughty list. "Telling a woman she should leave a hasty marriage in order to pursue her true love? That's not advice. That's—"

"Wishful thinking," Clarice shouted in his ear. "It's never that easy. Were there kids involved? Did someone in this love triangle have cancer?"

"Somebody always has cancer," Edith said gravely.

"You need all the facts." Mims stared at him levelly.

"All I had was a letter from a fan," Jason said in a voice some might call weak.

Actually, there had been no letter. Whatever numb-nut had come up with the idea of Jason Petrie doling out love advice should be fired. No woman in her right mind would come to him for love advice. He and his agent had cultivated his Casanova image for marketing purposes too well. He'd had to write a letter to himself, and in doing so, he'd drawn on a situation he was all too familiar with—his girlfriend dumping him for another man and rushing into marriage.

"You received a letter?" Clarice was incredulous. "That's odd. Who writes letters anymore? Folks your age write IMs, PMs, and DMs. They watch vlogs and tubers. Heck, I watch vlogs and tubers. Where have you been hiding?"

"Technology has never been my strong suit." He couldn't even figure out how to email on his phone. "Can I help you with something?" Volunteering for whatever activity they were recruiting for would bring this painful interlude to an end.

"Next time you want to give love advice, come to us first." Mims pushed the magazine aside. "Now for the reason we're here. I know we can count on you for the Date Night Auction." She wasn't asking.

"Just keep your advice column on the down-low," Edith said sotto voce. "Opinions like that make you seem like less of a catch."

This was too much. Jason planted his boot heels flat on the floor as if he were about to stand and walk away, a fruitless effort since he was trapped against the wall. "Ladies, I'll have you know I was instrumental in bringing Kevin and Mary Margaret together." The mayor and kindergarten teacher were getting married this summer.

The three elderly women burst out laughing.

Edith tapped her chest. "That was us."

Clarice clucked her tongue. "Completely."

"Didn't see you dancing in the club the night Kevin proposed." Mims rested their case by slapping her palms on the table.

Were they right? They couldn't be. But since Kevin wasn't here to defend him, Jason didn't argue.

"Not that we hang our hats on our matchmaking success stories." Mims leaned forward conspiratorially, lowering her voice. "We don't get belt buckles for every wedding bell rung."

"But we do keep track." Edith waggled her brows.

At which Clarice scoffed and shook her head. "Club business isn't any of *his* business."

Jason rolled his eyes. Everyone knew the widows loved to give Cupid a helping hand, and not always a subtle one.

"Regardless..." Thankfully, Mims prodded Edith from the booth. "You might want to wear one of those prize belt buckles of yours for the Date Night Auction. Your name always attracts a lot of donations."

"We'll work on drumming up bidders for you," Clarice said in that overly loud voice of hers. She used her walking stick to get to her feet.

"Work on?" Jason snorted like a hard-to-ride bull. He was a catch, dang it. They wouldn't need to drum up anything.

"Wendy Adams is always a generous bidder," Mims said sagely.

Wendy Adams? The quiet elementary school secretary?

"Darcy always bids on me," he mumbled through clenched teeth. That's what he and Darcy did. They had each other's backs.

"Oh." Mims stopped sliding out of the booth. "We don't encourage our widows to bid until they're at least six months into their widowhood."

"That's a rule." Leaning on her walking stick, Clarice frowned at him. "Although a one-year widow-versary is preferable."

"Rules?" Edith said in a quiet, rebellious voice, catching Jason's gaze and winking. "I've found most Widows Club rules to be more like guidelines."

Chapter Two

♥

There's been a mistake," Darcy said again.

This wasn't why I married George.

Some people in town already thought that she'd married George for his money. Now they'd think that she'd married him to get the judgeship too.

"It's no mistake, my dear." Henrik's smile tried to reassure. "This is what George thought was right."

Darcy shook her head. Since she was twelve, George had taken an active role in her life, from helping to find Darcy foster homes after sending her parents to jail to coaching her to wins in debate class to helping her pass the bar last December. George had been more than a mentor, and she'd have done anything for him, including care for him during the last year of his life. But this?

"I've only taken three cases to court." And she'd lost all three! There was the irony. George had presided over all her pro bono cases and had raked her over the coals for her poor performance. "What was George thinking?"

"You can't say this is news to you," Henrik said gently.

Darcy opened her mouth to deny it. And then closed it.

Earlier this year, when he'd known death was near, George

had argued Darcy should stay in Sunshine after he was gone and consider a judgeship—*his judgeship*, which was laughable, given Darcy had little legal experience and was a Jones. Who would vote her into office?

How she wished George were here to argue with today.

Henrik continued to regard her patiently. "Actually, it must have been fifteen years ago when George first told me you showed promise for the bench."

Darcy's jaw dropped.

Henrik continued to smile at her as if she were an unexpected ray of sunshine. "George said as much again last year."

"But..." She'd graduated from law school in Denver a little over a year ago and celebrated with a big, lights-out, don't-remember-the-details weekend with Jason in Vegas. "Are you sure it wasn't more recently?"

Henrik shook his head. "I remember the conversation last year vividly. We were having steak at the Bar None in Greeley. George was relieved to finally have found someone worthy to be his replacement. He'd mentored several lawyers, including his sons, but he said your qualifications were unique."

"But he knew I wanted to leave Sunshine."

"Yes. He mentioned that too." Henrik drew a piece of paper from his briefcase and handed it to her. "Perhaps this will clarify his rationale."

Dear Darcy,

If you're reading this, I'm no longer the sitting judge of Sunshine County. You are. I know the first thing you thought when Henrik told you the news—what was George thinking? You, of all people, know that I'm many things but I'm no fool.

Being a judge requires a big heart, a strong sense of justice, and a solid understanding of the law. You're young but you have all those things. And, in time, a judgeship will bring you the acceptance you crave based on who you are, rather than the man you married. What I'm asking of you is hard but so was growing up a Jones, marrying this old man, and passing the bar. Have a little faith in yourself. And me.

Warmly,
George.

Darcy read through the missive once more, just to be sure she hadn't misinterpreted George's chicken scratch.

"We'll get things signed and settled right away." Henrik rummaged around in a drawer until he found a pen. "If you still have doubts, consider this. What on your résumé sets you apart from all the other wet-behind-the-ears recent law school graduates?"

"Nothing." Other than the fact that it had taken her fourteen years to graduate college and law school and pass the bar.

"And would you agree that the phrase *appointed temporary judge* will look good on your résumé?"

That was a no-brainer. She nodded.

Henrik placed both hands on George's blotter and leaned forward, continuing to present his case. "And if you had to choose a judge for Sunshine and your only choice was between Rupert and Oliver, who would you choose?"

Neither. But Darcy wasn't going on record as admitting it.

"I rest my case." Henrik hit the intercom speaker on the green rotary phone. "Tina Marie, we need some signatures notarized in here." He released the button. "This isn't going to be easy for you, but George said you were the right woman for the job."

George had said a lot of things.

You'll gain respect by holding to your principles, even if they're unpopular.

Weather the storm.

Look forward, not back.

So many greeting-card-like sentiments. Darcy pressed her fingers to her aching temples.

George, I'd like to tell you a thing or two. Things they couldn't print on greeting cards.

Feel free, George seemed to snipe right back. *I can take it.*

Tina Marie entered the room on a huff and a muted grumble. Muted, but not inaudible. "We should be fingerprinting her for something else."

"Tina Marie, let me introduce you to your new boss, Judge Darcy Harper."

Tina Marie hit Darcy with the kind of look she normally reserved for repeat offenders.

Doubt throbbed in Darcy's temples.

Can I be Sunshine's temporary judge?

Have a little faith in yourself, George replied again, as clearly as if he were in the room.

Granted, Darcy had skipped her morning Coke so, now that it was midafternoon, her caffeine-deprived brain might be fuzzy and her imagination overactive. But George's voice sounded so real. And his encouragement...

Needless to say, if she did this, she'd need all the help she could get. Real or imagined.

If I do this...

She'd have to weather six months until the election, longer

if she had to wait to leave town until the new judge was sworn in.

Her mother would say this appointment was a hard pass, too long for a successful con. Especially when two seasoned, vindictive lawyers were gunning for her.

She'd have to endure negative public opinion and personal attacks.

Her brother would say a Jones could handle the scrutiny and stress.

She'd have to hear cases, most of which would be citizens with traffic citations they wanted to contest or drunk and disorderly violations they didn't want on their records. And she'd have to pass judgment, hand down sentences. All open to public record and censure.

Her father would say this was a new era for petty criminals since she—a Jones—could be soft on crime.

George had doled out punishments that he felt fit the offense. He always gave defendants a choice—a traditional sentence or a fine or restitution of George's own making, anything from carrying a sign up and down Main Street declaring their crime to sitting alone all day in a jail cell while disco songs blared through speakers as penance for violating the noise ordinance. But he'd established himself as a knowledgeable judge long before he turned sentencing into an art form. He could get away with it.

If Darcy took the position, the safer route for her was to stick to the letter of the law when it came to sentencing. No one could attack a judge who operated within the law's guidelines. Could they?

Quit doubting and take the job, George grumbled in her head.

"I'll need your identification." Tina Marie held out her

hand. "You may look like Darcy Jones, but you can't tell nowadays. Swindlers, liars, cheats. You never know who'll walk through that door."

This is it. Open season on Darcy Jones Harper.

Darcy's hand crept up to tug the neck of her white blouse.

She must have made a noise, because Tina Marie and Henrik peered at her more closely.

You're going to need a good courtroom face. Anybody can see you're afraid. George's voice again.

He'd been dead a month, and he chose today to haunt her?

Darcy shook her head. Six months. It felt more like a life sentence.

* * *

Noah brought Jason another beer, blocking his view of the door as it creaked open. "If you don't want to participate in the Widows Club bachelor auction, you should leave town and get back out on the bull riding circuit."

Jason pressed his palm over the scar in his thigh. His leg wasn't supposed to hurt. He'd been given the all clear to ride. But his leg had other ideas—nerves that unexpectedly tingled and the bone-deep ache of memory brought on when someone mentioned him returning to rodeo. Doc Janney claimed this would pass but couldn't say when.

"When are you returning to the circuit?" Iggy King settled in across from Jason and ordered a beer and a burger from Noah. He wore jeans, a navy T-shirt, and a ball cap, all of which were stained and dirt smudged. "Your wins always lead to an uptick in business."

Iggy and Jason had started Bull Puckey Breeding together. Jason had put up the money and Iggy was in charge of daily operations, but Jason considered them partners. They sold bull semen to dairy farms to keep cows pregnant and lactating and to ranchers who wanted an infusion of new blood in their herd. It was a lucrative business, more so when Jason was winning.

Jason kept his gaze on his beer. "Everyone gets something extra if I keep riding, don't they?"

His agent. His business partner. The Widows Club. Even his mother cashed in on his reputation. She had a yarn store in town but bred miniature horses on the side. Only Darcy hadn't cared about his career. The one thing she'd asked of him was that on the date of his retirement, they settle down and start a family somewhere that wasn't Sunshine. Getting out of town had been her condition. Waiting to get hitched until he retired had been his. Jason hadn't wanted to be an absentee dad like his traveling farm supply salesman father, who was now twice divorced.

Not that Jason hadn't been true to Darcy, apart from photo-opportunity kisses given for his corporate sponsors, which were usually quickly executed without so much as names being exchanged. Heck, he was practically an actor, playing a role. Despite that, his biggest fear had been realized. After a televised kiss, Darcy had blindsided him with that breakup and sudden marriage to the geezer who'd mentored her all through school. They hadn't talked. She hadn't realized—

Two of Darcy's friends, Mary Margaret Sneed and Lola Taylor, entered Shaw's, chattering as if they hadn't seen each other in weeks. They headed toward their usual booth near the pool table.

"Lost your nerve to ride, have you?" Iggy was a no-holds-barred friend, having gone to school with Jason since kindergarten. "Does that mean no more hopping on our bulls?" Which they sometimes did for fun. They were adults but still boyish at heart.

"I have plenty of nerve," Jason said, hackles up, palm instinctively pressing into his scar. "I miss bull riding. But don't forget I had two surgeries on this leg within the past year, leaving enough metal to set off airport security." Not to mention his heart was cracked and safety-pinned together. He wasn't ready to return. "I can let the youngsters have a go at some early prize money while my leg strengthens."

And besides, his eighteen-year-old protégé was competing this weekend at a rodeo in Phoenix. If Mark won, it'd almost be like Jason taking home the prize. Almost.

"You want me to believe your bones are creakier than your nerve? Or that pins in your leg are keeping you in town?" Iggy scoffed. "Dude, you've got connectors in your shoulder where they reattached your arm. Staples on your spleen. Play me a violin. Additional metal has never deterred you before. You received the all clear from Doc Janney a month ago."

Jason's hand moved across his thigh again. "Yeah, but..."

The door to Shaw's opened. Jason strained to see who was entering. Iggy's big head was in the way.

"Don't give me any *but*s, Petrie. I know why you're hanging around town. It's your Achilles' heel. Judge Harper died the same day as your medical release." Iggy smirked. Oh, he knew Jason. He knew him too well. "Darcy's like good wine. She was just widowed. You have to let her breathe."

It was the same message Mims had delivered—Darcy was temporarily off-limits.

But she wasn't off-limits to Jason.

She was his wife.

Chapter Three

♥

The moment Darcy entered Shaw's, she knew Jason was there. Her skin prickled the way it did during a lightning storm.

Ignoring her ex and the Widows Club board, Darcy walked across the bar to join Mary Margaret and Lola at their usual booth in back.

She pretended she didn't remember the strength of Jason's arms or the heat of his kiss. She pretended she hadn't seen a woman kiss him a year ago on the very television mounted on Shaw's wall. But one thing required no pretending. She was no longer unemployed. She was a judge.

And this makes you unhappy? George was apparently still in her head. *I wouldn't complain.*

Jeez, George. Don't dog me here.

Shaw's was a place to come to forget your troubles, not a place to be pestered by her husband's spirit. It was an institution in Sunshine that was as big as a barn, with exposed beams, a large bar in the middle, and a stage up front.

"How'd it go at the courthouse?" Mary Margaret tucked her long red hair behind her ears, her engagement ring twinkling.

Darcy fiddled with her wedding ring. The band featured a one-carat stone and sent out all the wrong messages to her detractors. But if she took it off too soon it would only add to the impression that she'd married George to sit on the bench.

What does it matter? You know the truth, George said.

"Are you okay?" Lola scooted over in the booth to make room for Darcy on her side. "You look like you've seen a ghost."

"More like hearing one." Darcy tugged an ear. "It's George. It's like he's in my head today."

"They say some people grieve like that." Lola should know. She did hair and makeup at the mortuary. "Sometimes I imagine I hear them talking while I'm getting them ready for services, sometimes from people I didn't know when they were alive. Don't worry about it."

"That makes me feel better." Darcy let out a deep, relieved breath.

Avery burst into the bar and hurried over to join them. "What'd I miss?" She looked Darcy up and down. "Other than this fashion faux pas. Girl, you're in mourning, not dead."

The bar wasn't crowded. The Widows Club board chuckled as if they'd been listening. Darcy slouched in her seat, certain Jason had heard every word too.

Tell Ms. Blackstone that you look like a judge, George groused.

Darcy sighed. After her wedding, she'd made a concerted effort to look and act like the staid wife of an elder statesman. But her efforts always felt like a big fail, and Avery was never shy about telling her so.

"Avery," Lola chastised, putting her arm around Darcy's shoulders, "leave it."

"No." Avery's head quivered quickly from side to side, sending her long black hair rippling about her shoulders. "My grandmother has the exact same pair of shoes Darcy's got on. She wears them to church every Sunday in summer." Avery slid in next to Mary Margaret, but she wasn't done. "And that blazer is so twenty years ago. The least you can do is pick an era, like Bitsy or Clarice, and stick to it."

Bitsy was an eighties girl, and Clarice was Bohemian seventies.

"You don't understand," Darcy said wearily. "Darcy Jones Harper wouldn't dress like you."

"Like me?" Avery laughed, glancing down, presumably seeing her fashionable black blouse and narrow-legged jeans. "What's that supposed to mean?"

"Pipe down. Both of you," Mary Margaret cautioned. "Jason's watching from over by the door. Don't make it worse."

Avery tsk-tsked, continuing at a lower volume. "Darcy's wearing granny sandals, a business suit that says she has no style, and her hair in an unflattering bun like she's run out of hair product. It can't get any worse than this."

"Unless Jason comes over and offers to buy me a drink," Darcy whispered fiercely. "You think I like dressing like this? You think I should have dressed like a trophy wife? That would have made things ten times worse."

Avery drew back, tilting her head as she considered Darcy's words. "Is this a trick question? I think it's a trick question. A year ago, you dressed like Jason's would-be trophy wife, which I wholeheartedly approved of. You rocked it. When you married George, you changed your appearance...and your...your everything. Hardly any drinks with the girls at Shaw's, certainly not on Sundays. And no clothes shopping trips with us to Greeley. Why?"

"I need a drink." Darcy didn't answer Avery. She'd already said too much. "Don't you need a drink, Lola? Let's all have a drink." She signaled Noah for a round of their usuals.

"I take it the courthouse thing didn't go well," Mary Margaret said tentatively. "Who's the new judge?"

"Yeah. Which of the Harpers was sworn in?" Avery asked.

Darcy hesitated.

"Maybe Darcy can't tell us until it's official," Lola said sympathetically. "You know, she's always so good at keeping other people's secrets."

And my own.

There was no way to sugarcoat the truth. "I was sworn in. *I'm* the new Judge Harper."

Darcy's announcement was met with silence.

Mary Margaret cleared her throat. "That's...great?"

"If unexpected." Lola's expression was as sorrowful as when she'd learned George had died. "Is this what you want? You were going to leave town and become a public defender."

"Darcy can't leave town now that she's a judge." Avery smiled. "But at least the robes will cover most of that." She made a circle in Darcy's direction with her hand. "I may be nagging you about your fashion style, but just so we're clear—I'm not giving your Louboutins back when you decide to embrace the real Darcy."

Embrace. Darcy wanted nothing more than to have a pair of strong arms embrace her, tell her she'd done the right thing both in marrying George and in taking the oath of office. Her gaze drifted toward Jason once more.

She'd only ever dated Jason. All through school and after. He was the man who knew almost all her secrets. The man who'd held her when her mother skipped town to evade a federal fraud charge. The man she'd turned to each time her father and brother were arrested. The man who'd celebrated with her when she'd graduated from law school, although her head pounded just remembering that hangover.

For nearly twenty years, Jason had been the love of her life. He had a square jaw balanced by a set of deep dimples high on his cheeks. His hair was a bright blond and his eyes a deep blue. And when he held her, she didn't feel like she was from the wrong side of town. She felt like a woman who'd found home.

"No, no." Mary Margaret snapped her fingers midair in front of Darcy. "Now is not the time to fall back on bad habits."

Her friend had no idea how far back she was falling—back to the Jones way of capitalizing upon opportunities that fell in their path. She should have refused to become judge. What did acceptance say about her moral fiber?

That I thought highly of it, George snapped.

Noah delivered a chardonnay for Mary Margaret, a cabernet for Lola, a red zinfandel for Avery, and a beer for Darcy. Although Darcy sometimes ordered wine, the irony of her drink of choice wasn't lost on her. She was blue collar, through and through.

Up until her wedding, she'd relied on her friends to help her shop for clothes, which might explain her fashion miss when attempting to present herself as Mrs. George Harper. What did it matter? The right career wardrobe gave a girl a big dose of confidence, but so did the right friends.

Darcy raised her glass. "Here's to me making something of myself." Hopefully it wasn't a fool.

They clinked their glasses.

"You were sworn in?" Avery sipped her wine. "On a Bible and everything?"

Darcy nodded.

"You've got to live by the letter of the law now," Mary Margaret pointed out. The voice of experience, since she was marrying the mayor. "No more speeding to Greeley for early-bird Black Friday sales."

"No more sneaking in alcohol to the midnight showing at the movies," Avery said mournfully, which was ironic since she managed the movie theater.

"No more making out in cars at the overlook near Saddle Horn Pass," Lola said wistfully.

That announcement brought the conversation to a screeching halt.

"You're married," Darcy said, stating what seemed to be the obvious. "You don't have to make out in cars."

"You try finding private time with a six-year-old at home." Lola smiled impishly. "Besides, the point is that you have to be the judge, 24/7."

"Sadly, I think this is what George trained me for." Things he'd said and done in their year together were starting to make more sense. "No more acting up or acting out." No more wild hairs or wild nights. Which meant she absolutely, positively could not hook up again with Jason.

That cowboy, like her old wardrobe, wouldn't buy her respectability.

But that fact couldn't stop the girl from the wrong side of the tracks from dreaming.

* * *

"What is this doing here?" Iggy tapped the love advice column Mims had left. "Don't tell me you're doing *that* again. That won't win Darcy back. I'm embarrassed for you."

Jason glanced over to Darcy. "That's not—"

"Look." Clarice sat down next to Jason, using what for her was probably a whisper. "Here's how it's done." She propped her walking stick against the table and then handed Jason her cell phone, sideways.

Jason was no good with tech. Never had been. He took the phone with a firm grip, the way he would grab a rope on a bull. The screen went blank.

"Are you giving him bedroom tips?" Iggy grinned and leaned toward the center of the table. "Lemme see."

"Jason, you're all thumbs." Clarice reclaimed her phone, worked some magic, and then showed him a video of a woman giving relationship advice. That is, if the subtitle was correct. Jason wasn't entirely sure, since Clarice was talking over the audio. "You want to understand where people are coming from, especially if this is the second—or fourth—time around for someone." Clarice nodded to Bitsy as she passed their table and headed for the one the Widows Club board had taken. "Listening is a form of investment in relationships, and conversely, relationship advice. Garbage in. Garbage out." Clarice toggled around to something else. "He's good too."

A boy of about nine or ten grinned onscreen and said, "Let me tell you how easy it is to get a girlfriend. First, always open a door for her."

Iggy howled. "Priceless."

Jason eased Clarice's phone back into her space, somehow managing to shut off the future Dr. Phil on her screen. "I get the idea. A printed love advice column is outdated." His agent had told him it wasn't well received anyway. But Ken had also said Jason's sponsors were getting antsy. To keep his endorsement paychecks coming, he needed media exposure, a return to the circuit, or both.

"Now, you can do the written word if you also do video." Clarice swiped her finger over her screen, bringing up a flowery banner—*Love Advice for Today's Singles*. "But above all, you have to have something relevant to say."

"Amen, sister." Iggy couldn't seem to stop laughing. "Folks like to hear from a modern, sensitive man."

"Which excludes me." Jason put his hand over her screen, creating a cascade of pop-ups. "I'm a cowboy, and if my reputation was based on fact"—which it wasn't—"a player."

Iggy laughed so hard that he fell over on the bench seat. He knew Jason was only serious about one woman.

"Being a cowboy is what makes you unique." Clarice frowned at her phone. "I could help you. However, the message has to come from a genuine place of caring, not hurt."

Was she calling him out on the whole Darcy thing in the column?

"Hang on." Iggy righted himself and nodded toward Clarice. "You mean, with a little help from you, that Jason's love advice could catch on?"

"Yep." With a press of a button, Clarice cleared her screen. "Hashtag trending."

"No." Jason hurried to put the kibosh on that idea, even though his agent might approve of the buzz. He shook his finger at Iggy. "I will not embarrass myself any further by pretending to know the female mind." If he had any real knowledge about women, he'd have seen Darcy's marriage to the judge coming. He'd have made sure she knew of their Vegas vows sooner.

"You're too young to understand women." Clarice tucked her cell phone in the bib of her overalls. "That doesn't mean you couldn't dispense insightful advice on any topic. But if it's love, I could prompt you."

"No," Jason said again. "I'm not a puppet."

"Don't throw the baby out with the bathwater. Clarice is offering to help." Iggy's grin meant trouble. "And I sense an increase in sales corresponding to this venture. How do we make this happen?"

Jason sucked down his beer, staring over the rim of his glass at Darcy, who looked no happier than he felt. She might have been with her friends but there was a furrow in her brow. She often wore her heart on her sleeve, and he could tell she was worried about something. He could ease her mind if she let him. He could release her dark-blond hair, hold her gently, run a hand along her soft curves, and whisper words of reassurance.

"We'd have to find the right room to record," Clarice was saying. "I've had success producing your mother's knitting vlog from her shop's storage room."

Both men were struck mute. Presumably, Iggy was as dumbfounded as Jason to learn Clarice was a video producer and that his mother had an online knitting show.

"Then it's settled," Clarice said. "I'm free on Saturday afternoon. All we need now is a topic."

Iggy grinned at Jason.

"Please." Jason wiped a hand over his face. "If it's expertise you're looking for, I'll talk about bull riding."

Clarice and Iggy shook their heads. Clarice glanced in the direction of Darcy. Iggy turned that way too. And then the pair looked at each other and nodded.

"You have another area of expertise," Clarice said.

"Women." Iggy snickered.

"Charming women." Clarice nodded sagely. "It's what you do best."

Jason stared at his wife. "That's where you're wrong. Whatever charm I had, I lost."

When he'd lost Darcy.

* * *

"I thought you were resigning from the club," Mims told Bitsy when she joined her at Shaw's.

Bitsy tugged at the shoulder pads of her sweater set, which had fallen off center, the same as her spirits. She wasn't sure why she'd come to Shaw's after walking out on their poker game earlier.

Oh, that was a lie.

Bitsy sat down. She wanted to know what had happened after she left. Had they taken up her cause or not?

She and Mims were alone. Clarice was sitting with Jason and Iggy. Edith was over saying hello to her granddaughter Mary Margaret, who sat with Darcy.

Bitsy's hands rested on her small black tweed handbag, which sat in her lap, ready for her to stay or go. Irrationally, she wanted to do both. "I'm twitchy," she admitted miserably. "It just came on all of a sudden."

Mims didn't bat an eye. "It's been coming on for the past year." She'd obviously noticed what Bitsy had missed.

Bitsy clutched her purse to her chest. "I can't do this again." Fall in love. "I can't lose someone again." Bury him.

"You know how love works." Mims's fingers clung to the edge of the table as if she too was troubled by Bitsy's twitchiness. "It's a chance. A risk. A gamble. Especially at our age."

Shiitake mushrooms. Her friends weren't going to help Bitsy find true love. "You didn't play poker at all, did you? You've started on Darcy and Jason."

Mims nodded. "Bitsy, we've been friends a long time, through a couple of your widowhoods. I've seen you get twitchy. Forget about men. If need be, a sleeping pill will make the nights pass quicker. We have so much to do—fund-raisers, matches—not to mention that your mother needs you."

"Helping others find love isn't the same as being in love." Bitsy made her decision. She swung her legs out of the booth. "You know I didn't ask for this." Not the twitches. Not the longing. Not the loneliness. "But I'm not sure I can ignore it." Although she'd try.

Mims set her lips, which made Bitsy hesitate.

"If I can't escape this, can you...at least...wish me luck?"

Chapter Four

♥

Beer had a tendency to go right through Darcy.

Her wine-drinking friends were on their second glasses and in no need of a potty break.

Darcy excused herself and slipped away to the bathroom. Shaw's was busier now, practically full. Thursday was the new Friday, after all. But thankfully, the ladies' bathroom was empty.

Darcy stared at herself in the mirror. At once-bright blond hair. At a face nearly devoid of makeup. With her hair pulled severely back from her face, her ears looked big and her eyes small. Her suit wasn't flattering. And her shoes... She wasn't as good at molding her appearance to the role she was playing as her mother had been.

George, why didn't you tell me you'd recommended me for your judgeship?

The voice in her head remained silent.

And Darcy knew why. Every time George had said she shouldn't settle for anything less than a court bench, she'd told him Jones girls were lucky to be allowed to take the bar. He'd grumble, trying to get the last word. She'd laugh, trying to discourage his delusions. What delusions? The clever old fox had pulled it off!

Darcy laughed now. A mirthless sound that echoed oddly in the empty restroom and foretold certain disaster.

On the way back to her friends, Darcy hurried around the corner of the hallway and nearly ran into Jason.

"Whoa." His hands landed on her hips.

Darcy's fingers came to rest on his elbows. It was purely reflex. She nearly rose up on her toes and kissed him. That was reflex too.

"Hi," he said, a slow twinkle building in his blue eyes.

She was wired to respond to that twinkle. She wanted to lean in and—

Judges don't neck in bars!

George!

Darcy blushed and dropped her hands. "Jason, I . . ."

"I've been meaning to ask . . . How are you doing since . . . ?" Since losing George, she thought he meant. "You look nice."

In her frumpy judge's-wife clothes? With her hair pulled behind her big ears? Darcy shoved his hands off her. "Friends don't lie to each other, Jason." She tried to dart past, but he was too quick, stepping in her path.

"Honey, nothing you change on the outside can change the way I feel about you in here." He tapped his chest. "That's why I know you'd never have married the judge if you didn't love him. He was such an important figure in your life. You've got to be hurting. Let me help."

His words nearly undid her. Everyone had offered condolences after George died. Everyone had asked how she was doing. But no one implied that she'd been in love with George and might be heartbroken. Only Jason. He'd always given her the benefit of the doubt.

"Darcy, you could be eighty, and you'd still be beautiful

to me." Jason's voice was deep and low, his tone heartfelt. "If you need anything, call me."

That would be unwise. George's stately voice filled her head.

It was good advice. Heartbreaking, but smart.

"I can't." Steeling herself against their attraction, Darcy lifted her gaze to Jason's. "Things have changed. I can't go back to who I was." The woman who loved Jason Petrie unconditionally and put herself second to his career.

"Things *changed*. Past tense." Jason gave her a small, hopeful smile. "And now they can change back. We can meet later and talk."

"Talk." She rolled her eyes. They both knew that when they were together, they never just talked.

"Just talk, I swear." Perhaps to prove it, he put his hands in his back pockets. "We never really had a chance to talk before you married the judge."

Darcy hesitated. He was right. They hadn't found closure after their breakup. And it was all her fault.

It had been June when they'd finally talked, a few weeks after the Event.

"The sponsors expect me to kiss their eye candy." Jason had followed Darcy around his small apartment as she collected her things, hobbling on crutches because of his recently broken leg. "You know that's part of the way I earn my paycheck."

"That's an excuse." Darcy dumped the contents of a bathroom drawer into the cloth grocery bag she'd brought. "That was no peck. That was a saliva exchange. And everyone saw." Everyone knew he'd betrayed her. Unlike the rumors or the more innocent pictures of him bussing a rodeo queen's cheek, here was proof.

"It's a reason, Darcy. Not an excuse. We had a plan, you and me."

She set the drawer on the counter and faced him. "A plan implies an end date. I've put my life on hold for too long." Traveling to see him compete on the weekends instead of studying for the bar. Taking terms off to follow him on the circuit. Languishing in bed with him the few times he was home during the season. "I have to think of myself, finish what I started, reach for my dreams."

That's what George had said when he'd proposed marriage.

"So this is a break?" Jason had followed her to the bedroom. "You need space to find yourself?"

"Yes." Darcy hadn't had the courage to tell him she'd married George the day after Jason had publicly betrayed her. They'd had a civil ceremony in Greeley, a union they were only just beginning to announce. Jason would hear about it soon enough. And so she'd stuffed the few clothes she kept at his apartment into her bag and then headed for the door without telling him this breakup was for good.

"Honey?" In the here and now, Jason slid a palm across her cheek and around to the back of her neck. "Do you want to go somewhere and talk?"

"I..." It was tempting. Darcy could go back to the way things were before. Dress like she remembered what sex was. Drink and dance at Shaw's like she didn't have a care in the world. Perhaps let her guard down and allow Jason to defend her honor the way he used to. But could he defend her marriage or her taking the judgeship without eroding his standing in the community? She couldn't drag Jason down like that. He had an image and endorsements to protect. "Jason, I...I can't."

Jason inched closer until she could practically feel his warmth. "But—"

"No." She pushed past him and on to her new life.

* * *

"Let's talk business," Jason said to Iggy when he returned to his table, smarting from Darcy's brush-off.

He'd recognized the longing in her eyes. He'd caught her staring at his mouth. And it was all he could do not to sweep her into his arms and kiss her back into his center of gravity. But this wasn't a strap-on-your-spurs-and-get-'er-done moment. Winning Darcy back was going to take patience, persistence, and thick skin.

"Funny you should bring up work." Iggy set his burger down. "A dissatisfied customer has come forward."

Jason didn't manage their company on the daily. He swiped one of Iggy's French fries. "Who is it and what have you done wrong?"

"*Moi*?" Iggy tried to look innocent.

Jason tipped his cowboy hat back. "Yes, you." Iggy had a habit of taking shortcuts.

"In this case, I'm innocent." Iggy cleared his throat, speaking loud enough to be heard over chattering patrons and the country song on the jukebox. "Tom Bodine wasn't happy with our product. He's claiming we sold him Samson's seed at a premium and he got bargain-basement lines instead."

Samson was a freak of nature. A humongous Brangus bull, a cross between a Black Angus and a Brahman. Tom Bodine was the wealthiest cattle rancher in the valley, and he'd built his empire with sweat and street smarts. If Tom felt he'd been cheated, he wouldn't let things rest until he had restitution.

"Did Tom…*accidentally*…receive product that wasn't Samson's?" After all, mistakes could be made and owned up to.

"Does it matter?" Iggy shrugged. "He's claiming his calves aren't holding true to the infusion of bloodlines we promised. His calves are small."

"But breeding is an inexact science." Jason relaxed a little, kneading the ache in his leg. "He could have genetic throwbacks." Runts in the litter.

"Not to mention his heifers aren't stabled. You and I both know many a cattle romance has occurred on the open range or even in a man's backyard pasture." Iggy smirked. "And his bulls are undersized."

Jason cut to the crux of the matter. "Tom blames us."

"Correct, sir." Iggy picked up his burger, pushing tomatoes and onions back in place. "Which is why we're meeting at Rupert's law office first thing Monday morning."

"Why not just talk to Tom?" Avoid all those legal fees and the potential for bad press.

Darcy's laughter drifted over to Jason. Too loud, too strained. He wished she'd tell him what was wrong so he could help. But in any case, she needed to hear him out. She needed to know they were married. He should have told her as soon as he'd learned of it himself. Perhaps then she'd never have married the judge.

"We can't just talk to Tom." Iggy rolled his eyes. "Because he's demanding a DNA test as proof that he received what he paid for."

It was Jason's turn to shrug. "Fine. Give it to him."

Iggy set his untouched burger back down. "A DNA test proves nothing. What if his heifers were impregnated in the open field before our product even arrived on-site? The DNA wouldn't match Samson's, same as if we'd sent him another bull's goods."

"You're right." Jason swiped another fry.

"Tom doesn't think so."

"And so, the battle begins." Jason settled back in the booth, staring at Darcy and preparing to dig in for the long haul on both the personal and professional fronts.

Chapter Five

♥

"What am I going to wear on my first day as judge, Stogey? The plain blue dress or the plain green one?" Facing George's old, cigar-brown French bulldog, Darcy held up one simple sheath and then another.

Stogey blinked, the canine equivalent of a shrug.

"Yeah, I don't think it matters either." Darcy shoved both options back in her small closet at George's house.

What's the problem? Your clothes are appropriate for work.

Yes, George. If I were twenty years older.

She was still annoyed that George hadn't told her of his plans and that he'd put a kink in hers.

Darcy moved to the sunroom with its cheerful white wicker furniture, charming bench seats, and bright-yellow pillows. Stogey followed along, wheezing a little. Darcy sat, bringing Stogey into her lap and rubbing his ears while she stared out at the pond in the back acreage.

In the fading light, the pond was calm. So much calmer than she was inside.

"In the legal world," George had told Darcy one morning as they sat in the sunroom, "you want to be the leaf that drops in the pond, not the rock. Minimize the ripples."

He'd been introducing the concept of being a part of the community without being in the community spotlight, which essentially meant go to work, go home, and don't make a public spectacle of yourself with a handsome rodeo star.

I meant don't cause a stir of any kind, George counseled now. *But by all means, ignore Jason.*

He just wants to talk. But Darcy smiled, remembering his heartfelt words and the tenderness of his touch.

Poppycock, George said at increased volume. *A judge and a rodeo star. There's a ripple you don't need.*

"I miss feeling attractive, Stogey. Call me shallow, but I feel more confident when I look pretty." Darcy tried to talk over George as she gave the dog a pat. "But I'm afraid Avery's right. Whatever I wear will be hidden beneath my judge's robes. I shouldn't worry."

The black robe. There was a new problem. She didn't have a judge's robe. And if she didn't have one by Monday when court resumed, she'd miss looking the part George had groomed her for. Darcy couldn't preside over court facing Oliver and Rupert without the baggy, black armor.

"I just remembered." Darcy glanced down at Stogey. "I still have George's robes." She hadn't worked up the courage to clean out his closet or his home office.

Stogey heaved himself into a sitting position and toot-a-tooted.

"Ew." Darcy waved a hand in front of her face. "So much for your special diet."

Stogey had a slew of issues—separation anxiety, digestive challenges, gum disease. Two days ago, he'd had eight teeth removed, top and bottom. Soft food didn't agree with him. But being alone didn't agree with him either. He'd clawed the heck out of the kitchen door today while she was gone.

"Come on, Stogey. Let's go raid George's closet." Darcy made her way down the hallway to George's room, pausing in the doorway to look inside, trying not to see George's frail body or the awkward tilt to his head that last day, trying not to hear his labored efforts to draw breath or recall how peaceful his lined features became when his heart had stopped beating.

It was easier to focus on the imprint of his bold personality. The big bed with its solid burgundy comforter. The two tall oak dressers with marble tops. The photograph of George in his naval uniform, regal head high. The portrait of him on his first wedding day, smiling happily with Imogene. Another with his arms around his two grown sons. The picture of Pearl, his longtime companion, beaming as she buried her nose in a bouquet of roses. A snapshot of Darcy and George when she'd graduated from law school. The frames crowded his nightstand, where he could look at them in his final days, along with a curling, unframed photo of Stogey as a puppy, carrying one of George's slippers.

"I'm dying, Darcy," George had confessed to her the day she'd seen another woman kiss Jason.

His belabored breathing... His sickly pallor... For the second time that day, she'd practically crumbled. "You're dying?"

"Not today," he'd reassured her. "But soon. My COPD means I'm a stroke risk."

She took hold of his cold hand. "What can I do?"

"I've never asked you for anything, Darcy." His craggy expression had softened, along with his voice. "But I don't want to die alone. I'm asking you for this one thing, to move in here and marry me. Let me give you one last gift, my name. You don't have to be a Jones anymore. And it would ease my mind to know you'll be part of my legacy when I am gone."

Unusual as his request was, Darcy hadn't thought on it long. George had turned her life around. She owed him everything.

Stogey waddled into George's bedroom, passing some silent-but-deadly stinkers on his way.

Darcy hurried across the room, overtaking the dog and his gas. She entered George's large walk-in closet. It was filled with wool suits, pressed white shirts, bolo ties, and cowboy boots. The wardrobe that defined who he was. In the corner, a collection of black robes hung from padded hangers.

Darcy slipped one on. George had been a tall man. The hem dragged on the floor. Worse, the robe could have enshrouded two of her.

If my parents could see me now, they'd…

Darcy scoffed without completing the thought. Her parents would applaud how she'd stolen a judgeship. Regardless of how she'd arrived at the position, she had to make George proud.

Something rustled, although neither Darcy nor Stogey had moved. A thin figure separated itself from the section of hanging suits.

Darcy jumped back, heart pounding. Stogey fell over, wheezing and whining a little despite his pain meds.

"Pearl." When Darcy's heart stopped racing, she dropped to her knees and helped Stogey to a sitting position, giving him a reassuring pat. "You scared me to death."

"His clothes still smell of him," Pearl said in a forlorn voice. She was a wiry woman with short gray hair and pale skin. She wore her waitressing uniform of black jeans and a black Saddle Horn T-shirt. The shirt was sprinkled with white cat hair.

George and Pearl had dated for decades. Pearl was against marriage and had broken up with him last year after he'd unexpectedly proposed. When he and Darcy married, Pearl made no secret of her disapproval of their union, which wounded George. When he'd been in that last decline, Darcy had encouraged Pearl's presence at George's side, going so far as to invite her to stay in the cottage on the property. The old woman and her cat still hadn't moved out.

Darcy stood. "Pearl, how long have you been in here?"

"Only a few minutes." Pearl fussed over George's suits. "I can't believe he's gone. I keep expecting him to walk through that door."

I had the honor to love that wonderful woman, George said in a melancholy tone.

"It'll get better." Darcy wrapped her arms around herself, hands lost in George's voluminous sleeves. She knew she should say more because she owed it to George to help Pearl through her grief. But Pearl grew touchy sometimes if she heard oft-repeated words of comfort. A change of subject was in order. "Did you know George recommended me for the judgeship?"

"Yes. What a ridiculous idea," Pearl said with a little laugh, recovering some of her characteristic prickly nature. "He was convinced those two sons of his would make tatters of his courthouse legacy. And now they're going to eat you alive if you can't fill George's boots." The old woman pressed a suit jacket sleeve to her nose and breathed in deeply. "He put a lot of faith in you."

"George gave you his heart," Darcy said in a voice she wished were sturdier. "But he left me to care for his legacy."

Stogey sat on Darcy's foot, staring up at her adoringly. It wasn't just his legacy George had burdened her with. The old Frenchie had come with the house. But even though she'd never been a dog person, Stogey was no hardship.

"If only he'd gone to the hospital. He might still be here." Pearl clung to George's suit sleeve as if his arm filled it. "I could be sitting and holding his hand now." She swung her gaze around, taking in the bottom of Darcy's robe. "You'll trip on the stairs to the bench if you don't hem that."

"Wouldn't that make Rupert and Oliver happy?" Darcy slipped out of the robe, intent upon returning it to its hanger.

But Pearl took it from her. "I'll hem this one. But the rest... This house, his office, his clothing are all I have left of him."

Darcy stared into the bedroom, seeing more than an empty bed. She saw the recent past.

"I should have married you when you asked, George," Pearl had said, clinging to his hand in those final days. "Then I could have taken care of you and your things properly."

Darcy hadn't missed Pearl's jab at her or the hint about an inheritance. Since his marriage to Darcy, Pearl, Rupert, and Oliver had often asked about George's plans to disperse his wealth. He'd never answered.

But at Pearl's confession, George had glanced at Darcy with a look so heartbreaking that she'd pitied him.

"Your patience... and kindness... will be rewarded," he'd said, although it wasn't clear whom he was talking to—Pearl or Darcy.

Not until George's will was read by a lawyer from Greeley did Darcy realize he hadn't provided for Pearl. He'd left everything to Darcy, which was a shock and hadn't made her popular with anyone, especially his sons.

Her father would say, "Finders keepers," like any good cattle rustler.

Her brother would say, "What a ride," like any good car thief.

And her mother would say, "Nice con," like any good hustler.

No wonder everyone in Sunshine hated Darcy. She had a family tree to fit her reputation as a woman who only had relationships with wealthy men. Didn't matter that she'd only ever been with two men in her life, or that Jason hadn't been wealthy when they first began dating. She was a Jones.

Inheriting George's assets was an unwelcome outcome of their marriage. Darcy planned to use a small portion of George's savings to start somewhere new. And then she'd sign over the bank accounts and house to Rupert and Oliver on the condition that Pearl be allowed to live rent-free in the adjoining cottage if she desired.

But that plan was now on hold. Darcy needed a roof over her head, preferably one with a gate to keep out the haters. And she suspected making a formal living arrangement with Pearl without gifting the main house to her stepsons would make those ripples George had wanted her to avoid.

Darcy knelt to pet Stogey, who rolled onto his back so she could rub his tummy.

"George doted on that dog." Pearl carefully folded the robe, aligning seams and smoothing the wrinkles. And then she bent over and slapped her knees. "Come here, Stogey."

Stogey closed his eyes and stayed put.

"Here, doggy-doggy-doggy," Pearl crooned as if calling her cat.

Darcy halted her tummy rub in case Stogey wanted to comply.

He didn't. He cracked one eye open but looked at Darcy, not Pearl.

"That dog is as stubborn as George." Pearl repeated her cat call.

Fearing another upset, Darcy set Stogey on his feet. "Go on."

Dutifully, Stogey waddled forward and accepted Pearl's pats, but he glanced over his shoulder at Darcy all the while.

* * *

Friday morning, luck was with Jason. The gate to the Harper fortress was open, providing clear access to the main house where Darcy lived and the small guest cottage Pearl was rumored to occupy.

Jason was just climbing up the front steps of Judge Harper's home when Darcy hurried out the front door with a gray-muzzled brown dog at her heels.

She frowned at him. "Did Pearl let you in?" If anything, Darcy's appearance was blander than yesterday, her brow more furrowed. She was practically wasting away in front of his eyes. "You shouldn't be here, Jason."

"We need to talk," he said gruffly because it was increasingly obvious that she needed someone to care for her. And he was determined that someone would be him.

"Okay, but you only have until Stogey does his business. Come on, boy," she crooned to the little brown dog, who tottered down the stairs. She led him to a low hedge. "How about here? You love it here."

It was a nice hedge in a yard that lacked the flowers Darcy had always dreamed of having. It was an impressive house, though. A rambling green midcentury modern with a circular drive, a large front porch, a portico on the side, and a garage in back. The old judge had given her things that Jason hadn't been ready to—marriage and the home she'd always wanted, even if it wasn't in the right flower-filled location.

Jason's phone buzzed in his back pocket. He took it out and glanced at the screen. It was his agent again. With a press of a button, he sent Ken to voice mail. "I can do that at least," he mumbled, thinking of Iggy and Clarice belittling his meager tech skills.

At the hedge, Darcy fidgeted, hair a muted gold in the bright morning sunlight. "What did you say?"

"Nothing." He had more important things to talk about than his cell phone abilities. "Do you remember that weekend in Vegas? Last spring? After your law school graduation?"

She scoffed, color rising in her cheeks. "I thought neither of us remembered much about that weekend."

"We had a lot to celebrate." In addition to Darcy's graduation, he'd won a particularly big purse and landed a large personal endorsement. "I was hungover for days."

"What about the lawn sprinkler head, Stogey? Don't you want to mark your territory?" Darcy trotted over to the corner of the lawn near the curving concrete driveway. "Or the rock? The rock always deserves consideration."

Stogey took his time sniffing his way from the hedges to where Darcy stood. He walked gingerly, with a slight sway. In fact, his eyes looked a bit glassy.

"What's the rush?" Jason asked, straightening his red-checkered shirt. "Doesn't the dog have a run or something he can hang out in?"

"Stogey? Stay outside?" She laughed mirthlessly. "George would kill me."

"George..." Jason shifted his booted feet, cleared his throat, and resettled his cowboy hat on his head. "George is gone, honey."

Darcy flicked a sideways glance his way. "Stogey would have an anxiety attack. He hasn't been himself since his oral surgery. He's highly medicated and completely out of sorts. I can't leave him outside alone."

As if to prove her point, Stogey lifted his leg and passed gas instead of urine.

"I'm going to be late to work." Darcy tapped her foot. Her black heels were low, and a disconnect from the sexy high heels he was used to seeing her wear.

But her legs...Her legs still looked mighty fine.

"Jason, tell me you didn't drive all the way out here to discuss a weekend neither one of us remembers."

"I was headed to the breeding business this morning but here's the thing..." Jason drew a breath. *Say it. Just say it. Just say it.* "While we were in Vegas that weekend, we did some crazy stuff."

"Jason." Darcy heaved a sigh and faced him squarely. "Usually, it's the woman who feeds a man that line, followed by *I'm pregnant*. Now, I know you aren't pregnant, and neither am I, so—"

"We got married."

The dog passed gas again.

Darcy paled. "That...That can't be. I'd know if we got married. *We'd* know if we got married. We'd have a license, a certificate, a paper trail."

"Everything was sent to my agent." Apparently that was the address Jason had put down on their paperwork. "It took weeks to arrive."

"But that was..."

"Last year. Yes."

"Which means when I married George..."

"You became a bigamist. Yes." He took no pride in pointing

out she'd broken the law. He knew how much she wanted to prove to everyone that she was different from the Joneses.

"But y-you...You never told me."

"I didn't find out until weeks later, when Ken received the envelope. If you recall, I tried to talk to you, but you wouldn't see me until—"

"I picked up my things from your apartment," she said slowly.

"Where you told me that we were taking a break, not breaking up." He allowed frustration to bleed into his words. "It totally blew my mind when I found out we were married. My agent told me right before a ride. I lost my concentration, and a bull stepped on me." Fracturing his leg in multiple places. "When you said we were taking a break, I thought I'd bide my time and tell you we were married when the moment was right."

"And then you found out I'd married George." She shifted her feet, again drawing his attention to her shapely legs.

He took a few steps closer to her, fighting a nerve jolt that nearly made him stumble, biting back a curse because his leg seemed to be getting worse, not better.

Darcy was staring at the dog and didn't seem to notice. "Why didn't you get it annulled?"

He'd asked himself that many times. "I worried filing for divorce—"

"Annulment."

"Divorce." He tipped his hat back again, so far it nearly fell off. "Give me some credit, Darcy. Even I know, when you consummate your vows, you call it divorce."

"Okay. Okay." Darcy closed her eyes for a moment. "We could file now."

Jason remained silent. He didn't want to file for a divorce.

He loved her. To heck with waiting for retirement to stake his claim.

"No." Darcy opened her eyes. "If we file now, I bet Rupert and Oliver would find out and then..." She reached out and shook Jason's arm. "You can't tell anyone."

The dog farted. Good timing, that dog. It gave Darcy pause, if only for a moment.

And then she was back to arm shaking. "Jason."

He covered her hand with his own. "I won't tell anyone on one condition."

Darcy smirked. "This better be good."

"My condition is simple, babe." Jason tried to give her a reassuring smile. "That we talk. You can explain why you married George." And he'd explain why their marriage should stand.

"No." She trotted across the grass to shoo Stogey from pissing on a garden gnome next to a small clump of flowery weeds, the only blooms in the yard. It was apparently the one area that was off-limits. "No."

"*No, Stogey, don't pee on that?*" he wondered aloud. "Or *No, Jason, I don't want to talk?*"

"No on both counts." Darcy glared at him, blue eyes flashing.

"This point is nonnegotiable." He was finally wedging a foot back into the door she'd closed when she married George. For the first time in over a year, he had the upper hand.

He was going to keep that winning position for longer than the eight seconds it took a bull rider to score.

Chapter Six

♥

B*igamist.*

This Jones apple hadn't fallen so far from the tree after all.

What would her stepsons think about that? Darcy shuddered to think.

But she was married. *They* were married.

Darcy squelched the sudden silver-lining notion that being married to Jason gave her bedroom rights. Just because she had rights didn't mean she should exercise them.

Rightly so, George said in her head.

Darcy didn't like the way George intruded into her thoughts about Jason. But she was running late. "Stogey, no scratching the door today." She tried to use her best sentencing voice, the one she'd been practicing in the bathroom mirror. She shut the pocket door between the dining room with its stuffy cherry furniture and the kitchen with its soft lemon-colored cabinets.

Stogey grumbled. Not a good sign.

Darcy gathered her purse and car keys from the butcher-block counter.

He sat on her foot. Also not a good sign.

She made the mistake of looking at him, staring into those

big, brown, worshipful eyes. She'd never had a dog before moving in here. How did owners leave them every day and go to work? She had to look away, dislodge her foot, and scurry out the door, feeling like a louse.

Stogey howled. There was a scrabbling noise. And then the scratching began.

Darcy froze on the bottom step of the portico.

"Someone sounds upset." Bitsy Whitlock, Pearl's daughter, walked up the driveway, looking 1980s chic.

"Stogey's going through a rough time." As were they all. *Bigamist.* Darcy clung to her purse strap, trying to hold in her secrets. "Are you looking for Pearl? She's not here."

"Mama just left for work," Bitsy said amiably.

Darcy hadn't interacted much with Pearl's daughter until George's death. But Bitsy had never treated Darcy as if she were a homewrecker. And for that, she was grateful.

"I stopped by to see you, Darcy."

Uh-oh.

Stogey's efforts increased. His howls became higher pitched and the scratching sped up. It was heartrending.

"I...uh..." Darcy tried to speak as if no small, furry creature were having a hard time being left behind. "I don't have much time to talk this morning. I...Oh, I can't do it." She caved, opened the kitchen door, and let the distressed stinker out. He was shaking and smelled like upset stomach. She sat on the top step and deposited Stogey into her lap, resigning herself to being late. "What a way to start my first day as Judge Harper."

"Go easy on yourself. It's normal to have good and bad days after a loss." Bitsy took a seat on a lower step nearby. "Can you spare a minute? I'm worried about Mama."

"Me too." Darcy rubbed Stogey's brown velvety ears. It calmed both of them.

Stogey heaved a shuddering sigh.

"What my mother had with George was unique. I get that."

I cherished her, George murmured mournfully in Darcy's head, *but I screwed up*.

"I know it sounds odd for me to say but you probably know..." Darcy considered her next words carefully. "George loved her deeply. It crushed him when she turned down his proposal of marriage."

"The same way Jason crushed your dreams," Bitsy said with a knowing nod. "I suppose, in a way, the two of you getting married made sense."

"Yes," Darcy said evasively. Everyone had been curious about her marriage, but they really only wanted to know one thing: Had she slept with the old man?

Props to me, George said, coming out of his funk.

Darcy chose to let that remark slide.

"I was hoping you could help me," Bitsy said in that soothing way of hers, rumored to have been developed over years in the customer service department at the cable company in Greeley. "Mama worries me. Do you have any ideas about how to help her get over her grief?"

"No." But how sweet of Bitsy to ask. This was the way families should be—caring for each other, lifting each other up in hard times. No doubt it was easier to be supportive when one wasn't locked behind steel bars.

"Bummer." Bitsy sighed. She wore a black velvet hair band on her bright-blond bob and a daintily flowered sweater set with white capris. Her ensemble accented her figure without saying, *Look at my feminine wiles*.

But she's not a judge, George pointed out.

But she's what I aspired to when I married you—fashionably classy. Darcy had overshot the mark and landed squarely in the church lady department.

George harrumphed.

"What's that?" Bitsy asked.

Had Darcy made a noise? Spoken out loud? She rushed on. "I've heard it's easier to diagnose a problem when you're on the outside looking in. But this is complicated. Pearl isn't really a widow, and I'm..."

A bigamist.

Criminy. She almost said it out loud.

Darcy stared at the expanse of back lawn sloping down to the pond. She'd always considered the yard plain. The one time she'd suggested adding clusters of planters and flowers, George had admonished her to worry about her studies. But now, she wondered how it would look.

It would look darn hard to care for, George snapped.

"I didn't mean to put you on the spot." Bitsy adjusted her sweater on her shoulders. "We both know Mama's squatting. You've been more than kind. I just wish I knew what to say to her."

She needs to forgive me, George piped up.

And you're just now realizing this?

If ghostly voices in her head could silently fume, George was fuming.

Stogey belched, reminding Darcy there were really only two people in this conversation and imaginary George wasn't one of them.

"I'm sorry, Bitsy. I'm a little distracted this morning." By bigamy and remorseful dead spouses.

"How are you feeling about being appointed judge?" Bitsy asked politely.

Darcy's gut response was to admit she was completely out of her element.

Don't sell yourself short, George snapped.

Darcy tugged her ear, trying to turn George's voice off. "I'm still in shock. Do I blame myself or George for the corner I'm backed into?"

What corner? You were headed for a life as a pregnant hausfrau, not a lawyer. I rescued you from that cowboy! George was angrier in her head than she'd ever heard him—dead or alive.

Darcy moved her hand from her ear to her temple. Was she really hearing George in her head? She'd never had thoughts like this in her life.

It had to be real because George wasn't done. *When Jason's mistake was televised, I knew the time had come to save you from yourself. Now you're in a position to make a difference in this town and what do you do? Doubt! Hesitate! Grab hold of your confidence and get on with it.*

"George could really set a person's teeth on edge," Darcy said, gritting her own. She had to find a way to deal with him the way she had when he was alive. "And I don't want to appear ungrateful because"—*Are you listening, George?*—"even though we didn't marry for love, we made each other happy."

Oops. If Bitsy hadn't known the truth about her marriage to George, she did now. Darcy braced herself for the older woman's reaction.

"Everyone approaches relationships differently." Bitsy gave Darcy a sheepish grin. "Mama was jaded after divorcing my father. She said she never wanted to pledge herself to a man again for fear she'd lose herself. George gave her love and space. I think she got scared when he proposed."

They fell silent. Stogey panted. Birds chirped. Darcy worried she'd said too much. And her dead husband turned tight-lipped.

Bitsy clasped her hands around one knee. "And now Mama's got all this energy bunched up inside of her, bottled up by grief."

"I think they had an unresolved argument." Darcy set Stogey on the porch.

Exactly so, George said.

Stogey trotted jauntily down the steps, tail wagging in time to his gas expulsion—poof-poof-poof.

Bitsy waved a hand in front of her face, taking it all in stride. "You may be right. What should we do?"

"I don't know. It's hard to win an argument with a dead man."

* * *

After all that had gone on Friday morning—a visit from Jason and then Bitsy, and then a trip to the vet—it was no surprise that Darcy was late to the office.

And Tina Marie was determined that she know it. "Judge *George* Harper was in every day at seven thirty. I'm here every morning at eight a.m."

It was nine.

Darcy stopped in front of her assistant's desk, her secret marriage to Jason pressing on the back of her tongue, fighting for release, along with a few choice words about her predecessor. *A pregnant hausfrau, George?* The longer she chewed on that, the more annoyed she became. Darcy cleared her throat. "I had to take Stogey to the vet. He's had a weird reaction to his pain meds."

Tina Marie bent her head over a case file as if she wasn't interested in listening.

"He's under observation." Darcy laughed self-consciously, shooting for casual and missing the mark completely. "Anxiety is no joke." Her own nerves were strung tighter than the trip wire to a booby trap.

"The dog was fine when the judge was alive."

"Right." Darcy retreated to her office. There was an overwhelming amount of folders on the big desk that hadn't been there the day before. It was going to take her hours to review everything.

Henrik had instructed Tina Marie to schedule the return to a working caseload for Monday, starting with sentencing hearings. Darcy had one office workday to catch up. The role of judge loomed large and daunting.

Don't you even think about walking away, George said sharply.

You lost privileges to tell me what to do, George, when you said you were saving me from myself.

"What's that?" Tina Marie asked.

"Nothing," Darcy said quickly. She didn't want her assistant to add talking to herself to her list of Darcy's faults.

Sheriff Drew Taylor popped in, looking handsome in his brown-and-tan uniform. "Lola told me you'd be here this morning." He'd married her last year.

Odd that Darcy used to think she and Jason would be the first of their friends to get married.

You were the first to be married—twice.

Not funny, George.

"What's that?" Drew asked.

"Nothing." Darcy was going to have to stick to her vow to stop talking to George.

"Congratulations on your appointment. Will you sign my search warrant?" Drew flashed Darcy a boyish smile and handed the paperwork over.

Her first official request.

Darcy took the documents with hands that trembled. "I believe this is where you provide me with just cause to search." She tried to smile and look as if she received requests for search warrants every day but her lips quivered as much as the paper she held. Search warrants often led to arrests, and in some cases, the separation of families, a state she'd been all too familiar with growing up.

Drew closed the door and pulled up a chair. "Nervous?"

On this side of a search warrant? "Yes. Clearly, I need to work on my court face."

Drew proceeded to explain the situation. It was as she'd feared. There were children living where Drew wanted to search. A single dad was suspected of fencing stolen jewelry. She felt ill but authorized his search warrant anyway.

After working through lunch, Darcy left at four to pick up Stogey.

"We switched him to a pain reliever that's an antipsychotic," the vet told her. "You should see a difference in his anxiety. If not, give us another call. If it's the antibiotics causing the gas...well, you'll be done in seven more days."

Upset by the day at the vet, Stogey trembled in her lap all the way home, where they found Pearl in the kitchen. She removed a small dish of lasagna from the oven. The altered judge's robe hung from a coat hook near the kitchen door. It looked freshly pressed and ready for public inspection.

Pearl, on the other hand...She looked like she'd been crying.

Darcy set Stogey down. He took refuge under the kitchen

table. He lay down, chin on his paws, and stared up at Darcy as if preparing for the worst.

"Would you like to eat with me?" Darcy asked Pearl tentatively.

"I'm not hungry." Pearl's voice shook the way a person's did when they were holding all the smashed inside parts together. It felt like Pearl was one tear shy of a complete collapse.

Most people, including you, are tougher than they look.

You're heartless, George.

I'm detached, which is the trait of all good judges.

"Here, doggy-doggy-doggy." Pearl made a half-hearted attempt to call Stogey, who didn't budge.

The woman needed something more than Darcy could give to get her through her grief. Something more…

"Pearl, you should take a memento from the house. Something that reminds you of George and gives you comfort, like Stogey gives me."

The older woman stared at Stogey and then lifted her gaze to Darcy's. There was enough sorrow in her eyes to last a lifetime. "George loved that dog." But increasingly, there was something more in her eyes. Something hard and calculating. "George would have wanted *me* to have Stogey."

"What?" Darcy didn't have to think twice. "No."

Pearl staggered back as if she'd been stabbed. Darcy grabbed hold of her in case she fainted.

"But you just said I could have anything." Anger built in Pearl's voice and she shrugged free of Darcy. "George loved him, and I want him."

They stared at each other.

"But you have your cat." It was the wrong thing to say.

Pearl drew a sharp intake of breath. Bitsy would be heartened by Pearl's glare.

Darcy wasn't heartened. She was unnerved. She moved between Pearl and Stogey.

Say something, George.

Silence rang in Darcy's ears, drowning out whatever George had to say. If he had anything to say. Because really, what man stepped between his mistress and his wife? George might be dead, but he wasn't stupid.

"You took George and now you want Stogey too?" Pearl's voice rang with indignation.

"Yes." Darcy couldn't have explained it. She just knew that Stogey had stolen a part of her heart and she couldn't let him go.

"You won't get away with this." Pearl shook her thin finger at Darcy. "I won't let you. That dog is mine. It was what George wanted because I'm patient and kind." She bolted out the door, slamming it behind her.

The sound echoed in the empty house.

No Jason. No George. No Pearl.

No family, real or bonded by circumstance.

"I'm alone, except for you." Darcy sank slowly to her knees, reaching for Stogey. "Come on, Stogey. Come on, boy."

Stogey tooted and stayed where he was.

Chapter Seven

♥

Saturday afternoon, Jason answered a call from his protégé, Mark Knox, on the first ring.

"Hey, dude. What's up?" He put aside the broom he'd been using and settled into an office chair at Bull Puckey Breeding, grateful for the distraction from trying to solve the impasse he had come to with Darcy. "Did you go eight seconds this weekend?"

"He did not." Spoken with sarcasm by a familiar, masculine voice that didn't belong to Mark. "Mark's in the hospital recovering from surgery. Why haven't you answered my calls? You think dodging your agent's phone calls and ignoring his texts is professional?"

Busted. "Don't act so surprised. It's like you've always said." Jason swiveled the ball cap he was wearing until the bill sat at the back of his head. "I'm a bull riding prima donna." Good thing he was sitting down. Lightning struck his thigh, causing his foot to kick out.

"I should fire you," Ken quipped.

"Isn't that my line? You're supposed to keep my sponsors happy and my bank balance high."

Ken scoffed. "Role reversal. You've got to be on the

money board or make a buzz on social media for that to happen."

Jason didn't want the reminder that he was remiss in the care and feeding of his career. "Enough about me. Why do you have Mark's phone?" When he'd taken Mark under his wing last year, Jason had convinced Ken to take him on too.

"Mark got thrown by a feral beast." Ken dropped the sarcasm. "New bovine blood from some ranch in the wilds of Idaho. That bull broke Mark's arm in two places. Good thing I was there to fill out the medical forms and sit at his bedside since you were AWOL."

Swearing, Jason turned his ball cap back around. "How is he?"

"Shaken, as anyone would be," Ken said crisply. Blood and gore didn't faze him. "It's Mark's first real injury, and he's beginning to realize he's not invincible. I was thinking about bringing him up for a visit instead of home to his mama, who is sure to say I told you so and beg him to stay in her care. Surprisingly, I feel you'll be able to talk him out of quitting."

"You want to come here?" That wasn't like Ken. He might represent rodeo competitors, but he was New York all the way. He'd never been to Sunshine.

"I'll make the sacrifice," Ken said dryly. "Besides, while you get Mark's head on straight, I'll fix whatever's ailing you and jump-start some contract negotiations with our new corporate partners. In terms of homework, you better have something more interesting to show me than a bull semen operation."

Jason pressed his palm into his aching leg scar. "Yeah. Fine. I'll clue you in on what I've been doing when you get here." Better to hold the news until Ken arrived that he'd been up to nothing but repairing his personal life and waiting for his leg pain to go away.

As soon as Jason disconnected, three members of the Widows Club board entered the office, shepherded by Iggy.

"And this is where we keep all our product before shipment." Iggy gave Jason a pleading look, one begging for a defensive save against the invasion of sweet, elderly women. "And look, here's a bachelor who actually agreed to be put up for auction. If you have Jason Petrie, you don't need Iggy King."

The reason for Iggy's plea became clear. He was rarely an auctioned bachelor. He much preferred bidding on bachelorettes to being bought.

Edith scurried over to a large, metal cryogenic unit, one of several in the room. "You keep the bull swimmers in here? Can I see?" She reached for the latch release, almost quicker than Iggy was in getting there to stop her.

"We don't like to open and close the cryo unit." Iggy leaned on the top, not as casual as he probably wanted to appear.

"I imagine it's like opening and closing your freezer at home." Using the toe of her hunting boot, Mims moved a dirty pair of coveralls on the floor toward the wall. "You wouldn't want to give their product freezer burn, Edith."

"Exactly." Jason mimicked Iggy, leaning on top of the next cryogenic unit down. Edith seemed the kind of woman who followed her curiosity gene rather than respecting someone's boundaries. "Other than looking for auction recruits, what brings you ladies by today?"

"You, of course." Clarice rested her arms on her walking stick. "You and that relationship advice vlog. It's Saturday. We had a date at the yarn shop."

Jason opened his mouth to deny his involvement, but then

he remembered that his agent was coming and expected him to have something in the works. This was just the kind of venture that Ken would disapprove of. Ken would make sure the vlog was over before it ever got off the ground. "Okay."

"Okay?" Iggy nearly fell off the cryogenic unit. He lowered his voice. "Does this mean you've given up on getting back together with a certain ex-girlfriend?"

"No. It means this better help me win Darcy back."

* * *

I COME BEARING GIFTS.

Jason's text arrived around dinnertime on Saturday and made Darcy's skin prickle. He'd attached a photograph of a package of pumpkin-and-oatmeal soft dog treats that promised to be delicate on a dog's system.

Darcy was curled in a chair in the sunroom, Stogey in her lap, watching the late-afternoon sun turn the calm pond a satiny blue gold.

It had been twenty-four hours since Pearl had demanded custody of Stogey. In that time, Darcy hadn't found the old woman in her kitchen, lurking in George's bedroom, or pacing the hallway. It hadn't stopped Darcy from listening for the creak of floors or the soft mumble of Pearl's grief. Hadn't stopped guilt from lingering in her thoughts like a bad meme stuck on repeat.

ARE YOU HOME?

She'd turned down an offer of dinner and a movie from Avery, mostly because she knew they'd end up at Shaw's later.

There'd be beer. There'd be a band. There'd be dancing. But a judge shouldn't be seen out drinking and dancing.

You'll get used to staying in, George said sternly.

Would she? It might be nice to create a ripple or two.

George harrumphed.

Jason sent a house emoji and a question mark.

Darcy smiled. "Those treats might be worth a try," she told Stogey, ignoring George. Nothing she'd tried to feed Stogey was forgiving on his medicated system. She didn't want to give Pearl a reason to take him away from her.

I CAN JUST HAND THEM TO YOU AND LEAVE.

A likely story, George groused.

Jason sent a picture of himself at the front gate.

It was a nice gesture, helped by his handsome, nonpressuring smile.

He's one of the few people in town who still like me, George.

George seemed to scoff in her head.

Jason's gesture was thoughtful, and given the fact that they were married, she couldn't avoid him forever. They needed to talk about next steps.

Talk. Her pulse quickened.

Unbidden, a troublesome thought surfaced: *And there are my conjugal rights!*

Judges are above hanky-panky! George was in fine form today.

"We're just accepting Stogey's treats," Darcy said aloud to drown out George in her head. She set the dog on the floor and texted Jason that he was to drive to the garage in back. It couldn't be seen from the road.

Darcy went to the security panel and unlocked the gate.

And then she darted into the bathroom, smoothing her loose hair and ruing the fact that she wore no makeup and was dressed in a faded Colorado University T-shirt over a pair of comfy gray leggings that were stained in random spots by colored bleach. There was no time to primp or change. Besides, he'd said she was beautiful no matter what she wore. This was his chance to prove it.

Judges are above—

"No one," Darcy finished over George's reference to hanky-panky. "Especially judges who have arguments with dead husbands."

Jason's truck rumbled past the house and to the garage in back.

Darcy slipped on her red Keds and led Stogey out to meet him. The afternoon light was fading, softening edges. She was a Jones. She wouldn't let it soften hers.

Jason hopped out of his big white truck. Darcy checked out her husband from the ground up. Brown cowboy boots, faded blue jeans, a dark-blue T-shirt that hugged all those muscles. He wore a ball cap over his blond hair. And then he removed his sunglasses and smiled at her, bringing forth those endearing dimples. Darcy's mouth went dry.

Thankfully, her Keds remained rooted to the ground. It was Stogey who rushed forward to greet him.

"You look rested." Jason knelt to scratch Stogey behind the ears, glancing around the property. "Sweet pond. Mind if I take a look?"

"Actually..."

He'd already set off toward the shore, where two green Adirondack chairs sat facing the water. He carried the bag of dog treats and a manila envelope.

She followed at a slower pace because he looked nearly

as good going as coming, and it'd been a long time since she'd allowed herself to look at any man the way a single woman would.

Not that I'm single. I'm married to Jason.

She did so love the way her cowboy walked, like the world was his oyster.

Not that he's mine in anything other than the legal sense.

George cleared his throat as if uncomfortable with her thoughts.

Jason sat in a chair and opened the bag of dog treats. "Let's give one of these a try, boy."

Stogey took the small biscuit and worked it around his mouth, whimpering as he tried to find a way to chew without hurting.

"Sorry." Jason gave him a pat, glancing at Darcy as she leaned on the back of the other chair. "Rosalie at the pet store said these are soft chews, but based on Stogey's reaction they might not be soft enough. Maybe you should save them until he recovers some more." He closed the package and smiled tenderly at Darcy.

His hand brushed lightly over his thigh. They'd been together so long that she knew how to translate the gesture. It was an unspoken invitation to sit in his lap. To have his arms around her. To talk the language they understood best.

What would be the harm—

Stogey belched and then gacked up what he'd eaten in the grass. He had a knack for bringing Darcy back to reality.

"If it's not coming out one end..." Darcy moved around the chair, intent upon comforting him.

Jason scooped Stogey up before she could reach him. "So much for promises made on the package." He scratched the little dog behind the ears, continuing to appear charming and nonthreatening with that display of dimples. "I brought something for you too." He nodded toward the chair she'd been hiding behind. The envelope he'd brought rested on the seat.

Darcy withdrew the contents—a photograph of them standing before an altar. She wore her hair down, a red dress, and her black Louboutins. *Those were the days.* He wore a black shirt, black jeans, and a huge belt buckle. He had her bent over in a hot kiss. *Yep, those were the days.*

Involuntarily, Darcy's gaze drifted to Jason's lips and his blond five o'clock shadow.

A vague memory tickled the back of her mind. Laughter. Deep kisses. And the irrepressible feeling that she had been loved that weekend. Not in the physical sense. Well, there'd been that too. But she'd been cherished.

And then a clearer, more painful image emerged of a cowgirl kissing Jason on television.

"Thank you for this," she choked out as thickly as dog gack.

"I wanted you to know it was real. I loved you."

Past tense.

Tears burned the backs of her eyes, fighting for release. She'd never wanted Jason to stop loving her.

You need to stay ahead of revelations like this in court. And work on that court face!

Zip it, George.

"I still love you, Darcy," Jason said tenderly. His words filled the fissure his use of past tense had made in her heart a moment earlier.

I love you too. Her mouth was too dry to say the words.

George surged forth in her mind. *Cheaters can't help you earn the town's respect.*

Cheaters like me, you mean? Because some would call bigamists cheaters.

Her comment to George went unchallenged.

Jason stared toward the pond, rubbing Stogey's ears. "We made a plan when we graduated high school, and we stuck to it for over a decade. It was so logical. We'd wait until we were ready to settle down to get married. We'd be in better shape financially, and we could go anywhere. But I think we realized in Vegas that the plan had to get thrown out the window. I don't know about you, but it was becoming harder and harder for me to leave you behind every spring. I think the alcohol swept all that logic away so that we could finally do what we should have done when we were eighteen— legalize the vow we'd made to love each other forever." He sighed. "But then we woke up and logic kicked back in."

Too bad memory had lapsed along with logic. Knowing they'd been married would have changed most of the decisions she'd faced afterward.

Woe is me, George grumbled. *You're a judge!*

"That day you saw me on TV..." Jason regarded her steadily. "That bull gave me eight seconds of a fight, but I hung on. I was blown away after the ride, ecstatic, running on adrenaline. And then...when that woman my sponsor selected kissed me...it meant nothing."

Darcy crossed her arms, pressing them tight against her chest in case her heart decided to leap out and take him back. "You don't kiss a woman who isn't your wife like that."

"She lip-bombed me. And I called you right away to explain. And an hour later. And all night long. You wouldn't take my calls."

Because you were with me. George chuckled.

Used by you, you mean. To keep control of your legacy.

Again, you got appointed judge! As if that absolved him of his machinations.

She'd been betrayed by two men. Darcy's chin rose so high it felt like her neck was trying to lift her above this moment. This pain. She refused to acknowledge the viselike grip anguish had on her chest. "You've laid it all out very nicely. But the one thing you've never said to me is that you're sorry." *And I don't just mean Jason, George.*

"I'm completely sorry," Jason said without hesitation, frustration, or defiance. He spoke the words sincerely with a shine to his eyes. "I lost the most precious thing in the world to me that day. You. And I've been trying to win you back ever since."

"It's too late." Why didn't those words come out stronger?

"Because of George? Because he could give you what your family and I couldn't?"

"Yes." She tried not to shift a muscle, not to squirm, not to let Jason know that she still loved him.

"I'm jealous of a dead man." Jason gave a dry, mirthless chuckle. "He gave you your dream." He set Stogey down and came to stand before her, wiping away the solitary tear she hadn't realized was on her cheek, resting his palm tenderly on her face. "I'm going to prove to you that we should be together. Now and always."

She struggled to keep herself from leaning into his touch, moving into his arms, or kissing him and admitting she felt the same way. What would rekindling their love solve?

The sunset shifted from a soft orange to a cold gray. The color of reality.

Greatness never came without sacrifice, George pointed out.

And she had sacrificed a part of herself this past year for this opportunity as judge, dressing differently and avoiding her friends. And now she had to protect Jason from the Jones taint of association.

Darcy stepped free of Jason's touch. "The reason we made that plan all those years ago was that I never wanted to hold you down. Everyone knew you'd be a world champion. I didn't want to be the simple girl back home, the Jones girl who kept you from living your life fully, the high school sweetheart you'd eventually come to resent when you kissed another woman and decided to move on." Her voice rasped, giving away how wounded she was. "And I especially didn't want to be the woman who was seen as holding on to her golden ticket, because that's what Jones women are known for."

What an irony, given that George's offer had given her the thing she'd wanted desperately to avoid with Jason—a reputation as a gold digger.

"I don't care that you're a Jones."

That was because she'd never told him the truth about the first twelve years of her life.

"You were never a noose around my neck, honey." Jason stared into her eyes and the love that shone there reached deep into her chest and squeezed what was left of her heart, pressing damaged parts together. "You were the best part of me. You were the woman everyone knew was loyal to me. The woman I was always proud to brag about."

George was oddly silent.

Darcy fought for a breath. "But now we're in two different places, Jason. You belong out there, and I..." She didn't know where she belonged. "I'm the temporary Judge Harper." A position that required her to leave the old Darcy, the woman who loved Jason Petrie, behind.

Chapter Eight

♥

"Where have you been all weekend?" Mama stomped in front of Bitsy on Monday morning. Pearl was working her shift at the Saddle Horn diner, looking more like herself than she had since George died. "Even those Widows Club friends of yours didn't know where you were." Mama pointed to Bitsy's three friends in the corner booth.

"Is everything okay?" Bitsy took stock of her mother, the diner, and her widowed friends. Everything seemed as it should be.

"I'm fine." But the way Mama snapped those two words contradicted their purported meaning. "Where were you all weekend?"

"I had a trip scheduled to visit Roger and the kids. Remember?" Her oldest son lived in the mountains above Golden. She'd wanted to run from her too-big bed and the disastrous two-year twitch. But even her adorable grandchildren couldn't keep her from tossing and turning on a narrow sofa sleeper two nights in a row.

"I tried to call. Over and over." Mama jabbed her finger at her. "You didn't answer."

Mama was out of her funk. Bitsy bit back a smile. "You

know my cell service is spotty up there. My phone was off the entire time." Hence the reason she'd had nothing in her call record.

"Technology never works when you need it." Mama huffed. "Never mind. I need you to come with me."

"Where?"

"To see Rupert Harper." Still wearing her apron, Mama dragged Bitsy out the diner door, much to the delight of the few customers in the Saddle Horn, including the Widows Club board. "I'm going to sue Darcy for guardianship of Stogey. George loved that dog, and he loved me, so we should be together. And now that con woman says he's hers."

"Oh, Mama. No." Bitsy recalled how Darcy had rescued Stogey from the kitchen Friday morning. She and that dog had a connection. "Let's have a cup of tea and talk about this." Damage control was required. Bitsy dug in her black ballet flats. "You've always been a cat person."

"No more talk." Mama dragged Bitsy forward with surprising strength. "I saw Rupert drive past a few minutes ago. He went into his office."

"But…what about your customers in the diner?" Her mother prided herself on her professionalism.

"Alsace can cover for me until we get back." Clearly Mama wouldn't be dissuaded.

It was a short walk down the block and across the street, too short a walk for Bitsy to collect her thoughts and devise a plan to stop this train wreck. Mama was back, but at what cost? Her lawsuit was groundless. Bitsy needed time to prevent Mama from making a big, costly mistake.

"It's locked." Mama rattled the handle on the law office's front door and then banged on the glass. "I know you're in there, Rupert."

George's younger son ambled to the front, exhibiting all the calm Bitsy needed to feel. He wore a nice suit and a blue silk tie the color of his eyes.

Bitsy rarely dealt with anyone who wore a suit. It was...He was...Shiitake mushrooms! Rupert seemed to move in slow motion to the tune of Duran Duran's "Save a Prayer," a song about seduction.

"No." Not the two-year twitch. Not now.

"Open up." Mama's cropped white hair stood straight up in the stiff morning breeze, making her eyes seem sharp and full of business.

Bitsy tucked her hair behind her ears, turning off the one-night-stand soundtrack as Rupert leisurely unlocked the door at the same speed that a man leisurely undressed a woman. She shut her eyes, trying to reboot, but his freshly showered scent reached her, as beckoning as fragrant sheets just out of the dryer.

Gah. She opened her eyes, no better off than before.

"Good morning, Pearl. Bitsy." That suit. Those eyes. That detached smile. It was the same chill he'd given them at the few holidays and birthdays they'd spent together with George. It was a smile that said Bitsy and Mama were dismissible. It should not be sexy. Rupert was a stick-in-the-mud. Handsome but far from perfect. Why did he, of all the men in Sunshine, flip her twitch?

She tried to argue, dredging up all the old, negative impressions of Rupert. His heavy, put-upon sigh. His patronizing smile. His snooty way of looking at everyone and everything.

She used to think it was a shame Rupert was such an egotistical jerk. He was attractive. He was well off, a man just passing middle age but not past his prime. He'd be a perfect recruit for some of the Widows Club events if he weren't such a bitter pill.

"What brings you by today?" He stared at Bitsy with that condescending smile.

The two-year twitch flared to life and said, *He'll do.*

"That's not right," Bitsy mumbled. She wasn't coming out of widowhood for a younger man who didn't even like her.

"What brings us by?" Mama grouched, elbowing Rupert aside. "A dog. It's my dog, and I want him."

"Mama, please." Bitsy tried to sound apologetic. The best thing that could happen would be for Rupert to send them on their way. Mama would continue to rail, but she couldn't escalate this beyond what it needed to be—a grief-ending grudge. "My mother feels she should have—"

"There are no *feels*," Mama snapped. "I was kind. I was patient." She raised a finger toward the ceiling. "I will be rewarded!" Mama cried in a voice filled with resentment. "He said it. And then she said I could take whatever I wanted."

"Uh-huh." Rupert checked his fancy watch. That watch. It went perfectly with his expensive suit and his expensive car and his expensive, custom-built home overlooking the river. His primary bedroom probably had an unfettered view of the water.

Bitsy wanted to bolt, to scurry down the sidewalk away from the two-year twitch and back to the safety of the Saddle Horn. But there was just one thing keeping her there—the suddenly attractive attorney needed to laugh off her mother's lawsuit. She added *obtuse* to his list of detriments. "Mama, you're going to have to spell it out for Rupert."

"D-A-R-C-Y." Mama crossed her arms and glared at Rupert. "Is that clear enough for you?"

"Darcy?" Rupert spasmed to attention and lost some of his aloofness. "Darcy Jones? What did she promise you?"

"It was the pair of them." Mama calmed down a bit now that Rupert was showing interest. "George and her. It was supposed to be my choice. And then she just up and changed her mind, as if George's wishes are of no consequence."

Bitsy sensed an opening. "Yes, about George's will…"

"What did you choose?" Rupert seemed genuinely interested. His smile was infinitely kinder.

Which was a shame since the flip side of Bitsy falling for someone was the fact that, years after they married, the man always died. Jim, Terry, Wendell. Three data points was a trend. If Rupert fell in love with her, it was a death sentence. It was practically a public service for her to squash this attraction!

"Stogey!" Mama plopped into a chair and crossed her arms over her chest.

"I'm sorry." Cursing the two-year twitch and ill-made plans, Bitsy hurried to make the situation clear. "We don't want to waste your time. As you might recall, Mama wasn't named in George's will. I tried to tell Mama she doesn't have a legal leg to stand on."

"I'll stand on my hands if it means I get what's mine." Mama's sharp chin jutted out.

Bitsy cast about for a way to defuse the situation. It was small consolation that this was the first time in a month she'd seen anything resembling her mother.

"I don't care about legs or the regularities of the law," Rupert said gruffly. "My father always said a person's word is their bond. I'll take your case."

"Really?" Bitsy's knees wobbled. She sank onto the firm

leather sofa, admiring the set to his chin, breathing in an aphrodisiac made up of bath soap and new leather.

He'll do, the twitch murmured in her ear.

What had she done?

* * *

"Overruled."

Monday morning found Darcy drinking Coke and practicing court procedure in the bathroom mirror.

She'd spent all day Sunday in the sunroom, wallowing in grief over Jason's declaration of love. But she was a Jones, one who'd used nepotism—no matter how unwittingly—to rise to power. She wasn't good enough for Jason. Someday he'd appreciate Darcy for not taking him back.

"Today is a workday, Stogey." Or it would be until someone found out she'd been a bigamist. Rupert and Oliver would happily march her down to the jail and strip her of her judicial robe and this house and—

Stogey tooted, staring up at her with soulful eyes. It might be a new day, but it was the same safe wardrobe and sensitive doggy routine.

Stogey's stomach was upset, and anytime she ventured near an exterior door, he pressed himself against it and stared up at her with those sad, sad eyes.

For Darcy's part, in addition to her out-of-fashion shoes, she wore clip-on pearl earrings and had her hair in that unflattering bun. For her first day presiding over court, she'd chosen a shapeless blue sheath and a matching jacket. Not that what she wore mattered. The judicial robe Pearl had taken in hung near the back door. Despite having been downsized, it still covered her completely. Regardless of coverage, her appearance didn't make Darcy feel competent.

Clothes don't make the man, George intoned.

"Said most men." Darcy gave Stogey one of Jason's dog treats, grabbed her purse, car keys, and judge's robe, and bolted out the door.

Almost immediately, Stogey began to scratch the door and whine, not just a little. This was a royal, the-sky-is-falling-and-I'm-falling-apart panic attack.

So much for the new meds.

Darcy got into the car and shut the door. Even with the windows closed, she could hear the dog's distressed cries and the scrape of nails on wood.

Awoo-woo-woo.

Alone. She knew what it felt like to be left behind, to have each of her family members arrested, taken away, put behind bars. She'd spent time in the foster care system, halfway houses, and juvenile detention centers. Before Jason, she'd learned to rely on herself and only herself. To keep her head down. To keep going. And to do it alone.

But alone... It hurt.

It was only with Jason that she'd felt she belonged. He'd helped her make closer friendships at school—with Avery, who'd introduced her to Priscilla Taylor and later to Mary Margaret and Lola.

Awoo-woo-hoo.

Stogey's cries pressed on her chest, rang in her ears, chilled her bones. There was no one to comfort Stogey. No one but Darcy.

With a sympathetic cry, she darted back inside.

Stogey hobbled away from the door when she entered, panting and looking as drained as she'd felt when she'd learned she'd married Jason in a drunken stupor. She grabbed Stogey's leash and small dog bed, scooped him up, and hurried back to the car, taking a moment to examine his paws, which thankfully weren't bleeding.

"This is not our new routine," she told him. "And you have to be good in the car."

Stogey licked her chin, sighed, and tooted.

"I can't wait to get you back on kibble, toothless."

Stogey rode into town in the place of honor—Darcy's lap. He stood the entire way, front paws on the arm rest, small black nose pressed to the glass. He only tried to vaporize Darcy twice.

"I don't have time to take you to the vet." She was already late by Tina Marie's standards, even though it was only seven forty-five. The vet wouldn't open for another fifteen minutes.

She slowed as they reached Main Street, obeying the speed limit. Jason's truck was parked at Rupert's law office.

Her stomach felt as unsettled as Stogey's.

What did those two have to talk about?

Bigamist.

She tried to remember more of her wedding to Jason, but all she recalled from that Las Vegas trip was a red, satin-covered, round bed and the luxury of room service.

Forget Vegas! Forget marriage! Forget consequences, inheritances, and legacies!

Jason had done so for over a year. She could too.

She pulled into the courthouse parking lot, braking hard when she saw Tina Marie's car parked in George's reserved spot. "No. That's just wrong."

Stogey whined. She wanted to whine along with him.

Luckily, she found a parking spot in the back underneath

an ancient pine tree beside the small park where employees liked to eat lunch. No one used the space because the tree dripped sap and needles. But hey, she'd found a spot. And there was a cool breeze this morning. All she needed to do was let Stogey water the tree, crack the car windows, and stow the dog in the car for a few short minutes until she told Tina Marie to move hers. Then she could come out, take Stogey to the vet, and park in her own space.

Easy, right?

* * *

Rupert's secretary showed Jason to a conference room, where Iggy paced.

It was a nice conference room, as those things went. Dark paneling, dark wood table, serious-looking leather chairs. It all added up to one conclusion: Rupert didn't come cheap.

Jason held his cowboy hat in his hands, turning it nervously, not quite knowing where to stand or sit. His impromptu visit to Darcy on Saturday hadn't led to the reconciliation he'd hoped for. But she hadn't declared that her love for him was dead. There was still hope. If only he didn't feel as if he were hanging on to a bull with a bad position and a premonition that he was about to be flung to the dirt.

"When Tom gets here, let me do the talking," Iggy said, disrupting Jason's thoughts. He'd put on a blue button-down shirt and black tie, although he still wore jeans and cowboy boots. "You don't have to say a word."

"I think that's Rupert's line." Jason gave his business partner a grim smile, subtly shifting his aching leg.

"Rightly so. Neither one of you should talk." Rupert entered carrying a thin folder. He sat at the head of the table and indicated Jason and Iggy should sit to his right, facing the door. "This is a preliminary meeting, the purpose of which is to gauge how much money it will take to avoid going to court."

"We're not paying a dime," Iggy bit out, clearly outraged.

"If you haven't heard, the interim judge is Darcy Harper." Rupert studied Jason, presumably because he knew they'd been an item since they were twelve, not because he knew they'd been married for over a year. "I'd prefer settling to taking a case before her. New judges are notoriously unpredictable."

"Wouldn't she declare herself unfit to rule the case or whatever the lingo is, given she used to sleep with Jason?" Iggy managed to both frown and smirk at the same time, as if he wrestled with both bad news and the joy of rubbing Jason's failures in his face.

"She might recuse herself." Rupert flipped open his folder. "Or either party could ask her to do so." He lifted his gaze to Jason. "Do we need to ask?"

Yes, because she's my wife.

No, because she's infinitely fair.

Jason shrugged, hoping it wouldn't get that far.

Rupert's brother Oliver entered, followed by a fuming Tom Bodine.

"Hey, Tom." Jason stood and extended his hand across the table.

Tom snubbed him, glaring at Iggy like dudes did before they threw the first punch in a bar fight.

Jason sat back down and did his best to look like this was just a couple of fellas getting together to talk about cattle. But it wasn't. Tom scowled at Iggy. Iggy stared at Rupert. And the Harpers? They were making small talk as if they were getting ready to watch a big game on TV. No big deal.

"What can we do for you, Tom?" Rupert asked.

Tom jabbed his forefinger on the tabletop. "I want what I paid for."

"You got what you paid for," Iggy said, half under his breath.

Tom had excellent hearing. "Prove it, Ignacio. Let's conduct a DNA test."

"Seems like a reasonable request," Rupert began in an equitable tone. And then his voice hardened as he explained how a DNA test would be inconclusive. "How does my client know your heifers were only impregnated by Samson's sperm?"

"Are you questioning my word?" Tom leaned toward Rupert, no longer scowling. He was glaring now. "Or my ranching ability?"

Oliver held up an arm and used it to edge Tom back into his seat. "We can all agree that the test means nothing. We'll settle for restitution. The purchase price refunded plus ten thousand dollars in damages."

"What damages?" Jason blurted.

Oliver gave him a cool look. "Suffering."

"Until we see your client *suffering*…"—Rupert let the word hang in the air before continuing—"we're only prepared to offer a refund."

"Refused." Tom stormed out, a heart attack waiting to happen. Seriously, the man had anger issues going back to his wife's death.

"Gentlemen, why don't you grab a cup of coffee while the legal teams confer?" Rupert gestured toward the conference room door.

Jason and Iggy returned to the reception area. Jason

poured himself a cup of coffee and then sat on a leather couch that looked as if it had just been delivered from a showroom. It smelled like it too. The coffee table was a tree slab with bark around the edges, rough and ready to snag someone's fancy clothes. Trendy, Jason supposed, but impractical as all get-out.

Iggy grinned, perching on the arm of that new sofa. "That went well."

Jason nearly dropped his coffee. "In what universe?"

"Tom didn't punch anybody."

"There is that." Didn't mean Tom wouldn't punch anyone later.

"Want to ride a bull today?" If Iggy was trying to make light of the situation, he was doing a poor job of it.

Jason's leg twinged, causing his foot to jerk out toward the coffee table. "Our bulls are so domesticated, they're not much of a challenge anymore."

"Still, you look like you could blow off some steam." Iggy tipped his hat back. "We can take the quad out on the paintball course." The one they'd made in one of the sloping pastures behind their business. "It rained last weekend. We can ride mud."

"No, thanks." They were good at getting stupid. But stupid didn't appeal to Jason today.

A few more minutes passed, and then the Harper brothers stepped into the hallway.

"See you in court this morning?" Rupert asked Oliver.

"I wouldn't miss her debut for free tickets to the Super Bowl." Oliver smirked. "She's going to fall flat on her face."

Jason assumed the "she" Oliver referenced was Darcy. Something fierce and primitive gripped his insides and balled his fists.

The Harpers chortled. Jason's jaw muscle ticked. And then Oliver left.

Rupert waited until his brother was in his fancy car to convey the bad news. "We couldn't come to an agreement. Looks like we're going to fight this out in court."

"Figures," Jason muttered, still upset that the two lawyers wanted Darcy to fail.

"Gentlemen." Rupert shook their hands, grimacing when Jason gave a bone-crushing squeeze. "I've got a brief to write and clients at the courthouse. I'll let you know when we've got a court date." He retreated down the hall.

"Come on, Ignacio." Jason tugged his business partner out the door.

"Where?"

"To court." He'd take any opportunity to prove to Darcy that they were better as a team, and he had a feeling that she needed a familiar face in her corner.

* * *

After twenty minutes of a dead-end argument with Mama in the Saddle Horn's parking lot, Bitsy was ready for a hot cup of tea, some comfort food, and a visit with her friends.

Mama veered away to check on her customers, as pleased as punch with the outcome at Rupert's. However, the Widows Club board was on its way out, which meant Bitsy would be drinking that tea alone.

"Come on." Edith marched past. "You're going to miss it."

"What?" Bitsy stared longingly at the booth the widows typically occupied, the one Alsace was bussing. The two-year twitch was ruining everything. "If it's club business…"

"You'll miss Darcy's debut as judge." Mims hooked Bitsy's arm, turning her around.

"Once the seats are filled, they aren't going to allow anyone else in." Clarice was already walking ahead at a good clip considering her walking stick. She had her hearing aids in and wasn't shouting.

"Hottest ticket in town." Mims patted Bitsy's arm. "You can tell me about your morning along the way, and I'll update you on Darcy and the Date Night Auction. You're curious, aren't you?"

Bitsy was. But the right thing to do would be to stay at the diner and continue her campaign to make Mama see reason.

Unbidden, Rupert's face came to mind, hard-edged and proud. Bitsy wanted to sigh contentedly. Conversely, she wanted to tell Mims about her attraction and beg her to talk her out of it.

Instead she allowed herself to be led away, caught up in the flow of things that were easier than heartbroken mamas and misdirected twitches.

Chapter Nine

♥

Darcy should have known Stogey would have a second meltdown the moment the car door divided them.

The howling. The desperate intent to dig his way out of her economy sedan. Darcy took a step back, testing the waters.

A-eee-hoo-wooooo!

A piece of faux leather might have been flung toward the passenger seat.

A couple entering the courthouse stopped and turned to see what the commotion was. At this rate, someone would report Darcy for dog abuse, and Pearl would get her way.

She grabbed a large cloth grocery bag from the back seat, tucked Stogey's small dog bed in the bottom, and then placed him in the bed. He settled in, as snug as a bug in a rug, staring up at her with love in his big brown eyes. "This is only for today."

She needed to calm down, take a breath, and run, because court began in thirty minutes.

Darcy's courthouse reception was no better this morning than it had been last week. The cold stares. The eye rolls. And then there was the impact of the stink bomb Stogey left in their wake—generating sounds of disgust and mean-spirited laughter.

They think it's me. They think I'm a bundle of nerves.

They're half-right.

"Good morning, Tina Marie. Don't park in my space again." Darcy didn't slow to gauge her administrative assistant's reaction to her command.

She shut the door to her office, tossed the black judge's robe over a chair, and unpacked Stogey and his bed, tucking them both under the desk. The apprehensive little dear circled several times before dropping down with a puff of air. And then Darcy collapsed into George's big, creaky desk chair with a sigh that was almost a wail. What was she going to do with Stogey? And more importantly, what was she going to do in court?

She didn't know.

Don't panic, George cautioned.

Too late. She was panicking, thoughts racing. She had to make a good first impression or she'd be outed as a fraud.

She should have taken yoga at some point in her life. It might have helped her center herself.

Or she should have learned how to phrase positive affirmations.

Stogey tooted.

Positive affirmations. Positive affirmations. Darcy needed a personal pep talk. She cast about her rattled brain until she came up with one.

This bigamist judge, who smells like old dog, is going to walk into that courtroom and command everyone's respect.

No. No. No. That hadn't come out right. It was horrible!

Semper fi. Seize the day. Run, Forrest, run. Those were positive affirmations.

I'm going to march into that courtroom and command every-one's respect.

Better. So much better.

Who was she kidding? She was a clunky, smelly bigamist. She was doomed.

Darcy put her head in her hands.

"Fifteen minutes to court," Tina Marie's voice crackled through the intercom.

A printed sheet of paper on George's desk listed the cases on the docket. Darcy opened her paper files, quickly reviewing each of the morning's cases. Reckless driving with witnesses. Reckless driving without witnesses. Indecent exposure. Drunk and disorderly. Darcy scribbled notes on Post-its for each one, including sentencing guidelines. She was going by the book, adhering to the letter of the law. No one could find fault with that.

All too soon, Tina Marie was barging in. "Heaven help us. Here we go." She marched across the office and through the door to the courtroom the way Darcy should.

Darcy stood and put on her voluminous robe and then gathered her case folders. "Wish me luck, Stogey."

The little dog stood as well, following her to the court-room door.

"No." Darcy shook her finger at him. "Stay."

Stogey went to stand in front of the door, staring up at her with those soulful eyes. And he didn't even toot.

Darcy tried to shoo him to one side, but he was determined to go where she did. "Okay. All right. Change in plan." She prepared the big grocery bag once more with his bed and tucked Stogey inside. "But you're not getting out. And please, no stinkers."

He gave her a toothless doggy grin that she took for agreement to her terms.

"Wish us luck." She opened the door and faced George's music.

"All rise for the *Honorable* Judge Harper."

Darcy didn't miss the sarcasm from Ronald, the bailiff. She dwelled on it like a bitter cup of tea, missing the rest of his introduction and call to order. She clumped up the steps to her seat, placing her stack of cases on the desk and Stogey underneath.

She'd been in courtrooms as a child, witnessing the justice system from the defense side. She'd watched George run the courtroom both when she'd clerked for him and after their marriage. She knew what to do, what to say, what procedure to follow. Except she'd never sat in his chair and been the focus of so many stares.

The courtroom was packed. It shouldn't have been. She was sentencing inconsequential cases today. There were her detractors in the front row—Rupert and Oliver, grinning like suited Cheshire cats. And her cheerleaders—Avery sat with Lola opposite the Harpers. Midway up the aisle sat the Widows Club board, including Bitsy, who looked guilt stricken. Was that an omen? And there, in the back, sat Iggy and Jason.

Jason. My husband.

Words stuck in Darcy's throat.

For years she'd dreamed of being Jason's wife. And now their marriage was going to ruin everything. Not just her temporary judgeship but her entire legal career!

"First on the docket," Tina Marie prompted in a voice loud enough that everyone could hear.

The courtroom shifted.

Darcy's gaze connected with Jason's.

Go on, he mouthed.

She drew a deep breath and drew herself up taller in the chair.

Beneath the bench, Stogey ripped a raspberry but not with his mouth.

The courtroom erupted in chuckles.

"Excuse me." Darcy glanced down at the first case, cheeks heating. "I've got"—*George's*—"my dog under the bench."

"There are no dogs allowed in the courtroom." Ronald stuck his thumbs in his utility belt.

If Darcy had to put Stogey somewhere, there'd be damages. Not to mention more injury to Stogey physically and emotionally. The dog needed a therapy dog.

A therapy dog...

"Stogey is an emotional support animal and will not be removed," Darcy said as firmly as she was able. She might have even fooled some of those present with her fake front of authority.

Lola gave her a thumbs-up.

Ronald stepped forward. "But—"

"My courtroom. My rules." Darcy stared at Ronald with false bravado. "First case for sentencing."

"Sy Smithcorn," Ronald said mulishly.

An old man stepped to the bench ahead of Oliver. His face was tan, thin, and just as wrinkled as his worn clothing.

The district attorney, Keli Connelly, stood next to Tina Marie's desk, holding all her case files in the crook of her arm.

Darcy opened the man's file. "Mr. Smithcorn, you've been charged with indecent exposure, to which you've pled no contest. This carries a maximum penalty of five hundred dollars or six months in jail. Do you have anything to say before sentencing?"

"My client is homeless." Oliver wore a knowing grin. It didn't escape Darcy's attention that he left off her title: *Your Honor*. Or that he was taking a pro bono case the public defender could be handling. "Mr. Smithcorn was washing his clothes down by the river."

"All his clothes?" Darcy asked.

"Yes, Your Honor," Keli said in a flat voice. "Mr. Smithcorn chose to do his laundry in the buff in full view of the highway. And then there was the dancing."

"I've never been shy about my assets. Ain't about to start now." Mr. Smithcorn guffawed. "And the Lord meant us to dance."

There's an image. George chuckled, showing up late for court.

"There's a time and place for dancing naked," Darcy said absently, trying to rationalize a punishment that fit the crime without dwelling on a naked old man busting a move. Fining the defendant would only result in a default, given the state of his financial affairs. Jail time would be a waste of resources, although, from the look of Mr. Smithcorn, he could use a free trip to the dentist. She perused the visiting judge's notes to buy time, catching the sleeve of her robe on a drawer knob. She tried to gracefully and unobtrusively free herself. "Were you arrested when the citation was issued?"

"Spent a night in the hoosegow."

Oliver chuckled, leading a chorus in the gallery.

Darcy felt her cheeks heat. "Gentlemen, this is a serious matter. May I remind you that the maximum penalty for indecent exposure in the state of Colorado is either a five-hundred-dollar fine or six months in jail."

"For doing my laundry?" Mr. Smithcorn was flabbergasted. He had a fairly clean record, having been picked up for vagrancy once and having one arrest for petty theft. "What's the world coming to? What's Colorado coming to?" He staggered to the edge of Darcy's desk and shook his bony fist at her. "Are you the devil? 'Cause you look like the grim reaper to me. Thin hands coming out of black shadows."

"Bailiff…" Darcy's heart scaled her throat. She'd been in enough rough spots growing up to be scared of a man entering her physical space. She swallowed her fears back down. "*Bailiff?* Bailiff."

Ronald leaned against the wall, smirking.

If Mr. Smithcorn had a knife…

If Mr. Smithcorn had a tendency toward violence…

"Bailiff," Darcy said again, weakly.

A cowboy in a white straw hat stormed the bench. Or rather Mr. Smithcorn. Jason grabbed the man by his elbows and dragged him backward. "You ask before you approach the judge, buddy."

Ronald charged forward, apparently considering Jason more of a danger to her than a derelict who'd threatened a member of the court.

"Order. Order." Darcy banged her gavel. "Mr. Smithcorn will spend the night in jail for contempt and return to receive sentencing tomorrow. The court will take a five-minute recess." She banged her gavel again.

"But we've only just started the session," Tina Marie griped.

Stand your ground. George's voice reverberated in Darcy's head.

Despite George's command, despite Jason racing to the rescue, Darcy was alone.

I'm not ready for this.

Instead of demanding to see Ronald in her chambers for dereliction of duty, instead of warning Oliver he too might be held in contempt if he continued to act like this was a mock trial for high schoolers, Darcy picked up Stogey's bag and fled out the door, through her office, down the hall, and out the back to the parking lot.

* * *

"Are you okay?" Jason hurried down the back steps of the courthouse to where Darcy was encouraging Stogey to relieve himself.

"I'm suffering a bout of self-loathing." Darcy turned to him, dropping the dog's leash in the process. "A Jones doesn't lose control of a crowd."

"You're not a Jones." Jason let her live with those words for a moment when what he really wanted to do was close the distance between them and wrap his arms around her to reassure himself that she was all right, and to reassure her that she could collect herself and give it another go.

"I'm not sure what I am anymore," she said on a shaky breath. "Thank you for stepping in back there. Mr. Smithcorn took me by surprise."

"Don't be hard on yourself. He would have taken George by surprise too." Jason came to stand next to her, in case she felt the need for a pair of strong, supportive arms. "Chalk it up to courtroom jitters. First days always suck. Why, I remember my first professional bull ride and—"

"Do *not* compare what just happened in there to you getting thrown off a bull." Darcy whirled, poking his shoulder. "I can't afford to be scared or uncertain. Before I walked in there this morning, my staff suspected I was incompetent. Now they have no doubt." She let her hand drop. It disappeared in the long cuff of her black sleeve. "And the town . . ."

"You've always worried too much about what others think." Jason moved closer still, lowering his voice to say, "George believed in you. And as your one remaining husband, it's my duty to remind you how awesome you are."

"Hush." Darcy glanced over her shoulder toward the courthouse.

He pressed his lips together, refusing to argue.

"It matters what these people think. They all believe I slept my way to the bench." She crossed her arms over her chest. "I have to earn their respect or this will all be for nothing." She pointed toward the courthouse. "I have to march back in there and be bulletproof."

"On that point we agree." He took her by the shoulders. "No one pushes Judge Petrie around."

"Oh, will you stop?" Darcy shook herself free.

"Regardless of what name you go by . . ." He brushed a stray lock of blond hair behind her ear. "You've got this. You'll get your share of blisters in there, and then you'll develop calluses."

Darcy nodded. But it was a glassy-eyed nod. She was still rattled. "Thank you. It helps to know I'm not always alone." She bit her lip as if she'd said too much.

Stogey whined. He'd crawled beneath a hedge. His leash was tangled in the branches. He was stuck, much like Jason and Darcy.

"I'll get him." Jason moved to the shrubbery and bent to disentangle the thin strip of leather.

"Darcy, can I talk to you?" Rupert stood on the back landing. His superior glance landed on Jason. "Alone?"

Jason took Stogey's leash and walked him far enough away

to pretend he was honoring his attorney's wishes but not far enough away that he couldn't still hear the conversation.

"Did Jason tell you that Tom Bodine is suing him?" Rupert asked in a tone a school bully would use to intimidate a smaller kid for his lunch money.

Jason clenched the leash.

"No." Darcy straightened her robe on her thin shoulders and lifted her chin.

Jason recognized her body language. Her stubborn streak was kicking in. No doubt she'd reached her limits for suffering fools in the courtroom earlier.

"You do understand?" Rupert was looking unexpectedly flustered. "If Jason's suit goes to court, you have to recuse yourself."

"If it comes to that, I'm sure you can present that argument," she said coolly.

Attagirl.

Rupert jabbed his finger in her direction. "You need a lawyer."

"No one ever laughs at your jokes, Rupert." Darcy's voice rang out. "It's my first day. My performance isn't criminal, while your attitude toward me borders on contempt."

"Ha! It's no joke." Rupert regained some of his tormenting manner. "You need a lawyer because I've taken on Pearl Conklin as a client. She's suing you for custody of Stogey. Given the length of her relationship with Dad, I have no doubt I can win."

Darcy lifted her chin higher.

"I'll be drawing up papers." Rupert smiled. And that smile said everything the middle-aged lawyer didn't. That smile said he wasn't going to let Darcy off the hook for marrying his father or taking the judgeship he'd publicly coveted. That smile said he was going to enjoy every ounce of pain and suffering Pearl's lawsuit caused Darcy.

Jason tugged Stogey toward Darcy.

"Get yourself a lawyer," Rupert told her.

"She is a lawyer," Jason shot back before Darcy could.

Rupert laughed. "She needs a good lawyer." He was still laughing as he flung the courthouse door open and returned inside.

"I should have expected this." Darcy's hand shook as she took Stogey's leash from Jason. "Everybody wanted something from George. I shouldn't be surprised that the one thing I want is up for grabs."

"What did you want from George?" Jason righted the robe on her delicate shoulders.

"I didn't ask him for anything." Darcy lifted her gaze to Jason and the grief he saw there pained him. "George promised to help me pass the bar and gave me a last name that commanded respect. He joked about a judgeship but he didn't say anything about recommending me as his replacement or..."—she huffed—"everything else he left me."

Jason's world tilted. She'd said nothing of George's love for her or hers for him.

Before he could ask her anything else, Tina Marie poked her head out the courthouse door. "If you're going to get through the day's docket, recess is over."

Chapter Ten

♥

"Brian Lang. Please approach the bench." Darcy opened the next case file.

George's robe chafed the back of Darcy's neck.

His chair felt too large. His shoes too big to fill. George had cowed the court, the lawyers, and his staff, while she'd face-planted in her first appearance as judge.

But before she'd been a Petrie or a Harper, she'd been a Jones. She'd forgotten that this morning. Now she was going to hit the ground running.

Oliver accompanied Brian to the podium, wearing a patronizing smile, probably gloating over her performance on the first case of the day. Representing the state, Keli stood with Deputy Wycliff next to Tina Marie's small desk.

Darcy replaced her smile with her court face. "Mr. Lang, you're charged with reckless operation of a motor vehicle, which carries a minimum ten-day sentence or a seven-hundred-dollar fine. You've pled not guilty but waived your right to trial. Do you understand these charges?"

"Because this case was initially heard by an esteemed judge . . ."—Oliver didn't hide his disdain—"I'd like to remind Your Honor of our position. Deputy Wycliff didn't see the incident in question. Therefore, we move to dismiss for lack of evidence."

"I'll grant a quick review." Darcy coughed to cover a gassy squeaker from Stogey.

"I cited Brian after he fled the scene of an accident he caused." Deputy Wycliff seemed offended that a plea of innocence had been entered. He was young and clearly passionate about upholding the law. "Brian cut Naomi off while passing her on the highway headed out of town. He forced her into a ditch."

"Hmm," Darcy said, assessing the situation before her.

On the state's side, the deputy's use of first names was a sign of his inexperience in court. It hadn't escaped Keli's notice. She frowned but stared at the wall behind Darcy.

As for the defendant, Brian smirked over his shoulder at Naomi, his ex-girlfriend. And that was interesting. *Ex-girlfriend.* Naomi and Brian's breakup had been more gossip-worthy than Darcy and Jason's. So many bitter, public displays initiated by Brian.

And Brian's attorney? Oliver had a good court face, as cold and haughty as his voice. "My client was exposed to an obscene gesture that distracted him during the act of passing. Mr. Lang wasn't the cause of anything."

From the gallery, Naomi snorted.

"Who distracted Mr. Lang and with what gesture?" Darcy asked, preferring to hear testimony than to read through it with everyone waiting.

"My client was caught off guard by Naomi Citi," Oliver continued to speak for Brian, who stood at his side, expression alternating between smugness and fear.

The smugness Darcy attributed to Oliver standing up and

defending him. The fear...She hoped she, as judge, struck fear in him. But her day hadn't been working for her so far.

"Just so I understand, let me recap," Darcy said. She'd have to do it without accusing Brian of being a vengeful idiot, which would only give Oliver ammunition to sneer at her some more. "Mr. Lang was passing and turned to look into the vehicle he was overtaking, which happened to be driven by his ex-girlfriend." Surprise! "Mr. Lang claims an obscene gesture was made by Ms. Citi and that startled him so much that he lost control of his vehicle and accidentally ran Ms. Citi off the road. Is that correct?"

"Precisely. We move to dismiss." Oliver's smile broadened, turning his expression toward winner face.

Prematurely, she hoped. "And Mr. Lang didn't stay at the scene to make sure Ms. Citi was all right? Or was he so surprised that he didn't notice her car was no longer in his rearview?" Darcy was proud of the fact that she kept incredulity from her tone. When Oliver didn't answer, she glanced at Naomi. "Ms. Citi, please approach the bench."

Naomi made her way from the gallery. She was a few years younger than Darcy and wore a simple gray sweater, slimming black trousers, and suede booties.

Darcy had serious bootie envy. "Is this account of events accurate, Ms. Citi?"

"Of course not." Naomi's voice dripped with disdain. "Brian pulled up next to me and kept swerving at my car. I jammed on the brakes and flipped him off, but he slowed down too. And he was so intent upon scaring me that he almost missed the truck barreling toward him head-on. We both braked. He cut me off. And I skidded into the ditch. Eight stitches." She lifted her dark bangs from her forehead, revealing a small, pink scar. She turned her face toward Brian. "Jerk."

"Objection," Oliver said.

Darcy waited for him to state his grounds. When he didn't clarify his reason for objecting, she said with great satisfaction, "Overruled." All that practice in the bathroom mirror was paying off!

Keli grinned, hugging her case files. Deputy Wycliff nodded, rocking back on his heels. Even Tina Marie seemed to approve. At least she wasn't rolling her eyes.

"I sentence Mr. Lang to ten days in jail, the minimum allowed by law." *Boo-yah!* That felt absolutely awesome. Darcy wanted to high-five someone, do a little dance, or kiss a certain cowboy.

Stop right there, George grumbled.

"What?" Brian clutched Oliver's arm. "You said this was nothing. You said she wouldn't know what she was doing."

"Shut up, Brian." Oliver pried Brian's fingers from the fine blue wool of his suit jacket. He glared at Darcy. "That's not right. You know that's not right."

"You mean that's not how the old Judge Harper would have done it?" Darcy refrained from rolling her eyes. "Didn't you tell me recently that my husband couldn't distinguish between the law and his imagination when it came to sentencing? And now you're complaining about sentencing per the law?"

Oliver's fingers closed around his tie. "You're basing a sentence upon hearsay. Deputy Wycliff didn't see the alleged event happen."

"I believe you're referring to witness testimony." Shoot. Darcy should have sworn Naomi in. Wasn't Ronald supposed to do that? Did she have to tell him first? She couldn't remember protocol. Darcy blinked back to the issue at hand. "That's not hearsay, Mr. Harper. The driver of the oncoming vehicle gave a sworn statement that supports Ms. Citi's written statement in the police report and also matches her testimony today." There. An excuse not to have sworn Naomi in immediately.

"I want a lawyer," Brian blurted, red-faced.

Oliver scoffed, hand tugging his poor tie. Italian silk didn't deserve such treatment.

Darcy sat back in George's large, creaky chair. "Mr. Lang, your lawyer is standing right next to you."

"I want a different lawyer." Brian stepped away from Oliver. He sent Keli a pleading look, which the district attorney ignored, as she should. She wasn't the public defender.

"Darcy, ten days is too much." Oliver abandoned abusing his tie and turned his aggression toward her. "You know what my father would have handed down."

Actually, she was too nervous to come up with a creative form of punishment for Brian's vindictive and dangerous crime. "Mr. Harper, may I remind you that I'm not your father. And that in this building you may be cited for contempt for not addressing me as Your Honor or Judge Harper."

In the back of the courtroom, Jason and Iggy chuckled. The Widows Club board tittered midgallery. And her friends in the front row gave her double thumbs-ups.

Darcy wanted to celebrate along with them, but she couldn't dwell on her small measure of success. Oliver was on the attack.

"My father would have given my client some outlandish option." Oliver's anger cut every syllable of his words into sharp pieces. "He would have offered my client ten days in jail or a night of volunteering in the emergency room in Greeley, where he was certain to see the grim effects of automobile accidents."

Dang. That was a good idea. Too bad Darcy was sticking

to the letter of the law. "I'm afraid it's too late for options," Darcy said smoothly, with a trill of power racing through her veins. "Ten days." She pounded her gavel.

Oliver took a step forward. "But—"

"Appeal the sentence to the county probation officer," Darcy said firmly, pounding her gavel again. She cautioned herself not to pound Oliver with it if he came any closer. "That is, you can appeal if you're still his legal counsel. In the meantime, Deputy, take Mr. Lang to the county lockup."

Oliver took another step toward the bench. "But—"

"Bailiff, escort Mr. Harper out of the courtroom and remind him of the perils of contempt of court."

"You." Oliver snapped at his brother before Ronald could react. "I thought you said she wouldn't be able to handle this."

"She won't." Rupert glowered at Darcy.

Apprehension closed around her, thickening the air and delaying a comeback.

This was only the second case of the day. Was every defense attorney going to challenge her like this? Most likely. But they'd think twice if she refused to give Rupert and Oliver an inch in the courtroom.

"Let the record show that the court is warning Rupert Harper that his conduct may be in contempt." Darcy smiled at her stepsons. She smiled the way generations of Joneses had when threatened—like she held a royal flush.

No one need know it was more like a pair of twos.

* * *

"Give it up, man," Iggy said to Jason at Shaw's on Monday night. "She's not coming. Judges don't hang with their exes, especially on a school night. Look. There's a blonde at the bar who's dressing hot and staring at you."

"Pass." Jason sipped his beer, not having looked at the blonde once.

He was thinking about how Darcy hadn't mentioned love as a reason she'd married George and how she'd told him that Jason's support made her feel less alone.

They'd known each other since the early grades of elementary school, but they'd bonded when they were twelve and both staying at a juvenile center in Greeley. He'd been sent there for acting out after his father left town. He'd stolen a kid's bike from school and then gotten into a wrestling match when the boy confronted him about it. His mother had been at a loss as to what to do with him so Judge George Harper had sentenced him to a weekend in juvy.

Darcy was staying in juvy due to an accessory charge of helping her father steal cattle. There'd been some question about her involvement with the crime. She admitted having been there but told Jason she'd fallen asleep in the back seat.

Back then, she'd taken one look at Jason and said, "You're angry. You'll never get out of here scowling like that. People—the ones who set you free—they want to see you smile instead. Just a little. It makes them think you've learned your lesson and are willing to obey the rules."

He'd been trying to work that smile to his advantage ever since, frequently with her. But it occurred to him that his smile and the pleasure of his company hadn't helped Darcy reach her dreams. She'd done that with George's help. And when she'd returned to the courtroom for her second case, she'd had a smile all her own.

"Darcy did good today, didn't she?" he asked Iggy.

"I got news for you, buddy." Iggy watched Priscilla Taylor,

one of Sheriff Taylor's younger sisters, as she tugged a cowboy from Tom Bodine's ranch onto the dance floor. "We
didn't spend all morning watching the Super Bowl. We sat in
court. The first hour was amusing. But I refuse to go into
a play-by-play of the rest or listen to you recap. We have a
problem, you and me. And I'm not talking about women.
Tom Bodine is a pain in the butt."

"I'm assuming our lawyers are battling it out." Jason
nodded toward Pris on the dance floor, moving in time to the
beat of a jukebox song. "Now, make this night worth it for
one of us. Go cut in and dance with Pris."

"She's past history." Iggy scowled into his beer, an indication that he might want to revisit the past. "Tom is our
current problem. While you were fixing your mother's fences
this afternoon for those mini horses of hers, three local
ranchers canceled orders."

"Dang. You think Tom Bodine pressured them to do it?"
Jason scowled as his gaze landed on Tom's employee on the
dance floor. "Talk about fighting dirty."

Iggy leaned forward, dark eyes blazing. "I think we should
countersue. Claim libel or damages or something."

"Pain and suffering," Jason muttered. "I have a feeling a
countersuit won't make Tom back off." But he was at a loss
as to what would.

Iggy slouched in the booth. "If you'd competed this weekend and won…"

Jason's leg twinged. "Okay, stop. Do you even know how
hard it is to ride a first-class bull after being off the circuit for
so long?" He sat up taller. "I can practically guarantee you
that I won't win the first few times I score a ride."

"You go to the gym every day. You have muscle memory.
I'm sure it's like riding a bike."

"For sure, it's that easy." Jason gave Iggy a scornful look that contradicted his words. "A two-thousand-pound bike with an inherent mean streak. Piece of cake."

"We need to get you some practice rides, is all. Maybe buy a new breeding bull, one who's rough around the edges." Iggy sobered, staring toward the dance floor as the music slowed and the cowboy drew Pris closer. "You know, I think Tom would be happier if he was dating someone. He's been a bear since his wife died. And then those twin boys of his hit puberty."

"Are you joining the Widows Club now?" Jason chuckled. "Dabbling in matchmaking?"

"He could use your love advice." Iggy's grin returned. "Maybe you should ask him to be on that video show of yours."

"That is the worst idea you've had all day." And Iggy was filled with bad ideas.

"Not so fast. Think about it. The Widows Club can't get Tom to participate in their functions." Iggy drained his beer. "Who would date him? Who knows? We'd have to learn his interests, and in doing so, we'd find a vulnerability in this court case. Does he sit at home and watch sports? Don't laugh. He's a grown man. It's not like he goes to bed right after dinner. And he's too cranky to be bingeing movies every night on the Hallmark Channel."

"You could always ask his twin boys." Jason caught Noah's eye, indicating he was ready for the check. "I hear they're working at the Burger Shack now." The teens never worked anywhere very long. Last fall, they'd briefly worked for Jason and Iggy. "Maybe they could help us understand where Tom's coming from and what woman in town would be perfect for him." In theory, a happy Tom would be less vindictive.

"Talk to the twins?" Iggy grinned. "That's a great idea."

Wait. What? "Please don't."

"It was your idea."

"It was all hypothetical. Imagine how Tom would react if he knew we were checking up on him." Jason fixed Iggy with a hard stare, not that hard stares worked on his business partner when he got an idea in his head. "We did give him the product he paid for, didn't we?"

"We did." But Iggy didn't look at Jason when he said it. That might have been because Pris began kissing her dance partner.

Or it might have been because Iggy lied.

Chapter Eleven

♥

Darcy?" Someone rapped on the sunroom window, interrupting Darcy's dream of Jason dressed only in chaps and boots as he carried her to bed. "Darcy?"

Darcy nearly fell off the window seat. She clutched Stogey with one hand, but the file she'd been reading when she fell asleep slipped to the floor.

Bitsy stood in the backyard near the sunroom window, waving in the early-evening light. Her black velvet headband was askew. She pointed to the kitchen door. "Can I come in?"

"Sure." Darcy set Stogey down, setting thoughts of bare-chested cowboys aside in the hopes that Bitsy had talked some sense into Pearl about possession of Stogey. Thinking of which, she'd forgotten to ask Jason about Tom Bodine suing him. She and Jason had a lot to talk about. Emphasis on *talk*. She couldn't let this marriage go on. But she couldn't bring herself to consider the options available for divorcing him either.

Don't tell yourself it's only your career and his at stake. Your heart is involved too.

Butt out, George.

"I was going to call." Bitsy didn't waste time on pleasantries, charging into the kitchen as soon as Darcy opened the door, banishing all thoughts of husbands. "But I had to bring Mama bananas for her banana nut bread." She held a pair of black bananas. "So I decided to come by and see how you're doing."

"My dog and I are fine." Darcy sat at the kitchen table. Stogey curled in a ball at her feet.

Bitsy grimaced but hurried on as she pulled up a chair and set the bananas on the table. "You'll be happy to hear Mama is more like herself."

"Grumpy? Bossy? *Decisive?*" Darcy emphasized this last. "After all, she decided to bring a lawsuit rather quickly."

Bitsy had the good grace to look pained. "I tried to talk her out of it. Honestly, I tried to talk *him* out of it too."

"Ah yes. Rupert is thrilled for a chance to come at me." He'd sensed blood, his condescending expression dimming today in the courtroom only when two of his clients had decided to change their pleas to guilty and throw themselves on the mercy of the court.

"He's rather intense, isn't he?" There was something odd in the tone of Bitsy's observation, almost as if she admired Rupert. And she was blushing.

Stogey ripped one of his raspberry gassers.

"Oh?" Darcy reached down to give the dog a pat. "Sounds as if you're intrigued by his intensity." *Do I use that tone when I talk about Jason?*

Yes, George grumped.

"Oh, how I hate this." Bitsy covered her face with her hands. "The last time it came around, I got married. Can you just see me? With him?"

Darcy sat back in her chair. "I think I missed something." She hoped, anyway.

Bitsy released a groan and dropped her hands. "You have to help me. I don't think I can resist him on my own."

"You lost me somewhere between the door and your request for help."

The older woman latched on to Darcy's hand. "I'm a widow-maker."

Darcy's pulse quickened. "As in...a murderer?"

"No, but I might just as well be. Every man I marry dies." Bitsy's features pinched. "My first marriage was a lifetime ago. I was in my twenties. We had two beautiful children, and then *BAM!* Jim died in a freak snow-skiing accident." Bitsy's eyes watered and she sniffed. "Time passed. Two years to be exact. I was restless. Lonely. And then I fell in love again. Terry was divorced. He had two kids. Years later, we married. Our families blended beautifully. And then *BAM!* He died while crop dusting." Bitsy didn't look at Darcy. She stared at those black bananas. "I told myself I'd be okay. I picked up the pieces. Moved on. I was going to be comfortable with widowhood. Time passed."

"Two years?" Darcy guessed.

Bitsy nodded. "I met a wonderful man, also a widower with two kids. Wendell and I got married."

Darcy remembered Wendell. Or, more accurately, she remembered the house Wendell and Bitsy had lived in—a charming Craftsman with a colorful flower garden. Darcy and her brother used to sneak by there the night before Mother's Day to pick flowers.

You ought to apologize for that, George advised.

You want me to apologize for every transgression? That'd take all day.

Just the ones that weigh on your soul.

Oblivious to Darcy's internal conversation, Bitsy was still reminiscing. "Christmases were big affairs, what with six grown children and their expanding families coming to town to visit. I was gloriously happy. And then—"

"*BAM!*" they said in unison, because Darcy had caught on to the trigger word.

"Heart attack." Bitsy laid her palms on the table, almost as if she were revealing her hand in a card game. "And now…"

"Time has passed," Darcy guessed.

"Yes." Bitsy pressed her palms over her cheeks. "Two years. And this morning, I saw Rupert, and something inside of me twitched."

"Rupert," Darcy said slowly, thinking back to George's funeral service with both Pearl and Bitsy in attendance. Rupert had snubbed Pearl, Darcy, *and* Bitsy. "But he's—"

"A jerk, I know." Bitsy rolled her eyes to the ceiling.

"And he's—"

"Younger than I am, I know."

Not by much. Darcy guessed maybe eight years or so. And Pearl was a few years older than George. She didn't understand the fuss. "If his age bothers you, why would you—"

"Fall for him?" Bitsy dragged her fingers down her face, no longer teary. But she looked pained. "I don't know. All I know is that's how I roll when the two-year twitch hits."

"So?" Darcy put her chin on her palm, happy to hear about someone else's love problems. "What are you going to do?"

"Do?" Bitsy blinked. "About the inevitable love and loss?"

"Don't jump ahead. The jerk hasn't expressed any interest in you." Darcy didn't sugarcoat it. "But yes. What are you going to do about Rupert and your mama and this two-year twitch?" And, more importantly, Pearl's lawsuit?

Bitsy opened her mouth. Closed it. And then said, "You were good in court today. Maybe a bit harsh on the punishments."

"Nice change of subject. I'm following the law, Bitsy." Darcy prepared to loop back around to the lawsuit at the first opportunity. "George was quite good at handing down unconventional punishments to fit the crime. His detractors hated it, including your darling Rupert. But based on the appeals I was told are being filed because of my decisions, my detractors would prefer George's sentences." Go figure.

"You're judging yourself by George's career," Bitsy said absently. "You'll never be like him."

"Thanks for the vote of confidence." Hurt, Darcy lifted Stogey into her lap, cuddling him close, needing someone on her side. Even if it was only a dog.

Stogey licked her chin, loving her no matter what kind of judge she was.

Blind loyalty. That's what she used to think she got from Jason. And if she discounted corporately arranged kisses, maybe that's what they'd had. If she still loved Jason, did that mean their marriage was inescapable, like Bitsy's twitch?

Stogey squeaked out some gas.

That's a no, George said.

"I didn't compare you to George as a put-down," Bitsy clarified. "George had his time. Now it's yours. You have to own it. It's like…" She straightened the set of her layered sweaters. "It's like finding a really cool vintage jacket and pairing it with a modern sundress."

That was saying a lot coming from Bitsy, whose entire wardrobe was vintage eighties.

Bitsy brushed Darcy's hair off her shoulder, the way a caring mother would. "Your hair is a lovely, sunny color. You should wear it down every day."

"You're changing the subject again." And yet part of Darcy fell for it. She ran her fingers through the hair she'd once flaunted with layered cuts and blended highlights. "I'm trying to establish myself in a man's world. I want them to focus on my work, not my looks."

Bravo, George intoned.

"Notice first impressions much?" Bitsy gave a weak chuckle. "Have you ever known a man to pay attention to an unfashionable woman? I put in decades at the cable company, and let me tell you that for women, dowdy is dismissible. Don't give the Harper boys any reason to disparage you."

Objection! George railed.

"I think I have to try it George's way first." With a heaping serving of Jones chutzpah.

"If it works." Bitsy patted Stogey's head. "Do you think Rupert is safe from me?"

"The femme fatale of Sunshine?" Darcy chuckled. "You're worried your love will eventually lead to his demise?"

"Don't joke. I've buried three husbands on my watch."

"I think you're safe. Rupert is in love with someone else."

Bitsy went mannequin still. "Who?"

"Himself, of course."

They both laughed.

"Seriously, Darcy, I don't know what comes over me when the twitch strikes. I shouldn't worry about Rupert. As you pointed out, he's wrong for me on so many levels. In his eyes, I'm not datable. It's not like you and Jason, practically perfect in every way."

Darcy remembered the way Jason had come to her after her court meltdown, so caring and supportive. "I have his friendship."

"And you have mine. But friendship won't keep you warm on long, lonely nights." Bitsy stood, paced, and stopped in front of Darcy. "Don't lose sight of the big picture as you take on this new career. You need to come into your own at work and in your personal life. Life is about more than a day job."

"Yes." Darcy couldn't resist adding, "It's about twitches and lawsuits."

"And which would you prefer if you could only have one?" Bitsy asked slyly.

Darcy didn't respond. It was a no-brainer.

Where Jason was involved, she'd take the twitch.

* * *

Bitsy stopped by Mims's house on the way home.

"How did it go with Darcy?" Mims ushered Bitsy into the living room, where there was a fishing show on mute.

Bitsy collapsed into a cushy chair. Her mission had been to gauge Darcy's emotional state. She wasn't going to tell Mims she'd let the conversation drift toward more personal matters pertaining to Bitsy's heart. "Not surprisingly, Darcy is more focused on her career than on Jason."

"But she's not anxious about becoming judge or over-wrought about George's passing?"

"No. Maybe we should hold off with the nudges until the end of summer." By then Bitsy wouldn't be rattled by the two-year twitch. "Darcy has a lot on her plate and busy people make fewer openings for love."

Mims shook her head. "We can't let up now. Clarice is all in on the video blog and giving Jason his nudges."

Nudges. That's what the widows called their activities, the ones they believed would lead toward a love match.

"Why don't I call in a few favors with some of our widowed sisters?" Mims picked up her phone. "I think Mary Margaret and Lola owe us a favor. And they might be able to help Darcy keep Jason top of mind."

* * *

I SAW JASON JOGGING PAST YOUR PLACE THIS MORNING. ♥

The text came in before six a.m. from Lola. She'd copied Mary Margaret and Avery. She was a die-hard romantic but not usually such an early riser.

It was hard not to picture Jason running. He had a good body. A great body. His scars were like magnets to her fingers, the marks of a fearless warrior. Her skin prickled just thinking about him.

Ahem. George came awake.

Darcy shuffled out to the kitchen for a morning can of Coke. It was best to wait for Mary Margaret to put an end to Lola's romantic intentions. She was the pragmatic friend in the group. But the airwaves were empty until after she'd showered.

I SAW HIM LIFTING WEIGHTS AT THE GYM.

That was Mary Margaret, absent any cautions about protecting Darcy's heart.

WHAT ARE YOU DOING AT THE GYM? Darcy asked. She wasn't aware Mary Margaret did anything to stay fit except dance.

I DROPPED OFF KEVIN FOR HIS WORKOUT. ☺ JASON WAS SWEATY.

Darcy didn't appreciate that Mary Margaret—who was practically married—was admiring Jason's sweaty muscles.
Really? George seemed pained.
Darcy made it to the courthouse with Stogey before the next text arrived.
HE SWUNG BY THE BAKERY FOR COFFEE. That was Avery. HAIR STILL WET BUT HIS BOOTS WERE ON.
"Really?" Darcy adjusted her grip on Stogey's bag, accidentally jolting him.
The dog reacted by releasing a stinker.
Darcy waited to respond until Stogey was safely under her desk.

WHO PUT YOU ON JASON WATCH?

Each of her girlfriends sent back laughing emojis.
But the damage was done. Darcy had trouble getting images of Jason out of her head.

* * *

"This is a bad idea." Jason paused outside the Burger Shack Tuesday afternoon. "I should be at the courthouse in case Darcy needs me."
The burgundy truck the Bodine twins drove around town

was parked nearby, a clear indication that at least one of Tom's kids was at work.

"Dude." Iggy rested his hands on Jason's shoulders. "Darcy is fine. In fact, she'll be better if our case never comes before her. We're going to go in there and we're going to be social with Tom's two boys. Maybe we'll learn one of Tom's weaknesses. Maybe we'll spot an opening that will appeal to a single lady. To those smart-alecky teenagers, we're just two clueless cowboys. They'll never know we're shaking them down for information on their daddy."

Jason shook his head. "This cowboy isn't cut out for sub-terfuge." Or technology. Or giving love advice. He'd stopped Kevin Hadley on the street this morning. The mayor had laughed when Jason suggested he'd had a hand in Kevin winning Mary Margaret's heart.

Given his track record with love, Jason should head on over to the courthouse with a bouquet of flowers, a box of chocolates, and a pair of knee pads upon which to grovel.

Still, the smell of grilled burgers was enough to allow Iggy to drag Jason inside the sparsely filled local institution. Mostly because he'd skipped lunch.

"Let me do the talking." Iggy walked up to the front counter, where one of Tom's identical twin boys was working.

"Welcome to the Burger Shack, Mr. King." The teenager, possibly Phil, gave Iggy a bored stare. "You look like you could use a late-lunch-slash-early-dinner double with mush-rooms and pepper jack cheese."

"And sweet potato fries," his twin, possibly Steve, called from the back, grinning as he hefted a cage of fries from the fryer.

"Perfect." Iggy reached for his wallet. "Plus a cola. And I'll pay for whatever Jason's having. You boys do realize you're in the presence of royalty. I'm a King, and Jason is a world champion." Iggy tried to laugh but it sounded like a donkey bray. He wasn't so good at this spy business either.

"Some advice?" The Bodine in the back came up behind his brother, peering over his shoulder so that it almost looked like the counter twin had two heads. "Save the comedy for comedians."

"Ouch." Iggy waited to say more until Jason placed his order for a plain burger, sweet potato fries, and a Coke. "Do you watch a lot of comedy on TV? Is that how you're such a good judge of humor?"

The Bodine working the register rolled his eyes as he gave Iggy his change. "Dad doesn't allow us to watch more than an hour of TV a day. That hasn't changed since we were, like, five."

Jason sensed Iggy was outmatched. He eased his hip against the counter, pretending indifference to the conversation. But he wondered... when had Iggy's antics lost their charm?

"Wow. Does your dad make you watch news?" Iggy tucked his wallet into his back pocket. "Perhaps while he's surfing an online dating app?"

"Dad doesn't date. And after dinner we always watch old home movies of our mom." The Bodine who might have been Steve salted those fries. "Dad cries. We cry. And then we all sing sad Christmas carols."

Jason sighed. Not because it tugged his heartstrings but because it was malarkey.

"Really?" Iggy looked like he bought into the narrative. How could the man be such a good Casanova and such a poor judge of character?

"No. Not really," said the Bodine cashier. "Dad told us he's suing you. We're not stupid. Whatever you're trying..."

He made a dive-bomber sound, shooting his hand from his shoulder to slap the counter. "Crash and burn."

Jason shook his head. "I told him this was a bad idea."

"Yeah." The other Bodine twin placed their cardboard cartons of fries on a red plastic tray. "Maybe next time you should come in one at a time. It'd look less suspicious. But thanks for playing."

"No hard feelings," the cashier said. "You can wait for your burgers at the pickup window."

When they had their food in a corner of the small dining room, Jason shook his finger at Iggy. "I told you so."

"Okay. We were bested by kids." But it hadn't hindered Iggy's appetite. He took a big bite of his double cheeseburger and took his time chewing. "I'll admit that was embarrassing. Do you think they're going to tell Tom we came in?"

"Wouldn't you?" Movement by the door caught Jason's eye. "Uh-oh."

"What?" Back to the door, Iggy froze, burger halfway to his mouth. "Did Tom just walk in?"

"Worse. The Widows Club board is here."

"Jason Petrie." Clarice hobbled up to him, wielding her walking stick authoritatively. "Didn't you say on Saturday that you'd be in your mother's yarn shop this afternoon? This is the second time you've stood me up."

"I didn't actually agree to—"

"My bad." Iggy slapped a hand on his forehead. "I completely forgot to tell Jason we'd set a date."

"I showed up late." Edith took the seat next to Iggy and swiped a fry, her short auburn hair almost as red as the ketchup. "Didn't matter. There was no cowboy in the back room giving advice on love. And Clarice was ready to record too."

Unabashedly eavesdropping, the Bodine twins burst out laughing.

Bitsy stood back, fidgeting with the strap of her black tweed purse. She glanced over her shoulder toward Rupert's law offices. Was her mother there discussing her lawsuit against Darcy?

"You're missing someone." Iggy pushed his tray of fries toward Edith. "Where's Mims?"

"The trout were biting." Edith sniffed. "We couldn't get her away from the river."

"Not even for romance advice videos." Clarice checked her cell phone. "Are you going to be done soon? If we're going to do this, we need to get started. Your mother said she had dinner plans in Greeley."

Jason pushed his burger away, having lost his appetite. "I hate to disappoint you, but I just don't think I'm qualified to give love advice."

"I beg to differ. Which one of us has a trail of pictures with women from every rodeo stop on the circuit?" Iggy tapped on his cell phone, pulling up Jason's website, the one Ken had paid to have created and kept updated. "And I'm talking photographic evidence." He angled his phone so Jason could see the screen. "Here's you with lipstick on your cheek. Here's another with your arms around two babes. And here's lip-smacking evidence that saliva has been exchanged."

The picture that had cost him Darcy. Just looking at it brought up the pain on Darcy's face when they'd talked at her pond, and shamed him.

Although now that Jason was looking at the montage of his rodeo career, he had to wonder why there weren't more pictures of him riding bulls. Was this his rodeo legacy? What a sickening thought. Still, he had to defend himself. At least to Iggy. "Every one of those women is wearing a banner or a hat advertising one of my sponsors." Jason's scowl deepened. "I'm paid to project an image." One that had filled his bank account. He could retire a wealthy man today, if he wanted.

"Like kissing's in your contract." Iggy blanked the screen on his phone, withdrawing his evidence. "I need a contract like that."

"Wowzer." Edith talked around a mouthful of sweet potato fries. "I thought bull riding was only about riding bulls."

"Me too." Bitsy no longer had a stranglehold on her purse strap.

"Finish up." Clarice pounded her walking stick the way Darcy pounded her gavel. "You're both coming with us."

"Where?" Jason muttered, preferring to head over to the courthouse to check on Darcy.

"To your mother's back room at the yarn shop." Clarice turned just as the door to the Burger Shack opened again.

"I thought I saw you through the window." A familiar, lean man in a rumpled pair of khakis and a white polo spotted Jason and stomped over. "It's worse than I thought. Much, much worse." Ken Tadashi stood over Jason, scowling. "You're carb loading."

"Ken always worries about my girlish figure." Jason recovered his shock and introduced his agent to the assembled. He extended his aching leg, trying to ease the tension without alerting Ken. "What did you do with Mark? Leave him at a bus stop outside the hospital in Arizona?"

"He insisted I drop him at home with his mother in Utah." Ken set his cell phone and rental car keys on a nearby table. "I'm tired. Worn down to my last nerve. That boy wants to quit, and the only hunger I see in your eyes is for greasy food, not another world champion belt buckle."

Before Jason could argue, the widows came to his defense.

"Jason, your agent seems a bit militant." Edith paused in eating fries to give Ken a disdainful look.

"Like he doesn't know exactly who works for who," Bitsy added, earning a nod from Iggy.

Clarice pounded her walking stick again. "Jason, don't say you need his approval to do the video today."

"Tell me I got here in time." Ken confiscated Jason's half-eaten burger and sat at the next table over. "You haven't filmed a sex tape, have you? Or developed a fetish for much older women?"

Clarice mumbled something about nothing being wrong with that.

Bitsy mumbled something about a twitch, glancing toward Rupert's office.

"You young men don't know what you're missing." Edith swiped Iggy's soda.

Iggy held up his hands in silent surrender of both beverage and conversation.

"No offense, ma'ams," Ken said belatedly.

"Some taken," Edith said in between soda slurps. "I'll have you know that we're all catches."

Ken wisely made a noncommittal sound and took a bite of Jason's burger.

"I'll have you know that Jason is going to do a vlog I'm producing." Clarice drew herself up as grandly as royalty, a disconnect with those two long, gray braids and hickory walking stick. "He's going to give relationship advice."

Ken choked, eyes widening.

"See?" Iggy nudged Jason. "He's overwhelmed by the brilliant idea of you as a love guru."

More like in shock.

Ken gave an awkward little laugh, setting the stolen burger aside. "Reality check. My client knows nothing about love." He laughed again. "But he can thank his lucky stars that no bull has ever ruined that pretty face of his. Jason still has sponsorship offers, despite not riding a bull in forever."

"I have offers?" Boy, did Jason need some good news right about now.

"Indeed." Ken tapped his cell phone. "You've received an invitation to be a spokesperson for a dandruff shampoo."

"Next." Jason waved his hand. "I don't have flakes."

"No one has to know that," Ken said swiftly. "We've also been approached about promoting a hemorrhoid cream."

Jason closed his eyes. "You're killing me." He'd never had those either.

"You're surprised it's devolved to this?" Ken gave another ruthless chuckle. "This is what has-been rodeo stars receive."

Anger pooled in Jason's belly, nearly as intense as the nerve pinging in his leg. "I'm not a has-been. I'm on a sabbatical."

Clarice tapped Jason's shoulder. "Can we go make our video now? Or do you want to listen to your agent talk about personal hygiene products some more?"

Jason stood. At this point, the relationship video gig had more appeal than hemorrhoid cream commercials.

Ken got to his feet too and moved those loafers in Jason's way. "Why do I know nothing about this video?" He shook his head. "I need to be consulted so that I can protect you and your image."

"My playboy image?" Jason countered. "Or my rodeo image?"

"Both!" Ken's voice shook with annoyance. He ran a

hand through his crisply cut jet-black hair. "I'm supposed to guide your career to maximize profit. You can't agree to projects without consulting me." Ken was militant. And on a power trip.

Anger thrummed in Jason's veins. "Can't or shouldn't? You're my agent, not my boss."

Clarice, Iggy, and Bitsy applauded. Edith was busy eating.

A primitive noise arose from Ken's throat. "As your agent, I have every right to demand to know who these people are and what they want from you." He looked Clarice up and down. "You're making a video. What kind of video? How will it be distributed? And what is my client's cut?"

"Young man." Clarice inserted herself between Jason and Ken. She had a slight height advantage and stared down at Ken as if they were boxers about to fight. "Do not imply we're taking advantage of Jason. We're talking legitimate relationship advice. Not bedroom banter. And it will be distributed for free on social media."

"Free?" Ken said mournfully. "It's worse than I thought."

"Not that Jason—or Iggy—know a thing about women." Edith inserted herself between Clarice and Ken. At a serious height disadvantage, she reached up and poked Ken in the chest with her finger. "But I think they have great entertainment value as a pair."

"No one will take them seriously," Bitsy added without bodying up to Ken. "Despite their number of conquests, neither one of them has ever been in a serious relationship."

"Hey," Jason said with bite. "That's not true. I was with Darcy for nearly two decades." He barely stopped himself from admitting they were married. "Don't say a word about Darcy," he cautioned Ken, hoping he'd get the hint that their marriage was still secret.

Meanwhile the Widows Club tittered, and the Bodine twins chortled. As reality checks went, this one stung.

"That woman was a saint to put up with you for so long," Clarice said, not unkindly.

"You should work on your grovel technique," Edith said. "Both of you."

Jason nodded. Today, of all days, he couldn't agree more.

"Ladies, let's ease up on the criticism." Iggy tried to salvage a lost cause. "I'm happy to be a confirmed bachelor. Proud of it, in fact. I can get company whenever I want it."

The old ladies' laughter deepened. The Bodine boys slapped their palms on the counter as if it were a drum set. Even Ken looked at Iggy dubiously.

"Ignacio, you've exhausted the dating pool in Sunshine," Clarice pointed out. "You either need to settle down or move on to Greeley. This experience will be good for you."

"Soul-searching." Bitsy nodded.

"Life changing." Edith had somehow worked her way back to eating the fries.

Ken frowned at all of them. Jason waited for him to crush the whole idea or spill the beans about Jason and Darcy being married.

But Ken surprised him. "Okay, ladies. I'll approve this experiment, but only for a limited run. And I want you to consider one thing." Ken fixed Jason with a hard stare. "Bringing in your exes for an episode. There's nothing like confronting your past to open your eyes to the present."

Jason was overruled by a chorus of feminine agreement, Iggy's crowing, and Bodine laughter.

"Tell me I get to watch," Iggy crowed.

"Don't you get it?" Jason tipped his cowboy hat back. "They want both of us. And our exes." In fact, they were implying neither man would find true love without this experience.

Iggy paled. "Hey. No. I was just defending my honor. I don't want to be filmed."

But the widows were all over the idea. In a matter of minutes, they decided that Edith would sit in a third chair as the interviewer for this first attempt and that other women would be brought in later.

"Are you sure about this?" Jason asked Ken. "Say the word and I'll back out."

His agent had no sympathy. "You want to stay in this small town instead of riding the circuit, you need buzz. You can give this little idea a whirl or I can close on one of those sponsorship offers."

"Dandruff shampoo and hemorrhoid cream? No." Jason rubbed his thigh, stopping when Ken noticed.

"I'll tell them we're considering the offers anyway, just in case this video thing crashes and burns." Ken finished off Jason's burger. "What's going on with your leg?"

"His leg is fine." Iggy slapped Jason on the back. "It's his heart that's in need of repair."

"Whatever you say, Ignacio." But Ken's brows were raised speculatively as he stared at Jason.

Chapter Twelve

♥

"Your Honor, may I approach the bench?" Rupert asked.

"Must you?" Darcy mumbled, while in her head George practically growled with annoyance.

It had been a long day in court with a stream of cases and intermittent Jason sightings via text—the latest from Lola, who'd seen him coming out of the Burger Shack with a well-dressed, dark, handsome stranger, to which Avery had responded with the google-eyes emoji.

Tina Marie was trying to catch up on their workload, shoving as many sentencing cases as possible through the system, presumably before someone realized Judge Darcy Harper wasn't qualified for the position. On the other hand, every defense attorney in the county, public and private, had tried to exploit Darcy's inexperience or undercut her confidence today.

It was approaching four o'clock, and Darcy's patience was at its end.

"Your Honor, may I approach the bench?" Rupert asked again.

The last thing Darcy wanted to do was allow Rupert, the object of Bitsy's twitchy affection, more time to complain about her sentencing in front of an audience. She was afraid her court face had fallen an hour or so earlier. And unlike yesterday, she had no supportive crowd in the courtroom.

It was sad to admit, but she'd expected Jason to enter every time the public door in the gallery opened. All those text sightings of him about town made it that much harder to keep her focus on court.

Instead of granting Rupert access, Darcy turned to her assistant. "How are we doing with the docket, Tina Marie?"

"I think we set a record for the highest number of cases in one day." Tina Marie might have been the only person in the room who looked pleased.

"Given that, let's postpone the final trio of cases until tomorrow." Darcy's gaze touched on each of the defenders present—Rupert, Oliver, and Reese Walter, the public defender. "I'll see you three in my chambers. Court adjourned." She rapped her gavel, gathered her case folders and Stogey, and made her retreat.

The three men traipsed into her office looking grim. They didn't sit, and neither did Darcy. She expected an immediate attack and wanted to face them on level ground. Her adversaries waited to engage until Tina Marie passed through the judge's chambers from the courtroom and closed the door behind her.

"This can't go on," Rupert said sharply. "Your sentences are ridiculous."

"They're too severe." Reese echoed Rupert's derision.

Gripping his tie, Oliver glared at her in silence, perhaps because they'd had multiple go-rounds on sentencing already.

Begin as you mean to go on.

It felt good to have George in her head. She didn't have to face them alone.

"I'm following the letter of the law." Darcy lifted her chin. "Isn't upholding the law what a judge is supposed to do?"

The three men exchanged glances and frowns.

In their hesitation, she found strength. "Don't be hypocritical. In the past I've heard each of you complain about George's sentencing," Darcy went on, increasingly convinced she was right. "Reese, I've heard you at Shaw's venting about punishments handed down. And you two...There wasn't a holiday or birthday that went by without you jumping on George's back about him being too lenient."

Again the three men exchanged glances. And then they looked down their noses at her, their scorn palpable. But they lacked arguments to back up what they wanted—a judge they could control.

It struck Darcy then. Too often she let others tell her what to do—bosses, professors, Jason, George. But this time, she held the power. The power to punish these men if they didn't treat her with the respect due her position. The power to continue to sentence the way she saw fit. They could complain to her. They could lodge complaints with the Judicial Performance Commission. But they couldn't do anything to her in the courthouse.

Begin as you mean to go on, George repeated.

"Get out of my office." Darcy didn't recognize her voice. She didn't recognize the woman who thrust her arm out and pointed toward the door. She was confident and certain, even in her clunky heels. Somehow she'd developed an intimidating court presence, not just a face.

Attagirl, George cackled.

"Get out," she repeated in a way she hadn't practiced in the mirror.

She didn't recognize the men who filed out of her office, tails between their legs.

Judge Darcy Harper.

She was beginning to believe it could stick.

* * *

"I'm only here because I'm your best friend," Iggy told Jason a few minutes after leaving the Burger Shack.

They stood outside Jason's mother's yarn shop in downtown Sunshine, mirroring each other. Arms crossed, hat brims pulled down low.

"Here's the thing." Jason tugged Iggy out of the way of Rosalie Bollinger, pet shop owner, who was walking her two dogs—a huge Saint Bernard and a small terrier mix. "This can die a quick and painless death if we go in there and have nothing to say. The Widows Club told us we're clueless about women. Why not play to that?"

"Brilliant." Iggy clapped Jason on the back. Whether he could keep quiet was another thing entirely.

Ken parked his rented Lexus in a nearby space and got out. "I could have walked here. This town is so small. I don't know how you stand it." His gaze caught on Avery Blackstone changing movie posters a block over. And then Tiffany Winslow cleaning the pharmacy window glass.

"The scenery is first-rate." Iggy elbowed Jason, chuckling.

Jason didn't laugh. Darcy wasn't part of the scenery. She was probably still in court without anyone watching her back.

"Don't look so grim, Jason." Ken joined them on the sidewalk. "It's always good to try new things. Who knows? You could be so smooth on camera that we land a rodeo announcer gig when you retire."

"The hemorrhoid ad is looking better and better." Iggy chuckled once more.

Jason shook his head.

"You'd think a man who climbs on bulls for a living would show a little more courage. Is this the studio or...?" Ken glanced around, perhaps looking for a recording studio. "Where are we going? Time is money."

"Right here." Jason opened the door to the yarn shop, directing Ken and Iggy inside. "Hey, Mom. You remember my agent, Ken."

"Ken. What a surprise." His mother set down her knitting needles and came around the counter. She wore a thin, neon-pink sweater she'd made and had her blond hair pulled back from her face.

Mom was a hugger. Ken was more the polite-handclasp, shoulder-bump type. Jason's mother sprang and wrapped her arms around Ken before he could dodge out of reach.

"Ken, you feel solid, like you're thriving. Jason must be earning enough money to feed you well." Mom released him and took a small step back. "But your wardrobe is a bit too citified for Sunshine. I've got just the thing to help you fit in."

In no time she had a black sweater vest on him.

Ken gave Jason a long-suffering look. "Does this not prove I'd do anything for you?"

"Will you quit dawdling?" Clarice yanked aside the curtain that separated the store from the storeroom. Her walking stick rested against the wall. "We're ready back here. The yarn insulates sound nicely, and Nancy needs to close up soon."

The storeroom was filled from floor to ceiling with color-ful yarn in boxes, in plastic bags, and in stacked skeins. A rug had been tossed on the floor and an oblong folding table tucked into the tight space.

The elderly widow positioned them behind the table—Jason in the corner next to several containers of baby-blue and -pink yarn, then Iggy, and then Edith blocking them in. They sat on a redwood picnic bench that his mother normally used to display baskets of yarn and knitted goods in the store window. Bitsy sat on a folding chair by the storeroom entrance. Clarice stood behind a tripod upon which she'd mounted her cell phone. Ken took up a space next to her.

"I'm having second thoughts," Jason said. The walls of yarn were closing in.

"Be a sport," Ken said with a significant tug on his sweater vest. "I'll send the video to a friend of mine in New York who manages social media influencers and another who produces rodeo coverage for the networks. We'll see what they think."

Jason didn't want to be a sport. This was going to suck. Big-time. It was like drawing a ride on the meanest bull at the rodeo. Things were going to end badly. Stomp-stomp. A bolt of pain struck Jason's leg. He grunted softly but refrained from massaging the pain away. Too many eyes were trained upon him.

"I can tell you right now, a yarn backdrop isn't your look." But Iggy, like Jason, was wedged in. "Or mine either."

"Just FYI, people. I have no idea what to say." Jason wasn't sure whom he was announcing it to, but it needed to be put out there.

"Follow my lead. I've been given notes." Edith looked at Clarice. "Tell me when you're ready. Oh, before that. We need a name for this thing. I thought we'd call it *The Relationship Threesome*."

"No," Jason ground out, horrified by the innuendo in a multigenerational, multigender crowd.

"*The Love Trio*?" Edith rebounded quickly.

"No," Jason said even more firmly this time.

"*Thoughts from the Throuple*?" Edith blinked innocently at the two men beside her.

Was it possible she knew what a throuple was and was yanking their chains?

Regardless, Jason rejected that too. "We're not calling this anything. It's a demo. Who cares if we have a title?"

"New York," Ken said simply.

"He's right. We have to call it something," Bitsy said in that soothing voice of hers. "Every video you see online has a title and names of those featured."

"We're not putting my name on this." Jason was back to choking out his words.

"It doesn't fly without your name," Ken said as if it had been decreed.

"Rock, paper, scissors?" Edith suggested, finger-counting the three of them. When they frowned, she said, "Final answer. *Love Advice from Two Cowboys and a Little Old Lady.* You can't argue with that."

"They won't." Ken checked his phone. "It'll do. Let's get this thing started."

"And we're live." Clarice made a lasso motion with her hand.

"Welcome to the inaugural session of *Love Advice from Two Cowboys and a Little Old Lady.*" Edith glowed, as if this were her big break in Hollywood. "During our chats, we'll learn what well-to-do, modern-day cowboys think about dating, relationships, and sex."

Iggy lowered the brim of his cowboy hat and slouched.

"No sex talk," Jason insisted. "This is PG-13."

"Dating, relationships, and celibacy, then," Edith pivoted without a crack in her smile. "Although I think we can all agree that celibacy is boring if it isn't a choice." She pinched Iggy's cheek the way a grandmother pinched a baby's. "Are you celibate?"

"Don't look at me," Iggy whispered, chin to his chest as if trying to hide his face. "I have a very active social life in that respect. Now the bull rider here…"

Jason did a slow burn, which involved glaring at Ken.

"Focus, Edith," Clarice murmured, making a move-it-along circular motion with her hand.

"Let's get right to our first topic—initial attraction." Edith glanced down at scribbles on a small notepad. She pointed at Bitsy. "Per our crack researcher, it's a scientific fact that both genders notice the face first." She paused, glancing up at Bitsy. "Hang on. Is that right? I would have thought men would notice a woman's bazingas and women would notice a man's behind. Is the face response significantly higher than other body parts? Was it close for men? I mean, bazingas have to be high up on the list." Edith looked at Jason, because Iggy's face was hidden by his hat brim, his shoulders shaking with barely contained laughter. "What do you notice first, cowboy?"

"I plead the Fifth," Jason said flatly. If he said anything, Darcy would hold it against him if she ever saw this debacle.

"I can't keep quiet. I just can't. I'm going with honesty." Iggy raised his head and cupped his hands in front of his chest. "Bazingas. One hundred percent bazingas. Not the size so much as the display. Let me know you're comfortable with what you've got, ladies."

Jason fastened the top button of his shirt, trying to look as buttoned-up and pious as possible. "I'm extremely uncomfortable with this topic. Can we go back to celibacy? I'm celibate and have been for—"

"No. We have to know everything about bazingas." Edith half turned on the bench to face Iggy. "One of our cowboys prefers confident bazingas over facial features. It's fascinating."

"Please," Jason said in a strangled voice. "No more bazingas."

"Are you a behind girl, Edith?" Iggy asked, clearly having forgotten they were being recorded.

Jason couldn't forget. He stared at Clarice's phone on that tripod and wished for a technological catastrophe.

Meanwhile Ken, Bitsy, and Clarice were grinning, which didn't bode well. Bazingas aside, couldn't they see this was a bust?

"I thought I was a fan of a man's backside until last Christmas." Edith grinned at their production crew. "It was his shoes that had me falling. They weren't orthopedic. They were expensive leather. Shoes are very telling at my age, an indicator of many things. Like his ability to be mobile and active." She winked. "Not to mention his net worth and his sense of style."

Iggy hung on every word. "What happened with the leather-shoe guy?"

Beneath the table, Jason punched his friend in the thigh and muttered, "Don't encourage her."

Edith tsk-tsked. "He was actually too active for me. His entire day was devoted to a rotation of dates with women. Keep in mind, he was retired. But his calendar was more tightly scheduled than an airport reopening for landings after a thunderstorm."

Iggy inched away from Jason. "So, you're downgrading to orthopedic shoes from now on?"

"I'm actually choosing celibacy for now." Edith squared her shoulders. "I thought I'd spend some time working on me."

"Do I really need to be here?" Jason demanded, half standing in his yarn corner.

"Yes!" everyone said.

Iggy hauled him back into his seat.

Ken gave Jason a hand gesture he took to mean *stay*.

"What attracts you first to a woman, Jason?" Edith prompted. "Go on. Don't be shy."

"A woman's personality." It was the safest answer on the planet, and Darcy couldn't find fault with it.

Iggy chuckled. "Oh, I can see her personality from halfway across the bar."

"Her character and moral fiber." Jason raised his voice, trying to rise above the innuendos being tossed about by Iggy and Edith.

"Personality isn't exactly a box you check at first sight," Edith said doubtfully.

"The fact that she has something she's passionate about," Jason floundered, trying to remember what had attracted him to Darcy when he was younger. She'd been such a badass at first, pretending she didn't care that her parents spent more time behind bars than in Sunshine. "I respect that a woman has a dream she's pursuing instead of hanging her hat on mine."

It was the truth, he realized suddenly. He loved that Darcy had never made him feel as if they weren't equal partners, both working toward success in their respective fields.

"Jason's a sensitive guy," Iggy said, smirking. "But counterpoint. I like to keep the banter light until the second drink."

"Don't you mean the second date?" Edith asked.

"Second drink on the first meet," Iggy clarified. "If I've got a chance, I'll listen all night." He wobbled his eyebrows suggestively.

"Great transition. Let's move on to passion." Edith referred to her notes again. "Do sparks have to fly from the get-go? This always seems like such a trap to fall into. From a woman's perspective, if you keep things platonic, the man may think there's no chemistry and not give the relationship a chance. However, if you give that kiss your all and someone thinks you're going to 'put out,' there might be hurt feelings. And if you do the bedroom rhumba too soon, you might be seen as fast and loose or, worse, desperate."

Jason bit back a groan. Judge Darcy wasn't going to like the direction of this conversation at all.

"You can't hold back on those first kisses, not if you want there to be a second," Iggy explained. "And you can always test that chemistry with restraint. At least I can."

Jason scoffed. "Says the man whose kisses have enticed many a first date into a first sleepover."

"And I say it with pride." Iggy puffed out his chest. "There's no shame to being young and attracted to confident bazingas. Insta-love is the foundation of many a great marriage."

"Says the man who has yet to be married." Jason tossed his hands up.

"Like you are?" Iggy arched his brows.

"Like I am," Jason growled. "I am nothing like you."

"Cut." Ken stepped in front of the tripod. "I think we end on Iggy's line about insta-love. That last part wasn't exactly flattering to you, buddy." He nodded toward Jason.

"And that's what we're here for, after all." Iggy got to his feet in the small space between the table and bench, helping Edith to hers. "Jason's reputation."

"Jason's career," Ken corrected crisply, "which benefits your bull semen business. You'd best remember that."

"Like you're going to let me forget," Iggy scoffed. "I'll always be second fiddle to the world champ."

Jason and Ken exchanged glances. Jason imagined Ken was registering the same thought: Iggy had serious envy issues.

Edith came around to the other side of the table, beaming at Jason. "You said some really nice things. Women love to feel their work and their passions are respected."

"And to know their men are proud of their accomplishments." Clarice joined Edith, smiling reassuringly at Jason, as if he'd done well.

He'd face-planted harder than if a bull had tossed him with a spin move.

On a positive note, Ken's contacts would probably take one look at the video and give a scathing review, advising Ken never to put his client in such an embarrassing situation again.

Edith blinked owlish eyes at Clarice. "Did you get my best side?"

"Yes, always," Clarice said briskly, although Edith had turned this way and that and Clarice hadn't touched her cell phone the entire time.

* * *

Chuckling, Bitsy walked down the sidewalk on Main Street toward her car.

If she was any judge, the video they'd made wasn't going to give anyone helpful love advice. But the widows were hopeful the ruse would give Jason something to think about when it came to his relationship with Darcy. And it might even make Iggy, the die-hard bachelor, grow up a little.

She paused at the street corner, checking for traffic before stepping into the crosswalk.

"Bitsy." A man called her name from down the block.

She turned, realized it was Rupert, and twisted her ankle.

"Ow. Shiitake mushrooms." Bitsy hobbled back to the corner.

"Are you all right?" Rupert put a steadying hand on her arm, the way a Boy Scout did when helping an old lady across the street. "I didn't mean to startle you."

"I'm fine." The initial throb of pain in her ankle was receding. There was a different throb lingering in her arm where he was touching her. Unlike Edith, she was noticing Rupert's face, not his shoes.

The compassionate smile. The deep blue of his eyes. The firmness of his skin. She could even smell a wisp of his aftershave.

Her gaze dropped to his feet, and it was just as Edith said. His feet were encased in fine leather, a sign of a virile man who had no need for orthopedic shoes.

She sighed.

"Are you sure you're okay?" Rupert took a few steps back, adjusting his grip on his black leather briefcase as he studied her.

Oh my. Oh my. Oh my.

In those few steps he'd taken, she'd taken note of his backside, and his gaze had dropped to her bazingas.

Were they confident?

She didn't dare look down.

This is not like me.

That darn two-year twitch had been encouraged by Edith's comments from the video blog.

"Are you sure you're okay?" Rupert's smile was no less kind. "Can I buy you a cup of coffee?"

What a smile! I should have had Mama sue somebody earlier.

"Yes. I'm just woolgathering." *Choose your words, Bitsy! You sound like an old maid!* "I mean, something Edith said just got caught in a loop in my head. I would love a cup of coffee." Maybe some caffeine would put her on her toes. And perhaps time spent with Rupert would quell his triggering of the twitch. Extended exposure to him in the past had always resulted in the confirmation of his almost loathsome character.

Loathsome seemed harsh. Perhaps *haughty* was a better word. *Regal.* Yes, that was even better. That was...

Bitsy wanted to thunk herself on the head. She was talking herself down from the Rupert-is-inappropriate ledge.

They walked toward the Olde Time Bakery, which made decadent pastries, rich lattes, and cups of flavorful French roast.

"Are you coming from court?" Bitsy asked. "How did Darcy do?" Too late, she realized how treacherous the subject was. Or...er...not too late. It was a superb question that would only bring out Rupert's dark side.

"You're a fan," Rupert said flatly.

"We're an odd sort of family, don't you think? We should all support each other."

"I can't get past what she did, and neither should you." The vibe he was giving off was non-twitch-worthy. Here was the Rupert of old.

And yet her attraction didn't wane. "Darcy made your father happy."

"And she made your mother miserable." Rupert held the door to the bakery for her. "Why defend her?"

It was time for a change in subject, normally something she was quite good at. Words escaped her. The image of his broad shoulders did not.

She scurried inside. The bakery was filled with enticing, warm smells. There were a few people in line ahead of them but no one she knew well enough to greet heartily and use to ignore Rupert for a minute or two.

"Did you file something for Mama's little grievance?" Lordy, she hoped not.

"I'm still trying to decide how best to present it. Cases of she-said versus she-said aren't impossible to win, but they are tricky to position based on the law."

"Take your time." Bitsy's eye caught on a chocolate-drizzled croissant filled with cream cheese. Premenopause, she would've been all-in on that.

They placed their coffee orders.

"And we'll split that chocolate croissant." Rupert pointed to the treat. "I saw you looking at it."

He'd been watching her? The twitch shuddered in her veins. "Oh, I couldn't."

"I couldn't either, not unless I only ate half." He gazed at her with that compassionate expression he'd given her on the street corner earlier.

A warm feeling engulfed Bitsy, a swirl of feeling that bound the two of them together and promised other decadent things to be shared—gelato, birthday cake, bottles of wine.

"I'll get us a table." Bitsy forced herself to turn away, to contain the urge to beam up at a man she was completely wrong for and could be the death of. *Widow-maker.* She avoided the more intimate tables in the back and chose one near a window and the sidewalk.

Rupert followed her, carrying a tray with their lattes, the croissant, and two forks. "How are you holding up?"

"Me? I'm fine."

"You look a bit harried." He made the first move on the croissant, breaking off a piece with a fork. "Busy day? Or has your mother been taking up a lot of your time?"

"You mean since your father died?" She felt compelled to make a move of her own, taking a big, flaky piece oozing with cream cheese. "I should ask you how you're handling his passing."

"But you won't." He took a sip of coffee. "You're too polite."

"And you discourage intimacy." That was totally the wrong word to use. Her cheeks heated.

Rupert raised an eyebrow, which only served to make him look more handsome.

"Friendship, I mean. You discourage it." She couldn't hold on to her dignity and not explain herself. "And community too. Don't pretend you don't know what I mean. You're a successful attorney in a small town. You buy anything that matters in Denver—your car, your furniture, your clothes. And despite years of our parents being companions, this is the first time you've asked me to coffee."

"A mistake on my part," he said smoothly. "I hadn't realized what a stimulating conversationalist you are."

"And just like any good lawyer, you divert attention from here"—she pointed at him—"to here." She pointed at herself, realizing they were alike in their ability to deflect.

"All right, I'll get to the point." Instead Rupert hesitated, smiling at Bitsy in a way that made her feel appreciated as a woman. Her bazingas might be confident after all. "I'm looking for a witness who might have overheard Darcy or my father declaring intent to give your mother the dog."

Shiitake mushrooms! She'd read his appreciation all wrong. He was looking for a star witness, not a star in his eye.

"George wasn't likely to have a conversation about something like that in front of anyone." Bitsy stabbed another piece of croissant. It broke apart, the way her twitch should be crumbling. She speared the lesser half. "From day one, that dog was his."

"And what about Darcy?" Rupert continued his gentle interrogation.

"We haven't spent much time together." Her portion of croissant fell to the table. "Is that why you asked me..."— Out?—"for coffee? To see if I'd be a witness for your case?"

He studied her—from her black headband to the ribs below her bazingas. "You'd make a compelling...witness."

He was toying with her. Bitsy shook her head. It was time to face facts. She was old enough to have babysat for Rupert when he was young enough to need a sitter. This twitchy infatuation with him was going nowhere. "Were you angry at Darcy when you weren't appointed judge?"

Rupert shrugged, half frowning. "She's a temp. The election in the fall is what matters."

"So you *were* angry." She watched him over the rim of her coffee mug. "Can I tell you something?"

"Please. Take the stand." He sat sideways, legs crossed at the knee, one hand on his mug, one eye on her.

"One of my husbands was a fantastic armchair quarterback. He could call plays and read defenses quicker than the television announcer. But he couldn't throw a football farther than across the living room. Not that it was his fault. He had a bum shoulder. But he was a fantastic referee. He called all the high school games."

Rupert's grip on the mug tightened. "You think I should be satisfied where I am."

"I think people who stop to appreciate what they've got are happier in general." She should listen to her own advice. Bitsy took the last bite of croissant, gathered her purse, and took one last look at Rupert's handsome face across from her. This was one of those moments that happened rarely and wouldn't likely happen again. She'd put an attractive, powerful man in his place. "Thank you for the coffee." All she had to do was walk away without looking back, without validating she cared what he thought.

She reached the door, willing herself not to glance over her shoulder.

She did.

Rupert was looking at her. And not with disdain.

Him, the twitch whispered.

Bitsy went the long way around the block to reach her car. If she hadn't, Rupert would have had a clear view of her rubbery-legged stride nearly the entire way. He would have known she, an older woman, found him attractive.

If he didn't know already.

* * *

"What's up with your leg?" Ken demanded when everyone else had left the stockroom. "And don't lie to me."

Jason considered doing exactly that. For about two seconds. "It's nothing. Nerve twinges, Doc says. He thinks it will fade in time."

Ken circled him, staring at his leg. "But you can ride?"

"Yeah. I mean, I haven't tried."

"Not even one of those old geezers at Bull Puckey Breeding?" Ken's intense gaze rose to Jason's face. "That's not like you."

Again, he tried not to admit anything. Again, he was unsuccessful. "Okay. I'm concerned that the twinge might disrupt my concentration during competition."

"We'll get you an appointment with an orthopedic sports doctor. No more of this country doc stuff. If we leave tomorrow—"

"I'm not leaving." Jason set his chin.

Ken propped his hands on his hips. "Because of Darcy?"

Jason nodded.

"Unless you're planning on retiring, I wouldn't let this *twinge* go too long."

Jason filled his lungs with air to argue, and...nodded.

His mother yanked open the curtain separating the store from the storeroom. "Ken, where are you staying while you're in town?"

"Oh." Ken hadn't prepared his answer to that question.

"Don't worry. You can stay with me." Jason's mother had the sweetest smile and the best of intentions. "Although I'm meeting friends in Greeley for dinner tonight, I always have the guest bed made up and ready for company."

Ken gave the sweater vest he still wore a little tug, an unspoken reminder that he didn't want to spend this visit ensconced in knitted wear. Which he would be if he stayed at the Petrie homestead. Jason's mother was overly protective of those in her sphere and showered them with knitted gifts.

Much as he enjoyed seeing his agent squirm, Jason interceded. "Mom, the guest bed is a twin and—"

"Ken is single," Mom said firmly while still maintaining

the sweet tone of a parent who made cookies from scratch. She treated all Jason's friends and colleagues like they were underage. "A twin is adequate. I can give you a key, Ken. Just make sure you're in by ten."

The men exchanged glances. Jason shrugged, as if to say, *I tried, man.*

"Thanks for the offer, Mrs. P," Ken said smoothly. "But I have to maximize my time with Jason. We have a lot of business to discuss, as you can imagine." He pushed Jason out the door.

They walked several feet down the sidewalk before Jason risked saying, "You know, I live above Iggy's garage. You can sleep on my couch, but frankly, you might have been more comfortable in my mom's twin bed."

"With her curfew? No." Ken pointed at his rental. "Get in. I could use a shower. Take me to your Batcave."

They got into his Lexus. It smelled like new. Like Rupert's leather couch. Like the way a successful man's vehicle should smell. Jason had lived like a vagabond for so long, saving money for his and Darcy's future, that he had a sudden urge to buy a ranch, a new truck, and a big, big bed.

"Have you told the missus that she's a missus?" Ken and his dry sense of humor.

"Yes. I'm giving her time to let things sink in." He directed Ken to Iggy's house. It wasn't far from downtown, but then again, nothing was in Sunshine.

From the driveway, Ken craned his neck to look at the garage apartment, making a disapproving noise. But he stayed quiet until they were upstairs in Jason's place. "I had no idea. This is wrong. You've earned more than a million dollars from prize money and endorsements. Why are you living like a ranch hand or a grocery store clerk?"

Jason bristled. "Because I was saving to buy a spread and build my wife a dream home. What does it matter where I keep my stuff? I'm never here anyway."

"No." Ken shook his head. "You're going about this all wrong. The way you live. The way you give Darcy all the time in the world to take a break or realize being married to you is a good thing. If you had the spread and a show of wealth, she'd be beating a path to your door."

"As would every other buckle bunny in America. I grew up without much. I don't need the trappings of wealth." But he didn't put as much emphasis on his words as he would have an hour ago, before he'd ridden in Ken's fancy rented Lexus.

Ken moved into Jason's bedroom and sat on the bed. "I've failed you. I should have come up here sooner. I'm cringing inside imagining you hobbling up those stairs with a cast on your leg. In the dark. In the snow."

"Barefoot," Jason added, straight-faced.

"Yes, barefoot!" Ken tossed up his hands. "This is all my fault. But I'm going to clear everything up. Your leg. Your love life. Your career."

"Maybe you should stay with my mother." Because Ken was beginning to sound overly nurturing.

His agent ignored him. "What else is going on with you? Tell me everything. I know there's more."

"Well . . ." Jason fidgeted, and not because of any leg twinge. He was embarrassed to admit another of his problems to Ken. "There's this lawsuit."

Ken clapped a hand over his eyes.

Jason explained about Tom Bodine. When he was finished, Ken did some deep breathing exercises. It was a good thing that Jason was used to Ken's method of reducing stress, or he might have been freaked out.

And then Ken stopped and pointed at Jason. "I know exactly what to do and where to start."

"You do?" Jason had a bad feeling about this.

"Yes. You're going to go tell your wife you need a place to stay while I'm here. Just a few days. During which time you can flash your pearly whites and repair whatever needs fixing at her place with those big muscles of yours. Also, ply her with promises of forgiveness, fidelity, and the house of her dreams."

"She's actually not impressed by wealth. And plus, she inherited the old man's money."

"Stop with the negativity." Ken waved his arms madly, very un-Ken-like.

"She'll never agree to let me stay." There was the little thing called her reputation.

"Stop." Ken glared at him. "Have I ever steered you wrong?"

"Need I mention dandruff shampoo and hemorrhoid cream?"

Ken scoffed. "You can do whatever your ego bends to, Jason. Now go. I need a shower and a power nap before I send out that video. Oh, and leave me a key."

Jason grinned. "Promise to be home and in bed by ten?"

"Go!"

Chapter Thirteen

♥

Darcy. What a surprise." Bitsy opened the door to her mother's cottage Tuesday evening wearing pink capris, a flowered blouse, and a look that was anything but surprised.

Wink-wink.

It had been Bitsy's idea that Darcy come to the cottage on George's property. She'd called Darcy just after five, suggesting the visit with the hope that it would weaken Pearl's resolve to sue. Darcy wasn't optimistic, but she was willing to try anything at this point. And so even though she was tired and hungry and intrigued by further Jason sightings, Darcy had changed into a pair of shorts and a T-shirt and come over as the sun disappeared behind Saddle Horn Mountain.

"Let her in, Bitsy." Pearl stood on a stool in the small kitchen. She was cleaning her cabinets, scrubbing with all her might in a T-shirt and jeans that looked like they might fall off her. The contents of her china cabinets were strewn about the counter, stacks of china and mismatched coffee mugs and glassware. "Darcy can haul out the trash when she leaves my dog here."

"I brought salad." Darcy and Stogey entered the cottage.

Darcy handed Bitsy a plastic container of salad she'd bought at Emory's Grocery.

"Mama doesn't eat enough vegetables." Bitsy thanked her. "Wasn't that nice of Darcy to bring you something? We were just talking about you."

"Pfft." Pearl kept scrubbing. "You were talking."

Darcy hadn't been in the cottage since Pearl had moved in. The one-bedroom bungalow looked different. Whereas before there had been some photographs of George, they were everywhere now. On the small mantel. On the two end tables. On the TV console cabinet. They weren't the typical pictures of a happy couple. They were just of George. Young George. Middle-aged George. Elderly George walking Stogey.

"Didn't there used to be a picture of you on the mantel?" Darcy asked Bitsy, who shushed her.

"Why are you here?" Pearl demanded, stopping her scrubbing long enough to glare at Darcy.

"I was wondering if you wanted to come over this weekend and box up some of George's things." That, too, had been Bitsy's idea.

"I can't. I'm devastated." Pearl pulled her features into something resembling a sad, insincere face. "Someone thinks they can have everything."

Bitsy and Darcy sighed at the same time. Stogey put his nose to the hardwood and waddled around the room and then into the bedroom.

"You see? Stogey feels at home here." Pearl resumed her scrubbing. "Let me and my dog wallow in our grief."

Stogey was unlikely to wallow in anything but the fuzzy blanket at the end of Darcy's bed.

A cat hissed in the bedroom. Stogey yelped.

"Stogey?" Darcy walked toward Pearl's bedroom.

"Do not cross my wallowing boundary," Pearl warned, stopping Darcy in her tracks.

"There's a time to wallow and a time to move on, Mama."

"Move on?" Pearl raised her voice so high that her words bounced off the ceiling. "I have nothing. Not even a dog to comfort me."

As if to contradict her words, Pearl's white cat strutted out of the bedroom.

"I don't think George would have wanted you to pine like this," Darcy ventured, craning her neck as she tried to see Stogey through the open door.

"What do you know?" Pearl grumbled. "You were only his wife." She paused before adding slyly, "And you didn't even share a bedroom."

"True," Darcy admitted without argument. That was how badly she wanted the lawsuit to go away.

"I was there when George needed me. When he lost Imogene. When he fell and broke a hip. When he came up with the cockamamie scheme about how to protect his legacy by stealing you from Jason."

Stealing me from Jason?

Bitsy and Darcy exchanged glances.

"I was there when he thought through the details of the bench appointment. I was there!" Pearl railed.

"You were there at the end too," Darcy said kindly, inwardly gnashing her teeth against another revelation about George.

"Everybody wants me to go on as if my heart wasn't broken." Pearl choked on a keening cry. "You both think I don't know about the stages of grief. But you can't be old and not know. I'm in the angry stage, and when you decide to give me what's mine, I'll be in the bargaining stage."

"Moving backward through the grieving process," Darcy murmured to Bitsy.

"Mama, you know George wouldn't have wanted you to act like this. Or to take Stogey away from Darcy."

"You're soft. You're both soft," Pearl wailed from her perch. "And George was the softest one of all, swayed by a pretty face into thinking she could take on those boys of his."

Bitsy gave Darcy an apologetic look.

Stogey dragged a black bra into the room, practically prancing with pride. It wasn't an old woman's bra, girded for a long day of support. It was a black, lacy underwire with purple trim.

"Hey." Darcy took it from him and with a start realized, "This is mine. Pearl, have you been rummaging in my drawers?" It was her date bra. And—*hello*—she hadn't been on a date since she'd been with Jason. She couldn't remember when she'd seen it last.

"Me? Sift through your underthings?" Pearl sank onto the top step of the stool. "Only a jealous woman would do that. And I was never jealous of you."

Darcy shook the bra. "I thought you only wanted one thing from the house." Stogey. "This wasn't even George's!"

"Mama." Bitsy laid a hand on Darcy's arm. "It's time to put a stop to the drama. George loved you. But have you ever considered that he gave everything to Darcy because she wouldn't be blinded by grief? Have you ever thought he spent all of his marriage to Darcy preparing her to take care of the town and you?"

If any of that had been George's plan, he hadn't told Darcy. But apparently he had been as secretive as she was. And he was silent now.

"You have to drop the lawsuit, Mama. Rupert charges by the hour, you know."

"But Stogey is mine," Pearl said emphatically. "She's a Jones. She's doing what Joneses do best."

Stogey gingerly clamped his toothless jaws on the strap of Darcy's date bra and stared up at her as if he wouldn't mind a gentle game of tug-of-war. His gums were finally beginning to heal. And that face...

There was no way Darcy was giving him up.

"Trust Darcy to do what's right, Mama. Tell Rupert there's no need for a lawsuit."

"You want me to...I'm standing here and only just now realizing that no one loves me," Pearl said mournfully.

"I love you." Bitsy hurried to her mother's side and wrapped her arms around her. "George loved you. You have to have faith."

"Don't 'Mama' me. I see the signs." Pearl pried herself free, stiffly indignant. "You're in cahoots with Darcy. And I saw the way you looked at my lawyer. Maybe you're in it with him!"

"Mama...please."

Darcy clutched her bra, picked up Stogey, and left the pair to unravel their emotions on their own. As a family. Of which Darcy wasn't a part.

Once she was outside, sadness slowed her steps. She didn't have anyone. If Pearl had her way, she wouldn't even have Stogey.

A white truck was parked in her driveway. Jason leaned on the truck bed, his silhouette outlined by the setting sun. Darcy's heart beat faster at the sight of him, at the memory of today's updates—he'd gone running, lifted weights, been seen strutting around town. What was he doing here? Someone should have warned her.

Darcy cut across the lawn to the main house the way a woman did when she wanted to avoid temptation.

"Your gate was open." Jason grinned.

She'd left it open to make it easier for Bitsy to leave.

Darcy set Stogey on the lawn so he could mark the perimeter before going in. Her steps resumed. But they were slower, less purposeful. "I thought we agreed we shouldn't be seen together. I thought I told you..." His larger-than-life presence blocked her memory of what she'd said, because with him she wasn't alone. With him she had family.

Jason took deliberate steps toward her with that swagger her friends had reported on. "You came away from that conversation with one impression—that you couldn't see me. It'll be dark soon. You live on a remote country road. Who's going to see us?"

"Like we're back in high school? Sneaking around by the river?"

Makes me glad I raised boys, George said, suddenly making an appearance when he'd been AWOL at Pearl's.

"I'm proud of you, Darcy. I didn't say it before." Tipping his cowboy hat back, Jason kept on coming toward her. "I'm proud of you getting not one degree, but two. Passing the bar. And now being a judge. That takes hard work, determination, and a thick skin."

He had no idea. "So does hanging on to a bull for eight seconds."

Say good night, Darcy, George encouraged.

Darcy held her ground, but she was no longer sure which ground she was defending. Her judgeship or her love for Jason. Her husband flashed her his dimples.

And then she knew what needed defending. In the cottage, she'd been the odd man out. But here... her heart wasn't just beating faster, it was swelling with love and the comforting familiarity that was Jason.

"What are you holding?" Jason was close enough to claim the bra, holding it up in its proper shape. "I remember this pretty thing, and the pretty thing who used to wear it for me."

Darcy had been Jason's girlfriend too long to be embarrassed by him touching her lingerie. "Well, before you go getting all sentimental over it, Stogey just found it at Pearl's house." She didn't want to think about Pearl rummaging through her drawers. She snatched it back. "It's going in the donation pile. Let someone else sneak around with it on."

Before she knew what was happening, Jason's hands landed on the swell of her hips. "I wish that we were still in high school, sneaking around the county for hidden places to make out. I miss talking to you, Darcy. Your love and support grounded me, but . . ." He let his sentence trail off and his gaze drop to the bra.

He let her imagination complete the sentence. He wanted a kiss. He wanted the warmth of her body pressed to his. Or maybe that was her imagination. Her wish.

Judges don't have time for hanky-panky!

"George." Darcy's head fell forward until it rested on Jason's firm chest. "Every time I get weak, he's there in my head, telling me what I should be doing. Or shouldn't, as the case may be."

Why don't you talk to Pearl, George?

She won't listen.

Jason stroked a hand over Darcy's hair, coming to rest on her bun. "He wasn't in your head in the courtroom, was he?"

"Oh, he was listening and commenting a little." But only a little. Not the way he seemed to jibber-jabber when she was with Jason. "When George was alive, he had a habit of letting me speak first when he grilled me about the law. I'm sure when he's good and ready, he's going to give me an earful about my performance on the bench." She rubbed her temples. "You don't think I'm nutty? Hearing him, I mean?"

"No." He said it so tenderly that she believed him. "The first year I left home, I heard your voice in my head. It was like I needed you with me, shoring up my doubts and keeping me company."

"Before you rode a bull?"

"No. Different times, like when I was driving to an event after I'd eaten dirt the night before. I'd see something you might have liked. A horse watching me pass by. The back seat of a car filled with balloons. A vendor at a rodeo selling fancy boots. You commented on everything I saw as if you were by my side. It made me smile. It kept me going week after week."

That had always been the hardest part of his career for both of them. A rodeo man was on the road at least eight months out of the year.

"You never told me that before," Darcy said softly, staring at the placket of his shirt. "I like that." But more than that, she liked that Jason understood that she heard George. Giving in, her arms slipped around his waist. "Did I argue with you in your head? Or nag?" The way George did.

"No. You were pretty much just along for the ride, pointing out the good stuff in life." They stood so close that his words vibrated through her. "If George's advice bothers you, just tell him to go away."

Darcy bunched the bra in her hands. "George doesn't like to listen to someone else's opinion." She doubted he ever had.

"Then tell George to shut up." Jason tilted her face up to his. "Tell him one kiss won't destroy your career."

His lips lowered, found purchase, and began a gentle journey to reacquaintance. On her sigh, he deepened the kiss.

It was lovely to be held by strong arms, to be kissed like she was the one thing in the world that sustained this man. It was lovely because George was as quiet as the pond on this still, twilit night. Darcy and Jason were together. That was all that mattered.

Her hands moved up his chest and across his stubbled cheek to spear through his hair, knocking his straw hat off. And then her hands met resistance...

"Hey." Jason pulled back a little, reaching to touch his ear and disentangle the bra strap she'd accidentally hooked over it. He tossed it to Stogey.

Darcy didn't care. She tugged him closer. "Kiss me again, cowboy, before George comes back and reminds me what I've got to lose."

And her cowboy did. Oh, how he did.

* * *

Something sat on Jason's foot.

He stopped kissing Darcy to look down.

The moon on the horizon illuminated Stogey sitting on top of his boot. They'd been leaning against his truck and making out like teenagers who couldn't stand for the night to end.

Darcy stepped out of his embrace, easing the bra from Stogey's chops. "George is back."

Jason inwardly cursed George and his place in Darcy's head. He picked Stogey up and scratched him behind his ears. The dog gacked, and gacked again, as if choking on something.

"Stogey." Darcy took him into her arms. "He always does

that when he eats grass. It's quite rude, but he doesn't actually vomit anything. I think he just regrets eating it." She turned toward the front porch, features shadowed because her porch light didn't come on.

"Wait." Jason scooped up his hat and fell into step with her. "Can't I at least walk you to your door and kiss you good night?" *Ask you if I can stay for a few days?*

"George says no." She climbed the first step. "We can't start up again, Jason."

He drew her back to him. "We're married and adults. We can do whatever we please. Take it as slow as one step at a time." He put his foot on the next stair up.

She shook her head. "This could be the way I get what I've always wanted."

"You always wanted me." He tried not to sound frustrated.

Darcy placed her hand over his heart. "I love you, Jason. I probably shouldn't admit it, yet there it is. But what good does that do me? I'm in a fight for my future. And if anyone knew we were married...If anyone knew *when* we got married, I'd lose it all."

"But you'd still have me." He brushed his fingers through her hair. "You want that, don't you?"

"I've learned a lot of things in this house," Darcy said softly. "About the law, about relationships, and about myself. I don't want to be in a relationship where my man is required to travel eight months out of the year and kiss other women under the guise of corporate advertising."

This was where Jason was supposed to say he'd do anything to be with her. This was where he was supposed to say he could retire. Heck, he'd missed the start of the rodeo season. He had enough in the bank. He could quit now with the staples and fasteners and pins inside him to prove he was man enough to win those world championships. He could quit and the leg twinges would be an annoyance, not a worry. But he had to be honest with her and himself.

"I want to be with you, Darcy. Only you. I want to live on a ranch with you, raise kids, take you to a bar like Shaw's on a Saturday night and tell anyone who'll listen how much I love you."

She inched backward. "But..."

He hated the way she drew away from him, the way her expression closed off, but they'd delayed talking for too long. "Do you remember when I left for the rodeo at eighteen? Do you remember what my mother said to me?"

Darcy nodded. "Go to college first. Get a fallback plan."

"But I knew in my gut that I had to be a rodeo man." He framed her face with his hands, willing her back to him, willing her to give them a chance. "And I know in my gut that the rodeo's not quite done with me. The same way I know that we—"

"We can't get back together, Jason. But..." She stared at him the way he'd prayed for months that she would, with love in her eyes. "I can't stop loving you. And maybe that means you're my fallback plan. Can't you leave town for seven months? Go get rodeo out of your system while I figure this judge thing out?"

"My gut says no." As did his suddenly twinging leg. Jason pressed a kiss to the back of her free hand, subtly flexing his aching thigh muscle. "But hey, a question like that...It's the kind of thing old George would say during sentencing. You can pay a fine or leave town for seven months."

"It is very George-like, isn't it?" She sighed.

He drew her closer, but not close enough. The little dog

in her arms was between them. "Maybe you're more like the old man than you think. Up here." He made a small circle on her temple with one finger. "Maybe that voice you hear in your head is the girl George wanted you to be." He ran a hand past her temple, fingers tangling in her silken tresses, tugging at those pins that confined her hair. "But no matter what voice you hear in your head, in my heart you'll always be mine." He leaned closer, coming in for a kiss. And she was going to let him.

Stogey chose that moment to pass a stinker.

"My chaperone." Darcy chuckled, stepping free of his embrace. "Love doesn't mean we don't have obstacles to overcome."

"I like to think of Stogey more like your good luck charm." And then, because he could, he leaned forward and kissed her again.

It was a different kiss from the ones in the driveway. Slow. Careful. Instead of combustible heat, there was tenderness. Instead of the urge to rip off her clothes, there was contentment.

This, he thought. *I want this.*

Not the empty adulation of the crowd. Not a photo opportunity kiss. Not the hawking of someone else's product. He wanted Darcy. In his arms. In his bed. In his life.

She drew back. "That was so slow it should have been boring."

It hadn't been, and they both knew it.

"That was a husband kissing his wife." Jason tugged her closer, careful of the dog. "That was coming home, darlin'. Don't even try denying it."

She didn't.

Jason pressed on. "Honey, I hate to ask this, but... I need

a place to crash for a few days." He explained about Ken's unexpected visit.

Darcy rolled her eyes. "Stay with Iggy."

"And cramp his style? Or worse, bear witness?" Jason shook his head.

"What about your mom?"

They exchanged a glance, both chuckling. Darcy knew his mother and her boundary-crossing, overly nurturing streak.

"Let me stay a few nights on your couch. I promise not to pressure you into anything. I'll just be here, guarding your back."

She studied him for a moment.

He was almost certain she'd refuse. But he didn't loosen his hold. He was good at hanging on as long as need be.

"George doesn't like it, but... okay."

Chapter Fourteen

♥

In the moment Darcy said okay…

In the instant Jason pressed a kiss to her forehead…

She had regrets. And those regrets sent her back in time to her early friendship with Jason.

"Jason. Darcy." Judge Harper entered the dining hall of the juvenile detention center and called them over. "I thought I'd stop by and see how you're doing."

Darcy obediently came forward. Joneses didn't mess with judges, even though Judge Harper was old and rich, her mother's kind of mark. She smiled and caught Jason's eye, silently sending him a message to smile as well.

He did. Jason had a nice smile, like her mother's.

Judge Harper looked at them both and then nodded. "I see you two formed an alliance. Good. Are you ready to go home?"

"Boy, am I." Darcy's smile practically split her cheeks.

Her mother entered the dining hall, which also doubled as a visiting center. She spotted Darcy, but instead of joining them, she sat on the bench in the corner.

Darcy took a step toward her.

Judge Harper held her back with a hand on her shoulder. He put his other hand on Jason's. "You know, most kids who come here more than once think they're smarter than the system. They use good manners. They smile. They pretend they've learned their lesson. But character can't hide behind a smile forever."

Darcy kept smiling, but her stomach did a little flip the way it did when she sat alone in Dad's truck on a dark road while he stole cattle.

"But you two have good character. And you're smart enough to know that your parents don't always set a good example." He glanced toward Darcy's mother and then at Jason. "It's hard to be an adult and always do the right thing. If you feel angry, hit a ball, not your friend's face. If you want a pretty dress, work hard for the money to buy it, don't steal."

Jason nodded.

Darcy nodded, but she didn't feel so good.

"Darcy?" Mom called to her.

Judge Harper let her go.

She sat next to her mother but she stared at her feet because everything Judge Harper had said had a ring of truth to it.

"Darcy." Mom took her hand. "Listen to me. Your father and me . . . We're going away for a while."

Darcy knew what that meant. They were going to prison. But they'd never gone at the same time before.

"Judge Harper has made arrangements for you to stay with a nice family in Sunshine and your brother to stay in Greeley." Mom's smile was off in a way Darcy couldn't explain. "I know you like to make friends, but you have to remember our life is secret. You wouldn't want to tell someone about me and make me stay away longer? Or spill a secret about yourself that sends you back here."

"No," Darcy said quickly.

"Good." Mom smoothed Darcy's hair. "You look pretty

today. Remember that people will like you if you show them what they like to see."

"Did I lose you?" Adult Jason stroked Darcy's hair and pressed another kiss to her forehead. "You went away for a second."

He didn't realize how far she'd gone. "While you're here, you need to park around back," Darcy told him, refusing to let him inside until he'd done so. She stood at the kitchen door, waiting for him to bring in his duffel bag. "There'll be no more kisses." No more temptation.

"I'm fine with that." He flashed a grin that brought out his dimples.

I want more kisses.

Darcy held on to Stogey the way a child clung to a security blanket. But as she opened the door to let Jason in, she experienced the first shaft of pure happiness she'd had in George's home.

The George she'd married had been tall and gangly, a skeleton of the hale man he'd once been. He'd blended in with the darkly paneled house with its heavy drapes and shuttered windows that protected his sensitivity to light. When he'd entered a room, it'd been with bowed shoulders, shuffling feet, and a booming, gravelly voice that defied the weakness of his physical being.

Jason was tall and broad, his blond hair a beacon in the shadowy house. He stood out, a ray of sunshine and energy. His boots scuffed the linoleum. His heels rang as he planted them to take stock of his surroundings. His smile and laughter were just what she needed. What she'd always needed.

More than she needed to launch her law career?

She was afraid to answer that question.

* * *

"This is the kitchen." Darcy clutched Stogey like a shield.

Jason hung his hat on a hook by the door, running a hand through his hair as he took in his surroundings. "I thought it'd be grander."

The house was dark. The lighting limited to small lamps. The door he'd come through was gouged at Stogey height. The kitchen cabinets were a soft shade of yellow, a faint attempt at cheerfulness. The butcher-block counters and small kitchen dinette tried to convey warmth. Overall, it felt like a place to sleep, not live.

"George wasn't into material possessions," Darcy said defensively.

"Except for that fancy iron gate." And its electronic security panel.

Darcy didn't argue. She gestured toward an alcove off the kitchen. "That's the sunroom." It had two rattan chairs, built-in white Shaker benches beneath the windows, and brightly colored pillows and drapes. "It looks out over the pond."

"It looks like it was constructed in this century." And lived in by someone other than George.

"He had it built for Imogene when she got sick." Instead of expanding upon that, she led him through a doorway into the dining room without saying anything.

The dining room needed no introduction. The table would seat at least twelve. The red cherrywood was out of fashion. Even he knew that, and Jason wasn't up on trends. It was big and ornate and ponderous on the soul. He was liking this house less and less the longer he was inside.

"Living room." Darcy paused, looking around as if seeing it for the first time. Or through his eyes.

The room was oblong, broken by a round brick fireplace in the center with a humongous black metal flue hanging from the ceiling. A small television was positioned in front of two matching green recliners, one more faded and worn than the other. The wood floors were stained a dark brown. The curtains black and drawn closed. On the far side of the fireplace was a piano with worn keys and a white couch with big orange flowers. The couch cushions didn't fit snugly against the couch back, as if they'd been washed and shrunk.

"The judge lived here?" It was hard to believe. He'd expected some luxury, more like Rupert's office. Instead it was more like... his apartment. And finally Jason understood what he'd been unwilling to believe in the kitchen. "He really didn't care about the finer things in life at all."

Unlike his sons.

"He cared about the law. He cared about people. And justice." Darcy held her head high, as if girded against Jason's poor opinion of the house she'd come to call home.

He slung an arm across her shoulder and hugged her to his side, the way friends do. "He was like us." Reluctantly Jason released her. He'd promised not to pressure her. This tour... this stay... it was a gift. An inside look into her life with George.

"He was like us," Darcy echoed hollowly. She led him down a dimly lit hallway.

He was going to take Ken's advice and make this place better for Darcy to live in, starting with installing bright light bulbs and opening those drapes. Somehow he'd repair the scratched kitchen door and whatever else needed upkeep.

"That's George's room." She continued past it without further discussion. "And this is his study, which is where you'll sleep." She paused and added, almost as an afterthought, "There's a sofa sleeper in there. I'll get you some blankets and pillows."

He dropped his duffel to the brown shag floor.

She led him past another room. "That's my bedroom."
Her bedroom.
It wasn't George's bedroom.
Jason almost sank to his knees to give praise to Jesus. Since that day outside the courthouse, he'd tried fitting Darcy's marriage into a business-deal-type box. But there'd always been that niggle of doubt. And now he knew.
Darcy didn't sleep with George.
He'd told himself for months that it'd be okay with him if she had. Their love—his and Darcy's—was different. He knew it to the core of his being. Whatever feelings she'd had for another man were separate from the love she had for Jason.
Didn't mean he hadn't had doubts. Didn't mean he hadn't lain awake long into the night and wrestled with jealousy.
But now he knew for certain. He knew, and he breathed a deep sigh of relief.
She led him back into the sunroom. "And that's it."
"It's not very big."
She shook her head, still clutching that dog, whose short legs hung limply over her forearm like those of a leopard sleeping on a tree branch. The dog was relaxed, but Darcy wasn't. She fiddled with her wedding ring, turning it with her left thumb. Not looking at anything. Not him. Not the dog.
He was missing something. Jason glanced around the kitchen. There was an empty bowl in the sink. He glanced around the sunroom. There was an empty Coke can on a coffee table. He hadn't seen signs of life anywhere else in the house. "You stay in these rooms." He made a sweeping gesture to indicate the kitchen and sunroom.
"Yes. I studied with George in here. At the table. In the sunroom sometimes." Her words were stiff. Stilted. Her gaze jerked about. "He spent a lot of time in bed. In the

dark. He was sick. Sicker than anyone knew. He needed help to get up, to get dressed, to get to work and back."

"You were his nurse?" His neck spasmed as his head jerked back. A reflexive response to a shocking revelation. "Tell me you didn't clean the house and mow the lawn too."

"He needed me. Not just for physical care but to ensure he went out on his terms." Darcy's blue eyes were huge. By degrees her chin came up. "I don't regret it. He turned my life around."

Thoughts and revelations flew by too fast to register.

She'd married a man who needed a caregiver, who insisted she study the law rather than work, who didn't tell her he was making her his heir. And then there was Darcy's insistence that she live up to George's standards. And the old man's voice in her head. He'd dangled Darcy's dream in front of her, all the while pulling strings.

Rage bubbled in his veins.

Jason prided himself on the fact that he didn't rail. He didn't demand to know exactly what had gone on under this roof while she was married to George. He didn't stomp around, lashing out like a wounded bull.

Instead he came forward, set the dog down, and wrapped his arms around her because he knew this woman better than he knew himself. She looked like a Jones, like she could take whatever obstacle life threw in her path. But inside, she was a delicate flower. "I'm sorry. It's all my fault. I wanted to make as much money as I could for us for as long as I could. And because of that you ended up here. I should have known you weren't happy. I should have taken one look at you and seen the truth." That she needed his help, his love, a flippin' rescue.

After a moment's hesitation, Darcy's arms circled his waist. "You don't have to be sorry. I made a choice. I knew it would be as difficult as being in foster care. In some ways this was easier."

Meaning that in some ways it wasn't.

"I loved George like a father. Without his involvement in my life, I would probably have gone to jail by now. What's a year of my life when weighed against that?"

The wounded bull banged around his chest, demanding action, retribution, revenge. But still, he held her tenderly.

"The town...Rupert and Oliver...Everyone's wrong." Jason drew her closer, wanting to absorb her into his very being so she'd know she wasn't alone. If he had his way, she'd never be alone again. "George gave you everything out of guilt."

Darcy shook her head. "I think he believed marrying me rescued me from becoming a stay-at-home mom instead of an attorney. I think he left me everything as payment for becoming Judge Harper. Not for seven months. But forever. I think he believed no one would make Darcy Jones a judge. I certainly wouldn't have."

Later, after he and Darcy sat for hours at the kitchen table—him holding her hand, her clinging to Stogey...after she brought him up to speed on her marriage, on her struggles to understand the law to George's high standards, on Pearl's angry grief...after she confessed her desire to give the money and properties to George's sons and Pearl and her fear of losing Stogey...after listening helplessly to her claim that she'd do it all again—Jason sprawled on the hard-coiled sofa sleeper mattress in George's study and stared out the open window at the blanket of stars, waiting for a star to fall so he could make a wish for Darcy, a wish for that fresh start she wanted far, far away from the web George Harper had woven.

Because she deserved to choose her own destiny.

George's office smelled like old wool suits, cigars, and

decaying books. It smelled of old money and old man. Of desperation in a man's last days.

Jason couldn't imagine devising such a plot. He'd grown up on a small sheep ranch owned by generations of Reeds, his mother's family. Their house, the house his mother still lived in, was a small farmhouse over one hundred years old. It was filled with antiques. He got a kink in his neck just thinking about the wood-trimmed antique love seat in the living room. It wasn't made for lounging. But Mom always said there was no reason to buy new furniture when the old held up. Dad had supplemented their ranch income (translation: paid the bills) with his farm supply salesman job. Those sheep were the first animals Jason had ridden on. His first horse had been a wild mustang his father received in lieu of payment. He'd learned to fall off without breaking a wrist on that horse. He'd grown up with socks mended so many times they were paper thin. Jeans he'd grown out of and tucked into his boots to avoid being labeled as a flood-wearer in school.

Money, the kind of money that allowed you to buy a car because it was Tuesday—it'd been a dream. Like Ken said, Jason had that kind of money now. It was just...the money wasn't as important to him as Darcy and her happiness. He'd been going through life grateful for the opportunity to climb on a bull and put his manhood to the test every week. He would have paid someone for the privilege. But by some twist of fate, they paid him.

So he could relate to this house not being a showpiece, to George and his passion for the law. But he couldn't relate to the way the old man had treated Darcy.

Jason punched his pillow.

Darcy, jeez. She'd lived here for nearly a year. The two times preteen Jason had gone before George, he'd been scared to death. And the judge had known it. He'd scared Jason straight when he'd sentenced him to juvenile hall.

As for Darcy...

George had also seen Darcy throughout her childhood and teen years. He'd known she was intent upon going to law school. One year, he'd even awarded her a scholarship so she could work fewer hours waitressing at Shaw's. George knew what Darcy wanted. And him being the type of judge he was—a man who presented you with hard choices and the hard truth about your life—he knew how to railroad folks down a path. He'd railroaded Darcy into marriage and a seat on the bench.

Slimy bastard. Jason punched his pillow once more.

I'm being judged without a trial.

Jason sat up, glancing furtively around the room. The voice had sounded garbled, ancient, almost the way he remembered George sounding the last time he'd seen him in December, when he'd taken the time to speak to Jason at Shaw's.

Jason lay back down. Darcy's belief that she heard George's voice in her head was getting to him.

That and his guilt for not recognizing the jam Darcy had gotten herself into.

Don't feel guilty, boy. Darcy rebounded, same way she's always done.

Jason jerked to a sitting position again, wide-awake and a bit unnerved. After a moment he whispered, "Get out of my head, George."

He thought he heard laughter. But there was no more commentary.

In the morning he convinced himself he'd dreamed the entire thing.

* * *

Darcy's alarm went off far too soon, jolting her out of a sound sleep.

She'd gone to bed last night comfortable with the truths she'd shared with Jason about her marriage to George but ruing the fact that she hadn't told him she'd been a juvenile delinquent.

She rolled over and stared in the direction of the alarm clock. The numbers were obscured. She must have left something on the bedside table.

She rubbed her eyes and sat up. The gray light of dawn peeping through the window revealed the obstruction.

A Coke can had been placed in a glass tumbler with ice, so that the can was kept cold. It blocked her view of the time.

"Jason?" Her bedroom door was closed but not latched. She smiled. This was their normal. He'd leave her an iced can of Coke in the morning and go for a run.

She turned on the bedroom light. A scrap of paper with two scribbled words sat on top of the can: *Love, Jason.*

Jason loves me.

She put Stogey on the carpet, where he stretched and yawned and released a characteristic toot.

She popped open the Coke and poured half its contents over ice. Jason would be out somewhere running, starting his day with miles logged while she slept.

"Just warming up," he'd say, flashing that trademark grin upon his return.

Darcy drank the soda while padding down the hall to the kitchen door. "Come on, Stogey." She put on a jacket over her pajamas, slipped her bare feet into plastic rainboots, and escorted the dog outside.

The sun was coloring the horizon pinkish orange, chasing away the mists clinging to the grass. The pond was still. She sucked down more Coke while Stogey went right out to the grass and relieved himself.

Love, Jason.

It might have been the caffeine and sugar surging in her system, but everything seemed on the track of rightness. Her judge's robes had arrived special delivery. Tina Marie was no longer openly hostile. And Stogey was promptly taking care of business outside.

Footfalls approached.

She and Stogey turned to see Jason jogging down the drive. Sweat soaked his hair and dampened his shirt. His tan legs were thickly muscled, despite the ugly-looking scars above his right knee.

"Just warming up." He slowed a few feet away and came to a stop with a lurch. He reached for his leg, almost as if he'd pulled a muscle, and then straightened and gave her a smile with all the dimples. "You should shower while I make eggs." He kissed her forehead and proceeded up the steps, limping a little and calling for Stogey to follow.

Darcy's skin tingled where he'd kissed her. She sipped her cold Coke. Stogey waddled toward the door, pausing at the top step to glance back at her, waiting.

Everything's going to be okay.

She didn't dare believe it.

* * *

"Do you want me to keep Stogey today?" Jason walked Darcy out to her car after breakfast.

"No." Darcy wouldn't look at him. "People would ask me where he was."

"And you wouldn't want to tell them."

You're her dirty little secret.

Jason scratched his head, glancing around. "Did you hear that?"

"What you said?" Darcy deposited her purse and laptop bag on the passenger seat. "Try to see this from my point of view." She came around to the driver side, Stogey at her heels.

"I do. It's just…" His hands found her hips, but he continued to scan the area for the source of the grumbly, masculine voice. "I'm your husband, not your dirty little secret."

So her career means less than yours?

"What's wrong?" Darcy framed his face with her hands. "You look like someone just pulled the rug out from under you."

"I was just thinking that…" He didn't want to admit he was hearing George in his head. He tucked her into his arms. "I was just thinking that my career isn't more important than yours. You made lots of sacrifices to support me over the years, showing up at events, loaning me money to stay on the road. I need to be willing to do the same."

Harrumph.

Take that, old man.

Darcy pulled back to look at Jason. "You do realize that you can't stay here more than a few days for exactly the reasons you just mentioned—helping to defend my position? As soon as Ken leaves, you have to go."

"I'm going to support your career, honey. Seven months isn't forever." And if Jason played his cards right, he wouldn't have to wait that long. He scooped up Stogey. "Go on. You're going to be late for work."

She continued to stare at him, a look of wonder in her eyes. And then she shook her head. "Nothing is ever as easy as it sounds."

"But it should be." He opened the car door for her, handed Stogey over, and then shut it when she and the dog were settled.

Darcy rolled down the window. Stogey poked his little head out the window, pink tongue hanging out.

"You know, there's a perfectly good Cadillac in your garage." He'd seen it through a window. It was much newer and in better shape than her old Toyota.

"That was George's car." Whatever lightness he'd brought to the morning disappeared from her eyes.

And this was George's house, but she was living in half of it. "Have a good day at work," he said with forced cheer and a wave. "Text me if you need moral support in the audience."

Some of the warmth returned to her gaze. "I'll be fine but thank you."

Jason stood in the portico until she turned out of the gate and onto the road leading into town. He went back into the kitchen, cleaning up the breakfast dishes. He carried his mug of coffee while he made a circuit of the house. It was still dark and dated, like his grandfather's home.

Harrumph, George seemed to grumble again.

Jason made a second circuit. This time, he counted light bulbs that needed replacing and opened the blinds and drapes, letting in bright sunshine. "Better."

That earned him another *Harrumph*.

The front door burst open. Pearl stood looking like an angry scarecrow in need of some stuffing. "What are you doing here? Stalking Darcy? I should call the sheriff." But instead of calling, she stomped to the front windows and closed the drapes.

If she'd done that before Jason knew the truth about George's illness and her behavior in the aftermath of his death, he'd have backed off and let her. But there was no going back. He had to help Darcy find happiness again. And that meant he had to help Pearl find happiness again.

While Pearl moved to the next window, Jason followed closely behind. "I'm staying here for a couple of days." He yanked the dark drapes to either side. "And I'm not a vampire."

"The light hurts George's eyes." Two windows down, Pearl clutched the curtains closed and glared at Jason.

"Nothing hurts George anymore." Jason took a step in Pearl's direction. "Shrouding this place in darkness won't bring him back."

Her face scrunched tighter than a stale prune. "I used to like you, Jason Petrie."

"Same." Jason had eaten many a breakfast at the Saddle Horn, where she worked. He approached the old woman with caution, giving the curtain she held a tentative tug. "You know, when my dad left us, my mom wouldn't get rid of his things for months."

"Hoping he'd come back?" Pearl said on a shuddering breath, deflating.

Jason shook his head. "Pretending everything was normal. That she wasn't shattered inside and one big angry mess." He didn't feel the need to share that, at twelve, he'd been ill equipped for the loss too. If anything, his scars ran deeper and had taken longer to heal because no one had told him he could channel his anger in a new direction until he'd met Judge George Harper. "When my father left us for another woman"—and her kids—"he thought we'd be happier without him, if only because he was happier."

Selfish SOB.

That was 100 percent Jason's inner voice.

"People know I'm one big angry mess," Pearl said, staring toward the two green recliners in front of the television.

"People knowing doesn't help make you any less angry." Jason had taken all that anger and channeled it into riding bulls, the only things he could find that were angrier than he was.

"I always thought George and I were on the same page." Pearl's voice lacked the fierceness she'd charged in with, and her face lacked the prune-like anger. But her fingers still clutched the black drape. "But then he realized the COPD was getting the better of him and he was too proud to drag around an oxygen tank and wear a cannula so he could live longer. He wouldn't listen to me or his sons or the doctor. He'd sit in that chair." She gestured toward the worn green recliner. "And he'd worry about one of his boys becoming judge. He'd worry they'd reverse the good he'd done and give new meaning to who Judge Harper was and what he stood for. He'd worry you'd get Darcy pregnant and she'd give up on practicing law. And somewhere along the way, after he asked me to marry him and I refused, the lines between the two worries must have blurred and . . ." Her words were nothing more than a whisper, a bitter wisp of air. But they were an admission that George hadn't been in his right mind and that she hadn't been able to stop him from enticing Darcy into a marriage bargain. "George thought I'd be so happy he'd found a Harper he could mold into his own image. He'd thought I'd celebrate his *marriage*." She raised faded blue eyes to Jason's face—faded, yes, but still brimming with anger in need of an outlet. "And now . . . sometimes . . . even though I loved him . . . I want to celebrate on his grave."

Me too.

But Jason couldn't lose sight of this piece of the puzzle.

George, sick and facing death, low on oxygen his brain needed, might have lost that bit of himself that should have drawn a line where Darcy was concerned. It wasn't an excuse for what he'd done. But it was a reason.

Jason took Pearl's hands from the curtains and then folded her gently into his arms. Pearl might not have done right by Darcy, but she was his friend, and collateral damage as far as he was concerned. "It's better to lay blame where it belongs, rather than with someone who was just looking for a little help." His beloved Darcy.

Criminy, George. You left a mess.

Like you've done any better.

The bull inside Jason's chest huffed.

Everything will be all right if our women forgive us.

Easy for George to say. He wasn't the one trying to fix things.

Pearl was as tense as a strung bow. She didn't cry. She didn't yell. For now, she was keeping all that raw emotion she'd told him she was feeling inside.

The way Darcy did.

But Jason knew this was just a moment of calm in Pearl's stormy grief. She was like a long-stabled mare in need of a day of freedom in a big pasture. A day to rage, to lash out, to...

"Why don't we take a drive out to the cemetery?" Jason moved the old woman to arm's length. "You can show me where he's buried. I think you and I have some graveyard dancing to do. I hear from Lola that's all the rage."

Harrumph!

Chapter Fifteen

♥

N o. That can't be right." A man's voice carried into the courthouse hallway.

Darcy hurried past, judge's robe billowing behind her. For once she was early to work.

"That's not a five. It's an eight. This is ridiculous." An elderly man stomped out of the traffic clerk's office, which opened early on Wednesdays. He nearly ran Darcy over. "Sorry, I...Darcy? Darcy Jones?"

"Yes?" She peeked at Stogey to make sure he was all right in her bag before taking a good look at the man.

He wasn't wearing a suit and tie, and his hair was now more white than gray, but she remembered him immediately as one of her mother's marks. Her stomach dropped.

"I almost didn't recognize you. It's been a long time but you look just like your mom." He caught her arm. "It's me. Nathan Dickinson. I was your mother's boss." He gave a self-conscious laugh. "Or I was twenty years or so ago, before she got sent to—"

"I remember you," Darcy said quickly, also recalling how her mother had coached her to pretend she was terribly sick and possibly dying. She gave him a small smile to cover for the fact that she didn't want Nathan reminding her coworkers that her mother was in prison for bilking him. "Nice seeing you again."

Nathan caught her arm again. "Look at you. You look so healthy. And you're a judge?"

"Yes." Darcy knew it had been a mistake to put on her judge's robe in the parking lot. But she'd run out of hands to carry everything—purse, laptop bag, Stogey, her robe on a hanger. She gave her arm a polite pull, trying to free herself.

Nathan didn't let go. "Listen, I got this traffic ticket, and I totally misread the date to pay. I thought this was an eight." Nathan dropped her arm and pointed to the court date on his citation. "They say it's a five and that I'm late. But you . . . Oh, ho ho. You can fix this, right?"

"No. Sorry." Freed, Darcy headed for her office. She made it three steps this time before Nathan claimed her arm once more.

"But it's not fair. These old eyes. It was an honest mistake," he said, like this was her problem.

"They have payment plans." She tugged her arm, harder this time, heart pounding.

Frowning, Nathan positioned himself between Darcy and her destination. "And you can fix it. For old times' sake." He laughed mirthlessly. "You owe me."

Fear shuddered through Darcy because she probably did, if for no other reason than that he deserved more than an apology from the Joneses.

"Problem, Your Honor?" Amazingly, Ronald the bailiff appeared at her side, hands on his utility belt, scowling at Nathan.

"Oh, you know how small towns are." When Darcy tugged

this time, Nathan let her go. "Everybody knows everybody. Nathan was just saying hello." Darcy continued on to her office.

"And asking for a favor," Nathan said in a way that said he'd hold a grudge because she hadn't granted him one.

"Man up and pay your fine," Ronald said before following Darcy to her office. "You okay?" he asked when they reached Tina Marie's desk.

"I'm fine. Thank you for stepping in." She'd been caught off guard.

How am I supposed to handle situations like that, George?

He didn't answer. He hadn't been in her head all morning.

"You shouldn't wear your robes outside of the court-room." Ronald pointed a thumb over his shoulder toward the hallway. "Everybody wants a favor or to tell you about their grudge regarding a judgment, just makes it worse if you advertise who you are."

"That's why Judge George had a gate installed at his house," Tina Marie said without looking up from her computer screen. "Not to keep out the baddies from seeking revenge but to prevent every yahoo he'd been neighborly with from stopping by to have him take care of a ticket or a grievance." She scribbled a note on a pad. "Wish I had a gate at my house. Folks stop by there sometimes too."

"Oh." Darcy felt better toward George for leaving her a gated house. She set Stogey's bag down and lifted him out. "Thanks for the advice. I'll be more careful from now on." Still a bit shaken by Nathan's arm grab, she went into her office while Stogey received his morning greeting from Ronald and Tina Marie.

Darcy sat down and glanced at her calendar, startled to realize that this weekend was her mother's birthday. She wasn't good about calling or sending cards to her incarcerated family but she made it a point to visit once a year.

Tina Marie entered, placing a sheet of paper in front of her. "I need your signature."

"What's this?" Darcy didn't recognize the form, and Tina Marie hadn't brought in her notarizing supplies.

"A request to have Stogey tested to be certified as an emotional support animal." She reached down to give him a pat. "I also scheduled a quick online appointment with a clinician to declare you in need of one."

Darcy paused, pen poised above the signature line. "He has to pass a test?" He was still a bundle of anxiety. And she...Darcy didn't want to go on record as needing an emotional support animal. Rupert might use that against her. "Is this necessary?"

"If you want to go by the rules, yes." Tina Marie stared at Darcy, some of the animosity that had been mellowing returning. "You do want to do this by the book?"

"Yes. Of course." Darcy rushed to sign. "Everybody has an emotional support animal nowadays, right?"

"Not me." Tina Marie whisked the form away. "Not George. But you seem jumpy."

* * *

"Where have you been?"

After he parked at the courthouse, Jason's boots had barely hit the pavement before Iggy was on his case. He took a seat on a picnic table bench next to Ken and across from his cantankerous business partner. The smell of garlic permeated the courthouse park grounds.

The Garlic Grill food truck was doing a brisk lunch

business from the curb. Kimmy Belmonte had gone from making her special sandwiches at the deli counter at Emory's Grocery to operating her own food truck. To say it was popular would be an understatement.

"Seats are at a premium wherever the Garlic Grill is nowadays." Iggy shoved Jason's sandwich order at him. "I had to tell three different people that your seat was taken. Where've you been?"

Jason opened his tuna garlic pesto salad sandwich and breathed in deeply. "I was dancing on someone's grave at the cemetery."

"I don't like where this is going." Iggy crumpled his sandwich wrapper, rolling it into a little ball. "You mean literally?"

Jason nodded. Pearl had demonstrated her clogging talents on George's grave before collapsing in the grass for a good cry.

I'm not sure I deserved that, George groused.

Jason laughed because the old man most certainly had.

"Are you feverish?" Ken stopped eating his salad and laid his palm on Jason's forehead. "Tell anyone who asks about graveyard dancing that you have no recall because you were feverish."

"You're feverish for ordering salad instead of a sandwich." Jason bit into his.

"I'm gluten-free." Ken stabbed his fork into a tomato wedge. "You'll need to drop gluten if you don't stop packing on the carbs. Jeez, your pantry looks like it was stocked by a teenage boy."

"Cowboys don't count carbs." Jason opened the water bottle Iggy pushed his way.

"Cowboys don't dance on their..." Ken scowled at Iggy as

if he didn't want to complete that sentence in front of Jason's business partner. He leaned in and lowered his voice. "Cowboys don't dance on their ... *lover's* dead husband's grave."

Yeah, he'd almost said *wife*.

"Never fear," Jason said. "I wasn't the one dancing. It was Pearl."

Ken's fork hovered midair. "Who?"

"The judge's ex-girlfriend. Keep up, man." Iggy gloated over Ken's confusion. "We have good news. Tell him, Ken."

The wind whispered through the pine branches above them. The rear courthouse doors banged shut. Jason glanced toward the rear exit, where Darcy had fled after her first case on Monday. Two men sat on the steps and lit cigarettes. Darcy was nowhere in sight. He imagined her eating her lunch at her desk.

"Earth to Jason." Iggy snapped his fingers in front of Jason's face.

"You have good news," Jason said, returning his attention to the table. "Those orders that were canceled are back on the books?"

"Sadly, no." Iggy didn't look bummed about it, though. "It's about our love advice video."

Jason groaned, glancing at Ken. "You heard back from New York already."

"Don't act like it's a death sentence." Ken stirred his salad. "My New York contacts say the camera loves you. And they believe there's something to the chemistry in *Love Advice from Two Cowboys and a Little Old Lady*. The bad news is they say it needs work before we can sell sponsorships and make money doing it."

"Sweet, right?" Iggy shot his rolled sandwich wrapper into a nearby trash can. "We could be sponsored."

"Don't expect much more than T-shirts and free samples." Jason set his sandwich down. "Tell me you're messing with us, Ken. I wanted this to go away. Remember the fan ridicule after I wrote that love advice column?"

"This is different and good for you. Have I ever lied to you?" Ken shook his fork at Jason. "Don't answer that. But in my defense, I only lied to you for your own good. But this... This could be a thing. You have all the elements of a home run—a straight man, a wild card, and a fool."

"Me being the straight man." Iggy reached across the table and slapped Jason's shoulder. "I could be a thing."

Jason rolled his eyes, knowing full well who played which roles. Edith was the wild card and Jason was the straight man. "I hate to ask, but what changes did they suggest?"

"More of you, obviously. A tighter topic. You know, don't bounce around so much. And more relationship drama with details."

Relationship details? Darcy had practically sworn him to secrecy when it came to where he was staying. Jason struggled to swallow the bite of tuna fish stuck in his throat. "I'm not getting personal or dramatic."

"I can be dramatic." Iggy tilted his cowboy hat rakishly. "Ask any woman who's dated me."

Ken leaned forward. "Thank you for volunteering, Ignacio. We'll bring in one of your exes for the next installment."

"But... but..." Iggy sat back and nearly fell off the bench backward. "No. It's got to be Darcy. She and Jason... Their story has some juicy details."

Shaking his head, Jason washed his tuna fish down with water. He needed a clear voice to argue against this.

"For obvious reasons, we need a special segment just for Darcy and the golden boy here." Ken picked at his salad, thankfully not voicing what the obvious reason was—their marriage. "No. It's got to be you at first, Ignacio. You're going to be the star of the next segment."

"That's Mr. King to you." Iggy frowned. "I'll only agree to this if you agree to my terms. When we get sponsors, you have to represent me."

Ken gave Iggy a hard look that made Jason's partner squirm.

"Representation is putting the cart before the horse." Jason hoped, anyway. He was still banking on the video to be a failure. "You've forgotten one thing."

"What's that?" Iggy blinked.

"You have to find one of your ex-girlfriends who's willing to go on camera." Ken smirked, clearly enjoying putting Iggy on the spot.

"Oh."

A fancy little red sports car sped by with the top down. Barbara Hadley, who considered herself the first lady of the town, sat behind the wheel, laughing, her shoulder-length blond hair flying behind her.

"Best head on over to Prestige Salon." Jason tried really hard not to smile. "You know that's where Barb's headed. If you hurry, you can ask her to be on the show before her next customer shows up."

"We're not exactly on friendly terms anymore," Iggy admitted, chewing the inside of his cheek.

"Are you on friendly terms with any of your exes?" Ken asked sharply.

Iggy shrugged. "I think I'm on record as admitting I'm not into long-term relationships. It's a position that runs counter to what most women are looking for in a man."

"I'll take care of getting this Barb woman to participate."

Since he'd arrived in town, Ken had been tossing out promises like shills passed out leaflets on the Vegas strip. The agent was usually true to his word but he'd never met the town's queen bee. "If this venture pans out, Mr. King, I'll represent you. Now make yourself scarce so I can talk business with the client whose earnings currently pay my bills."

Iggy gave a mock salute and ambled off, walking like he was on top of the world.

Jason and Ken ate in silence for a few minutes. The lunch crowd dwindled, returning to the courthouse. The day was clear and bright, as sunny as the town's name. The breeze. The rustling pines. After being inside George's house and being privy to his secrets, the day was a literal breath of fresh air. Jason wanted to bring that feeling to Darcy.

"Checked in with our protégé, Mark, this morning." Ken cleaned out the last of his salad. "He's practically retired. What is it about these kids that makes them quit?"

"Oh, I don't know. A couple thousand pounds of hurt?" Bull riding was about compartmentalizing fear and suppressing the flight instinct, all while operating at peak physical performance. "I believed in him. Poor guy."

But you didn't train him. You mentored him with tips and words of encouragement.

Jason frowned, refusing to take criticism from a figment of his imagination. He shifted on the bench, causing a nerve to send a white-hot bolt down his leg.

"You think you let Mark down?" Disapproval etched Ken's features. "I think he may not have had what it takes in the first place. Riding a bull never brought him back to center the way it does you."

"You think bulls bang some sense into this hard head?"

"Yeah." Ken stared at Jason as if trying to read his mind.

"I'm not going to sugarcoat this. I'm worried about you and that leg of yours."

"By the time I win Darcy back, I'll be fine."

Ken didn't look convinced.

"Don't worry. I'll hook up with the circuit in June and you can make that mortgage payment due on your fancy apartment in New York City." Jason polished off the last of his sandwich.

"You're at a turning point." Ken slid farther away from Jason on the bench and turned to face him. His khakis and polo shirt were crisp and new, unlike Jason's faded blue jeans and worn gray checkered button-down. "Have you ever wondered if this so-called nerve damage might be your body trying to tell you it's time to retire?"

"Like it's all in my head? Not a chance." The physical pain was too severe to be a figment of his imagination. "You know why I'm here. What's at stake for me personally. But rodeo…Rodeo is my life." The bright lights. The clang of the bull's bell. The unending motion. The accolades. "Rodeo is who I am."

Rodeo is a young man's game. You can't play God forever.

Clam up, George.

"Jason, rodeo is who you are until it's not anymore." Ken nodded sagely, seemingly on the same page as George. Despite being Jason's age, his agent wasn't one of the best in the rodeo business for nothing. He'd probably seen and handled every situation and emotion from his clients. "Do you honestly think you'll be riding bulls ten years from now?"

"No." Jason scowled. "But I want to be in the kind of shape where I could. If I wanted."

"And yet you haven't given any thought to life after the limelight." When Jason began to protest, Ken held up a hand. "If you're going to linger in Sunshine, use that time for more than just winning back your one true love."

"Without rodeo, I'll be like everyone else." Like Iggy, whose glory days had been in high school. Heck, most folks in town thought he and Iggy were interchangeable already— two cowboys who refused to settle down, preferring to chase a good time. Jason gritted his teeth.

"And what happens to your image, the one I sell to America, when you and Darcy get back together?" Ken held up his cell phone screen so Jason could see it. He'd brought up Jason's website and was scrolling through picture after picture. "Look at Jason Petrie's smug mug with all those babes. Every man wants to be him. Every woman wants to be with him."

"That's not who I am." That man was more like Iggy.

"Listen to what I'm saying." Ken put his phone facedown on the table. "I want you to be happy. Making money for me, but happy. But in order to do that, I need you to think about what's going to make you happy besides winning Darcy back. Because if you retire without a promotion plan, all the offers I field for you are going to be like dandruff shampoo and hemorrhoid cream."

Jason laughed, and it was almost as if George were laughing along with him...er, at him.

Ken sat back, surprised for once. "This amuses you?"

"You have plenty of time to plan for my post-riding career." Jason pounded his fist on the picnic table when what he wanted to do was pound his aching thigh. "Because I'm not retiring."

Ken stared at Jason too long. "I know what's good for you. Trust me to fix the tangled threads of your life." He gathered his trash. "As long as you take care of the other loose end."

Jason didn't have to ask what the loose end was.
Ken meant Darcy.

* * *

Darcy and Stogey came home to pots of flowers gracing the
front porch and lining the portico. The porch light outside
the kitchen door was new and came on as Darcy parked
the car.

They entered a warm kitchen. Chili simmered on the stove
and the aroma of cornbread filled the air.

For a moment, she expected Pearl to march into the room
demanding Darcy eat while it was hot. For a moment, something tickled her intuition. The house felt different.

She set her purse and keys on the counter and hung up her
judge's robe as if it were her jacket.

"Perfect timing." Jason emerged from the sunroom carrying a beer. He set his on the counter and got a cold one for
her out of the fridge. "Dinner is ready, or it can wait until
you enjoy your evening cocktail."

She accepted the beer because who wouldn't need a drink
after presiding over a case argued between her stepsons?

"Tough day at the office?" Jason set Stogey's food on the
floor. "You need a hot shower? A foot rub?" He stared at her
feet in those clunky heels and for whatever reason, he didn't
look at them with disgust.

And she didn't even have nail polish on!

"The flowers outside are nice." Darcy took a generous
swig of beer while her overworked brain began registering
things. The role reversal, for one. She was usually the one
who greeted Jason with an adult beverage, a tempting proposition, and a hot meal. While she pondered that surprise, she

gestured toward the dining room with her beer. "Why is it so light in there?"

"Oh. Pearl and I opened all the windows today. You know, aired things out. Spring cleaning or whatever they call it." Jason stood leaning against the counter, looking too casual, too innocent. "And I replaced a bunch of light bulbs."

"You and Pearl?"

"Yes, ma'am."

She liked Jason like this—dimples popping in and out, him trying to keep a secret. But the part about Pearl… "You're joking, right?"

Someone rapped on the kitchen door. Without waiting to be told to come in, Bitsy burst into the room. She spotted Jason and threw herself into his arms. "Thank you."

Darcy raised her brows and her beer, toasting whatever Jason had done to undo Bitsy. Perhaps he'd cured her of the Rupert-induced twitch.

"Mama turned a corner today." Bitsy stepped out of Jason's arms and then launched herself at Darcy, giving her a big hug. "She may have gotten her groove back."

It sounded like Jason choked back a laugh. Darcy couldn't tell because he turned his back on them and stirred the chili. "Do you want to stay for dinner? I made plenty."

"No. I had barley soup with Mama." Bitsy released Darcy with a small laugh and went to stand in the doorway to the dining room. "Will you look at that? The place isn't so gloomy with all that natural light streaming through the windows. Even Mama commented on it." Bitsy spun, clasping her hands together and facing Darcy as if waiting for her cue to burst into song. "I've decided I need a little makeover. Would you like to go shopping with me this Saturday?"

Yes!

She longed for the old Darcy's wardrobe. Or a pair of four-inch heels. She set her beer down on the counter and forced herself to say, "I can't." She may have made headway winning over her staff but she had a long way to go with Rupert and Oliver. They continued to be displeased with her by-the-book performance. Dressing like Mrs. George Harper was her best defense.

"What Darcy means is she can't shop Saturday morning." Jason had turned. He'd picked up his beer and was working those dimple-popping smiles. "I'm taking her to visit her mother. But she can meet you at the mall in the afternoon. Shopping always lifts her spirits. And then you can drive her back."

Darcy stared at Jason without really seeing his dimples, the gleam to his blond hair, or the warmth in his blue eyes. The same feeling that had swept over her last night rolled back in like fog along the coast. This man knew her. He remembered her mother's birthday. He remembered that she got maudlin after visiting her in prison. A man like that . . . A woman didn't just throw him away to reach for a career. No. A man like that deserved a woman who loved him just as deeply. Who was as good a barometer of his moods as he was of hers.

Darcy's gaze dropped to her sensible shoes. She hated them. She hated them worse than Avery hated them. And the reality was she wasn't a bulletproof judge with her hair in a bun and those clunky shoes on her feet.

The fashion choices of Mrs. George Harper were eroding Darcy's confidence. She needed to find a happy medium between the woman she'd been in her twenties and the woman who was Sunshine's judge.

If only she knew where to start.

Chapter Sixteen

♥

It wasn't unusual for the Widows Club board to meet more frequently during spring, their peak season of fund-raising events. In the next few weeks, they were hosting a bachelor auction, a bake sale, and a fashion show.

Bitsy found the board at Shaw's sharing a platter of loaded nachos and a pitcher of iced tea. "May I join you?"

"Don't act like you aren't one of us," Mims said gently, bumping Edith with her elbow.

"You've been on the board longer than I have," Edith said with a sigh.

"But...I resigned." And Clarice wasn't moving over to make room for her at the table.

"You didn't formally resign." Clarice wiped her fingers and then shoved over to make room for Bitsy on the seat. She tossed her gray braids over the shoulders of her purple tie-dyed T-shirt. "If you don't submit your resignation in writing, the board can't pass a motion to accept your resignation." She grinned. "I'm a stickler for rules. I should know if you're on the board or not."

Bitsy sat stiffly, holding her black tweed purse in her lap. "Still, I'm distracted by thoughts of romance. I shouldn't be. I'm too old, too dated."

"You shouldn't be human?" Mims asked ever so gently. "You shouldn't be lonely or have your breath caught by someone you find attractive? Even if it doesn't work out?"

"If that were the case, I wouldn't be on the board at all." Edith passed Bitsy a small plate. "Love has no expiration date."

Clarice poured Bitsy a glass of tea. "What was it Edith said the other day? We're widows, but we're not dead." She chuckled.

"But..." Bitsy floundered. "You ordered and made sure there was a plate and a cup for me. I didn't even know I was coming."

"We wanted you to feel welcome if you did." Mims turned the platter of nachos so that Bitsy could take some from an untouched portion of the plate.

"I love you," Bitsy said tearfully. "I love you all."

They ate nachos and drank tea while they talked strategy about helping Jason and Darcy patch things up.

Rupert entered and took a seat where he could see her, cuing the Duran Duran soundtrack in her head. Before Noah took his drink order, Jason's agent joined him.

Bitsy nodded toward the pair. "He'd be a moneymaker at the bachelor auction." Meaning Ken.

"They both would," Mims said matter-of-factly. "And there's nothing from keeping a board member from bidding on one of them."

Nothing but a lack of courage.

* * *

"How did you make this happen? Barbara Hadley is Sunshine's resident diva." Jason walked toward the yarn shop with his agent, rolling cramped shoulders. He'd spent the morning replacing some rusty rain gutters at Darcy's house.

"I can move corporate mountains and stubborn bull riders to my will." Ken walked and answered email without tripping over his own two feet. "What's one small-town prima donna?"

"You must have Mafia roots I don't know about."

"Japanese yakuza? No. Everything I learned about crisis management I learned from my grandmother."

"She must have been a force of nature."

"She still is," Ken said without looking up from his screen. "How's it going with Darcy?"

"Good." It had been days since Jason had taken Pearl to dance at the cemetery. Since that time, he'd played the role of dedicated house-husband to Darcy, except without spousal privileges. Still, he wouldn't trade his time with her at the house for anything. Darcy lifted his spirits the same way he seemed to be lifting hers.

George made a sound of reluctant approval in Jason's head.

Ken lowered his phone and touched Jason's arm, bringing him to a halt on the sidewalk. "What would you do if a doctor told you no more bull riding?"

Had his shoulders been sore? They weren't now as he threw them back. "I'd tell him I know my body and what it's capable of."

Ken tucked his cell phone in his back pocket. "Even if there was an increased risk of serious injury?"

"More serious than a compound leg fracture?" Jason crossed his arms over his chest.

"Possibly," Ken allowed. "Men die from bull riding every year."

"Your point?" Jason planted his boots more firmly on the pavement. "And do not say it's time for the retirement talk."

Ken rolled his eyes. And he wasn't an eye-roll type of guy. "See? This is the problem with professional athletes. They've been driving themselves to their physical limits for so long that they don't know when to quit and smell the roses."

Your agent wants to put you out to pasture.

"Shut up, George."

Ken's brows drew together. "Who's George?"

Before Jason could reply, his mother opened the yarn shop door and waved them inside. "How are my boys doing?" Although it was spring, Mom greeted them with fine-gauge scarves, which she wrapped around their necks like leis in a Hawaiian greeting. Red for Ken. Blue for Jason. "Are you staying out of trouble?"

"Always." Jason hugged his mother and veered to the back room and the wall of yarn. He headed toward his spot, eager to get this video session and talk of career ends over with.

"Clarice." Ken placed his scarf around her neck. "Everything ready? This is our second shot. We won't get many more."

"Thankfully," Jason mumbled, greeting Iggy and Edith before taking his place smushed against the nursery-colored yarn.

The bell over the front door rang.

"Barbara, I haven't seen you in forever," Jason's mother said sweetly from the other side of the curtain. "Have you taken up knitting?"

"No." The chill in Barb's answer said it more plainly than words: she was unhappy joining the little people. "I've lost my senses and accepted an invitation to participate in this...thing."

"It's so fun," Mom gushed. "You'll get addicted to it."

Barb's laughter lacked any warmth.

"Holy snakeskin," Iggy murmured, tugging down his shirt. "It's happening."

"Nobody say a word," Edith whispered. "She might bolt." *Batten down the hatches.* Even George was leery.

Jason's mother held the curtain aside.

"So this is where history is being made." Barb stepped into the storage room and paused. Every short, blond hair was in place. Her makeup tasteful and flawless. She wore a formfitting black dress with tiny pink polka dots and midnight heels that weren't made for walking anywhere outside a bedroom. "It looks like someone should be knitting. And that someone won't be me."

There was a moment of awed silence, and then everyone talked at once.

"I'm so glad you came," Mims said.

"What a pretty dress." Clarice fingered Barb's sleeve. "It's a tad busy for the camera. Do you have a jacket?"

"She can borrow my sweater." Bitsy removed her thin white sweater and made as if to put it on Barb.

The mayor's ex-wife warded her off with a graceful pass of her hand. "I'll be fine. And the camera will love me."

Iggy stood and swallowed, a loud sound that drew everyone's attention. "Yes, I just gulped. My queen." He gestured toward a folding chair on the right of Edith. He and Jason were trapped in the corner to Edith's left.

"We just need you to sign a waiver." Ken produced a document and a pen.

Barb perused the page. "This is cookie-cutter and not what we agreed to. I have conditions."

"And here we go," Jason murmured. He'd been in the same class as Barb in school. She was pricklier than a wild berry bramble.

"First, I'd like my full name, title, and business to show on-screen every time I speak." She fluttered her false eyelashes at Ken.

Clarice frowned. "I don't think—"

"Piece of cake in the editing room." Ken talked quickly over their producer. "A request like that never goes in the talent contract."

Jason wasn't sure that was true.

"Barbara Hadley, Owner, Prestige Salon," Barb said in distinct tones. She drew her hands outward, as if she were pulling taffy. "All together. Every time."

"Your word." Iggy pounded his chest. "Our command."

Barb signed and then settled into a chair, drawing one of the microphones closer to her.

You young people never read anything you sign, George said in rumbly disapproval.

"I'm sorry, but . . ." Clarice hobbled near. "I hear your wrist bangles. And those earrings. Can you remove them?"

"No." Barb sounded offended that she'd ask. "It's my ensemble."

"Maybe just the bracelets?" Mims stepped forward. She'd been fishing earlier and still wore her tan fishing vest. "I can hold them." More like confiscate. She yanked them off Barb's slender wrist. "I'm storing them right here, in my bait pocket."

For a second Barb froze, looking horrified. But it was only a second before she regained her detached, regal expression.

"I guess you won't be needing me for this segment. This is Iggy's feature." Jason stood, contemplating how he'd get out from behind the table.

"Stay where you are." Edith reached across Iggy and swatted Jason back down, not that he had a way out. "You're the glue that holds this thing together."

"The marquee that attracts viewers." Ken nodded without looking up from his phone.

More like the sacrificial lamb. George guffawed.

Jason rued the day Darcy had told him about hearing the old man in her head.

Everyone settled, even imaginary George.

"I'm ready. Let's do this." Clarice tapped her phone. "Take it away, Edith."

"Do you have my good side?" Edith twisted her red bangs over her eyes.

"Yes, and we're rolling," Clarice snapped.

"Welcome to *Love Advice from Two Cowboys and a Little Old Lady*," Edith began. "Today, we're talking about relationships that sputtered and fizzled out. Why? In the hopes that we can all learn how to make love last."

Barb might have scoffed. If she had, it was an elegant noise, and no one dared look.

"I bring the perspective of bachelors everywhere," Iggy said with a tip of his hat.

"And I call him out on his bull." Edith struck a pose, one shoulder thrust forward.

They both turned to Jason. Well, Iggy turned. Statue still, Edith swiveled her eyes in Jason's direction.

Right. Jason was the glue. "I'm just the clueless man who wants to win his...lover back." He'd almost said *wife*.

"Brilliant," Clarice whispered, clenching a fist in front of her face.

"Why do relationships fall apart?" Edith asked, speaking slowly and rolling her chin forward over and over, like a horse running in slow motion.

"Cut." Clarice tapped her phone and then stomped forward with her walking stick. "Edith, what are you doing?"

"My job?" Edith held up her hands.

"Which is?" Clarice huffed.

"Moderating while showing viewers my best side. You see, if I hold my chin up just so it smooths out my wrinkles."

"As does Botox," Barb said coolly. "Administered by a doctor the first Saturday of the month at Prestige Salon. Can we get that on film?"

"Oh." Edith blinked at Barb. "Do you offer senior discounts?"

"No." Barb sucked in her cheeks and stared at her fingernails, which were impractically long and the same pink as the dots on her dress.

"A shame." Edith was back to enunciating and chin extensions.

"Edith, stop," Mims said in an authoritative tone of voice that had both Jason and Iggy lowering their hat brims. "Your job is to draw out conversation, not become a meme."

"Excellent point." Clarice turned about and returned to the tripod.

"I don't know what a meme is," Edith said under her breath to Iggy.

"I'll show you later," he promised.

"From the top," Clarice commanded, tapping her phone.

Edith and the two cowboys repeated their introductions without as much posturing by their host.

"We're lucky enough to have a couple here who've broken up." Edith extended a hand toward Iggy and then toward Barb. "They're going to take us through what attracted them to each other first. If you caught our last episode, you'll be betting on confident bazingas." Edith executed an exaggerated wink.

Unused to the widows, Ken tossed his hands in the air and then toward Jason, as if expecting him to step in for a save.

"Right," Jason said smoothly when Edith took a breath. "We're going to fast-forward past attraction and what worked for this charming pair and jump into the deep end to discuss why the relationship failed. Now, our top-notch researcher, Bitsy, tells us that most relationships falter because of a lack of communication." The factoid was right there on a Post-it note on the table in front of Edith. Jason turned to Iggy.

"Don't look at me," his business partner said. "I texted her."

"I don't think booty calls qualify as communication," Barb said smoothly. "Now, at Prestige Salon, customers can always enjoy a spa day after a trying breakup."

Jason was beginning to see how Ken had enticed Barb to participate. She was turning their love advice into a salon infomercial.

"Booty calls," said Edith in a slow, wondrous way. "Let's pause to explore the term for some of our less socially active viewers. Is it always a call? Could it be a text? An email? A PM? Or a DM?" She raised the brim of Iggy's hat higher. "Your thoughts?"

"Yes?" Iggy said in a small voice. "Please don't ask me about swiping."

Jason pulled his friend's hat brim back down.

Edith moved on. "At what time would these booty communiqués come in? Do you wait up in anticipation of one? That would seem counterproductive to beauty sleep."

"Nobody waits up." Barb stared down her nose at Edith.

"But what if you're asleep and you miss the call? Er... text...or...?"

Honestly, Jason had been lost at "DM."

"If you miss the call, no matter what the message vehicle,

then you miss *the call*." Iggy lifted his hat brim with the knuckles of one hand. "If you know what I mean."

The man was no good at keeping his head down and out of the line of fire. Barb's eyes had narrowed. Edith drew a breath as if preparing to ask for a detailed description of the nocturnal activities of the dateless and desperate.

They were off track. Jason leaned forward, trying to catch Edith's eye. The message from New York had been clear—limit the sidebar conversations. He might not want the show to be a success, but that didn't mean he wanted to make a fool of himself. "Messages of this nature have nothing to do with couples and successful communication."

Edith's brow furrowed.

"It's all a moot point." Barb's entire body flinched, as if she was fighting the urge to get up and go. But she held on to her smile. "You shouldn't make a booty call in the middle of the night to the person who's in the same bed as you."

"There goes half of my social life," Iggy muttered, rubbing his jaw. "I thought it was charming."

Jason sent the camera a look, and he hoped that look said Iggy didn't speak for the male species. "A relationship is about relating to one another. Listening to the events of their day, their frustrations, their hopes for tomorrow. Talking about what drives you nutty and makes you unsure." That's what he and Darcy had been doing these past few days. Well, he'd been a good listener. He hadn't told Darcy about his leg.

"Yeah, I don't do that." Iggy sat back, crossing his arms over his chest. "Serious stuff isn't fun."

Grow up, George rumbled.

For once, Jason agreed with George.

"What Jason is referencing sounds like girl talk, doesn't

it?" Edith nudged Barbara. "You work in a salon. You probably bond with ladies all day long."

Clarice was biting her short fingernails.

Barb's careful smile broadened. "Actually, I own—"

"But we're talking about relationship fails," Edith said. It was unclear whether Edith knew she needed to get back on track or whether she was onto Barb's course of action and dead set on sinking that ship. "We're talking about how couples drift apart, which is why we've brought Barbara in. She's a recent divorcée, free to pick and choose the cream of the crop in Sunshine, which is why she chose...Iggy?" Edith ran out of steam. She patted Iggy's shoulder. "You mucked it up, didn't you? Texting instead of actually pushing words out your mouth."

Iggy pressed his lips together, quiet for once.

"I mean you were trying to advance above your pay grade with Barbara." Edith gave a small chuckle. "And then what?" She turned to Barb. "You slept through an ill-timed booty call and realized things weren't quite the way they should be?"

"I thought this was a PG-13 show." Jason went for the save.

"I didn't call her, okay?" Iggy said tightly, perhaps realizing this was a mess of his own making. "Barb is great. But I didn't call on the regular. And that was that. End of story. She deserved better."

"I did." Barb crossed her arms over her chest and glared at Iggy. "As the business owner of—"

"Do you forgive him?" Edith asked breathlessly. "At least enough to be civil when you see him around town? Or perhaps to take him back?"

Barb didn't answer, but something like a growl arose from the vicinity of her chair.

Clarice must have had her hearing aids in, because even she glanced in Barb's direction.

But Edith... She must have had cotton in her ears. She just kept on digging. "I mean, as a mother and a business owner, it's imperative to forgive, don't you think?"

"Yes," Barbara ground out, eyes shooting unforgiving daggers at Iggy.

"Oooh." Edith squeezed their arms. "I think we're having a breakthrough here. Barbara, in the spirit of learning, we'd love to hear your perspective on what went wrong between you and Iggy. You know, he is a work in progress. And I'm sure all our viewers would find this helpful."

"Well..." Barb glanced at the camera, looking unsure for once.

As one, Jason and Iggy leaned forward to catch every word.

"He didn't compliment me on the way I looked."

"Oh, that is poor form." Edith gave Barb a sympathetic glance. "I find you lovely."

"Thank you," Barb said stiffly.

"In a cold, untouchable kind of way," Edith continued matter-of-factly. "While Iggy works that dusty, rumpled look that can be dangerously attractive. If one is willing to look past some things."

"What things?" Iggy demanded.

Edith scoffed, as if his faults were as plain as day. "Obviously, the interruption of one's beauty sleep with texts after midnight. The tendency to look so far ahead that you don't see the beauty in front of you. And the fact that you don't invest in a woman by listening to her everyday concerns." Edith snapped her fingers in front of Iggy's face. "Earth to Iggy. Did you not hear a word of what was being said today?"

There was a moment of awed silence.

Awed on Jason's part, at least. Here he'd thought the entire session was being hijacked by Edith and somehow she'd managed to bring it all around. Although Barb had barely said a thing.

And from the look on Barb's face, she had a lot to say. None of it pleasant.

Before she could air any of her grievances, Clarice called, "Cut!"

* * *

"That was so much fun." Edith hooked her arm through Bitsy's as the Widows Club board headed toward Shaw's for the early-bird specials. "What did you think, Bitsy?"

"It was fun," Bitsy agreed, slipping on her sunglasses. "I think you missed your calling, Edith. You were brilliant."

Edith preened. "Thank you. Doesn't all Jason and Iggy's talk just make you want to reach out and ask a man for a date? I wonder if David knows about modern-day dating and booty protocol."

Mims chuckled. "I thought we weren't chasing after David anymore." She and Edith had vied for the widower's attention last holiday season.

"If David saw my best side, he might put me back in his dating rotation. There's nothing wrong with an occasional free meal, is there?" Edith dropped Bitsy's arm and turned to Clarice. "Well? What are my chances?"

"That I got your good side?" Clarice tsk-tsked. "With one camera, your good side is your nose. Focus on the goals of this thing, Edith. We're nudging."

Goals? As in plural?

Bitsy slowed, letting Edith and Clarice move on with their discussion. She stared into the craft store, pretending to be interested in a display of quilted hot pads with tulip motifs. But her mind was whirring around Clarice's mention of goals, plural.

Mims stopped next to Bitsy. She and her vest smelled mildly of fish guts. "Thinking of taking up quilting?"

"It isn't just Jason these videos are targeting, is it? You're trying to nudge me." Bitsy could feel her face scrunching into a frown.

"You're complaining? You did ask for our help, after all." Mims linked her arm through Bitsy's and turned her toward Shaw's. "So you got a reminder that relationships aren't all flowers and nights out on the town? If your feelings are strong enough for someone, you can get past that."

"Can I? I had my eyes opened to how cell phones make dating more complex." Was Rupert into DMs and booty calls? Bitsy suppressed a shiver. "I'm not sure I'm up to the modern-day dating scene."

"You'll be fine," Mims reassured her. "Because if I know you, you'll fall for a man who understands what's important to you and sees the world from the same page."

She and Rupert on the same page? Bitsy stumbled over an uneven edge in the sidewalk.

Mims had no idea how wrong she was.

Chapter Seventeen

♥

Oh. My. Goodness." Darcy turned into her driveway and slowed the car to a crawl.

Jason was painting a rain gutter from on top of a ladder next to a flowerpot filled with red geraniums. Normally she'd take a moment to appreciate the flowers, but Jason didn't have a shirt on.

All that golden hair. All that tan skin. All those perfect muscles and imperfect scars.

That's my husband.

It was a good thing George was no longer in her head. But Pearl was. Or more accurately, she was on Darcy's mind as she stood outside the cottage watering a newly planted rosebush.

The old woman didn't return Darcy's waved greeting.

Her snub didn't matter. Not when shirtless Jason awaited her.

Stogey had ridden all the way home in her lap, front paws on the arm rest. He saw Jason and wagged his tail at speed, releasing a stinker.

"Like I needed a spritz of eau de dog." Darcy parked beneath the portico and let Stogey out, steeling herself to the vision of all that man candy.

Stogey ran to the base of the ladder and whined. Darcy wanted to do the same thing.

Or perhaps put on her second-best date bra and some halfway-decent heels and drag Jason down to Shaw's to blow off some steam on the dance floor, get a little buzz on, and then bring her cowboy back home.

"You're quite the handyman," she said. "Love what you've done with the place." She loved looking at the blooms but not as much as she loved staring at his bare torso.

"I'm a man of many skills." Jason hopped off the ladder, set his brush on top of the paint can, and then pulled Darcy into his arms for a kiss.

She didn't protest. In fact, she pressed herself closer and deepened that kiss.

When he drew back and would have stepped away, she held him near. "That was just what the doctor ordered," she said.

"Bad day at court?"

"I played Judge Evil Stepmother to Rupert and Oliver." It had been exhausting but she was feeling rejuvenated now.

"I know some games that don't involve judging." His breath was warm against her ear. "And the first move usually begins with a kiss."

"Oh, let's play." She lifted her face on a sigh.

Jason didn't immediately bring his mouth to hers. Instead he kissed his way down the column of her throat. Traced her collarbone with his tongue from one side to the other. Dropped kisses up the opposite side of her neck. And then finally—when her knees were as weak as her resolve— kissed her.

And kissed her.

And kissed her.

This time when he pulled back, he stepped away. "I'll be in the kitchen, Judge." He picked up Stogey. But his gaze was hot and on Darcy. "If you want me."

She did. And she would have thrown herself at him if only he hadn't reminded her of what was at stake.

For both of them.

* * *

"What's taking you so long in there?" Jason called from the kitchen on Saturday morning.

Darcy was rummaging in her top drawer for a clean pair of socks. "I have nothing to wear."

Nothing appropriate for both a prison visit and shopping at the mall. Nothing that made her feel like a cross between the old Darcy and Judge Darcy Harper. She wasn't even sure what that would look like but she knew for sure she had nothing in her closet or chest of drawers to fit the bill.

"'I have nothing to wear.' The plight of women everywhere." Jason came to stand in her bedroom doorway.

"The plight of women who purged their wardrobes to avoid making waves." Darcy wore boy jeans and a conservative blue blouse. She planned to put on Keds if she could find some no-show socks.

She dug deeper, past granny jammies and a pair of Spanx. Her fingers bumped into something solid. She pulled out a small knitted drawstring bag, a gift made by Jason's mother. From it she withdrew a set of ceramic salt and pepper shakers. The mallards, male and female, were designed to lean on each other the way married couples should.

"What's that?" Jason came into the small bedroom and to her side, bringing with him the fresh smell of soap and a strong desire to lean on him. He'd brought sunlight and flowers to George's dark home. And he wanted to bring the steadfast love they'd once shared.

All she had to do was say the word. If only she could find the right one and protect him at the same time.

"These were my mother's. They were probably stolen." But there were few things she considered more precious, because they reminded her of those rare days in the kitchen when the Joneses had seemed like a normal, happy family. "Mom's idea of a meal was slathering mayonnaise on bread, salting it, covering it with shredded cheese and slices of celery, and putting it in the broiler."

Jason chuckled. "She managed to put some basic food groups together."

"She wasn't exactly a broccoli-and-brussels-sprouts mom." Darcy fitted the shakers together and placed them on top of her dresser. "Sometimes I was so hungry I couldn't wait for it to cool down. And then it'd burn the roof of my mouth."

That was the problem with memories of her childhood. They were bitter and sweet. When the Jones family was together, there was laughter but not a lot of much else that was permanently good-feeling.

"You should put those shakers in the kitchen," Jason said softly, as if there were someone else in the house to hear. "There's nothing of yours anywhere in this place."

Darcy half turned to face him, appalled. "I'm not moving in."

Jason looked around her bedroom, at the open closet and hangers with clothes—hers. At the small dresser that was also filled with clothes—hers. At the endearing old dog who was also now hers. He didn't have to say anything. Technically she had moved in. It was Darcy who needed to clarify things.

"I meant...I'm not staying. This house...This life...It's all borrowed. In seven months, I'll be moving on." She wasn't going to be elected in the fall. This was temporary, just like her time here with Jason. She reached deeper into the bag, withdrawing a small, rhinestone-studded heart on a tarnished chain.

"That wasn't stolen." Jason's shoulder brushed against hers. He gently stroked the heart with one finger the way he might have stroked the hair of a newborn.

Throat clogged with emotion, Darcy remembered the day he'd given it to her.

"Your family may come and go," Jason had told her as he put it around her neck on her fifteenth birthday. "But you'll always have my heart."

Years later, Darcy could tell by the way Jason looked at her—love brimming in his eyes—that he remembered that moment as well.

"You still have my heart, Darcy," Jason said gruffly, sliding his arm around her waist.

She put the necklace and the salt and pepper shakers back in the knitted bag. "You know what George would say. *Don't look back.*"

Jason's brow furrowed. "He might also say, *Watch where you're stepping as you move ahead.* We should talk about next steps, Darcy. We still love each other. That's something to be proud of, not hide."

"You're right, but there's just too much coming at me." It pained her to admit she wasn't perfect. "If we go public, the ground I gained recently will be for nothing. Not to mention the potential damage to your career."

Jason might have argued but for the knock on the front door.

"The gates are locked." Darcy grabbed her Keds, resolving to go sockless. "Do you suppose it's Pearl, coming to say she's dropping the lawsuit or that she's moving back with Bitsy?"

"One of those things might be true," Jason allowed. "It might be Pearl."

Stogey managed to speed-walk to the front of the house ahead of them, crop dusting the air from the exertion. He reached the door just as Pearl opened it.

"I couldn't go to work without coming inside." Pearl walked through the living room, circling the round fireplace. "I can feel George here today. Can't you, Darcy? The way he was before he got sick, before the mess he made last year."

Said mess sat on the circular brick hearth, pulled on her Keds, and made a noncommittal sound.

"You can hear George?" Jason said in an odd voice. "Can you see him?"

"No. I can't explain it." Pearl's voice rose an octave. "But I feel him. He's right here. He's right..." She picked up a tiki ashtray. "He's right here. We got this on our trip to Hawaii. There's still cigar ash in here. See?" Instead of holding it out, she clutched the ashtray to her chest and ran to the far corner. "And here. In this eight-track player." She punched a button and filled the room with the Eagles' "Take It Easy."

The old woman was working herself up to the frantic state she'd been in since George had passed. Nothing had changed. Not permanently. It made Darcy wearier than ever.

"Pearl. Honey." Jason went to the ancient stereo and turned off the music. He gently pried the tiki ashtray from the old woman's grip and set it aside so he could take her hands. "These are just things George enjoyed. George isn't here. He's in your heart. And he always will be. You just have to slow down and listen. And maybe find it in your heart to forgive him."

They were genuine words. Darcy should have spoken them. A week ago, she had. But that was before Bitsy encouraged Darcy to intervene in Pearl's grief, before the lawsuit, before the bra, and before the true weight of George's job had fallen on her shoulders. And most importantly of all, before Jason entered the house and told her she deserved better.

Tension pressed on Darcy's chest, keeping her silent and still.

Likewise, Pearl didn't move. Didn't speak. Her eyes darted in Darcy's direction and then away, as if this visit was an olive branch and it was Darcy's turn to reach out.

To live up to the standards George had for Judge Harper.

"He's right, Pearl." Darcy came to her feet and joined the pair on the far side of the room. "George was never mine, not the way he was yours. He loved you and only you. Maybe if you listen hard enough, you'll hear him. That big laugh. That bossy voice."

"I can almost hear him telling Stogey what a good boy he is." Pearl withdrew her hands from Jason's. Her gaze fell to the floor as she wiped her nose. "You must think I'm making a fool of myself. An old, love-struck fool, that's what I am."

Jason and Darcy hurriedly assured her that wasn't the case.

But Pearl refused to be soothed or convinced. "He's gone now." She marched to the door, opened it, and paused. "George wouldn't like Jason staying here. It sends the wrong message. You know what a stickler he was about his reputation." She didn't look either of them in the eye. But in a blink she was gone.

The slam of the door echoed in the house. Stogey waddled over to the foyer and sniffed the air.

"There's a lot that needs fixing around here," Jason said in the same detached tone of voice he'd used when Pearl first came in.

"There's a time to dog-paddle and a time to float." Darcy drew upon one of George's maxims. She made her way to the kitchen to collect her purse. "I'm floating, not fixing. Can you imagine Pearl's reaction if she knew we were married? Can you imagine the town's? Because she works at the Saddle Horn, which might just as well be called the Gossip Central."

Jason was hot on her heels. "You can't ignore our marriage forever, on paper or otherwise."

"You're right." She faced him, aching because she couldn't give him what both of them wanted. "It's not fair to you. It's not fair to me. And for darned sure it's not right that we love each other but going public would complicate our professional lives. Look at me. I don't have an agent or a lawyer to guide me through this mess. One misstep and..."

"I have an agent. And a lawyer on retainer somewhere." Jason came to her, placing his arms loosely around her waist. "You focus on being a judge. Let me take a burden off your shoulders."

"You make me sound like a princess." Someone who wasn't strong enough to rule alone.

"Having spent time recently with Barbara Hadley, the queen bee of Sunshine, I'll take Princess Darcy any day." He kissed her nose. "Now come on. It's your mother's birthday. Can't keep her waiting."

"And I promised Bitsy I'd go shopping with her this afternoon. I hardly know what to buy."

"Don't you dare feel guilty about buying anything," Jason said, holding open the kitchen door. "Including shoes. You always did love your shoes."

Footwear was the one area in which Darcy felt confident in her fashion choices before her marriage to George. "Would you quit being perfect?"

Without warning, Darcy was swept off her feet and thoroughly kissed. And when Jason was done making her breathless, he didn't draw away. "I'm not perfect, honey. Every time I kiss you, I hope it chips away at that resolve of yours. Every time our lips connect, I hope you drag me to your bed. Every time I tell you I love you, I hope you'll say love is all we need. Perfect?" He shook his head. "Not by a long shot."

Oh my.

Darcy didn't dare say anything for fear she'd capitulate.

He still hadn't gotten a verbal reaction to that near-perfect speech a short time later when Darcy sat in Jason's truck with Stogey in her lap.

"You can't bring him to prison or the mall," Jason said without dimples in his cheeks or sparkles in his eyes. Since their hot kiss in the kitchen and her resulting silence, he'd been snappy.

"You know I can't leave Stogey behind. Think of what he'd do to that door you repaired." He'd sanded the door and filled the gouges. All it needed was a coat of paint. She rubbed the ruff beneath Stogey's neck. "Besides, as soon as he passes his test, he'll legitimately be my emotional support animal."

Stogey licked the window.

"See?" Darcy gave the dog a back rub. "He likes going on car rides. And he likes you. He'll keep you company while you wait for me."

Jason scoffed and started the engine. "The least George could have done was own a manly dog, like a German shepherd or a Doberman."

"Stogey is manly."

And to prove it, the little guy belched.

* * *

An hour later, Jason parked in the visitors' lot at the state penitentiary. "I'll stay with Stogey while you visit."

"Thanks." Darcy wanted to ask her mother some questions without Jason around. She handed the dog over. "How do I look?" She brushed her hair off her shoulders, fishing for a compliment to bolster her spirits.

Jason took his time answering, arranging Stogey in his lap. "I'm in a catch-22 here, honey. If I say you look beautiful, you'll bite my head off. And if I say you look like a respected judge, you'll bite my head off." He went nose to nose with Stogey. "And who knows what you'll do if I tell you how fantastic your legs look in those jeans."

That's my man.

Darcy grinned. "Just because we're keeping this marriage platonic doesn't mean you can't give a girl a compliment." She hopped out of the truck and marched toward the main entrance, lightened spirits turning heavier the closer she got to her mother. She signed in. Went through a thorough screening. Wondered what her reception would be like. Put money in her mom's account. Waited in a large room with the rest of the visitors of prisoners in good standing until her mother was escorted in.

"You came." Mom's face brightened when she saw Darcy.

In her midfifties, Meredith Jones was still striking, even in orange. Gray mixed in with blond gave her hair the look of expensive highlights. They didn't allow much in the way of makeup on the inside—foundation, shadow, lip gloss. Mom applied it with a skilled hand.

Darcy gave her a hug. "Of course I came. It's your birthday." Too many of her birthdays had been celebrated this way.

They sat across from each other at a table. Mom stared at Darcy as if she was a sight for sore eyes. Or as if she was sizing her up for shady purposes. And didn't that sum up Darcy's opinion of their relationship?

Regardless, Darcy forced her words and her smile to be cheerful. "How've you been? You look thin." Wiry. Hardened.

"Menopause." Mom shook her head. "It's tougher to endure than the attitude of some of the violent offenders in here." She reached for Darcy's hand, earning a reprimand from a guard. Other than hugs of greeting, no touching was allowed. "Tell me all the news. Or at least the news I haven't heard since my *last birthday*, when you told me you married old George, which was a coup, even by my standards. Word reached us that he kicked the bucket and that you're the new judge. You've already got a reputation and everything."

"A reputation? It's too soon for reputations." The last thing Darcy wanted to admit to was her situation. She deflected. "Have you heard anything from Eddie or Dad?"

"Your father and brother are fine. Stay on point." Mom brushed aside Darcy's attempt to change the subject. "Word is you're tough on crime."

"You say I'm a tough judge like it's a bad thing." Darcy clasped her hands in her lap. "Are you sure they aren't still talking about George? My...my husband?"

Mom shook her head, leaned forward, and whispered, "Be careful, Darcy. Ease up on those severe sentences. To pull off a proper long-term scam, you can't make enemies."

"My being a judge isn't a con." But Darcy squirmed in her chair, giving her discomfort away. "I...I earned this chance."

"Sure you did." Laughing, Mom sat back in her chair. "I'd expect you to say nothing less. Half the success of a hustle lies in becoming who you say you are."

A chill crept down Darcy's spine. "I didn't scam George." But she had tried to become someone else.

Her mother ignored her. "People hustle every day. They just don't call it that. They make subtle changes to please their spouse or anyone they're in a relationship with."

That chill spread to Darcy's limbs. "Like a relationship with your daughter?"

Her mother didn't even flinch. "We were talking about *your* grand scheme. This will be hard for any Jones to top."

The cold inside Darcy gave way to the heat of anger. "There is no grand scheme. I have a law degree."

"I know."

"I passed the bar."

"I know."

"I was appointed interim judge on a recommendation."

Mom quirked her eyebrows. "Whose?"

Some Jones she was. Darcy had let her emotions get the best of her and fallen into her mother's trap.

"I'm not college-educated, Darcy, but I'm no dummy. Judges are old, plucked from a pool of experienced, practicing lawyers." Mom waited until a guard had passed to continue. "I can't tell you how proud you've made me. I worried when I entrusted you to George's care that you were too much of a follower. But you proved me wrong. You got more out of old George than I ever did."

Darcy's stomach roiled. She wished Stogey were sitting in her lap. She wished her fingers were curled around Jason's. "I'm nothing like you. Marriage, a judgeship, a house. Everything was George's idea."

"Really?" Mom laughed. "You're a Jones unicorn. A natural hustler. You look at something. You want it. And without much effort, it drops into your lap."

"It wasn't like that." But Darcy's stomach continued to roil.

"Oh, you're a unicorn, all right." More laughter.

Darcy wanted her mother to stop laughing, stop presuming Darcy's life was one big con. She had no choice but to go on the offensive. "And in this unicorn scenario, are you my fairy godmother?"

Mom stopped laughing but continued to grin. "Who else would you credit with teaching you a lost art until it became second nature? And now you need to turn your skill toward the ones who helped get you here." Her tone turned as hard as the look in her eyes. "I come up for parole review in a few months. You need to speak at my hearing. You know, tell them that I'm reformed."

"Will you be?" Darcy whispered. The abandoned child inside her longed for it to be true. But she didn't need George in her head to realize her childish hopes had no place in her adult world. "Don't bother answering that. I can't make any promises for or about you."

In a blink it was a seasoned convict sitting across from Darcy, a felon searching for a weakness to exploit, not her mother. "Where did my little girl go, I wonder. You used to ride shotgun when your brother stole cars and your dad pilfered cattle. And you were a good student of the game. You showed promise at reading people, at fitting into a role with just a change of your hair."

Darcy stared at her hands. "You're wrong. I was just a kid."

Mom scoffed. "You have a conscience now? If you did, you'd never have married old George. Admit it. You knew George's marriage offer was too good to be true. A nice, upstanding girl would have turned him down flat. On some level, you knew what was going down. And now you'd do anything to protect the ground you've gained, including keeping the details of your marriage to George secret from all those upstanding friends of yours."

Her accusations pressed on Darcy's chest, rang in her ears, chilled her bones. Why?

Because she's right.

No. I loved George. I owed him a last wish.

But it had come with benefits—tutoring, the protection of his name, a job recommendation.

If George had proposed to Avery, she'd have laughed in his face. And if Lola had accepted, she wouldn't have changed her personality or her wardrobe. If Mary Margaret suspected she was a bigamist, she'd immediately hire a lawyer to straighten out her mistake.

I am the horrible person most people in Sunshine think I am.

"You're starting to see." Mom nodded. "If the truth came out, you'd have no one in your corner. No one but us Joneses."

Yes, Darcy was starting to realize that what little pride she'd gained in her performance as judge was undercut by the way she'd gotten the position in the first place. Jason gave her the benefit of the doubt because she'd cared for George. Her friends might as well. But the town...

Darcy stood on legs that shook. "I have to go." Because she was thoroughly disgusted with herself.

Her mother got to her feet. "But we haven't talked about how you're going to get *me* out of here."

"I'm not." She couldn't do that to George. Or Judge Darcy Harper.

"You can't leave me here." Mom shook her finger at Darcy,

raising her voice. "How dare you. I'm the reason you're where you are today."

"Jones!" A guard yelled, making them both look. "Settle down. Show some manners."

"You're right, Mom. You created this unicorn," Darcy said, relying on her court face and her sentencing voice to cover her pain. "But you're not the reason I feel remorse. That came from the feisty old man who watched over me, the decent foster parents who took me in, the big-hearted friends who made up my real family, and the cowboy who loves me. Being a Jones isn't something I'm proud of, but I've always tried to do right by you." Darcy drew a big breath. "But that ends today. Good luck to you, Mom." Darcy fled the room, shaking. As soon as she was free of security, she ran. All the way across the parking lot.

Jason stood at the truck bumper, holding Stogey's leash. He took one look at her and opened his arms.

She fell into them, allowing herself to draw from his strength and be comforted by his love. And Stogey's too. He stood on his hind legs and rested his front paws on her calf. "You're my family." A cowboy and a stinky, toothless dog.

"Always," Jason said simply.

"I don't deserve you." How could she look forward and plan a life with Jason when she hadn't resolved her past?

"Oh, you deserve me, all right." He wiped the tears from her cheeks.

Darcy stared up into his eyes. They were the same color as the clear blue sky, the color of innocent wishes and girlish dreams. "No matter how hard I try, a part of me will always be a Jones."

"Being a Jones is what makes you special." He kissed her nose. "Because you always triumph over that part of yourself."

Did she? Darcy wanted to believe him.

"I can tell by your expression you have doubts." He kissed her nose again. "You're the girl who stayed after school to study in the library because you knew that was the only way to get into college. You're the girl who worked full-time and stayed in college even though it took you years longer to graduate."

"That says nothing about me not being a Jones."

"Doesn't it? Look around at the friends you've accumulated—their quality and integrity reflects on you." He smoothed the hair away from her face. "And look at me, the man who loves you. I'm still that boy who walked you home after school, the guy who'll wait for you, no matter what. Through college and law school. Through internships and clerkships. Through a marriage to another man and an appointment to a lofty office that not even you dreamed of attaining." He pressed his lips tenderly to hers, drawing her close enough to soak in his warmth, almost close enough to erase the Jones in her. Almost. "I'm good at waiting for you to find a place in life where we can be together."

"With a white picket fence, a dog, and a passel of kids," she murmured, because that had always been their dream.

But increasingly, a feeling was building in her chest, the belief that she didn't deserve him, because as much as she wanted to deny it, she just might be the woman her mother had raised her to be.

And she couldn't think of a way to protect Jason or to disprove her suspicions.

Chapter Eighteen

♥

I'm so glad I asked you to go shopping with me." Bitsy couldn't stop herself from giving Darcy a hug. She'd been incredibly nervous about stepping outside her 1980s comfort zone. Having only sons, it wasn't like she could call on her grown children for a fashion assist. "You look fabulous today, so much more like yourself."

"You mean with my hair down and wearing Keds?" Darcy watched Jason drive away with Stogey in his lap. She had a sad look on her face and a defeated note in her voice. "Not exactly judge-like. Shall we go in?"

"Just another minute." They'd met in front of the biggest department store at the mall in Greeley. Bitsy peered inside, wondering how to lift Darcy's spirits. "I arranged for a personal shopper. He's meeting us here. I hope you don't mind."

"Why would I mind you being spoiled?" Darcy smiled but it wasn't big enough to wipe away her melancholy.

"Well...I might have told Sonny we were both in need of a wardrobe makeover."

"Bitsy." Darcy had the whole courtroom persona thing down. The slight frown. The stern tone.

"Don't argue. I need to gracefully transition to this century." *Goodbye, shoulder pads.* "And you need to gracefully transition from a hot, single lady to a respected woman of the court. George didn't do you any favors trying to make you look matronly."

"Thanks?" Darcy almost smiled. "But—"

"Hello." Sonny Baker waved as he crossed the parking lot toward them, cutting off any arguments Darcy might have made. He was a distinguished-looking older gentleman wearing a charcoal-gray polo and pressed khakis. "Sorry I'm late."

"You're right on time, of course." Bitsy accepted his air kisses, wondering why she couldn't get twitchy over Sonny, who was single, older, and charming. "This is Darcy Harper, the woman I told you about."

"It's a pleasure, Your Honor." Sonny took Darcy's arms and held them outstretched. "I take it we're going from Sporty Spice to Kate Middleton fashionwise?"

"You caught me on a bad day." Darcy drew her hair forward, across her cheeks, as if trying to go incognito. "I used to idolize the fashion of Sarah Jessica Parker, but on a country girl's budget."

"Lucky for you, SJP and Duchess Kate both adore Alexander McQueen. And as head buyer here, I stock plenty of affordable look-alikes, options that will help bring out the true inner you."

Surprisingly, Darcy didn't protest.

Bitsy fidgeted, trying not to because Darcy needed the courage the right wardrobe would bring just as much as she did.

Perhaps sensing Bitsy's nervousness, Sonny fussed with the drape of her sweater. "And never fear! I've got several things to make my favorite Widows Club board member look fabulous for her newfound beau." Sonny swept them both inside. "Everything awaits us upstairs, including champagne."

"Oh, I couldn't. I'm driving," Bitsy felt compelled to say.

"Darling, you'll need alcohol to loosen your grip on your beloved shoulder pads." He hooked his arms through theirs and marched them across the store to the elevator. In a matter of minutes, they were upstairs in a private area with two small dressing rooms, chilled champagne, and a rack of clothes.

Every outfit Darcy tried on looked better than the last. Skirts and blouses. Dresses and pantsuits. High heels, wedges, and flats. Darcy had a figure that looked good in practically everything.

Meanwhile, Bitsy was having a crisis.

"Bitsy, my love, come sit with me." Sonny drew her down to join him on the bench upholstered in green velvet. "I've picked out lovely looks for you. And with every outfit, all I see is you working on deepening your frown lines." He smoothed his thumb across her forehead and then handed her the glass of champagne she hadn't touched.

"They're beautiful clothes," Bitsy agreed, sipping the tart bubbly. "Everything is wonderful. It's just..."

"Too expensive?" He tsk-tsked. "I was going to give you both an employee discount. Your fashion show fund-raiser brings us lots of customers every year."

"No. Not really. It's just... My body is no longer made for cinched waists and scoop-necked blouses." Not to mention leggings. She hadn't had the courage to step out of the dressing room with those on. She swallowed more champagne, wishing she were home in Sunshine and twitchless.

Sonny frowned. "You said you wanted date clothes."

"Yes, but... I want my date clothes to be comfortable and

the reflection in the mirror to be…" She felt the forehead creases this time.

"Bitsy, your body isn't thirty. Love the curves of your prime." Sonny patted her hand and then got to his feet. "But I'll take the blame. I may have pushed too far." He gathered the items he'd hung in her dressing room and replaced them with an entirely different collection of clothes from the rack. "These will flatter without emphasizing any one area."

Spirits bolstered, Bitsy gamely returned to the changing room. She emerged a short time later in a dress that fell gently past her knees. She twirled. "This checks a lot of boxes." No cleavage. No belt. And the tiny blue print flowers made her feel delicate. If only it had…

"If only it had shoulder pads." Sonny came up behind her, beaming in the mirror. "I can read your mind."

"Yes." Bitsy chuckled. "I might have the courage to switch out a few items, but you'll have to pull my sweater sets out of my cold, dead fingers."

Sonny wrapped his arms around Bitsy's shoulders and gave her a friendly squeeze. "Clothes should express who you are and the mood you're in. I'd never burn your sweater sets."

Darcy emerged from her dressing room wearing a white mandarin blouse over maroon slacks. "This has such a high neck. I'm not sure it's my style."

"I wanted something for the judge that would make a fashion statement at the neckline of your black robe." Sonny released Bitsy and moved to fiddle with Darcy's blouse, tugging it down at her waist and priming the stiff neck. "Those robes are extremely dull and made to show a man's collared shirt and tie. You need a necklace or a something stylishly feminine to let people know you may be the law, but you're also a woman."

"Oh." Light dawned in Darcy's eyes. "Like Ruth Bader Ginsburg. She's always got something going on at her neckline. What a fantastic suggestion."

"While simultaneously being hard to pull off," Bitsy noted. "Not many women's fashions go up high on the neck. Most go down."

"True that." Darcy gave herself a critical look in the mirror. "If I go the jewelry route, George had quite the collection of bolo ties. Some might pass for chokers. I don't think I can bring myself to wear pearls, even if I had any."

"You have plenty of time to figure out your courtroom style," Sonny said. "Experiment. Both of you should experiment."

Darcy and Bitsy spent a few moments checking out each other's outfits and handing out compliments.

"You don't think I'm being ridiculous?" Bitsy asked Darcy, holding out her skirt. "Going for a new look?"

"Rupert isn't going to know what hit him." Darcy's fingers tugged at the hem of her blouse. "You don't think I took advantage of George?"

Was that what was bothering her? "Heavens no. Even Mama couldn't twist that man's arm once he set his mind to something." Bitsy hugged Darcy. "Don't you dare believe what the gossips say. If anything, George took advantage of you."

Darcy drew a shaky breath. "Thank you for inviting me. I needed something to shake off the blues and someone I trust to do it with."

"We're an odd sort of family," Bitsy said, repeating the sentiment she'd told Rupert. "Brought together by George and Mama."

"A family of our choosing." Darcy gave Bitsy a watery smile. "I hope I don't disappoint you."

"Families don't disappoint, my dear." Of this Bitsy was certain. "They support. No matter what."

Darcy turned away, murmuring something that sounded like, "If only that were true."

* * *

"This is cool." Ken sat down in an Adirondack chair near the pond at Darcy's place. "The inside of the house was rough. But out here, it's like your own private park. The flowers are a nice touch. Hope Darcy liked them."

"I scored points. And I'm just getting started on this place." Jason planned to build a gazebo and picnic table near the water. He might be further along if he hadn't taken to skipping rocks across the pond.

Darcy might not want to stay in the house forever, but Jason wanted it to bring her joy while she was here. She'd been so upset after visiting her mother. He didn't like seeing her cry.

That's the only reason I tolerate you, George said gruffly. *You treat her right.*

Jason had positioned a small cooler filled with ice and beer between the two chairs. Darcy had texted to say she was staying in Greeley with Bitsy for dinner.

"We needed some time alone to go over a few things." Ken examined the beer label before opening it. "Gluten-free beer. You spoil me."

"I have a favor to ask, Mr. Fix-It." Jason opened his own beer and settled back with Stogey in his lap. "How can we make the record of my marriage disappear? Darcy is worried about it." Jason was beginning to believe they needed one big do-over.

"My gut reaction is that you can't." Ken picked at the beer's paper label, uncharacteristically glum. "If you let me, we'll get ahead of the story and make a statement. We may lose a sponsor or two but as soon as you're back on the circuit, we'll make that up. It won't be easy for Darcy. She broke the law."

"Whoa, whoa, whoa." This was unacceptable. Jason's entire body tensed, sending a bolt of pain through his leg and startling Stogey enough to make him flinch and pass gas. "What happened to Mr. Fix-It? Darcy unwittingly broke the law."

"Drunken memory loss doesn't exactly conjure up the sympathy of the public." Frowning, Ken sipped his beer. "Give me a copy of your marriage license, and I'll see what I can do."

"Marriage license?" Jason blinked. "All that was in the envelope you gave me was the photograph."

"No license?" Ken chuckled. "Seriously? This might be easier than I thought. Hold the damage control endeavors."

"Hey." Jason sat up, catching on. "We don't have an official marriage certificate."

You're hopeless, George said. *The both of you.*

"No license, no bigamy." Ken nodded, reaching over to pat Stogey on the head. "I'll call Monday to check."

Relief had Jason slouching deeper in the chair until he realized, "Being married is the only bargaining chip I have with Darcy, besides you staying in my apartment."

"Dude, love shouldn't require negotiations. You need to tell her it might not be real."

Jason's mind spun around the odds of Darcy kicking him out if she found out they weren't married. "I won't tell her until you confirm it. I don't want to get her hopes up in case the license got misplaced."

Wrong, George intoned.

A bird swooped across the pond. Stogey's ears perked up and he gave the area a good look-see. The bird disappeared into the trees before Stogey located it. He sighed and settled back in Jason's lap with a gentle belch.

What are you feeding my dog?

"Cheese pizza." At Ken's sharp look, Jason scratched Stogey behind his ears. "It gives the dog gas. You said we had other business?"

"I've given it a lot of thought and come to a conclusion. Iggy must go," Ken said simply.

Jason startled, nearly losing Stogey and his beer as he jolted upright. "Get out. He's my friend."

Ken's somber expression said he wasn't joking. "Listen to me. Step outside of yourself and look at your business situation rationally. The man's ineptitude generated a lawsuit. He was resentful of you being considered the star of a little video show. And I've seen the state of Bull Puckey Breeding. I can't imagine your books are any cleaner than your floor." Ken paused to drink some beer. "How am I doing?"

Perfect, George said.

George... "I can't get rid of Iggy. We've been friends since we were five. We're partners."

"With a legally formed partnership and everything?" Ken set his beer on the cooler and turned toward Jason. "I thought not. Do you even know how much money you bring in each month?"

He should be able to answer that question. "You think he's cheating me?" Jason refused to believe it.

Stogey turned and licked Jason's chin, wagging his little tail as if that tail wag was needed to lift his spirits.

Actually, it was.

Ken scoffed. "You think you can prove he's not?"

Again, Jason didn't answer. Iggy was a lot of things, but a thief? He didn't think so.

It's always the best friend, George whispered.

Or the trustworthy judge, Jason snapped back.

"What was that?" Ken gave him a concerned look that was short-lived because his cell phone buzzed with a message.

"Nothing," Jason grumbled, thinking about the picnic Iggy was throwing tomorrow at Bull Puckey Breeding to celebrate their fifth year in business. Now wasn't the time to hash this out with him.

A hummingbird darted past, wings louder than a bumble-bee. Again Stogey perked up. Again the bird was gone by the time he got to looking around.

He's as slow about birds as I am about my business practices.
Now you're catching on, genius.

"George, you are so annoying," Jason said under his breath.

"What was that?" Ken didn't look up from his cell phone.

"Nothing."

Something created a ripple in the pond. Stogey yawned.

Ken set the phone aside and reclaimed his beer. "Have you told Darcy about your video project? Imagine the fun we could have revealing you weren't ever married."

There's a reason why she's still wearing my ring, George said in that superior voice of his.

"Don't even joke about it." Jason scowled at his ringless left hand, thinking about the rock Darcy wore and the much smaller engagement ring he'd bought for her last year.

That's going to keep you up at night. George chuckled.

Out on the road, out of sight, a vehicle engine downshifted. It was too early for Bitsy and Darcy to return. He'd checked on Pearl in her cottage before Ken arrived. Which left...

Him clueless.

A black truck rolled past the portico, kicking up dust. It came to a halt next to Ken's rental car.

Jason turned. The setting sun was in his eyes, and he couldn't immediately recognize the man who got out. "Who's that?"

"Not to worry." Ken stood. "I invited him. Hey, Tom."

"Tom? Tom Bodine?" Jason set Stogey on the ground and got to his feet. Stogey waddled up to greet their visitor.

Tom strode across the grass toward them as if he owned the place. He wore a blue chambray shirt and his trademark black cowboy hat. "Evenin'."

Jason moved to the water's edge, picking up flat, smooth stones. He skipped one, sending a series of ripples across the pond.

"Thanks for coming." Ken indicated he should take a seat. In Jason's chair.

You mistakenly gave up that ground, George said in that know-it-all voice.

Jason threw another stone. It hopped once and sank.

"I brought whiskey," Ken said. And surprisingly, he had. He produced a knitted bag that looked suspiciously like something Jason's mother would make. It held a bottle and three glasses—real glass tumblers, mind you. Nothing but the best for Ken Tadashi.

He represents you, doesn't he? Be grateful he's not like your friend Iggy. George was prickly today.

"Nothing but the knitted best," Jason muttered, earning a sharp glance from Ken.

Tom took the generous pour of whiskey that was handed to him. "Nice place. George never had me out here."

"It's a fixer-upper." Apparently Ken had taken charge of

the conversation, the same way he took charge during negotiations with Jason's sponsors. "Someday my client will grow up and get a place of his own."

The client in question swigged whiskey from the glass he held in one hand, shaking stones in the other.

Tom made a noncommittal noise.

So far, whatever negotiations Ken had up his sleeve had stalled out. The men drank. Stogey lay on his back and squirmed, giving himself a good back rub.

"Have any trouble finding the place?" Ken continued his role as the good host.

Tom grunted. "It's Sunshine."

Jason nodded. Just about everyone knew where everyone else lived in Sunshine.

"Have you thought any more about my proposition?" Ken asked, earning a dark look from Jason, who hadn't authorized any propositions.

For a businessman, you leave too much business to others.
Thanks for the tip, George.

For sure, Mr. Fix-It needed to nurture his client-agent relationship by opening channels of communication. Iggy wasn't the only one who needed a tighter rein.

"My boys told me you're shooting a movie in town." Tom chuckled. "They're partial to those slasher horror films over cowboy flicks. Personally, I have no use for Hollywood cowboys."

"It's not that type of film," Ken said with good humor, grinning at his client—the supposed Hollywood cowboy.

Being the butt of the joke, Jason didn't even crack a smile. He felt like glaring and scowling at everyone, which was Tom's modus operandi. When had their roles been reversed?

Jason sipped his whiskey, focusing on the bite of alcohol as it went down.

"Tom, as I told you, there's an opportunity for you to brand your beef regionally. Bodine Beef." Ken passed his hand through the air like he was painting a billboard. "Grocery stores like a way to differentiate unbranded products, like milk and meat. And by pursuing a branding strategy, you can tack on a little premium with each sale."

"And the Hollywood cowboy would advertise my brand." It wasn't a question. And it wasn't a happy statement. Tom delivered it like a dig at Jason and waited for a reaction.

Instead of rejecting the idea out of hand, Jason felt it wise to keep quiet but not silent. He dropped the rocks in the shallows, where he could find them later.

If Ken was unnerved by Tom's goading, he didn't show it. "As I proposed, Jason would be a spokesperson for Bodine Beef for one year. You can use his image on your promotional material, gratis. And Bull Puckey Breeding will refund your purchase price." Ken sat forward, resting his elbows on his knees. "But in exchange you'll drop the lawsuit, including the claim for suffering."

"And no more pressuring other ranchers to cancel orders," Jason found himself adding, although he was in awe of his agent's wheeling and dealing. In awe, but still annoyed that he'd been kept in the dark.

"I don't know." Tom swirled what was left of his whiskey. "I consulted with my attorney today. He informed me that there'd be other costs involved in branding Bodine Beef. Creating the brand logo, licensing, hiring a salesman."

Like that was a hardship. It was Jason who was bending over backward here. He set his jaw, ready to bid Tom and his demands good night. He'd start a fire in the fireplace and wait for Darcy to return. He'd pull her into his lap and she'd kiss away this feeling that his life was spiraling out of control.

And whose fault is that? Ignacio isn't the only cowboy in Sunshine who needs to mature.

Jason ground his teeth over losing an argument with a dead man. Worse, a dead man whose ring his wife still wore.

"I said we'd help you get a leg up on profit." Ken was using his business voice. Everybody who knew Ken knew that tone meant the best and final offer was about to go on the table. It was time for Tom to pull up a chair or pass. "I didn't say we'd finance your venture. That is…"—he slid Jason a calculating look—"unless you're considering giving us part ownership in Bodine Beef."

"Part owner! You got some nerve." Tom stood, tossing the rest of his whiskey in the grass. "I'm owed, not the other way around."

Stogey got to his feet, sniffing the air. Jason picked him up to keep him out of trouble. That dog would try to ingest anything, from grass to whiskey-soaked grass.

"You sit on our offer for a couple of days," Ken said calmly. "Tell your lawyer to put a dollar figure to the value of our endorsement. It's worth more than your request for suffering."

Tom's fingers clenched around the glass, almost as if he were considering smashing it against something. Instead he set it on the chair and left them.

Jason waited for the truck engine to roar to life and the truck to pull out of sight before he said anything to Ken. "I don't appreciate not being consulted before you made Tom an offer. He wants a piece of me for free."

"I didn't tell you before because I wasn't sure he'd bite." Ken finished his whiskey and stood. "You complain about dandruff shampoo and hemorrhoid money, so I bring you beef. Which has the added benefit of getting you out of that jam your so-called business partner backed you into and has an opportunity for an extension after year one's freebie. Let me do my job so you can do yours—go legit with Darcy and ride some moneymaking bulls." Ken tightened the cap on the whiskey bottle, shoving it back in its knitted bag. "Just don't compete until after you've seen an orthopedic specialist."

My job. When had Jason's job stopped being about an eight-second thrill? He had more than a leg to mend and his talent to keep up. He had an image, an agent, and a business partner to manage. He had to do a better job at this adulting thing. If not for himself, for Darcy and the life he was itching to start with her.

About time you caught on.

George . . .

Chapter Nineteen

♥

I just want to go on record as saying we're in this together," Jason said to Darcy on Sunday, just as they pulled up to his mother's house on their way to his company's picnic. "If it becomes public knowledge, I'll make a statement about how I knew all along and didn't tell you."

"What brought this on?" Darcy scratched Stogey behind the ears. "Did Rupert find out that we're married? Is Pearl going to use it against me to get Stogey?"

"No. Nothing like that." Jason frowned, gripping the steering wheel. "I just wanted you to know that I plan to do a better job living up to my responsibilities both personally and professionally. And we..." His gaze came to rest on Darcy's left hand. "How much longer are you going to wear George's ring?"

Darcy spun her wedding ring, torn between her choices. Go slow and shelter Jason from the bad press her bigamy would elicit, because there were no long-term secrets in today's world, or hold tight to the love he offered now and hope he never asked more about her past? "I don't know?"

"Sometimes I feel as if George gets priority over me." His tone, his clenched jaw, his firm grip on the steering wheel...Something was eating at Jason and had been since before she'd returned from Greeley last night. "Do you want to be married to me or not?"

"I—"

"Darcy, it's so good to see you." Nancy climbed into the back seat and buckled in. There was an awkward silence. "Did I interrupt something?"

Jason and Darcy both denied it.

"Good." Nancy handed Darcy a round, frilly knitted item that was jailhouse orange. "Ken suggested I branch out with merchandise. I made you a scrunchie."

"Oh." Darcy tested its elasticity and then used it to make a low ponytail.

"And Jason, I made one of those bands you wear beneath the knee to strengthen your joints." Nancy passed a copper-colored knitted band to her son.

"My joints are fine." But the way Jason said it contradicted his statement.

"Your leg, I mean," Nancy amended.

"What's wrong with your leg?" Darcy stared at his jeans-clad thigh.

"Nothing." Jason accelerated as if they were late to the party.

"He gets twinges," Nancy said.

"*Mom.*" Jason kept his eyes on the road.

"Don't feel bad about not knowing, Darcy," Nancy said primly. "He told Ken and I overheard."

"That doesn't make me feel better." Not at all. Darcy clutched Stogey to her chest.

"It's just a twinge." He was trying too hard to make light of that fact.

Things dropped into place for Darcy, images of Jason

unsteady on his feet. "You almost fell when you were running! And at the pond when I thought you were encouraging me to sit in your lap..." She suddenly remembered Nancy was in the back seat. To heck with it. "You were rubbing out the *twinge*, weren't you?"

"Everyone needs to take a breath," Jason said woodenly. "Every once in a while the nerve around my pins gets irritated and takes me by surprise. No big deal."

"You said something similar when you had a cracked rib," Nancy noted.

"And a concussion." Darcy leaned back to take him in. "Is this why you haven't returned to the circuit?"

"I'm in town to support you," he ground out.

Darcy wasn't so sure. "And if I said I'd wear your ring instead of George's, would you head back out on the circuit tomorrow?"

Nancy gasped.

"You need me here," Jason said gruffly, his features carved in stone.

"Did you ask Darcy to marry you?" Nancy leaned forward, all ears.

"No," Jason snapped.

Darcy didn't deny it but she didn't answer Nancy either. "This explains why Ken's here. He'd never let you compete if you weren't ready. Have you seen a specialist?"

"It's just a twinge," Jason reiterated as if it were no big deal. He used the same tone and words when she talked about her Jonesness. He'd always been good at downplaying the negative.

They drove in silence the rest of the way to Bull Puckey Breeding. It was located in a big metal barn filled with pampered bulls and high-end cryogenic equipment. There were several corrals and pastures in back. The picnic had been set up near the fence lines of both. Iggy stood near a large, smoky gas barbecue, surrounded by several picnic tables and the Widows Club board. Nancy hurried to join them, carrying a dish holding cubed bread and spinach dip.

Carrying the carrot cake she'd made, Darcy managed to get between Jason and the beer cooler in the truck bed before he could lift it out. "I'm an excuse, aren't I? The personal reason you give as to why you haven't joined the circuit this year. You aren't just hiding the truth from me. You're being dishonest to the rest of the world."

His brows lowered, but he wouldn't look at her. "I'm here because I love you."

"And because your leg twinges," she said bluntly, not willing to let that slide. "Will it ever heal?" She looked him up and down. "I wish you'd retire. I wish you didn't feel the need to risk your life because it makes your ego feel better."

Jason's blue gaze was dark and stormy. "Why can't you wear my ring?"

"Because it won't solve anything," she whispered back, ready to weather the oncoming storm.

Other vehicles began to pull in. Friends greeted them.

Jason and his turbulent mood moved on. He carried the beer cooler to Iggy.

Darcy followed at a slower pace. Mims took the carrot cake Darcy had made and found a spot for it. Stogey took up a shady spot beneath the food table, presumably waiting for a morsel to drop. Darcy didn't have the heart to keep him with her in the hot sun.

Nancy put an arm around Darcy's waist. "Doc Janney told him nerves sometimes take longer to heal."

Darcy leaned into her mother-in-law. "I've seen him

stumble. I've seen him massage his thigh as if it hurt. Bull riders can't afford a twinge."

"Bull riders don't talk about bumps and bruises." Nancy sighed. "He won't ride until he's one hundred percent."

"I hope you're right."

More guests arrived. A game of cornhole was set up. Darcy found herself surrounded by friends on the sidelines, watching Jason take on Kevin, watching for any sign of the mysterious twinge.

"I see hints of the old Darcy." Avery gave Darcy's conservative skirt and blouse a once-over. "More stay-at-home mom than babe on the arm of a rodeo champ, but you're getting there."

"You're giving me grief for moving from dowdy to conservative." Darcy practically growled at her girlfriend. "Judges don't show cleavage or wear short skirts." Both of which could have described Avery's outfit.

"Missing your old life?" Avery teased.

"No." And it was true. Thanks to Sonny, Darcy was comfortable where she was landing fashionwise.

"Come on, Kev. Use those college football skills. Attaboy!" Mary Margaret spared Darcy's ensemble a glance as her fiancé tossed a beanbag at the target. "That'd pass for a kindergarten teacher outfit. I like it."

"It's good to have you back," Lola said softly.

"She never went away," Avery said. "She just didn't have as much time for us."

Lola gave Darcy a quick hug. "She knows what I mean."

And Darcy did. Lola meant the guard Darcy had put up as Mrs. George Harper had come down, along with her hair, if she hadn't been using Nancy's knitted scrunchie.

"I used to play softball." Edith elbowed her way to the

front of the rapidly expanding audience. "Same type of pitch. I should kill at this game. Who's up for a challenge?"

Before anyone took the widow on, a car pulled up out front.

"Who's that?" Lola was taller than Darcy and craned her neck to look over the attendees.

Edith plowed her way to the other side of the onlookers. "It's Ken and Rupert. I challenge you to a game of cornhole, Ken. New York City versus Sunshine. What do you say?"

"You're on." Jason's agent cut through the crowd to reach Edith, nodding a greeting to Darcy.

Avery gripped Darcy's arm. "Do you know His Hotness?"

Darcy nodded, and explained who Ken was.

Rupert took up a position across from them. Someone handed him a hard seltzer.

"What's Rupert doing here?" Avery muttered to Darcy. "Is he keeping tabs on you?"

"Why else would he be here?" Mary Margaret turned her attention back to Kevin's play. "Kev, you overshot the mark. Focus."

"This is a gentleman's game," Jason said, taking aim. "There's nothing at stake but pride on this shot." He threw his beanbag. It went in. His arms shot up as if he'd made a touchdown. "Winner! Winner. Winner. Winner." He poked Kevin's arms with every word.

"Jason, have you seen our new bull?" Iggy was turning burgers. He pointed toward the rear of their building. "He came in this morning. Unhappy gentleman. Just your type."

"You bought a new bull?" A frown flickered across Jason's face, one mirrored on Ken's features. "I mean, yay. We bought a new bull." He walked toward the barn.

"It'd be quite a treat for our friends if you rode him."

Iggy poked a fork at the burgers while he prodded Jason with words.

"No," Darcy said, although not in the shout she wanted to.

Jason glanced back at her, breaking his stride.

Or rather, his stride was broken by a twinge.

* * *

"How do I look, Mims?" Bitsy fiddled with her blouse at the shoulders, but instead of pads, her fingers bunched a thin layer of polyester. Panic sent shock waves to her knees. She needed those shoulder pads like she needed her lash-extending mascara.

"For the fifth time, you look lovely." Mims took Bitsy's hands. "Rupert's been looking at you since he arrived. Be human. Grab a diet cola and go make a pass at him."

"Oh, I couldn't. A woman my age—"

"A woman your age has heard every line in the book. Go toss one at him." Mims grabbed a can from a cooler and pressed it into Bitsy's hands. "Make us widows proud."

"Right." Bitsy clung to the wet, drippy can. "Twitch or no twitch, I can do this."

Mims turned Bitsy so that she faced Rupert. He laughed as Edith wound up her arm and released a beanbag that thwacked against a tree several feet past the cornhole target. Pushing Bitsy's shoulders, Mims propelled her forward.

Rupert laughed again. The sound filled Bitsy's chest with all kinds of warm feelings.

"I can't do it." Bitsy dug in her black patent leather flats. "I can be happy the way things are."

"Give the twitch a try." Mims was an outdoorswoman. She was stronger than Bitsy, braver than Bitsy, more willing to pull the trigger when a target came into her sights. Mims didn't falter. Step-by-step they moved closer to total mortification. "Chin up, smile on, bazingas forward."

Rupert turned toward them, his movements slowing as Duran Duran belted out the sultry chorus in her head from "Save a Prayer."

Oh, there was trouble. Bitsy was moving toward it. Mims didn't have to push any longer. Bitsy came to a stop next to Rupert, who was practically glowing, his dark hair tousled in the breeze, his shoulders filling out his teal polo shirt.

"I don't suppose you've ever owned a white summer suit," she said, still stuck in an eighties moment. "The kind you wear when you walk barefoot on a tropical beach."

Rupert's smile broadened. "Nope."

There was a screeching beat of silence.

"Oh." That almost sounded like a wail. Bitsy's cheeks burned with embarrassment. "I don't know what comes over me sometimes." Just the times when he was near. "I just blurt out whatever thought comes in my head." More like Edith than she cared to admit. "Can we blame it on low blood sugar?"

"We can." He took her elbow and guided her back to the food tables. "Can I buy you a hot dog for lunch?"

"You'd do that?" She tried laughing. It was a joke, after all. Everything at the picnic was free.

"I'm a little surprised at what I'm willing to do for you, Bitsy." He reached the main table and handed her a paper plate.

Something banged the barn at the far corner, and then a big bull trotted out into a small enclosure.

"Cowboys and their toys." Rupert's tone was critical as his gaze swung in the direction of Darcy joining Jason near the enclosure holding the bull.

"I'd say Jason can handle that." Bitsy leaned a bit closer, emboldened by the need to protect Darcy. "And I don't mean he can handle the bull."

Rupert's expression was haughty. "Don't ask me to approve of *her*."

Bitsy selected some strawberries. "I don't think Darcy needs your approval when it comes to who makes her happy. But your support would make her job easier."

"I'm sorry." Rupert set his empty plate back on the stack. "May I speak honestly?"

"Always."

"I'm getting mixed messages from you." Rupert shook his head, a slight smile touching his lips. "Or maybe I'm the one sending out dual signals."

The temperature rose in Bitsy's cheeks again, and she was afraid this time it spread across her chest. She'd never been a graceful blusher, but she refused to let a little thing like humiliation keep her from protecting those she cared for, which now included both Darcy and Rupert.

"It's all right." Bitsy rubbed his arm consolingly. It was a nicely muscled arm and... She swallowed, forcing her thoughts back on track. "I'm in the uncomfortable position of not knowing what I should be doing. Am I supposed to attempt to mend a rift between George's family and mine? Am I supposed to watch out for a young widow who I adore and admire?" She glanced around before lowering her voice and continuing, "Or am I supposed to look at a handsome, younger man and think I have a chance at—"

"Hey, Jason!" Iggy called. "Let's ride that bull!"

The crowd around the cornhole game turned and moved as one, rushing to the tables nearest the fence, jockeying for a position at the show.

"What were you going to say?" Rupert stroked Bitsy's shoulder.

And she wasn't even wearing shoulder pads!

When Bitsy didn't answer right away, Rupert stared down his nose at her like the chilly man at George's Christmas parties. It didn't matter what she'd been about to say. He was up and she was down on things that mattered.

"Nothing but a twitch." Bitsy took her plate of strawberries and joined the crowd at the fence, telling herself she'd been saved tremendous embarrassment.

When in reality, she'd probably suffered through the worst.

* * *

"Jason, what are you doing?" Darcy dogged his steps through the barn to the supply room. "Are you trying to prove a point?"

Adrenaline poured through Jason's veins as he anticipated riding that bull. They had a small corral with a bull chute in back for just these moments. Iggy had been right. This one was an ornery beast, unhappy with his new digs. The bull would be pissed at anybody who tried to ride him. Forget that Iggy had purchased him without consulting Jason. This was like receiving an unexpected gift on Christmas morning.

"I love riding bulls, Darcy. You know it and I know it." Jason dug in the plastic bin where he kept his bull riding ropes. All the pent-up frustration over his situation with Darcy, all the weighty decisions that needed to be made about his business, including Ken's management input, they all fueled the adrenaline rushing through his veins.

"What about your leg?" Darcy hugged her arms around her waist, lingering by the door, not that there was much room for her to stand next to him. The supply room was something of a mess. Less was stacked on the shelves than was stacked on the floor.

"Doc Janney said my leg is fine. Riding bulls makes me feel alive, and look what landed in my lap. A bull in need of blowing off some steam." Same as Jason.

"Something's going to land, Jason. And it's going to be you." Darcy predicted. "Don't do this."

He chuckled. "If a bull gets the better of me, that makes me feel like a man too."

"You sound like a teenager about to do something really stupid." She poked around a nearby pile of stuff. "At least tell me you have a vest and a helmet somewhere."

"Somewhere…" He wasn't sure where. He dug in the next bin.

"Are you the scheduled entertainment?" Ken appeared in the doorway, a slight frown on his face. "I don't recall approving this."

"Always with the jokes." The adrenaline needed an outlet. Jason's hands were beginning to tremble like a rookie rider's. "You're not the boss of me, Ken."

"Jason and I are going to ride that bull," Darcy said in a loud voice that dared anyone to contradict her.

For once Ken was caught flat-footed. He stared at Jason, speechless.

"That's not funny, honey." Jason found the padded vest and helmet in a nearby bin. "You can barely ride a horse, much less a bull." Not to mention she was wearing a skirt today.

"I'm not joking." Darcy had that determined look in her eyes and a firm set to her mouth. "I've ridden those mechanical bulls before." She didn't admit she'd only ridden on the low setting. "I'll go first."

Jason sent a pleading look Ken's way.

"I've always liked you, Darcy," Ken said, returning to form. "You always have Jason's best interests at heart."

"Likewise," Darcy said, siding with Ken.

"Okay," Jason said slowly, an idea taking shape.

That's an asinine idea, George said, having read his mind.

"I could choose not to ride today on one condition." He captured Darcy's gaze.

She raised her brows.

"You have to agree to wear my ring."

"This is not the way to ask a woman to commit to you," Ken said, as if Darcy couldn't hear him. "How about we all step outside and have a beer?"

Darcy pushed Ken out of the room and closed the door. She turned, a furrow in her brow. "I can't."

"For seven months?" Jason put his hands on his hips.

Darcy shook her head. "It's not fair to you. I think we should take a break, at least until our legal issues are straightened out."

The air left Jason's lungs in a whoosh, as if he'd just been thrown. "You don't mean that."

She looked pained. "You're not thinking this through. You're famous, and I'm a felon. I could go to jail for eighteen months for bigamy. I don't care how well you ride bulls or how well Ken writes a statement about what happened, your name will be mud if word gets out. And if I wear your ring, word *will* get out. I'm trying to protect you."

"By pushing me away?" Jason dropped his rope, his vest, his helmet. He had one last card to play. "Honey, I have something to tell you. You may not like it at first."

She brushed a hand through her hair and growled in frustration. "You sound like you're about to tell me there's been a miracle and you're pregnant. Why am I the husband in this relationship?"

Jason didn't laugh. He picked his way to her side. "Hear me out."

"No." Darcy took a step back. "I lied to you."

The bottom dropped out of Jason's world. He stopped in his tracks. "About George?"

"No." Darcy shook her head. "When I was a kid, I told you I wasn't like my family. That was a lie." Her brow furrowed. "I stole. I stole what my family told me to. Mostly food. Before Eddie went to jail, he was teaching me how to hot-wire a car. The reason I was in that detention center was because I was leading that heifer into the trailer for my dad so he could catch another."

"I don't care." Jason was so relieved she hadn't confessed her love of George that he swayed back on his heels so he wouldn't fall to his knees. "They were your family. They expected you to do those things. Once they were gone, you were a fine, upstanding citizen."

"I was. When I was with you. When I was with you, any crime, no matter how small, seemed wrong." Tears filled her eyes, but when he would have closed the distance between them, she held a hand out to keep him away. "But then last year, as soon as that woman kissed you, George proposed. And I knew on some level it was wrong to agree, even if I loved him in my own way and owed him the success I'd achieved. And then when I signed the marriage certificate, it was like my family was in my head, telling me I should change everything about my appearance and my life the way my mother would have, had my marriage been a scam."

"You were trying to shelter yourself and George. I refuse to believe your mother was egging you on."

Voices in heads shouldn't be discounted, George said.

Jason bit his lip to keep from shouting at George. But really, George was to blame, and Jason said so.

Darcy shook her head. "He was paranoid about his sons taking over his seat. But he remembered every detail of the law. I molded myself to my image of Mrs. George Harper. Don't blame George for that."

"Of course I'm going to blame George. He's been the voice in your head since he died." *Working double duty in mine.*

"I don't hear him anymore. I'm alone." Her voice cracked on that last word. "Or I will be as soon as you leave for the rodeo. And then heaven only knows what trouble I'll get into."

Jason clenched his jaw. "I love you. And..." Dare he say it? What choice did he have? "And there's a slight possibility that we may not be married. In which case, you wouldn't be a felon." There. Problem solved.

Darcy's jaw dropped.

Jason quickly explained about the lack of a paper license. "Ken's going to get to the bottom of this on Monday. So you see, there's nothing to worry about."

"You've known this since yesterday? You've known and you didn't tell me? Just like you didn't tell me about your leg? Is this why you've been moody?"

"No." He scowled. "Not entirely." George had goaded him into a contest of size and ownership.

Darcy opened the door and backed into Ken, who quickly sidled out of her way. "And here *I* thought I wasn't good enough for you. That's it. We're through."

Ken stood on the other side of the door, clearly having heard everything. The door wasn't that thick. "It's time to take a breath and regroup." He stood in Jason's way.

"Ken…" Jason swore as Darcy disappeared through the outer door. He was angry and frustrated and trapped. "Maybe taking a beat is how you deal with trouble in your world but that's not how I deal with it in mine."

Ken crossed his arms.

"Get out of my way!" Jason shouted, grabbing a pair of spurs. "I'm riding that bull."

* * *

Pennywhistle had never been ridden.

According to his breeding papers, that was the ornery beast's name. Pennywhistle.

You'd think with that moniker he'd have been a bit better trained. But no. It was a chore to get Pennywhistle into the chute. He kept charging Jason.

Burgers were served. Beer was consumed. Just not by Jason.

Anger refused to let him give up. Darcy thought she wasn't good enough for him. Darcy, who'd been manipulated by George.

Don't suck me into this. George was sounding decidedly chipper.

Iggy helped Jason put the strap and rope around the bull's chest. "He's raw, isn't he?" Iggy sounded positively gleeful.

"He'll do, Iggy." Jason wasn't giddy. He was grim. The argument he'd had with Darcy lingered at the back of his throat. He didn't want to admit he'd been wrong, but that was the impression he had.

Pennywhistle was chuffing louder than a freight train. He was one mean-spirited bull. His anger should have pleased Jason. It didn't.

Jason's leg twinged as he climbed the chute rails, nearly

sending him tumbling backward. It should have shaken some sense into him. It didn't. Jason was more determined than ever to prove to himself that nothing could stop him from bending life to his will. All he needed was a strong grip and the determination not to let go.

He balanced on the top rung, checking his vest and helmet, tightening his gloves. The guests were cheering him on. Everyone except Ken and his mother. They stood apart from the revelers. Darcy was nowhere to be seen.

This should have been Jason's moment. *Hometown rodeo star proves his skill on a bull two-thirds the size of the monsters he normally rides on the circuit.*

It's okay to back out, George said. *Doesn't mean you're any less a man.*

But it meant exactly that to Jason. He'd never backed down from a challenge or a dare in his life.

"Almost ready." He lowered himself onto the bull, who protested by bucking, but only half-heartedly, since there wasn't much space to move in the chute. Jason tightened his grip on the rope. "Hit it."

Iggy released the gate.

The bull leaped sideways. Jason hung on.

The bull bucked. Jason stayed on.

The bull spun. Jason's nerve shot fire through his thigh. He lost his leg position and flew through the air and landed in the dirt.

Iggy distracted the bull while Jason dragged himself to the fence. His right leg was burning with pain. Only pride kept him from dragging his leg behind him. Somehow he managed to climb stiffly up the rails and sit on top. He was sweating just as heavily as if he'd lasted the full eight seconds.

The crowd receded, kindly giving Jason some space to reclaim whatever dignity he had left.

You'll find that dignity shelved next to maturity, George muttered.

The bull trotted past, tossing his head as if he'd like a second go-round.

Ken hung his arms over the top rail. "I think we need a professional consult."

"Make the appointment. I'll go see your orthopedic specialist."

"You need that too." Ken glanced up at him. "When I said *professional*, I meant relationship professionals."

Criminy. "You meant—"

"The Widows Club."

Chapter Twenty

♥

Betrayed.

It stole Darcy's appetite.

After getting a ride home from Lola, Darcy had packed Jason's duffel and left it out by the locked gate, the security code to which she'd changed.

Stogey had sat down next to Jason's duffel while she walked away, his loyalties in question. She'd had to pick him up and carry him to the house.

This morning, the duffel was gone.

Darcy drank her morning Coke in the sunroom, right out of the can. There'd been no tumbler of ice waiting. No love note. She threw away the stack he'd left her during his stay. The pond was rippling from the wind. There was no man skipping rocks at the pond's edge. No shirtless man puttering around the house. Stogey moped and refused to touch his breakfast. He barely tooted.

She was heartbroken, but Darcy knew she'd done the right thing. Jason had known how upset she was over being a bigamist, how worried she'd been that Rupert or Oliver would discover she was a felon. And he hadn't told her there was a possibility it was all a misunderstanding.

When Darcy went to the cottage to give Pearl the new gate code, she clutched Stogey to her chest as if afraid Pearl would steal the one being in her life who couldn't be disloyal to her.

She went into work, half expecting to see Jason at the courthouse. He wasn't. She and Stogey arrived promptly at seven thirty. Her hair was down, and she wore wedges instead of the chunky-heeled, hated sandals, and a wraparound green dress that actually made her look like a young professional.

No one commented on her appearance all day. Or treated her with any more or less respect.

Take that, George.

He had no comeback. Not surprising, since she hadn't heard him for days.

Tina Marie poked her head into Darcy's office that afternoon. "Is it okay if I load up next Monday's schedule with divorce cases?"

"Can we take a day of marriages on the rocks?" Former-bigamist humor. Darcy might have given in to her stomach upset several times that day if only it wouldn't have given rise to pregnancy rumors.

"You can do it, Darcy." Tina Marie gave her a smile, one of the few she'd had since they'd begun working together again. "You're tough."

"Thank you." Darcy lowered her voice. "But I'll never be as tough as you." It was the truth. Tina Marie was protective of the office of judge, no matter who sat on the throne. "You've somehow managed to run through enough cases that there's light at the end of the tunnel."

"It helps that you're the hanging judge."

Darcy sat back, stunned. "You mean like George?"

"No." Tina Marie's tone changed. They'd come a long way

since Darcy's appointment, but there were still hard feelings. "George created alternative sentences that put those brought before him between a rock and a hard place. There was no easy way out. But by allowing them to choose, it put them in charge of their fate. No one blamed George for their lot in life after being arrested."

Darcy nodded. Everyone blamed her. The lawyers. The defendants.

"You, on the other hand, you represent everything they hate and fear about the law. There's no pleading with you. It's cut-and-dry." Tina Marie smiled, but it was a grim smile, an I've-accepted-my-lot-in-life-until-retirement smile. "Yep, you're the hanging judge. Won't help you preside over divorces on Monday, though." Tina Marie returned to her desk.

"*You've already got a reputation,*" her mother had said.

Darcy drew Stogey into her lap, needing to feel less bloodthirsty than Tina Marie had painted her. She knew the right thing to do was step down as judge. She just had to work up the courage to do it.

Henrik knocked on the doorframe. "Can I have a moment, Judge Harper?"

"Of course." Darcy indicated he should take a seat, wondering what she'd done to bring him out here. Had Rupert heard her confession to Jason?

Henrik closed the door behind him, shutting Tina Marie out. A bad sign. He took his time sitting down, unbuttoning his suit jacket, and taking stock of the office. A really bad sign.

"I haven't changed much in here," Darcy said self-consciously, glancing around at the dark paneling and traditional painting on the wall. "It still feels like George's office." Except she kept the heavy drapes open to let in the natural light.

"But you've changed a lot in the courtroom." Henrik nodded toward the door opposite the one he'd come in.

"Is there a compliment in there somewhere?" It didn't feel like it.

He studied her for a moment. It was different from the way he'd studied her the first day they'd met. "Our office has received some complaints."

It was almost a relief to know why he'd come. "About sentencing."

The hanging judge.

It was better than a rumor that she was a bigamist.

Henrik nodded. "You know, when George sat the bench, this was one of the lowest-crime districts in the area. And the lowest rate of repeat offenders in the state."

"No one ever said George was soft on crime. And I'm not either." If Darcy was going down, she was going down swinging.

"You're adhering to the guidelines," Henrik allowed. However, it felt like there was a *but* in his assessment somewhere.

Darcy didn't give him time to tack that on. "Aren't judges supposed to uphold the law of the land?"

"Most don't hold to the letter of that law." Henrik scooted forward in his chair, leaning his forearms on the desk. "If the minimum sentence is ten days, they might give them two nights in jail. Perhaps stipulating that the sentence be carried out over a weekend so that a citizen might not miss work."

Darcy settled back in her chair, hands clasped over her stomach, which wasn't happy with the tacos she'd had for lunch. "I'm not entirely clear on the course of this conversation, Henrik. Are you censuring me?"

"No." He glanced toward the courtroom. "But there have been complaints filed. Several were registered with the clerk of the court of appeals for this district. It's unusual for so many to be filed so soon after an appointment."

Darcy nodded. She was a special case. "And what did these complaints allege?"

"Erroneous decision." Henrik cleared his throat. "You know, the thing that made George a good judge wasn't his compassion for his community. It was his sense of humanity. He knew who he was and who he wanted to be. He cared for people. And through that caring, he earned their respect."

Respect. The lack of it grated on her nerves.

"Henrik, George wasn't perfect." The man had had rough edges up until the day he died. "I'm sure he had several complaints filed against him." Most likely for the same thing.

"And he'd admit that if you brought it up." Henrik nodded.

"He'd admit..." Darcy hugged herself. Her mouth was dry. She'd been furious with Jason for keeping the revelation that their marriage might not be legal a secret. But the secrets in her professional life were weighing her down too. "I need to admit something."

"Besides you marrying George for something other than love?" He didn't say it with acrimony. In fact, Henrik shrugged. "I think you know how George and I felt about the alternatives for the position."

He didn't care? Darcy frowned. "You could have appointed Reese or Keli." The public defender and district attorney.

"George talked to them privately a few years ago. Neither one was interested in the position. Reese has a health issue, and Keli had more personal reasons for turning the opportunity down." Henrik shook his head. "No, it was you. It was always you we pinned our hopes on."

"And how's that working out for you so far? You came here to tell me I suck as a judge." Darcy drew herself up

when what she really wanted to do was slump over her desk
and admit defeat. "You should have told me you knew about
my marriage to George from day one."

"Would that have made you feel better?"

"No. Yes. Maybe."

"Precisely. Not even you have sorted out how you feel
about the path that brought you here." Henrik got to his
feet and went to stand behind his chair, leaning on the back.
"You have regrets. There are words and actions in everyone's
past that they regret. Learn to forgive yourself."

"But—"

"I want you to be the best judge Darcy Jones Harper can
be. And if that means a little soul-searching to figure out who
you are and how you want to proceed, so be it." He stood
smiling at her ever so gently. "In time, Sunshine will forget
how you became judge if you're a good judge." He'd said his
piece, and he left.

Darcy slumped in her seat. Forgive herself? She'd have
to forgive others first. Jason and George were at the head
of the line.

Darcy stared at the dusty bottle of whiskey on the book-
case on the far wall.

She wasn't one for drinking on the job. Or drinking alone.

It was time to belly up to the bar at Shaw's.

* * *

"You've been avoiding me." Jason ran down Ken at his
mother's yarn shop late Monday afternoon because he hadn't
received word on his marital status.

"I've been busy." Ken wore a dark-brown sweater vest over a
tan polo shirt and was reviewing a paper list of some kind.

"Go easy on him." Mom snagged Jason in an exuberant hug. She wore a black, lightweight sweater with bell sleeves, reminiscent of Darcy's judge robe. "I'm thrilled to say Ken has shown me how to sell my knits online. He set me up with a website and everything."

"Clarice agreed to take pictures of her merchandise and post them online." Ken tucked his cell phone into his back pocket and gestured toward Clarice in the back room, who held her camera over a pair of mittens.

"It sounds like you've fixed everything," Jason said evenly.

"Not everything, but close to it." Ken grinned.

Ken never grinned.

Grinding his teeth, Jason led the way to the door. "Say goodbye to the kind ladies, Ken."

"Goodbye, kind ladies." He bowed.

Jason held the door, rolling his eyes. "Come on, Mr. Fix-It. I'm overdue for an update."

"Coffee?" Ken asked.

Jason nodded.

They walked toward the bakery. It stayed open until six on weekdays to feed the town's caffeine cravings.

"I did get some news today, and you're not going to like it." Ken nodded to Tiffany Winslow as they passed the pharmacy. "Turns out you're not married."

Jason swore. The wind carried the word away. "I know it's not right to pull for something that makes Darcy a felon, but I was really hoping our marriage was legal."

Ken tsk-tsked. "You'd be a lot calmer if you ate fewer carbs."

Jason swore again. Louder. His leg threatened to cramp.

They crossed the street, nearing the movie theater.

Avery came rushing out the front door, dressed up for date

night in high heels and a skirt that showed off a lot of leg. "I'm ready."

"Give me a minute," Ken said in a voice unburdened by lost loves and missing marriage licenses. "You look fantastic. I'll be right back."

They proceeded down the street.

"My life is in ruins and you have a date?" Jason settled his hat more firmly on his head, the way one does before throwing a punch.

"I'm allowed a personal life." Ken smoothed a hand over his fresh haircut, undoubtedly obtained at Prestige Salon.

"You're fired." He'd stand by Iggy before Ken.

Ken sighed. "I told you I'd fix this, and I will. You have to have a little patience. Rome wasn't built in a day."

"Like you called in the professionals and they had all the answers." Jason's hands fisted. He'd wait to pop Ken in the nose until they reached the bakery. There were napkins at the bakery to capture the blood. Mom would be upset if her sweater vest was permanently stained.

"I made those calls, Jason. And do you know why?" Ken narrowed his gaze on Jason. "Because I'm an adult. Which means I have to keep my eye on the professional ball. I can't just show up and cheer on my clients. I have to wipe up their blood and patch up their marriages. I have to schmooze potential clients and laugh at their bad jokes. I can't just sit and twiddle my thumbs and wonder how serious twinges are. I have to approach the problem as if I'm the guy who's going to fix it."

"Like I can't." Jason shuffled his feet.

"That's always what I assume. Yes." Ken blew out a breath.

This was why Ken was such a good fixer. He didn't shirk his responsibilities. He didn't get married in Vegas in a drunken stupor and send the documentation to someone else. He didn't let anger dictate the choices he made. With Ken, the buck stopped here. Jason had the good grace to stare at his boots and be thankful his agent had developed such skill. And while he contemplated the worn boot leather, he gave a moment of consideration to what his life might look like if he embraced adulthood. It wouldn't include eight-second rides on angry bulls. It wouldn't include days spent alone in a truck driving to the next big rodeo. That didn't mean he'd spend every day shooting the breeze with Iggy at Shaw's. Jason would have days filled with things needing to be done. Not that he knew what those things were yet. But those nights. His nights would be filled with the company of a warm woman and a loyal little dog. At least at first.

They stood in front of the bakery. Ken gestured to it as if giving Jason an invitation to draw back and—

Edith waved at Jason through the window. She sat next to Bitsy and Mims. A glance over Jason's shoulder showed Clarice trailing behind them, working that walking stick, gray braids swinging.

"I thought you were joking about the widow consultation." Jason scuffed his boot across the pavement.

"It's no joke." Ken opened the door for Jason. "It takes a strong man to ask for help where he least wants it."

And for a strong man of Sunshine, the last place to go for help was the Widows Club.

* * *

Darcy stepped into Shaw's and let the door hit her on the backside.

It was a weekday happy hour. The bar wasn't busy.

There was no one at her regular table in back.

Darcy hurried to the bar and ordered a beer. She set the bag with Stogey in it on the floor.

"We don't allow pets in here," Noah said firmly.

Dang, he had good eyes. "He's my emotional support animal."

Noah slid a beer in front of her. "Therapy dogs require a special jacket."

"It's in the wash?" She gave her former boss a pleading look. They both knew she was lying.

Noah shook his head and walked to the other end of the bar to take care of two customers who had been hidden by a thick post. It was Lola and Drew.

Darcy picked up her beer, her purse, and her dog and scurried over to join them. "I don't mean to interrupt date night, guys. But can I just sit here and pretend like I have a life? I'll be quick about downing this beer, I swear."

"Sweetie, you stay as long as you need." Lola's head rested on Drew's shoulder. "Becky's at her grandma's house. We're here for a cocktail, then it's on to dinner and a movie."

"Not necessarily the movie." Drew's smile grew slowly. "And maybe not even dinner."

Lola laughed. "How was your day? Getting any easier?"

"The short answer?" Because the long answer was too complicated. Darcy glanced at Drew. "Everybody hates me."

Lola sat up. "But not Drew."

Both women stared at him, waiting for an answer.

"I don't hate Darcy," he said on cue in a neutral voice. "But if she wants to be elected in the fall, she needs to think about the sentences she's handing down."

"I'm the hanging judge," Darcy explained to Lola. "Isn't that what folks want? A judge who's tough on crime? George was tough on crime." If Oliver had been in her shoes, he'd be a hanging judge. Rupert too.

She took a generous swig of beer, imagining what Rupert would look like in her clunky grandma shoes.

Drew patted her consolingly on the back. "Do you know what prison does to someone?"

"Well..." She thought of the hard planes of her mother's face.

"You put a petty criminal in a confined situation. They're bitter because their freedom has been taken away. And they're locked up with a bunch of other people, mostly hard-core criminals who are full of advice about how to become a harder-core criminal. Not to mention they bond over their hatred of law enforcement and laws in general." Drew paused, possibly realizing who he was talking to. "Sorry. You might know someone like this. Someone who went to jail for what might have been a starter crime? Someone who, upon release, became a repeat offender?"

"You're talking about my family." Darcy ran a hand through her hair. She wasn't finding her stride fast enough for the community. "You're saying the way I sentence perpetuates the system."

Drew held up his hands. "It's just one man's opinion." Which happened to align with George's opinion.

If they'd been texting, she'd have inserted the "mind blown" emoji.

Lola and Drew finished their drinks.

"We're headed out," Lola said, threading her arms into her sweater. "Unless you'd like us to stay until you finish your beer."

"No. Don't worry about me. Go on to dinner."

"Or somewhere with a nice view of the valley," Drew said slyly.

"Don't break any laws," Darcy said around a weak smile. All too soon, she was alone at the bar. "Noah, can I have some peanuts or snack mix or stale popcorn?" Anything to make it look like she wasn't pathetically alone in the bar. "And you forgot my coaster."

"You want me to turn on Oprah, too?" He nodded toward the baseball game on television as he placed a small bowl of snack mix in front of her. He slapped a round paper coaster on the bar and positioned her beer bottle on top of it.

"Don't be so judgy. Aren't bars supposed to be where you go to drown your sorrows? Where you reminisce about the good ol' days?" She shoved a handful of snack mix in her mouth.

At her feet, Stogey raised his nose and sniffed.

Darcy passed him a square of Chex. "It's brown, so it must be made of wheat." The vet had warned her about feeding Stogey people food. But wheat was healthy.

Noah looked aghast. "You can't feed your *therapy dog* in my bar."

"Have me arrested." Darcy gave Stogey another square. "We're out of here as soon as my beer is finished."

"Hold up. Darcy's in a bar on a weeknight." Avery slid onto a stool next to her. She was wearing the Louboutins Darcy had given her. "And she's not wearing my grandmother's shoes."

Ken took the bar stool next to Avery. "Hey, Darcy." He must have run into Mrs. Petrie earlier, because he wore a sweater vest over his polo.

"We're on a date," Avery confided with a sideways glance at Ken, who was texting.

"Talk to her while I wrap this up." Ken finished his missive and flagged down Noah. "What kind of signature cocktails do you have?"

"Beer on tap," Noah deadpanned.

"Funny. We'll have two Moscow mules," Ken said just as flatly. His phone flashed and he picked it up. The man was always wheeling and dealing.

But had he learned whether or not Darcy and Jason were legally married? She didn't dare ask with Avery present.

"Nice shoes." Darcy stared at Avery's feet. "My toes are having second thoughts about giving them to you." Louboutins beat wedge heels any day.

"If you miss these shoes that bad, I can rent them to you." Avery knew how to make an extra buck and how to toss a challenge.

"Rent?" Darcy scoffed. "I loaned you those shoes once. Gratis."

"And then you gave them to me. So if you want to rent them, you can. With terms and conditions. Embedded in the fine print will be that my grandmother will want her shoes returned." Avery turned her back on Darcy, facing Ken. She did the hair toss thing, flinging her locks dismissively in Darcy's direction.

Her hair smelled good, like the frizz-reducing spray Darcy had given her during the purge.

"Can I get you a refill, Darcy?" Noah asked, multitasking while he made those mules.

"I better not. Two beers and I might wrestle those shoes off Avery's feet."

"I heard that," Avery said over her shoulder. "And by the way, it's spring. You could use highlights."

Darcy ran her fingers through her hair. She didn't need to look in a mirror. Avery spoke the truth.

Ken leaned past Avery to catch Darcy's eye. "I need to ask you for a favor."

"Not now." Darcy worked on finishing her beer.

Jason burst through the door, started toward Darcy's usual table, but stopped when he realized it was empty. He took stock of the room. His gaze landed on her.

Darcy's heart went *ka-thump*.

She drained her beer. "Time to go." She reached down for Stogey's bag.

It was empty.

* * *

In the time it took Jason to find Darcy at the bar, Stogey waddled up to him and sat on his boot.

"You're a lifesaver, little man." Jason scooped the dog into his arms and strode over to Darcy, taking a seat next to her. "I'll have what she's having, Noah. And give her another."

"I shouldn't have a second beer." But she didn't refuse either. She held herself stiffly, perhaps waiting for the verdict on their marriage.

"Have another, Darcy." Ken draped his arms over Avery's shoulders. "I'll protect your shoes, honey, while Jason asks Darcy a question. He knows the one."

Jason frowned. Ken and the widows had a ridiculous idea for Jason to win Darcy back. "Didn't I fire you?"

"I ignore the ranting of temperamental clients." Ken glanced at Noah. "Can you at least make Jason's beer low carb? He's in training."

Darcy made a guttural sound and slapped her hand on the bar top like she was wielding a gavel. "Ken, did you tip off Jason that I was here?"

"That's what I always liked about Darcy." Ken twined his fingers with Avery's. "Can't get one past her."

Darcy reached for Stogey. Jason held him back. The jostling earned him a canine gas bomb.

"What do you feed this dog?" Jason looked deep into Stogey's eyes to make sure he wasn't medicated again. "Onions? Chili?"

"Chex Mix?" Darcy had the grace to look embarrassed. "And it was just a couple."

"No dogs allowed." Noah delivered their beers. "Especially ones that smell like that."

"He's a therapy dog," Darcy protested, albeit weakly. Her hair was askew, as if she'd run her hands through it and given up halfway.

Noah put his hands on his hips. "Put your therapy dog back in your bag or you'll have to leave."

"Come on." Jason slid off the bar stool with Stogey in his arms. "Let's get a booth." He waited for Darcy to get off the bar stool before heading for her usual table.

"No questions." Darcy set their beers on the table and then took Stogey, placing him in his carrier in the corner. "Just information. Go on. Spill."

No way was he spilling the good stuff first. She'd leave. "You're drinking at Shaw's."

"I had some day." She told him about the complaints against her and how Tina Marie had called her a hanging judge. "It seemed appropriate to have a drink. And then I got here and even Drew cast shade on my performance."

"Has George approved of your work?"

"George is oddly…absent." She ran her fingers through her hair once more. "You know, I don't think he's spoken to me since you came to stay."

I found a more interesting pupil.

Jason waved a hand in front of his face as if chasing off a pesky fly.

Stogey crawled out of his carrier and crept into her lap. He scanned the table for morsels, of which there were none, and then gave Jason a mournful look.

"We shouldn't be seen together." Darcy drank from her beer.

At the bar, Avery had her arms around Ken's neck and her back to them. Ken swept his hand through the air, encouraging Jason to get things moving.

"It's like Ken has superhuman hearing or something," Jason muttered. "I'm sorry I didn't tell you our suspicions right away about the license. Things between us have been tenuous, and I didn't want you to get your hopes up."

Darcy leaned forward, expression fierce. "Things between us were not tenuous. They were good, except for the fact that you didn't tell me you were injured or that we might not be married."

"I apologize for not coming clean with you. It won't happen again."

Stogey rested his chin on the tabletop, staring at Jason as if he thought filet mignon was being delivered to the table next.

Darcy stroked his head. "Let's be honest. Part of my frustration is about my job. I should resign." She took a sip of beer and then stared Jason square in the eyes. "I should resign and you should retire."

"Neither one of us is a quitter," Jason said none too mildly.

"I'm not quitting. I've decided to come clean, which will necessitate the retirement of the hanging judge." Darcy dug in her purse, presumably for her wallet or her car keys. "If Iggy shows up, which we both know he will—he has a radar for you in bars—he can finish my beer. Text me what the Vegas verdict is. I just can't do this anymore."

"Hold up. What do you feel the need to confess?" And why did she feel it would mean she'd have to quit?

"This." She flashed him the rock of a wedding ring. "A string of bad decisions that ended with me being judge. I feel the need to cleanse my soul. Sounds cliché, but you felt better after you told me the truth about Vegas, didn't you?" She got to her feet, gathering her purse and Stogey's tote bag. "They'll probably run me out of town, but I deserve it."

"This isn't the answer." The judgeship was important to her. She brought work home every night.

She sighed, a sound that said she'd decided that was the only avenue left worth pursuing, including the branch of her journey that involved Jason.

He had to do something. He had to say something. "I hear George in my head," he blurted.

I don't want to be drawn into this.

Darcy stared at him.

Jason nodded. "Since I moved into the house. He's rather annoying. Doesn't butt out of things that aren't his business, and he stays out of things that are his business, like you and Pearl."

"Prove it." She leaned forward, drawing Stogey to her side and pushing her beer out of the way. Her eyes narrowed. "What does George say about me telling the world I married him to get to the bench?"

To zip it and quit prosecuting herself.

"He doesn't think you should. He thinks you should stop judging yourself."

Darcy shook her finger at Jason. "You tell him I know

what he did. He and Henrik...They knew about my juvenile record. George knew I was all wrong for this."

She's always so certain she deserves nothing.

"When she deserves the world," Jason murmured, heart swelling with love for her.

"I'm going to tell the world the truth about me and George and...and everything," Darcy said sharply, slapping a twenty on the table and stuffing Stogey into his bed-in-a-bag. "Let them be my jury."

"Okay." Jason lifted his beer in a toast and drank some. "I think I know where you can do that."

"You're kidding me." She regarded him suspiciously.

"Nope. Ken wants you to be on my interview show. Here's your chance to come clean." That wasn't exactly how the widows had coached him to ask her to participate, but the point was to get Darcy to talk to him with moderators in his corner. And selfishly, Jason didn't want Darcy to tell anyone the truth about George. It would only give them a target to shoot at. And Darcy had spent too many years as someone else's target. "You come, and I'll tell you if we're married or not." He told Darcy the date and time, and to meet at the yarn shop.

"Okay," Darcy agreed, if hollowly. "I'm going to do this."

Jason nodded. He saw Bitsy enter the bar and signaled her that Darcy needed a ride. She headed over, stopping to greet Ken and Avery.

Darcy continued to linger. "Do you hear me in your head? Or is it just George?"

"Just George." He tapped his temple and drank in her sweet face. "But I wish you were with me. I wish you'd whisper when it's appropriate to take your hand or wrap my arms around you or draw you close."

Her cheeks pinkened. Her gaze touched his lips.

"But I'll wait until you give me the word."

She sighed. "I'm not good enough for you."

"Do you really want to be a judge?"

His question surprised her. Darcy's head drew back a little, and she blinked rapidly. "I think I do."

"Then you should own it. Your way. Not George's. Hair down. Heels high. Sentences that make sense to you, because you're a Jones and a Harper and possibly a Petrie."

"Why do people have faith in me in this job?" she whispered, clutching Stogey and his bag to her chest. "Why don't I have it in myself?"

Jason leaned forward, lowering his voice. "Honey, you're Judge Darcy Jones Harper Petrie." Or she could be. "The odds have always been in your favor. All you have to do is look forward, not back."

Her eyes widened.

I used to tell her that, George said softly as Darcy made for the exit.

"Yeah, well, she didn't believe it when you said it." Jason could only hope hearing it from him would make the message sink in.

* * *

"Is this beer taken?" Iggy slid into the booth across from Jason only a few minutes after Darcy and Bitsy left.

"That was Darcy's but she left it to you." Jason sipped his beer, continuing to contemplate the way he'd run his life for the past few years and coming to the conclusion that he hadn't done such a great job when he wasn't riding a bull. He needed to make some serious changes in his life. And he wasn't the only one.

"It's still cold." Iggy drank it down happily.

Jason stared at his childhood friend. "I swear, if someone walked away from a pizza, you'd swoop in to get the last slice."

"No joke. Good pizza and good beer should never go to waste." Iggy removed his baseball cap and ran a hand over his hair. "You up to trying to ride Pennywhistle again tomorrow?"

"No." He wasn't riding again until he got the all clear from the orthopedic specialist. "Iggy, tell me the truth about Tom Bodine's order."

Iggy held up the empty beer bottle, catching Noah's attention. "What does it matter?"

Jason reached across the table, grabbed his business partner by the neck of his T-shirt, and yanked him forward until they were nose to nose. "I'm an honest man. I won't tolerate anything but honest business dealings." He shoved Iggy back in his seat.

"Hey, I'm your partner." Iggy straightened his T-shirt. "Not to mention your friend. How much have you had to drink?"

"One beer. Not even." And he'd lost the thirst for more. Introspection tended to do that to a person when they admitted their own flaws. "Let me tell you about this *partnership*. I put up all the money into the business. I pay you a salary. Technically, you're my employee. But because I love you like a brother, I called this a partnership."

Iggy sat back, looking like he could use something stronger to drink than a beer.

"So when I ask you if Tom Bodine was given what he paid for, I want you to tell me the truth. Or so help me, I'll find a new partner." He pounded his fist on the table.

You've been hanging around too many judges.

Zip it, old man.

Noah approached the table. "Everything okay here?"

Jason stared at Iggy.

"Everything's fine." Iggy waited to say more until Noah was a safe distance away. "I'm ninety percent certain he got the right vials."

Jason bit back a curse. "Iggy..."

"Truth." Iggy set his beer down and held up his hands. "We've been going through part-time workers like rain through my fingers. We did a double collection one day from two different bulls and..." He shrugged. "That's where the ten percent doubt comes in. I'm sorry, man. It won't happen again."

"You're dang right it won't." Jason did swear this time. "This is my name. My reputation."

"It is called Bull Puckey Breeding." Iggy, being Iggy, couldn't resist a dig. Or a mischievous smile. "Not Jason Petrie Breeding, which would sound stupid."

Irrationally, Jason wanted to laugh. Because that was Ignacio King. A jokester.

"Here's what's going to happen." Jason pushed his beer aside and leaned on the table. "We're going to hire someone to work full-time. They'll help you keep the place clean and in order. And they'll be trained in product collection."

"Okay, you're the boss." Iggy smirked.

Jason didn't like that smirk. He reached across the table and pounded his fist near Iggy's beer. "You didn't let me finish. Ken is going to send someone to examine the books. If the accounts are in order..."—he slowed down, just in case Iggy had something else to confess—"then he's going to present you with a partnership offer."

Iggy stopped smirking and sat up taller. "For reals?"

"For reals." Jason nodded, drawing back. "You'll have to buy into the business. He'll present you with options to do this." He glanced over at Ken, who was having an intimate discussion with Avery. He was going to have to unfire him, because Ken was worth his weight in gold.

"Thanks, Jason. Seriously, man. You're the best. And the books...The books are clean."

"Good." Jason clasped his hands on the table. "There's one more thing you have to do for me. And it's not going to be pretty."

"Anything." Iggy nodded.

"We're shooting one last episode of *Two Cowboys and a Little Old Lady* on Sunday."

"I'll be there, man. I promise." Iggy raised his beer to his lips and then set the bottle down untouched. "Is this the Darcy episode?"

Jason nodded.

"Oh, man. I wouldn't miss this for nothing."

Chapter Twenty-One

♥

"All rise for the Honorable Judge Harper."

It didn't escape Darcy's notice that she'd earned an *Honorable* from Ronald. She was earning their respect with her performance and she couldn't have been prouder. But would that be enough that people like Ronald and Tina Marie could get past the nepotism?

Darcy settled Stogey under her desk and sank into George's big, creaky chair, making a mental note to have it oiled. "What do we have on the docket this morning?"

Hopefully, it was something to keep her mind off Jason, who seemed to have a closer relationship with her deceased husband than she did.

"Tina Marie? Ronald? Anybody?" Darcy snapped, immediately apologizing for losing her temper. She shouldn't have worn her hair down today. She should have kept it as conservatively fastened as the locked door on her temper.

"I'm sorry, Your Honor." Tina Marie stood. She hadn't had a schedule of cases ready this morning, claiming lawyers and defendants weren't cooperating with scheduling. She'd been trying to pull in some cases today that had originally been scheduled for later in the month. Tina Marie handed Darcy a folder. "Up next."

"This is the case of John Borrington versus the people." Keli came to stand next to Tina Marie. "Petty theft. Harassment. Lying to a police officer. We're here today for sentencing."

Glancing at the case file, Darcy felt like she was facing down a Jones relative.

The sheriff moved to stand beside Keli while Darcy familiarized herself with the case. She read the defendant the range of penalties for his crimes. "Mr. Borrington, I've perused your case file." Darcy hadn't been impressed. "You've been given many opportunities and yet you continue to return to this court."

"It wasn't my fault. I therefore plead not guilty." Mr. Borrington was apparently representing himself.

"You entered your plea in front of Judge Johnson." And he'd waived his right to trial, which seemed the norm in this district. Darcy glanced around the gallery to make sure Reese wasn't available to advise this man. "Before I sentence, let's hear from the sheriff first."

Drew came forward. "Mr. Borrington stole a package delivered to his neighbor, all of which was captured on the victim's video doorbell. When confronted about it, Mr. Borrington kept returning to the victim's porch and shouting obscenities, daring the victim to call the authorities."

"All of which, I assume, is in the video evidence referenced."

"Yes, Your Honor."

"Objection." Mr. Borrington seemed pleased to know court protocol. "I move that the video is inadmissible when considering an appropriate sentence."

"On what grounds?" Darcy asked.

"I was being recorded without permission."

Oh, it was going to be one of those days. "I wasn't aware

that thieves had rights regarding being caught on camera. Overruled."

"But ma'am—"

"You mean Your Honor?" Darcy's fingers curled around her gavel handle.

Jason, Rupert, Ken, and Iggy entered the courtroom and found seats together. Apparently, their case was coming before her today.

Darcy gave Tina Marie a significant look, one that she hoped said, *Next time warn me*, and then turned her attention back to the issue at hand.

"Your Honor, there was no sign warning that I was being recorded." Mr. Borrington continued his amateur efforts at defense.

"Your Honor." Keli interrupted. "Mr. Borrington is raising arguments he presented at his hearing. These have already been addressed and dismissed by Judge Johnson."

Oliver, Tom Bodine, and his twin boys entered the courtroom and found seats.

"Thank you, Ms. Connelly." Darcy stared down the defendant. "Mr. Borrington, to my knowledge, no law has been passed in the state of Colorado regarding warning people they shouldn't break the law because their crime will be recorded." Darcy waited a beat. "In fact, a trespasser waives any expectation of privacy. I'm warning you that you're coming very close to contempt by breaking with court protocol."

"But Your Honor." Mr. Borrington rolled his eyes. "How can I be trespassing when I'm not inside Turly's house?"

This man was yanking her chain. He'd known the moment he'd crossed the sidewalk that he was on his neighbor's property. That was Petty Crime 101.

"Excuse me, Your Honor." Rupert pushed through the

swinging door from the gallery and came to stand beside Mr. Borrington. "My client pleads guilty and throws himself on the mercy of the court."

"I thought Mr. Borrington was self-represented." Darcy gave the defendant a hard stare.

He must have been related to the Jones family. He didn't flinch. "My lawyer was late."

Or Rupert had taken pity on the man who stood alone in front of the hanging judge.

Darcy narrowed her gaze. "This court operates under the sentencing guidelines allowed by law, which for this incident is up to six months."

Someone in the gallery gasped. Jason wore a concerned expression.

Don't look at Jason.

"But my kids." For the first time since stepping from the gallery, Mr. Borrington looked remorseful. "It's not my fault. My wife left us last year. My boss downsized at the feed store. It's unfair. And now this. Who'll watch my kids while I'm in jail? It's not fair that they're punished too." He pointed out his children—a girl of about eight and a boy of about ten.

Tears fell down the little girl's cheeks.

Darcy remembered those days. Sitting in the courthouse hallway. Sitting at home waiting for her parents or someone to tell her what had happened. Sitting in school and being unable to concentrate because she didn't know what home situation she'd face after the bell rang.

Rupert remained silent, staring at Darcy. He knew something of her past. He knew it was much like that of the little girl sitting in the gallery.

She flipped through Mr. Borrington's file, searching for his criminal history. Petty crime. Petty crime. Drunk and disorderly. She turned her attention to Mr. Borrington, and in his face she saw her father, a man who wasn't going to repent.

"Tina Marie, call social services."

"What? No!" Mr. Borrington was livid. "Please, Your Honor."

"Yes, please," Darcy said, feeling anger fill her chest. "Tell me how your children need a good role model in their life, someone who'll stick around but teach them to be a bully and to cut corners by stealing." Her voice strengthened. "Tell me how you don't serve them vegetables or help them with their homework. Tell me how you always think about yourself first instead of what your actions are doing to their future."

"Your Honor." Rupert tried to interrupt.

She waved him off. "Tell me how you want your children to be upstanding citizens who never see the inside of a prison, much less a prison cell. Tell me why you shouldn't have these innocent souls put up for adoption today, this minute, in the hopes that they can have a chance at a better life."

Mr. Borrington's face was pale.

"Objection," Rupert said, although it wasn't much more than a whisper.

"On what grounds?" Darcy demanded, suddenly weary.

Rupert glanced over his shoulder at the children in question. And then he swung his gaze back to her. "On the grounds that I need to speak to you privately in judge's chambers."

He'd broken protocol. Rupert never broke protocol.

The little Borrington girl tried unsuccessfully to stifle a sob. Darcy felt like sobbing herself.

"Court will take a five-minute recess." Darcy pounded her gavel, grabbed Stogey's bag, and led Rupert into her chambers. She lifted Stogey into her arms. "You have four minutes, Counselor."

Rupert set his briefcase down on one chair. "I don't think you want to hear what I have to say."

"I'm sure I don't, but I've found that, as Judge Harper, I have to listen." To him. To Henrik. To Tina Marie. Everyone with an opinion about Judge Darcy Harper. Everyone who seemed to have forgotten that she was still just plain old Darcy Jones underneath these robes. A woman who'd only ever wanted to be respected and make a positive difference in the world.

"I miss my father." Rupert seemed surprised those words had come out of his mouth. He stared at her blankly. "I miss the way he lorded over this court because it was rare that I got anything past him."

Darcy frowned. "I realize I'm a huge disappointment—"

"I'm not finished." Rupert didn't pause to see if she'd give him the floor. He took it. "I miss his booming laughter and the way he could look at someone and know if they were remorseful for what they'd done and needed a second chance, if they needed a hard lesson, or needed to be put away." He pointed toward the courtroom. "That man needs a hard lesson, and you know it. You're about to let your past get in the way of doing what's right."

The truth pressed on Darcy. But she waited to hear Rupert say the obvious: that she wasn't fit for the bench.

Rupert drew himself up. "Now, instead of feeling ashamed of where you come from, go back in there and present that man with a choice. The kind of choice you wish your father had been given." Rupert grabbed his briefcase and returned to the courtroom.

"I think he just respected me," Darcy told Stogey. Respected, not disrespected.

Stogey let out an awful stinker. Darcy didn't care.

Respect was all she'd ever wanted. Respect without feeling as if she didn't deserve it. Passing the bar hadn't given her respect, just as wearing a black robe hadn't. The people closest to her—Jason, Avery, Lola, Mary Margaret, even Pearl and Bitsy. They gave her respect but she'd earned it by being a true friend, a loyal lover, a caring family member by marriage.

She had to earn respect. Her way. By making judgments that made a positive impact in her community. By being honest and fair.

What was happening to the Borrington family wasn't fair or just. A mom who'd abandoned them. A place of business that had fallen on hard times and let him go. Mr. Borrington was a single dad trying to make everything work. Darcy could make a difference here. Suggest support sessions for single parents and that Mr. Borrington be evaluated for anger management. The alternative would be jail time but she was certain he wouldn't take that route.

She stared into Stogey's big brown eyes. He licked her chin.

Stogey wasn't stately. He wasn't entirely healthy. But he loved nurturing people. Hospitals and airports had emotional therapy dogs. Why couldn't her courtroom have one?

"Come on, Stogey. No more bag for you. You've got a job to do making friends in the gallery." She just hoped the dog figured out how to do his job quicker than she'd figured out hers.

* * *

"Your ex had John Borrington's nuts in a vise," Iggy whispered in Jason's ear as Oliver explained to Darcy the suit Tom wanted to bring against them. "Maybe we should have asked her to recuse herself."

Under the grinning gazes of the Bodine twins, Jason shushed his business partner.

Jason had been surprised that Rupert had stepped forward in John's case, more so when Rupert's private conference with Darcy had resulted in her returning to the bench much calmer and kinder. Since when was Darcy on good terms with her stepson?

It was bad enough Jason was in court, not the rodeo arena, and without his cowboy hat for this preliminary hearing. But if Rupert and Darcy were on friendly terms, he was unsure of anything. And the way Darcy looked—with her hair down and a glow to her cheeks—Jason wanted to patch things up with her now. Today.

Iggy bumped his shoulder slightly. "Quit mooning."

"Let me see if I'm understanding you, Mr. Harper," Darcy began in austere tones directed at Oliver. "Your client can't prove whether he received the goods he paid for or not. Is that correct?"

"Yes, Your Honor." Oliver's fingers drummed over his tie.

"The suit claims suffering." Darcy glanced down at the papers in front of her and then toward Tom. "The exact manifestations haven't been listed in your brief. What are they?"

"What are they?" Oliver also looked at Tom.

Darcy leaned forward. "How have you suffered from this situation, Mr. Bodine?"

"I've been angry," Tom said at volume, as if he weren't angry all the time.

Oliver clenched his tie and looked pained.

In the chair next to Jason, Iggy turned his head, eyes wide and mouth shut. But Jason bet he knew what Iggy was thinking. For once, things were going to go their way on this lawsuit.

Darcy glanced toward Rupert. "And what efforts has your

client made to address Mr. Bodine's concerns or attempt to make reparations?"

Rupert got to his feet. "Your Honor, my client offered to refund Mr. Bodine's money. That was rejected. My client then offered to refund his money, provide him with replacement product, and provide free endorsements for one year by Mr. Petrie. That offer was also rejected."

"And the reason for rejection was…?" Darcy tossed the ball back to Tom and Oliver's side of the courtroom.

"Your Honor." Oliver cleared his throat.

"They're idiots," Tom said, loud and clear. "Why would I trust them a second time to provide me with quality sperm?"

Someone in the gallery choked on a laugh, earning a stern look from Darcy.

Small paws rested on Jason's calf. Stogey gazed up at him adoringly. Jason picked the dog up and put him in his lap. Stogey stood on his hind legs and put his front paws on the table. He leaned over and licked Iggy's cheek.

Someone giggled. Darcy's lips might have twitched upward but she didn't look Jason's way.

"Mr. Bodine, it sounds as if you're saying nothing Bull Puckey Breeding could do would be enough to make up for what may or may not have been a mistake. Would you agree with that statement?"

"Objection!" Oliver choked out. "This isn't a trial."

"But we're determining if there is merit to this lawsuit or not." Darcy had a confidence she'd lacked on her first day sitting the bench. Jason thought it was hot. "The very definition of a frivolous lawsuit is one brought for the sole purpose of harassing, annoying, or disturbing the opposing party."

"Took the words right out of my mouth," Rupert murmured, sitting down.

"But all lawsuits of this sort are compensatory, making up for damages incurred." Oliver might have made a stronger case had he not been yanking his own tie.

Darcy passed a hand in Tom's direction. "By your client's own admission, Mr. Harper, it's less about damages and more about punishment."

"Are you saying I can't sue your ex-boyfriend?" Tom demanded in his loudest voice yet. "I want a new judge."

The courtroom was quiet except for Stogey's soft panting.

"It won't matter which judge you go before, Mr. Bodine. You can't sue just because someone made you mad, especially when they made you generous offers of compensation."

Tom's jaw worked. "But—"

"And I'd consider what kind of example you want to set for your children." Darcy nodded toward the Bodine twins, who were sitting in the front row. "If you're a bully, your children will be bullies. I suggest the two parties return to the bargaining table. Legal representation will inform this court in one week of their progress."

Earlier, Jason had thought Darcy looked hot. Now she was smokin'.

For once, the Bodine twins were somber.

Tom's face was ruddy. "But—"

"Be careful, Mr. Bodine," Darcy warned. "Your behavior is bordering on contempt. If you can't come to an agreement, the court will rule in favor of the defendant." She banged her gavel. "Next case."

Jason tried to catch Darcy's eye on the way out, but she wouldn't look at him.

And then Iggy was pummeling his shoulder as they joined Ken in the hallway. "We won, we won, we won, we won."

"As usual, Mr. King," Ken said, "your celebration is premature."

* * *

Stroganoff was simmering on the stove when Darcy got home from work.

The gate had been locked. Had Pearl let Jason in?

Darcy half hoped that she had. The afternoon session of court had been... She'd been... Well, it'd been glorious to finally feel as if she knew what she was doing in terms of court procedure and sentencing. She was in the mood to celebrate with a hot kiss and a cold beer.

Not that she should be celebrating with Jason. But that's who first came to mind.

Who was she kidding? That's who always came to mind.

Darcy set Stogey and her purse down. "Hello?"

Pearl came in from the dining room. "Do you know how many magazines that man kept over the years? Don't guess. I'll tell you. All of them." She washed her hands in the sink and then stirred the stroganoff. "It's almost done. There's a bowl of salad in the refrigerator. And a gift for you on the counter."

The box on the counter had a bra inside. Plain, white, and her size.

"What's this?"

Pearl shrugged. "I owed you a replacement. I shouldn't have gone through your drawers or taken it. I don't know what I was thinking. Grief sometimes makes people—*me*—do stupid things." She met Darcy's gaze evenly. "I've been listening for George the way Jason encouraged me to and I...I'm sorry."

"Oh."

Stogey wagged his tail at Pearl's feet, begging.

"You'll get some, Stogey, don't you worry."

Her changed attitude broke Darcy's stupor. "He shouldn't. People food can upset his stomach." And she didn't need him tooting more than he already did. It made people in the gallery giggle and make faces. Darcy washed her hands and poked her head in the refrigerator. "Are you expecting company?" The salad was enough for two.

"You think I don't want salad?" Pearl tsk-tsked.

"You're eating with me?" Darcy was shocked.

"I owe you an apology for the way I treated you." Pearl slowly eked the words out of herself as if it cost her some pride. "I was like a wounded animal."

"A wounded honey badger," Darcy muttered.

"The love of my life slipped away from me." Pearl didn't raise her voice or stomp around. She tapped her forehead. "Here, as the man I knew slowly disappeared in character. And here." She tapped a spot over her heart. "As he slipped from this earthly plane."

Her words touched Darcy, more so because she hadn't thought she'd ever hear an apology from George's ex. It sparked her own need to make amends. "I never should have accepted George's proposal. I should have found another way to help him."

Pearl waved a hand between them. "Pfft. You were a baby."

"Not hardly."

"You were. And you carried your broken heart around in a basket for everyone to see." Pearl framed Darcy's face with her hands. "You married him a vulnerable young woman, and now you're a judge. I heard what you did today with that Borrington fella. That's what George wanted. For you to show people that Lady Justice has a heart."

"I didn't get there on my own." Darcy covered Pearl's hands with hers. "You won't believe this, but Rupert coached me."

"Really?" Pearl's hands fell away. "George would be proud of that too. Good heavens. I miss him so very much."

Darcy's heart went out to her. "Pearl." She slipped off her wedding ring. It didn't matter if she and Jason ever got back together. It was time to take the ring off. "George bought this for you. I think you should have it." Instead of Stogey.

Pearl gasped, accepting the ring with trembling fingers. "When George proposed, he surprised me. I thought he understood that I didn't want to get married a second time. I said no but I should have realized that George was a better match for me. If only he'd told me he loved me. If only I'd have given it more thought. If I had, I might have given him a different answer." She slid the big diamond on her finger. It glittered as if it had found the right home.

"When George proposed, I told him he should ask you again," Darcy said softly. "He said he'd only botch things up worse."

"I forgive him." Pearl blinked rapidly but a tear still managed to escape. "And I hope, wherever he is, that he can forgive me."

"I'm sure he does." Darcy smiled.

"Come on, let's eat." Pearl turned to the stove. "I can't stay long. I have the breakfast shift tomorrow."

Darcy got out the silverware. "Does this mean you're dropping the lawsuit for custody of Stogey?"

"No. Did George teach you nothing?" Pearl's sudden gaze over her shoulder was piercing. "Never make a decision about a lawsuit without consulting your lawyer first."

Chapter Twenty-Two

♥

Are you sure you want to do this?" Ken opened the yarn shop door for Jason the Sunday after Darcy had dumped him at the barbecue. "I'm a miracle worker but even miracle workers can't always make it rain."

"This is going to work," Jason said with more confidence than he felt. Darcy could have tracked him down any time this past week and demanded to be told if they were married or not. She hadn't. It gave him hope. That, and that he had Ken and the Widows Club on his side.

"My boys." Jason's mother greeted them at the door with hugs and bottles of water.

"What?" Jason glanced at the bottle. "Where are my knitted goods?"

"Right here." Mom slid a knitted sleeve over each of their bottles. "I saw these made by a machine in Greeley and thought I'd give it a try. Ken, I made yours like the Statue of Liberty. And Jason, yours is you. A cowboy with a hat. Can you see it?" There was a desperate note to her question.

"Yeah, Mom. These are great." Despite his reassurances, Jason didn't see her vision. Other than Ken's being a tarnished green and Jason's being several shades of brown. But he was nothing if not supportive. "Hot sellers for your website?"

"Jason..." Shaking her head, Mom gave him a stern look like the one she used to give when she caught him sneaking in late. "Don't humor me. I haven't sold any. It's a fail, I know." His mother may have been an avid knitter, but she knew when to admit defeat. "Still, it'll keep your cold bottles from sweating."

"It's the thought that counts." Jason hugged her again.

Mom targeted his agent next. "Ken, you're not wearing any of your sweater vests."

"It's a bit warm outside, Mrs. P." Ken cleared his throat. "I wore it on a date last week."

"Oh, such a sweet boy." Mom patted his cheeks.

Jason felt an eye roll coming on. Ken was a shark, not a sweet boy.

The bell rang over the door and Darcy entered. She wore blue leggings, a black tank top with a fancy knitted sweater over it, and a wary expression. Except for the cautious vibe, she was looking more like herself. Jason might not buy any knits from the shop, but he'd seen that sweater in the window last week. It was nice of her to support his mother.

Stogey trotted up to Jason and sat on his foot, staring up at him as if to say, *Check out my new jacket.* He wore a red-and-black service dog coat.

"Are you shopping for finished goods from me, Darcy?" Smiling at Jason, Mom went into yarn shop owner mode, holding up a pair of blue knitted baby booties. "Or have you finally decided to learn how to knit?"

"Sorry to disappoint, Nancy, but I'm here for my interview." Darcy submitted to a hug nonetheless, and she didn't look as if it was a hardship. She'd always gotten along with his mother.

"You will have so much fun. I hear a lot of laughter with this group. Here." Mom handed her a bottle of water with a white knitted sleeve. "This one is supposed to be the Easter Bunny."

"I see whiskers?" Darcy turned the knitted water bottle sleeve this way and that.

"I'm trying not to get discouraged." Mom set her shoulders back. "After all, it took Thomas Edison one thousand tries to make the light bulb, and I'm only on ten tries at water bottle sleeves."

Clarice held the drape aside for them. "We're ready."

Bitsy and Mims sat near the curtain, talking quietly. Iggy was teaching Edith how to do the floss dance in the space between the tripod and the table. The yarn lining the walls seemed brighter and more colorful than before. There was no roar of the crowd, but they all turned to Jason, smiling in greeting. He was in a battle for Darcy's heart. But it wasn't an angry battle, as when he rode a bull. It was a chess match with a team behind him.

Edith stopped dancing and held up a water bottle with a pink knitted sleeve. She drew Jason aside and whispered, "Are we supposed to give airtime to your mom's product? I can't tell if mine is supposed to be a piglet or a baby."

"This show has no sponsors," Ken said firmly from behind Jason. He tugged Edith's knitted sleeve from her water bottle and shooed those who worked in front of the camera toward the table. "Take your places. Did everyone sign their nondisclosure agreements?" He flipped through a stack of papers that Clarice gave him and then counted heads. All of them, not just Darcy.

Jason and Iggy scooted behind the table and sat on the bench, with Edith at the end.

Darcy was given a chair next to Edith and asked to sign one of the nondisclosure agreements. She glanced up at Ken. "What's this for?"

"We're developing a new web show," Ken explained casually. "It says you agree not to talk about what goes on here, including what's said. It's just protecting the intellectual property."

Darcy's brow clouded but she signed after reading it, a process interrupted when Stogey leaped into her lap.

She reads before she signs, George said with pride.

As soon as Ken was behind the tripod, Clarice said, "I'm ready. Good luck." She nodded to Jason. "Take it away, Edith."

"Welcome to *Two Cowboys and a Little Old Lady*," Edith began, leaving off the love advice part of the title.

"I bring the perspective of bachelors everywhere." Iggy tipped his hat.

"And I call them out on their bull." To emphasize her point, Edith gave Iggy a stern look.

Darcy stopped rubbing Stogey's ears.

"In this episode, I'm the guy who's just trying to figure love out." Jason gave Darcy a reassuring smile, hoping she wouldn't make a run for it. "Today, we're talking with the love of my life, the woman I lost because of stupidity, Judge Darcy Jones Harp—"

"Hello," Darcy cut him off, perhaps afraid he'd add Petrie to her list of last names. She waved at Clarice and her phone.

Point to Darcy.

Jason held on to his smile. Now came the tricky part. Letting Edith and Iggy pick apart his past. "For those who don't know the story of our breakup—"

"It involved a babe working for one of Jason's sponsors, which means the kiss was legal. Contractual even." Iggy rubbed his hands together. "You can't object to a legally binding contract, can you, Your Honor?"

"Um…" Darcy's gaze roved the room.

"She can." Edith elbowed Iggy. "If you say you're dating, if you say you're in a relationship, if you say she's your girl-friend, another woman's lips are off-limits. And I know a certain sports agent who should have said so before recommending Jason sign any kissing contracts."

Iggy wasn't letting the monetary piece go. "But his income, his image, his—"

"Chance at something real and lasting?" Edith scoffed. "It requires fidelity."

Darcy raised her hand as if they were in a classroom and she wanted the opportunity to speak.

Iggy ignored her. "What if Jason was an actor? A film star required to kiss other women."

"He's not an actor." Edith scoffed again. "He rides bulls for a living."

"Which is a young man's game," Iggy pressed on. "In order to establish a long-term income, men like Jason must branch out. Endorsements are a way to extend a career in the world of rodeo."

"Was he endorsing a mouthwash? A toothpaste?" Edith should have been a lawyer. She made Jason sound almost irredeemable. "A product related to hygiene?"

Jason held his breath, hoping she wouldn't bring up dandruff shampoo and hemorrhoid cream.

"Nope." Iggy hung his head. "It was a brand of cattle feed."

"Then I rest my case." Edith clapped her hands once. "Jason is guilty and should apologize."

Darcy held her hand higher. She needed to learn that good manners weren't going to help her on this panel.

"I did." Jason finally got a word in. "I apologized. I groveled."

"Were flowers and jewelry involved?" Edith leaned forward to catch Jason's eye.

"No, but I did bring dog biscuits." Jason tipped his hat to Darcy.

In return, Darcy gave him a small smile and lowered her hand to pet Stogey.

Point to Jason. Bonus points, considering Darcy hadn't walked out. The widows had assured him she wouldn't but he hadn't been certain.

"Dog biscuits?" Iggy slapped a hand over his eyes. "All these years by my side and the man has learned nothing about apology gifts."

"Shush." Edith waved a hand across Iggy and toward Jason. "Did you promise never to accept money to kiss another woman?"

"No." Jason didn't think he'd agreed to this line of questioning. "But it goes without saying that I won't."

Ken's lips pressed together in disapproval. Kissing women was a lucrative sideline, like asking someone in the drive-through if they wanted fries with that.

"Did you ask Darcy to forgive you?" Edith persisted in her interrogation of Jason.

"Yes."

"With dog biscuits," Iggy muttered.

"I forgave him," Darcy said in a small voice. "But then he did something else."

Her statement sucked the air out of the room, probably because neither Jason nor Ken had told their coconspirator cast and crew about the marriage piece to this equation.

"There's always something else unearthed in a tragedy," Iggy murmured to Edith.

"Yep," Edith murmured back. "The plot thickens."

Per the Widows Club plan, that catchphrase was Jason's cue to transition to the land mine of Darcy's insecurity regarding her past. He had something different in mind. "She's right. After she forgave me, I revealed something else." He paused for dramatic effect, during which time Darcy leaned forward slightly and looked in the direction of his legs. *Wrong, honey.* "I don't know if I'm married."

It seemed like everyone in the room gasped, even Ken, who had known Jason was going to go rogue.

"Dude." Iggy gaped at Jason.

"Excuse me. I came here today to be interviewed about my position in town." Darcy tried to redirect. "I thought you'd ask me about how I came to be a judge."

That wasn't what anyone wanted to hear or part of the Widows Club plan to help Jason win Darcy back. All eyes swiveled to Jason, brows raised.

"I was appointed," Darcy blurted, talking quickly now. "Recommended by my...my husband, George."

"May George rest in peace," Edith said solemnly. "He was right to recommend you."

Darcy's chin lifted. Jason suspected Edith's acceptance of the situation wasn't what Darcy wanted to hear.

"I want to get back to the question of marriage." Iggy gave that awful, braying laugh of his. "As in dude, why don't you know if you're hitched or not?"

"I'm interested in that answer too." Darcy patted Stogey's ribs so hard that he burped.

"The plot thickens." Edith swung around to stare at Jason.

He grabbed a skein of baby-blue yarn and squeezed it like

a stress ball. The state of his heart rested on the next few minutes. "I've participated in a marriage ceremony," Jason said carefully. "More like a commitment ceremony."

There was another round of gasps.

Darcy's eyes flashed. Her patience was waning.

"It was in Vegas," Jason continued before Iggy or Edith hijacked the conversation. "I had some drinks and don't remember it at all. A few weeks later, Ken received a picture of our wedding in the mail. I regret it because a marriage based on love should be memorable." And legally binding. "And both parties should be sober." A given.

"For the ceremony, at least." Iggy had half turned to face him too, blocking Edith's view. "But dude, I gotta tell you. I'm hurt. I always thought I'd be your best man."

"This is a disaster." Edith stared at Mims, crumpling her notes. "The plot is so thick it's pea soup."

Iggy took Jason's skein of yarn and began kneading it like bread dough.

Darcy sent Jason a look that seemed to say: *This is no longer funny.*

It was never funny.

Like you had a sense of humor, George.

The expression on Edith's face was thunderous. Obviously she didn't like being out of the know. "Jason, the plot—"

"I know, I know. The plot thickens." He gave Darcy a gentle smile, the kind of smile a husband gives to a wife when he knows she's annoyed and he plans to do something about it. Just not yet. "A marriage should be the expression of a couple's love for one another. It should be a day worth remembering. A proud day when you pledge to love, honor, and be the best friend of your spouse. You should invite friends and family. The ones you were still on speaking terms with."

"Not your aunt Midge," his mother said from where she peeked through the curtain. "She always said you had a pointy head as a baby."

Jason chose to ignore that comment. "And you should shower each other with rose petals and chocolate and sweet wine for people who don't like wine." Like Darcy, who still looked annoyed with him.

"None of this is in my notes." Edith smoothed the page of her scribbles, squinting at it. "Iggy?"

"I got nothing, Edith." Iggy twisted the baby-blue skein. "I was supposed to be his best man. I feel like I've been shorted."

"Darcy, I want to start over." Jason put a hand over his heart. "I would love to marry you again, this time with a license to make it legal. Because our ceremony wasn't right." He winked at Edith. "For all the previously mentioned reasons."

"Holy fudge nuggets," Edith whispered. "Is he proposing?"

"Yes." Iggy pulled his brim down. "Badly. Especially when you consider he already married her and must have asked before."

Darcy blew out a breath, took in another, and then stared at Jason, saying nothing and going nowhere, waiting.

"I'm actually not proposing," Jason admitted. "I'd like to reserve that privilege for another time."

I have an idea about that. George the romantic.

Jason rubbed his temple.

Clarice tapped her phone. "People, Darcy came for an interview. I suggest we return to the script and give her one."

"Ah, my cue." Edith peered at her notes. "We haven't covered the feeling of inadequacy in a relationship."

"There is no inadequacy between the sheets if you have an

attentive, giving partner." Iggy was right back in the swing of things.

Edith tipped his hat up. "Have you practiced being a better listener? We're not talking about bedroom rhumbas."

"I've heard there was a marriage," Iggy admitted mournfully, with a disapproving look Jason's way. "Which often leads to tales of bedroom woe."

"We're PG-13, people," Jason reminded them. "Besides, we're not talking intimate inadequacies. We're talking about the feeling that one person in the relationship feels deficient when compared to the other. Or to other people in town."

Scowling, Darcy sat back in her chair, crossing her arms around Stogey and pulling him to her chest as if it were the dog that needed shielding, not she.

"This is deep." Edith turned her notes over. "Darcy, care to comment?"

"No," Darcy said flatly.

"Please, dear." Bitsy jumped into the fray from the sidelines. "He means well. We all do."

Darcy blew out a breath. "Okay, I'll play along. Insecurity in our relationship? Always. I'm a Jones. Every time I make a mistake, that's what people say. *Well, of course she'd do that. She's a Jones.* Why would Jason want to go through life with me?"

"Love," came the chorused answer.

"That is the crux of it, isn't it?" Edith said softly. "What do feelings of being different matter if you love each other? A difference in age, a difference in education, a difference in where you come from... None of it should matter."

"I'm not sure how much weight my opinion carries, but Edith is right." In a surprising move, Iggy patted Jason on the back. "Congratulations are in order for your marriage.

And regrets for the fact that it wasn't legit. If your best man had been there, he might have rectified that situation."

Ken sighed and rolled his eyes. He had every right to. If both he and Iggy had been present, Ken was the more likely savior.

"Darcy, you believe you won't be elected this November." Jason wasn't asking.

"You had a rocky start." Trust Edith not to pull her punches. "I've heard nothing but glowing reviews this past week. Oh, and Iggy hired the infamous Mr. Borrington."

"Sadly, it wasn't my idea," Iggy admitted, sticking with honesty when it came to their partnership. He cast a thumb in Jason's direction.

That got to Darcy. She blinked suddenly teary eyes.

"That just makes it harder to walk away from everything." Darcy sniffed. "I'm finally hitting my stride in the courtroom, but it doesn't matter. I cheated to get this by marrying George. No matter what argument George presented about him needing me to be his wife, I should have said no. I loved him but it was platonic love."

Her statement created another one of those gasping pin-drop moments.

Jason wished he were closer to Darcy so he could take her in his arms. "Honey, you can't call your appointment cheating when you didn't know what George had planned. Give the old man some of the credit and some of the blame. Then forgive yourself."

There were choruses of agreement. Stogey nuzzled her chin.

"You don't understand." Darcy glanced around in apparent surprise. "How can you not see that I didn't earn this? How can you not think poorly of me after I confessed?"

"Because we disagree on principle." Edith raised her hands

toward the rafters. "Lots of friends don't align on every opinion or every little thing. Take my friends, for instance. They love the strategy of poker and I hate it because I don't think that way. Now, I could say, obviously, that they're wrong for liking poker, but until they change my opinion or I change theirs, we have to respect each other."

Bitsy and Edith exchanged smiles.

"I've told you before, Darcy," Jason said gently. "I don't think you cheated the system. And as for other disagreements we've had, I've been a rodeo man since I was eighteen, and I've seen my share of the winner's circle, but I think I've got to hang it up. It's time I accept that a man doesn't have to prove his worth on the back of an ornery bull. A real man prioritizes what he values in life and tries to enjoy every moment with the ones he loves."

"Is there a condition with this?" Darcy hugged Stogey, who belched. And for the first time, Jason realized she wasn't wearing George's wedding ring. "You'll retire if I keep quiet and see out my term. Is that it?"

"No. There should be no conditions on love," Jason said. "But I don't think you need to go airing your dirty laundry. That's nobody's business but your own."

"Dirty laundry?"

Darcy set Stogey on the floor and gathered her purse.

You're losing her.

George…

George, of course! "George asked you to give up your dream when he got you that appointment as judge. All you ever wanted was to leave town and become a public defender. And all I ever wanted to do—when I wasn't angry at the world—was be with you."

Darcy stiffened. "That's not true."

"Which part?" Jason was ruing that he hadn't changed the seating arrangements. He couldn't get his legs free to climb over the table and stop Darcy from leaving. "Clarice, cut, will you? Don't go, Darcy. Please. I'm being honest. I'm not retiring because of you or the twinge. I'm retiring because I can't pursue other dreams I have if I don't. I want to start a family. I'm ready to settle down. And all this…" He gestured around the room. "All this was to give you the opportunity to talk about the situation with George and the judgeship and for you to hear that it doesn't matter."

"The people in this room care about me. They'll forgive me a mistake." Darcy pointed toward the door. "But the people out there won't be as forgiving. And yet they need to know the truth because I'm a public servant. And one way or another, I'm going to tell them."

"No one is perfect, nor do they expect you to be. And nobody is liked and accepted by everyone they know," Jason said, feeling desperate. "George gave you a break, Darcy. Everyone in this room has been given a break a time or two. Don't think you can't use a leg up just because your last name used to be Jones."

It was the wrong thing to say. No matter how much she tried to separate herself from her family, she'd always identify as one of them. Darcy's face shuttered, and she headed for the door.

Ken stood in her way. "Just a friendly reminder that everyone signed a nondisclosure agreement. Everything discussed here is covered in the purview of that document, from screws to nuts. Or in this case, from retirement plans to judicial appointments to marriage details."

"What?" Darcy glared at Ken and then at Jason. "You're saying I can't talk about how George made sure I got his job? Not to anyone?"

"Not to anyone," Ken confirmed.

"You could challenge the contract in court," Jason said with a half shrug. She'd resent him for the legally binding agreement. Didn't matter that he hadn't wanted it to come to this. "But until then, maybe you should think about what a jury of your peers here today concluded about the past year—not guilty."

"Hear, hear," Mims said.

Darcy pushed past Ken but Mom was there to keep her from racing out the door.

* * *

"Not guilty," Darcy muttered angrily, heading toward the yarn shop door.

"Oh, Darcy, honey. Have you seen these adorable berets?" Jason's mother inserted herself in Darcy's path.

Chest heaving, Darcy came to a halt. "NDA or not, I'm going to tell the truth."

"Don't worry." Bitsy came to stand at Darcy's shoulder, holding up a hand to keep Ken back. "We signed Ken's thing. Our lips are sealed."

"But so are mine!" Oh, Darcy was mad. Lesson learned. Never sign anything without understanding it fully. And never, ever sign anything handed to her by Ken Tadashi. She gave him a dark look before hurrying out the door.

Ken followed her out, stiff as starch. "I feel like I should tell you that this wasn't Jason's idea."

"But he ran with it, didn't he? He keeps telling me that I have nothing in my past to be ashamed of but then he traps me into silence." Stogey sat on her foot and stared at her as if she could do no wrong.

"Darcy…"

She scowled at Jason's agent. "What?"

"I'm sorry the marriage wasn't real." Ken actually appeared remorseful. "You guys are great together." He touched her shoulder, like a soft attaboy. "Don't be mad. Like Jason said, you wanted an audience, one that would judge you, and we gave you one."

It wasn't the right audience. "This isn't over."

"By all means, engage a lawyer. Bring it to a judge." Ken had his hard-bargain face on.

"I have to go." Darcy swung her purse at Ken, missing him by inches.

Before she succumbed to the urge to swing again, she scurried down the sidewalk with Stogey at her heels.

Stogey was probably wondering when he'd get his next meal.

Darcy was wondering where she was going to find a lawyer to represent her.

* * *

"So, that was fun." Ken entered the yarn shop's storeroom, which had cleared out except for Jason.

Darcy and the widows had left several minutes before. In the main store, Mom was helping Kristy Brooks select a pattern for a baby sweater.

Jason still sat on the bench next to the wall of yarn. His elbows were on the table. His chin in his hands. His heart in the trash. "Define fun, Ken."

"Anytime I can inch my clients closer to their dreams, it's fun." Ken sat on a folding chair, as prim as a choirboy.

"Did we gain anything?" Jason scoffed. "Do you think we can hold Darcy off until the bachelor auction?" That was the

Widows Club plan B. Stall and hope, in the meantime, that Darcy would come to believe she wasn't the villain here.

Like I am?

I hope you don't plan to haunt me the rest of my life, George.

There was a sound in Jason's head, much like an old man's chuckle.

That didn't bode well for the rest of Jason's life.

"It's hard to say if the NDA will stand up to a legal challenge, even if we only need it to hold until the Date Night Auction on Saturday." Ken shrugged. "Did you get a chance to review the partnership documents for Mr. King?"

"Yes. Have I told you that I don't speak legalese?"

"Many times." Ken's phone buzzed. For once he ignored it. "I should probably tell you there will be no broadcasting career. And this little ensemble will not be picked up by any web channel. That was a red herring." And from his tone, he was having regrets.

"I thought there was something fishy about that." Jason plucked a pink skein of yarn from the shelf and threw it at Ken. "Why the ruse?"

Ken caught the yarn, using it like a floppy pointer around the room, from tripod to folding chair to Jason. "Because this... It got you shook. And sometimes when you're used to being top dog, you need a little shake."

Disapproval heated Jason's veins. "You're lucky I like you, Ken."

His agent tossed the yarn back. "And that I make you decent money."

"That too."

"It was amusing, though." Ken got to his feet, half smiling, testing the waters between them with raised brows that invited Jason to the same wavelength. "Edith and Iggy could take that show on the road."

Jason groaned. "Please don't tell them that. Iggy would love to be state-fair famous."

Ken sighed. "They would have been a good act at small venues."

"But they would have tested your patience." Jason stood and edged clear of the table. What was left of his heart was heavy from the continued loss of Darcy. "Any word from my favorite cattle rancher?"

Ken held the drape aside, clearing Jason's path to the exit. "Tom has decided to counter. A refund and a double order of product from Samson, the collection of which he will supervise."

Dang, that was smart. "Approved." It was no less than Bull Puckey Breeding deserved.

They said goodbye to his mother and went outside, where the sunshine and bright green of the town square tried unsuccessfully to chase Jason's cares away. He hoped Darcy was all right. He hoped she'd think about how many people in one room found no fault with her journey to a judgeship. But they were deflated hopes.

Ken glanced up and down Main Street. "You know, I have to leave town soon. I have other clients with problems just as devastating as yours." He sounded like he might miss Sunshine.

"But you'll stay for the bachelor auction?" Jason's big effort to get Darcy back.

"I'll stay till the end." He clapped Jason on the back, surprisingly hard.

Chapter Twenty-Three

♥

Armed with coffee and still-warm scones from Olde Time Bakery, Darcy knocked on Rupert's office door Monday morning.

Jason and Ken had outmaneuvered her. *Not guilty?* She expected Jason and her friends to understand her decision. But Rupert and Oliver? Not a chance.

She'd spent most of Sunday night tossing and turning, trying to decide what to do. By morning, it was easy. Stick to the original plan—leave Sunshine and Jason and start fresh elsewhere. She was a Jones. She wasn't above fleeing town with Stogey before the lawsuit was settled. Although she wasn't a die-hard Jones. First she had to confess the truth about her marriage and its benefits to someone who wouldn't consider her innocent.

Her heart felt empty, but she was determined to start over with a clean slate. The brisk morning air swept past her ankles beneath her long skirt and chilled her toes, which were in her wedge sandals. Stogey pressed his nose against the glass, wagging his tail when he saw Rupert approach.

Rupert opened the door but didn't let them in. "Did you have an appointment?"

"You know the answer to that question." Darcy raised the cardboard tray with two coffees. "I brought caffeine and scones. Are you going to let me in or not?"

He hesitated, stroking a hand over a very expensive-looking teal tie that would be a classy accent underneath a judge's robe.

Darcy touched the piece of turquoise holding one of George's bolo ties in place at her neck, suddenly unsure.

With a put-upon sigh, Rupert stepped aside. "You aren't going to make this a habit, are you?"

"No." Darcy followed him, moving slowly, still wrestling with second thoughts. "Unless you hurt her."

"Who? Pearl?" He led her into a nicely appointed conference room.

"No. Bitsy." Darcy dropped the end of Stogey's leash on the floor, put the bakery tray on the table, and deposited her purse and laptop bag on the floor.

Rupert dropped heavily into a chair, as if he'd stumbled in the act of sitting.

"Let me get to the point." Darcy settled more gracefully into her seat. "I need legal advice."

Rupert's eye roll indicated his disbelief. Or perhaps he was scornful of Stogey, who'd managed to tangle his leash around the wheels of Rupert's chair. He bent to unclip Stogey's leash.

"Please don't roll your eyes." A month ago, Darcy wouldn't have had the courage to talk to her stepson like that. She removed the coffees from the cardboard carrier. "You're the one who told me I needed a good lawyer."

"You need a lawyer for the situation with Pearl." Rupert sat back up, smoothing his pretty tie before picking up one of the coffees. "I'm not giving you legal advice beyond that."

"We'll see." Darcy hoped to appeal to his curiosity. She broke off a piece of scone. "You can advise me on a different matter, especially if I settle out of court with Pearl."

"And, of course, you need advice today. Right now." His tone suggested he'd expect no less from her.

Darcy drew her typed offer from her laptop bag and placed it upside down on the conference table. "I have my offer right here. Can you advise me or not?"

Rupert's entire being seemed centered on the paper on the table. "As long as your need for counsel doesn't pertain to the animal in question. By the way, we're not settling for anything less than full custody of Stogey."

She shook her head. "My plan is to keep Stogey—"

"Unacceptable."

"—and give you and Oliver the main house, along with George's money, but only if you allow Pearl to live in the cottage rent-free." She handed him the contract she'd drafted to do just that. "If that's what she wants."

Rupert took a moment to review the document and then set it down on the conference table. "You're trying to buy a judgeship. You think giving us this will keep us from running against you."

"I was actually planning to resign and let you two boys duke it out for the appointment."

"How unexpected." Rupert had a good courtroom face. He didn't so much as blink at her announcement. He took a sip of his coffee, leaning back in his chair. She could practically see the wheels spinning in his head. "What new legal trouble have you gotten yourself into?"

"Are you accepting my case?"

"My retainer is high."

He needn't have told her. Darcy could tell by the fancy

furniture in his office and his expensive taste in everything, including the engraved pen on the table.

"I don't care. I need a lawyer and client confidentiality." And closure for this chapter of her life. "Can you give that to me? Now?" She couldn't carry out her court duties *and* fight this case.

"I have a boilerplate contract you can sign but I'll only offer it to you if you agree to one stipulation." He almost smiled. "I need you to stay in your position until I say so."

"I get it. You've got some jockeying to do with Oliver. Let's just do it the old-fashioned way and shake hands for now." She thrust out hers.

He met her halfway. "What is this issue that requires such urgency?"

"For obvious reasons, I'm a public relations mess."

"And..."

"And the man I thought was my husband has blocked me from telling the world the truth about my appointment."

Rupert dribbled coffee on his expensive tie.

* * *

"Mama, are you okay? Where's the fire?" Bitsy hurried inside the cottage. She'd been so hopeful that Mama was doing better but Mama had called and demanded Bitsy come over right away.

"Rupert's coming over." Mama sat knitting in front of the television, her cat in her lap. "Do you think Darcy caved to pressure and is giving me the dog?"

Bitsy wasn't sure she wanted to take a guess or hear the answer. Besides, she was twitchy from the news that Rupert was coming over. She was wearing a sweater set today, with shoulder pads. And her hair was pulled back with her favorite big black velvet bow. Shiitake mushrooms! She was too retro for a younger man.

"I loved George for decades," Mama said. "And for decades I didn't expect anything." She set her knitting aside and got to her feet. She was slower now that the anger wasn't driving her, careful with her steps. "I didn't want anything from him either, just the pleasure of his company. And then everything went sideways. His marriage. His death." She glanced at her hand and—

Darcy's wedding ring!

"Darcy is giving you Stogey, isn't she?" Bitsy didn't need to ask the question. She knew the answer. "Look, I know you think you need Stogey to fill the place where George used to be, but you and I, we'll take care of each other, no matter what. You don't need George's dog. Let Darcy have him. She needs his love." Darcy was willing to bear the blame for every action George had taken. Until she shed that remorse, she'd never follow her heart and accept Jason's love.

"Pfft." Mama pushed away from her. "And who will take care of you when you spend your life savings caring for this old bag of bones? Where's my lawyer? He should've been here by now."

"Mama, when Rupert gets here, you have to tell the truth. You're not a dog person. George knew that. He wanted Darcy to have Stogey."

"Pfft. I know what George wants. It's like he's in my head." She walked toward the back of the house. "It's you who needs to face some truths."

"What?"

"Hello." Rupert knocked on the doorjamb. "Can I come in?"

The back door banged closed.

"Yes." Bitsy hurried to greet him at the door, noting his bright-blue eyes, their color brought out by the green hue of his shirt and tie. "You look ready to hit the town and attract a lady's attention," she blurted, immediately adding, "Ignore that. I meant you look very nice today, ready to go someplace nice. Like court." Her cheeks felt like they were on fire. "I'm going to stop talking now."

He smiled at her warmly, the way a man smiles at a woman he finds amusing. "I'm not dating anyone, if that's what you were getting at."

Bitsy froze. "You're...uh..." *Recover! Recover!* "You're a fine, fine young man. You should be dating...perhaps someone your own age."

His smile expanded. "Age is just a number."

Her whole body heated the way it used to when she went through the hated menopause. "I didn't mean to pry. You just..." *Cover. Quickly.* She raised her chin as if she were Edith and didn't care a whit what outrageous thing she said. "You just look very handsome today."

He chuckled. "And you assumed I dressed to catch a woman's eye."

"Let's be fair." Because nowadays you couldn't tell. "It could be a man too."

He guffawed. And when his laughter had diminished, he said, "I have a personal shopper. And if you tell my brother, I'll deny it, night and day."

A secret. Bitsy hadn't shared a secret with a man in what seemed like forever. "My lips are sealed."

He sat on Mama's sofa, opened his folder, and took a pen from his pocket. "Where's Pearl? She needs to review some documents."

"Mama?" *Please come rescue me.* "Mama?"

The house echoed.

"Excuse me." Bitsy hurried toward the back of the house, checking the bedroom and the bathroom. She'd said something about Bitsy facing Rupert and the truth. Realizing she'd been set up, Bitsy returned to Rupert, wondering how much she should tell him other than, "She's gone."

"Do you think…" He smiled pleasantly. She'd never seen him smile pleasantly at her before. "I mean, would you like to have a drink with me while we wait for her to come back?"

"All Mama has here is water and coffee."

"I've got an idea." Rupert closed his folder. "Let's head over to Shaw's."

"But…what if she comes back?" Bitsy knew Mama wasn't coming back. She'd said her piece and was leaving Bitsy to pick up the rest of the broken pottery.

"We'll leave her a note." Rupert stood, smoothing his tie.

And look! It had a stain. Was that why he seemed so self-conscious today? So…human?

He continued to wield that pleasant smile. "What do you say? Is it a date?"

Bitsy nodded, numbly telling herself it was only a little word that started with *d*. It could take on any number of meanings.

Surely he was just thirsty and wanted a bit of company.

Although if that had been the case, wouldn't he have asked for a glass of water?

* * *

"Hey, Jason, I need you to review some stuff." Ken entered Bull Puckey Breeding's office. "Do you have a minute?"

"You can talk while you help us with this new bull. We need an extra pair of hands." And Jason was in need of a distraction from Darcy. However, Pennywhistle was a handful. "We sent John to Denver for some more collection tubes. We're going to run out today."

Iggy zipped up a pair of stained coveralls. He tossed Ken a pair also in need of a good washing. "We can talk and work at the same time."

"No, no. I'm part of the brain trust." Ken held up the coveralls by his fingertips.

"Man up." Jason already had his coveralls on. "You'll be holding Carl. He's our teaser bull and gentle as a kitten."

Ken shook his head. "That's a hard no."

"Hurry it along so we can get the shipment in the mail today." Iggy herded Ken out of the office. He opened a stall door and clipped a lead rope onto Carl's halter. "Stand here and wait until we call you to come in."

Jason walked past them toward Pennywhistle's stall. A better name for the bull would have been Buttkicker. He was barely manageable. In fact, when Jason reached his stall, the bull banged the door and let out a deep, unhappy moo.

"Calm down, fella," Jason said.

"Hey," Ken called. "Shouldn't I tell you what the documents are before we start this? In case I'm injured and can't give you my opinion."

"He does have a good point." Iggy joined Jason at Pennywhistle's stall.

"But it makes me happy to make him wait." Jason smiled. He could use a little levity. He was pinning his hopes on the fact that Darcy always bought him at the Widows Club bachelor auction. She'd buy him, and then everything would be all right.

Correction. Then you'll have the opening you need to work on love.

Jason grimaced. George was such a stickler for details.

Pennywhistle complained again. He had massive shoulders, a white face, a red hide, and a shifty look in his eyes, one that said, *Proceed at your own peril.*

"Stay in Carl's stall, Ken." Jason opened Pennywhistle's door. "Tell me why we bought this bull again. He isn't even halter trained."

"He's kind of like you." Iggy joined Jason in the stall. "Very photogenic."

Their boots rustled through the straw as Pennywhistle glared at them.

"Hey, buddy. Look what I got. Feed cubes." Jason held them out to the side. "Sweet as candy. Come on, I know you want some."

Pennywhistle lifted his head and sniffed, let out a long moo, and practically lunged toward Jason's hand, knocking the treat to the ground. He bent his head to eat the fallen cubes.

Jason snapped on his lead rope and gave him a couple seconds to gobble up his reward before tugging his head up. "Why do I have a bad feeling about this?"

"Sorry, man," Iggy said. "I wish we had a few more days to work with him before this."

"Then you shouldn't have put his picture and vitals up on the website."

Pennywhistle lifted his head and gave them the stink eye.

Jason gave the lead rope a tentative tug. "Easy, fella."

And that's when it all went to hell.

* * *

"I'll have a wine spritzer," Bitsy said softly to Noah when she and Rupert were seated at Shaw's.

"Give me a bottle of that hard cider and some popcorn." Rupert loosened his stained tie and removed it as Noah left their table. "I used to come in here and order the sweet potato fries," he confided to Bitsy in a deep, low voice. "But then I hit forty and had to let my pants out at the waist."

"How...Uh...How old are you?" Bitsy told herself she only asked for the bachelor auction coming up. She tried to smile but her lips felt so uncooperative.

"I'm fifty-seven. You probably know, but I've had a bout of cancer, been divorced, have two kids living in Denver." He was reading out his vitals the way they'd be listed on one of those online dating sites.

"I'm sorry. I didn't mean to pry." *Oh yes I did.* She stored away the most important piece of information he'd dropped— cancer. For his own good, she should scurry on home.

"Oh, you meant to pry, Bitsy." Rupert leaned forward, lowering that voice of his to bedroom levels. "And I meant to let you."

The jig was up! "I should go." Mortified, Bitsy shifted in her seat, placing her hand on the table for leverage to make her escape. Mama would have to face her lawyer on her own from now on.

Rupert's hand covered hers. "Don't go. I haven't dated anyone since my wife took half my retirement."

Bitsy stared at his strong, tan hand, frozen.

"And that came out all wrong. I'm not here to talk about my failed marriage or your mother's court case. I'd just like..." He withdrew his hand and closed those brilliant-blue eyes. "I just miss female companionship." He heaved a sigh. "I miss the flirty banter. The way a woman sees things in the world differently. The sound of a woman's laughter, particularly at one of my jokes." He opened his eyes and stared at her, waiting for her to answer.

Stay or go?

Cancer. She brought such bad luck to a man's longevity.

And a younger man. Such a taboo.

If their positions were reversed, no one would bat an eye if they dated or...

Do not think about or*s*. Three-time widows didn't tempt fate with fourth husbands.

But three-time widows could enjoy the company of a man occasionally, maybe have some kind of arrangement the way George and Mama had.

Bitsy blinked. "I wasn't aware you had any jokes."

Chapter Twenty-Four

♥

Jason, Iggy, and Ken rolled into Shaw's as battered and bloody messes.

"Drinks are on me." Ken led the way. Seeing as how he was the least battered member of their crew, Iggy and Jason let him.

They sat at the bar. Jason had done a sweep before claiming a stool. If Darcy had been there, he'd have been trying to charm her into a conversation.

"You boys look like something the cat dragged in." Noah looked at their dirty, dusty clothes. "At least show me that your hands are clean."

They weren't. He sent them to the men's room while he poured them a round of beers.

"When did Noah become such a wet blanket?" Iggy leaned against the wall while Ken used the lone sink.

"When his dad retired, I think?" Jason watched Ken wash his hands, his wrists, his face, and behind his neck. "Jeez, are you gonna take a bath?"

"I was dragged through a layer of straw and filth by Carl the teaser bull." Ken moved on to the paper towel dispenser. "You're lucky I'm still riding adrenaline or I'd scurry back to your place and take a long, hot shower."

"We told you to stay in the stall with Carl." Iggy had no sympathy. He washed his hands well and gave his face a quick rinse.

"How was I to know you meant with the stall door closed?" Ken shook his head. "Or that the bull who dragged you from one end of the building to the other would be singing a mating call?"

Pennywhistle had dragged both men, despite their digging in their boot heels. The entire stable of bulls had been riled.

After Jason washed up, the trio returned to the bar, where beer and bar mix awaited.

"Now seems like the time to get some work done," Ken said. "Before I get distracted by alcohol or women."

Jason gave the bar another quick look-see. There were no women in the bar except for Bitsy, who was sitting with Rupert. Bitsy and Rupert? Jason caught her eye and raised his glass. Good luck to that. Whatever that was.

"First off," Ken said, "we have cause to celebrate. Tom has officially dropped the lawsuit."

"Sweet." Iggy clinked his glass to both of theirs. "I'll invite him over to get his goods and we'll be done with it. Won't happen again."

Jason was grateful for Iggy's reassurances. "What else do you need to get off your chest, Ken?"

"Oh, not much. We're being countersued." Ken drank deeply from his beer before continuing. "Darcy is challenging that nondisclosure agreement. She hired Rupert." Ken turned on his bar stool to face the older lawyer. Iggy and Jason followed suit.

"That was fast." Too fast. Jason felt numb. There were still days until the auction. Days during which he'd hoped Darcy would accept herself and the decisions she'd made to get to this point.

Bitsy pointed toward them, drawing Rupert's attention.

The lawyer took in the trio and laughed.

"Can we counter-counterfile or something?" Jason needed a ray of hope.

"I'll get in touch with our New York lawyer tomorrow and see." Ken's attention was suddenly magnetized to his pinging phone and incoming messages.

"Here's to Ken, your fairy godfather." Iggy raised his glass, clinking Jason's. "I gotta get me one of those." He sniffed Ken's shirt. "Maybe one who smells better."

* * *

"Good morning, Your Honor." Rupert entered Darcy's office midweek and closed the door behind him. His blue suit fit him impeccably. His black leather shoes had a mirrorlike shine.

"My lawyer has news for me?" Darcy finished zipping up her robe, in awe of Rupert's efficiency. He and Tina Marie would be quite a force in the courthouse after she stepped down.

"I called in a favor. We go before Judge Johnson in Greeley on Friday." Rupert set down his briefcase. He looked decidedly chipper today, possibly because he was that much closer to a judgeship. "As for your other lawsuit, Pearl is dropping her claim to Stogey in return for the rent-free cottage, and my brother and I have agreed to your terms for the house." He bent to give Stogey a pat.

His words lifted a weight off Darcy's shoulders. She hadn't realized what an emotional burden George's property was on her spirits. How much lighter would she feel when she was no longer a judge? Light enough to take Jason back? "And the money?"

Rupert picked up Stogey and put him in her arms. "We think you deserve the money."

"That doesn't make me feel good." Quite the opposite. That money felt like the spoils of a con.

Rupert took her by the shoulders. "Then give it away to charity, someplace that will help at-risk kids, like you were."

"What a great idea." Darcy drew a deep breath, studying the chiseled planes of Rupert's face and wondering why they no longer seemed so hard. "Why are you in such a good mood? Forget that. Why are you being so nice to me?" She gave a little gasp. "Did Oliver agree that you should be the interim judge? Let's call Henrik and get him out here immediately."

"We decided..." Rupert released her and retreated to the chair with his briefcase. "We decided neither one of us wants the job."

Darcy had a good guess as to why. "You looked up the salary schedule."

"I plead guilty, Your Honor." Rupert grinned. "We'd be taking pay cuts to fill Dad's shoes."

"But...I was going to leave town. It's all I ever wanted."

"Is it? Monday morning when you hired me, you told me you wanted to go somewhere you'd be respected and be able to make a difference." Rupert came to her once more, took her shoulders once more. "And I'm telling you that whatever reason you had for leaving, you don't have one anymore. Oliver and I...We misjudged you. We directed our anger at you instead of our father."

"But..."

"You're becoming a good judge. The seat is yours. If you

still feel there are amends to make, make them from the bench by doing what I know you can do best—seeing the person, not the crime."

If Rupert and Oliver—her mortal enemies—didn't hold her marriage to their father against her, perhaps Jason was right. Perhaps it was time to accept what she'd done and what George had done and move on. Darcy drew a breath, shedding another layer of weight from her soul.

Stogey nuzzled her chin.

"I . . . I don't know what to say."

"Well, I hope you say you'll stay, because it seems like Judge Darcy Harper has a chance at a long run on the bench." He grabbed his briefcase and opened the door. "My father would be proud. Not only that, he'd encourage you to find the one man who could help you make a long judicial run bearable. Strike that." He smiled. "I'd encourage you."

Weak-kneed, Darcy leaned on the edge of her desk, listening to her heart without guilt clouding her vision.

Tina Marie marched by, heading for the courtroom. "Are you ready?"

Darcy squared her shoulders. "Yes."

Chapter Twenty-Five

♥

On the night of the bachelor auction, Mims confidently took the stage at Shaw's to a round of applause. "Thank you all for showing up to the Date Night Auction to benefit the Sunshine Boys & Girls Club. Our bachelors—"

The crowd whooped it up, including Darcy. Their enthusiasm was infectious. Electricity skimmed the hair on her arms. Jason was in the crowd of bachelors on stage, looking just as handsome as ever.

"Our bachelors for auction tonight will be available for pre-screening for the next few minutes on stage. Gentlemen, we're still taking names if you feel left out." Mims stared down at the crowd. "Those in the mood to buy, please remember, bidding starts at one hundred dollars. This is a cash-only event. Winning bidders also pay for dinner and drinks afterward. But this is strictly an eyes-only auction. No touching our bachelors. That is, not until you've won your man. And..." She gestured for the crowd to quiet down. They did not. She tried to shout over them anyway. "And all bidding must be done from the floor. We have a new consequence regarding the stage this year. There will be no shenanigans. If you come up on the stage, you are automatically volunteered for the next auction and your bid is..."

"Pris, please go home." Drew was here in an official capacity as crowd control, but he was scowling at his sister. "I don't want you bidding on some random cowboy just because he looks at you twice."

Pris frowned at him but kept on drinking her beer.

"I can't believe you showed up tonight, Darcy." Lola smoothed Drew's uniform over his shoulders. "We're here because it's an anniversary of sorts. But I thought you were trying to control that image of yours."

"I came to support Bitsy." Who was going to bid on Rupert. Darcy cast her gaze around, unable to find her. "I'm undecided about bidding on Jason."

"Bitsy's over there." Lola pointed to a place far in the back. "If she's bidding, that's the worst place to be."

Darcy excused herself and made her way to Bitsy, who wore a beret and dark glasses. "What happened to taking life by the horns?"

"I came, didn't I?" She grimaced.

"But you look like you aren't going to bid."

"This is mortifying." Bitsy knotted her fingers. "If I bid on Rupert, everyone will know I like a younger man. And yet, I can't not be here."

"You know it's ten times worse to get up on that stage." Darcy tugged her forward. "Come on. Think of this as rescuing Rupert. You'll have a nice dinner together. People are probably going to be talking about Pris Taylor. She's got on her bidding face and a deep-seated need to put her brother in his place."

"But what about you?" Bitsy shouted. "Are you bidding on Jason?"

"Um…" Darcy shrugged and led the way to the bar.

Bitsy ordered a rum and Diet Coke.

"Shouldn't you be helping run the auction?" Lola asked Bitsy.

"I'm on a hiatus from the club." The older woman shoved her dark glasses back on.

The auction kicked off with Tucker Napier, who went for nearly two hundred dollars, put up by Tiffany Winslow. She and Pris squealed at her winning bid.

"A great start for a good cause." Mims led Iggy to the middle of the floor amid a wave of catcalls. "That's right, ladies. This is the first time we've convinced this confirmed bachelor to participate."

"He's blushing," Pris cried. "How adorable."

"Do not bid on him," Drew commanded, only to be shushed by Lola, who wrapped her arms around her man and kissed him.

"Say a few words, Mr. King." Mims held the microphone in front of him.

"Hey, y'all. I'm proud to be a cowboy." He paused for the squeals of enthusiasm. "And a man of few words." He tilted his cowboy hat rakishly, drawing more cheers from the bidding pool near the front of the stage.

Pris was wearing a blouse meant for trouble and an expression to match. She stood on the bar stool's rungs, thrusting her hand into the air and shouting, "Two hundred dollars."

Iggy's mouth fell open.

Pris sat back down as the bidding rocketed up to three hundred, to the delight of the crowd.

"Aren't you going to jump back in?" Darcy shouted at her.

Pris shrugged, yelling back, "It's best to let a man wonder sometimes."

Drew clapped his palms on Pris's and Darcy's shoulders. "As your older brother, Pris, I forbid you to date Iggy King." He gave Darcy a look and said, "Don't encourage her."

Pris's hand shot up. "Three hundred ten dollars!"

Lola pulled a scowling Drew back into her arms.

"Do you want a date with Iggy or are you just pushing Drew's buttons?" Darcy asked.

"Both." Pris had a mischievous grin that rivaled Iggy's.

"Three twenty-five."

The crowd quieted, highly unusual for auction night. But the bidding was unusual too.

"Was that Barbara Hadley?" Darcy craned her neck, trying to find the bidder. "It was."

Pris set her jaw. "Three thirty."

"Three thirty-five." Barb again.

The crowd parted for Barb, not only because she was the town queen bee and the mayor's ex-wife, but also because everyone loved a good fight over a love interest.

"Don't let Barb get him," Lola said to Pris. She and Barbara had a not-so-pleasant history.

"Loan me a twenty." Pris got to her knees on the bar stool. "Three forty."

Iggy posed for the bidders, making muscles.

"Three forty-five," Barb countered, staring right at Iggy.

And the way he stared back... There were sparks.

"Three fifty." Pris looked down at their group. "I really need that twenty."

Lola held up her hands. "I didn't bring my purse."

"Don't look at me." Drew grinned. "I'm pulling for Barb to land trouble, not you."

"Four hundred dollars!" Barb raised her bills in the air.

Pris froze for a second and then climbed down from the stool as Iggy's sale was made final. "Don't say a word, Drew, or I'll tell you what the twins did for spring break this year."

Their youngest siblings were in college and, by the sound of things, were spreading their wings.

Drew wisely kept quiet.

Next on the block was Charlie Taggert, who went for $150 to Nathan Nunes, which was no surprise. They'd been sweet on each other since high school.

Darcy couldn't see Jason. But she could tell by the way Bitsy stiffened next to her who was coming up for sale next.

* * *

"Another first for us." Mims looped her arm through Rupert's and led him to center stage.

He was wearing a black suit with a black shirt and tie. He looked dangerously handsome and out of Bitsy's league.

Her heart scaled her throat. She'd never bid on anyone before. She'd never wanted to.

But her pulse was pounding, sending her a message: *Him, him, him.*

She swigged the last of her rum and Diet Coke. Noah had gone light on the rum. She wasn't getting what she wanted—a numbing of the persistent two-year twitch. They'd agreed to casually date. There'd been no discussion about her bidding on him at the bachelor auction.

"You've got this." Darcy squeezed her hand.

"I shouldn't have come." Bitsy hated to be the center of attention. And what if she was outbid, as Pris had been?

"Nonsense." Darcy smoothed the set of Bitsy's blouse on her shoulders. "You have to bid. You and Rupert... You don't make sense, which means you probably do make sense, if that makes sense."

"You're making no sense, Darcy," Lola said over the crowd noise.

Him, him, him.

Bitsy shook her head. "I will not bid."

"Rupert is a lawyer," Mims read from a card. "He's divorced with two kids in college." She glanced up at him. "Did you write this? It makes you sound rather dull."

Instead of answering, Rupert held his arms out. "But I'm a well-kept dull."

The bidders clustering near the stage chuckled, but they were young. In their twenties mostly. What interest did those young ladies have in a middle-aged man who admitted he was dull? Rupert was about to get his ego checked.

Bitsy wrung her hands. Rupert was scanning the crowd. For her?

Darcy covered Bitsy's hands with one of her own. "Don't bid unless you feel up to it."

"Who'll give me one hundred dollars?" Mims wore her soldiering smile, the one that said she expected this to go south quickly but she'd do her best to salvage the situation.

"One hundred dollars." The voice, small and feminine, came from a far corner of the stage.

The crowd around the bidder shifted and murmured.

"Who bid on him?" Bitsy craned her neck. Why was it okay for a younger woman to bid on an older man?

More importantly: Would Rupert be happy to have a date with a younger woman?

Bitsy ordered another drink. "Tell me when it's over, Darcy."

"Sold!" Mims said almost immediately. "One hundred dollars. Thank you very much."

"Do you want me to find out who bought him?" Darcy stood on the bar stool's rungs. "I can't see."

"No, please. No. I don't want to look . . ." Desperate? Overly curious? Hurt? "*Interested.*" Or worse, heartbroken.

Shiitake mushrooms. The twitch just wouldn't get the message that she was casually dating, not falling in love.

"Don't look now, but Rupert's coming over," Lola announced.

Sure enough, Rupert was navigating his way through the crowd toward them with a pretty young thing behind him. She had bright-purple hair and good taste in clothes.

"Bitsy, I'd like you to meet my daughter, Shareen." He hugged the woman who'd won him—his purple-haired daughter! "We'd like you to join us for dinner."

Him. Him. Him.

"And this is Darcy, who's related to us by marriage." Rupert gave Darcy a warm smile.

Bitsy couldn't have been happier if Duran Duran had been blaring from the speakers.

* * *

Jason stepped onstage.

He was wearing his good cowboy hat, the tan felt one that Darcy had given him one Christmas. He had on his black boots with the silver tips, the ones he'd bought when he'd won the world championship the first time. His shiny belt buckle made the biggest statement. It said, *I'm here. I'm the boss.*

His gaze sought out Darcy. She was at the bar with some of their friends but she was watching him. They'd never participated in one of the Widows Club charity auctions without buying each other. It was tradition. But tonight, he felt as if this was the year she'd break with tradition. Forever.

He swallowed thickly.

"Jason Petrie may need no introduction, but I'm going to give him one anyway." Mims beckoned him to center stage.

"World champion bull rider, not once but three times on the circuit. Businessman. Entrepreneur. And a homegrown special kind of wonderful."

"Can I add something?" Jason took the microphone before she could protest. "I'm also not qualified to be up here this evening."

The crowd of women shifted uneasily. A few phones came out as people held them up to snap photos or record his announcement.

Mims reached for the microphone, but Jason stepped in front of her, blocking the move. "This is supposed to be a bachelor auction. Well, I'm here to say that I'm not available because... I'm married."

Several women in front wailed.

Jason turned to look at Mims. "Calm down." And then his gaze found the woman he'd considered his wife for the past year. "I'm still up for bid, but I'd like the bidding limited to my wife. The woman who went through a commitment ceremony with me. The only woman I could ever love."

The bar heaved a collective "*Huh?*" and turned about as folks tried to locate a woman who'd lay claim to him.

Calling Darcy out was a risk. If she didn't come out of her shell and claim him, he didn't know what he was going to do. Jason handed Mims the microphone.

"Bidding will start at one hundred dollars," Mims said, but without wind in her sails.

Crickets.

Darcy had her arms crossed over her chest and was glaring at him. Around her, their friends were huddled, heads popping up and down as they stared first at Darcy and then at Jason.

"Let me tell you about my wife." Jason had center stage

and he was determined to use that spotlight wisely. "If my wife's other husband was still around, I'd have words to say. He put too much on her shoulders without making sure she had someone strong at her back."

You know I can hear you, George grumbled.

Still no bid from Darcy.

"But my woman never cracks under pressure. She tries to do right by everyone, even if it means she puts herself last." The crowd quieted, practically leaning into Jason's words. "That doesn't mean she's perfect. She's made mistakes. Heck, so have I. I don't know anyone who doesn't have regrets. But isn't that what makes us each more interesting to one another?" Jason spared a glance at the people closest to the stage. "We go through life growing and changing and it's rare that you find people who click when you're five and when you're twenty-five. Those people...Those friends..." His gaze found Iggy, who was sitting with Barbara. They exchanged a knowing smile. And then Jason found Darcy once more. "Those significant others...You have to stand by them, through thick and thin. You have to cherish them, through good times and bad. You have to love them, even when outside forces throw complications your way."

No bid had been made. Not by Darcy or anyone. Mims looked worried.

"Are you sure your wife's in the room?" someone asked.

"Way to leave a man hanging," someone else said, giving rise to laughter.

Jason didn't feel like laughing.

"One hundred dollars." The masculine voice came from the stairs leading to the stage and belonged to—

"Ken?" Jason frowned. "We're not married."

"But I'm your agent, and I'm bidding on you." Ken

climbed to the top step. "In fact, if I'm the highest bidder, I want you to come with me to New York."

Probably to see an orthopedic specialist. Jason frowned. He'd already decided his career as a bull rider was over.

"You're on my stage," Mims growled, signaling to Clarice, who stood behind Ken.

"And if my wife is the highest bidder?" Jason still held out hope that Darcy, in her quest to live a more honest life, would come forward and claim him.

"Shouldn't she answer that question?" Ken turned toward the bar. "Mrs. Commitment Ceremony Petrie, are you going to bid or am I going to get this man at a bargain-basement price?"

More heads turned in the direction of the bar. This time they were rewarded.

"One hundred dollars and one cent," Darcy called crisply, color high in her cheeks.

Jason's leg twinged hard enough to make him stumble. Later, he'd swear up and down it was the joy of Darcy claiming him outright that nearly swept his feet out from under him.

"It's Darcy." The statement rippled through the crowd, along with "It's the judge."

Darcy held her head high.

"I know you can do better than that," Ken challenged into the microphone. He'd wrested it from Mims, who was subtly trying to grab it back. "This auction is for charity. Two hundred dollars."

"You're on my stage," Mims repeated, her words projecting through the speakers.

A few people caught on and chuckled.

At the bar, Priscilla Taylor drew Darcy into the huddle.

Jason realized the error of his ways. He should have made sure Darcy had enough cash to outbid anyone, but especially his deep-pocketed agent.

"Two fifty," someone in the audience shouted. It didn't sound like Darcy.

"Three hundred," Ken said automatically. "I could do this all day."

"Stop." Jason grabbed Ken's shoulder. "Stop now."

"Four hundred." Ken didn't back down. He lowered the microphone and said, "This is how you create buzz."

"And ruin my chance to get the girl." Jason barely contained the urge to pop his agent in the nose.

"Five hundred dollars," Darcy shouted. She climbed on top of the bar. "Five hundred dollars to charity and to keep the man I love by my side."

Jason threw his hands up in the air and whooped.

Mims grabbed the microphone from Ken. "Sold to Darcy Jones Harper...Petrie? And look who's up for auction next. Ken Tadashi, New York sports agent and occasional wearer of knitted vests."

"What?" Ken whirled on the Widows Club president. "I'm not up for bid."

"Young man"—Mims took Ken by the arm—"did you not listen to the rules? If you come up on stage, your bid is void, and you are, in effect, volunteering to be put up for auction. Now, ladies and gentlemen, Ken is a looker and a talker. He needs someone smarter than a fifth grader and stubborn as a mule. Where's my first bid?"

Jason didn't wait to hear more. He hurried down the stairs and made his way to Darcy's side.

Finally, George said. *Now I can focus on my unfinished business with Pearl.*

Chapter Twenty-Six

♥

Darcy pushed her way through the crowd to Jason and would have thrown her arms around him, except he tripped at her feet.

Or ... he'd gone down on one knee?

Darcy gasped. "Jason, are you all right?"

Around her, bids were flying for Ken. She thought she heard Avery's voice down in the front row.

But in front of her ...

"Honey, I'm okay. That wasn't a twinge." He flashed her a dimple-filled smile. "I hope you're serious about taking me back, because I want to make things legal."

"Is that a scrape on your cheek?" Had he been bull riding again?

He nodded. "I'm not retired from bull *handling*." He tugged a blue velvet box from his back pocket and opened it to reveal a sparkler that suited her more than George's ring ever had. He took her hand and slid the princess-cut diamond on her finger. "I know you're serious about being judge, but if you're elected to office, we can start having kids, right?"

Darcy laughed. "What happened to no conditions?"

"Three hundred!" That sounded like Pris, if only because Drew shouted, "Pris, no!"

"These are plans, not conditions." Jason grinned at Darcy, flashing those dimples. "I love you, honey. We should have done this a long time ago."

"I couldn't." She shook her head. "Not because of your career and not because I'm a Jones and no one in town respects my family, but because I didn't respect myself. I needed to resolve my past here." She tapped a place over her heart. "Inside. Even though people were telling me the opinions of others didn't matter, it took me spreading my wings and gaining confidence in myself to believe the opinion that matters most is my own."

"Is that a yes?" Jason's eyes sparkled, and his dimples flashed.

Someone nearly tripped over him.

Darcy drew him to his feet. "You thought proposing to me in a crowd at Shaw's was more romantic than proposing to me when you were rip-roaring drunk?"

"I'm proposing right now because I can't wait to start our life together with babies of our own besides Stogey." Brow wrinkling, he glanced around the floor. "Where is Stogey?"

"Pearl agreed to babysit tonight. She says George always wanted her to be a dog person." Darcy missed Stogey like nobody's business. But he might have been trampled in the crowd and she wouldn't have missed Jason's performance for the world.

He wrapped his arms around her. "Say you'll be mine, honey. Say you'll marry me again, and this time we'll do it up right. I know you've always dreamed of a traditional church wedding with a fancy dress and flowers."

"Not a quickie Vegas ceremony with a red dress and Louboutins?"

He ignored her. "I've had my eye on some property out by the river. We can establish a herd of our own and maybe I can start a school for young bucks who think they've got what it takes to ride a bull. I think I have something to give back to the bull riding community, more than words of encouragement."

"You don't mind if we stay here in Sunshine?" Darcy slid her arms around his neck. "I know we always talked about leaving but I think you're right. I might just have a chance at winning the seat when it comes open in November. With you by my side, I think I can make a difference, the way I wanted to."

"The way George wanted you to." He kissed her then as the crowd roared over Ken's sale to Avery.

Later, when they'd been given a booth for their date and the well-wishers had stopped coming by, Darcy couldn't resist asking Jason, "Is George still in your head?"

"No. I think he...I think he moved on to Pearl." Jason's fingers tangled with hers. "The Date Night Auction was all his idea. He knew you always bid on me. But you know what? It doesn't matter whose idea it was. The Widows Club is going to take all the credit, same as always."

About the Author

Melinda Curtis is the *USA Today* bestselling author of lighthearted contemporary romance. In addition to her Sunshine Valley series from Forever Romance, she's published independently and with Harlequin Heartwarming, including her book *Dandelion Wishes*, which was made into a TV movie entitled *Love in Harmony Valley*. She lives in Oregon's lush Willamette Valley with her husband—her basketball-playing college sweetheart. While raising three kids, the couple did the soccer thing, the karate thing, the dance thing, the Little League thing, and, of course, the basketball thing. Now when Melinda isn't writing and Mr. Curtis isn't watching college basketball, they do the DIY thing.

Want more charming small towns?
Fall in love with these Forever contemporary romances!

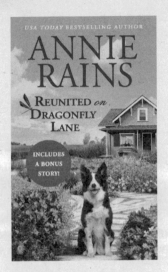

REUNITED ON DRAGONFLY LANE
by Annie Rains

Boutique owner Sophie Daniels certainly wasn't looking to adopt a rambunctious puppy with a broken leg. Yet somehow handsome veterinarian—and her high school sweetheart—Chase Lewis convinced her to take in Comet. But house calls from Chase soon force them to face the past and their unresolved feelings. Can Sophie open up her heart again to see that first love is even better the second time around? Includes the bonus story *A Wedding on Lavender Hill*!

DREAM A LITTLE DREAM
by Melinda Curtis

Darcy Jones Harper is thrilled to have finally shed her reputation as the girl from the wrong side of the tracks. The people of Sunshine Valley have to respect her now that she's the new town judge. But when the guy who broke her heart back in high school shows up in her courtroom, she realizes maybe things haven't changed so much after all...because her pulse still races at the sight of bad-boy bull rider Jason Petrie.

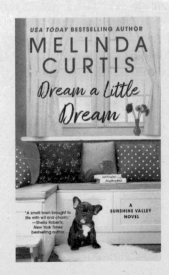

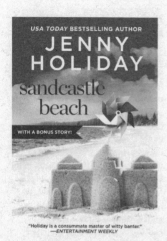

"Holiday is a consummate master of witty banter."
—*ENTERTAINMENT WEEKLY*

SANDCASTLE BEACH
by Jenny Holiday

What Maya Mehta really needs to save her beloved community theater is Matchmaker Bay's new business grant. She's got some serious competition, though: Benjamin Lawson, local bar owner, Jerk Extraordinaire, and Maya's annoyingly hot arch nemesis. Turns out there's a thin line between hate and irresistible desire, and Maya and Law are really good at crossing it. But when things heat up, will they allow their long-standing feud to get in the way of their growing feelings? Includes the bonus story *Once Upon a Bride*, for the first time in print!

A WEDDING ON LILAC LANE
by Hope Ramsay

After returning home from her country music career, Ella McMillan is shocked to find her mother is engaged. Worse, she asks Ella to plan the event with her fiancé's straitlaced son, Dr. Dylan Killough. While Ella wants to create the perfect day, Dylan is determined the two shouldn't get married at all. Somehow amid all their arguing, sparks start flying. And soon everyone in Magnolia Harbor is wondering if Dylan and Ella will be joining their parents in a trip down the aisle.

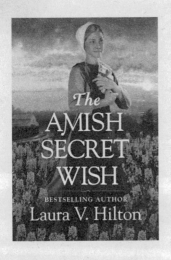

THE AMISH SECRET WISH
by Laura V. Hilton

Waitress Hallie Brunstetter has a secret: She writes a popular column for her local Amish paper under the pen name GHB. When Hallie receives a letter from a reader asking to become her pen pal, Hallie reluctantly agrees. She can't help but be drawn to the compassionate stranger, never expecting him to show up in Hidden Springs looking for GHB…nor for him to be quite so handsome in real life. But after losing her beau in a tragic accident, Hallie can't risk her heart—or her secrets—again.

HER AMISH WEDDING QUILT
by Winnie Griggs

When the man she thought she would wed chooses another woman, Greta Eicher pours her energy into crafting beautiful quilts at her shop and helping widower Noah Stoll care for his adorable young children. But when her feelings for Noah grow into something even deeper, will she be able to convince him to have enough faith to give love another chance?

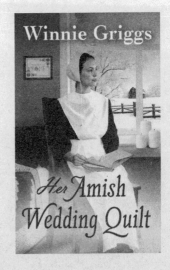

Discover bonus content and more on
read-forever.com

ONE LUCKY DAY
(2-IN-1 EDITION)
by Jill Shalvis

Have double the fun with these two novels from the bestselling Lucky Harbor series! Can a rebel find a way to keep the peace with a straitlaced sheriff? Or will Chloe Traeger's past keep her from a love that lasts in *Head Over Heels*? When a just-for-fun fling with Ty Garrison, the mysterious new guy in town, becomes something more, will Mallory Quinn quit playing it safe—and play for keeps instead—in *Lucky in Love*?

FOREVER FRIENDS
by Sarah Mackenzie

With her daughter away at college, single mom Renee isn't sure who she is anymore. What she *is* sure of is that she shouldn't be crushing on her new boss, Dr. Dan Hanlon. But when Renee comes to the rescue of her neighbor Sadie, the two unexpectedly hatch a plan to open her dream bakery. As Renee finds friendship with Sadie and summons the courage to explore her attraction to Dr. Dan, is it possible Renee can have the life she's always imagined?

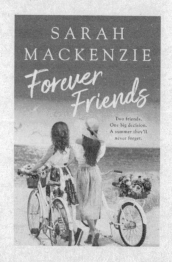